The Girl Who Could Not Die

Daniel Basil Lyle

LylePublishing

Sulphur, Oklahoma

The Girl Who Could Not Die

Copyright © 2019 by Daniel Basil Lyle

ISBN 978-0-9985937-2-2

Published by LylePublishing
505 W. 12th Street, Sulphur, OK 73086
(www.LylePublishing.com)

Printed by CreateSpace, an Amazon.com company. Available from Amazon.com and other retail outlets. Also available as an ebook on Kindle and other devices.

LCED01022020

DISCLAIMER and FORWARD

Although this book draws heavily from some of the author's own experiences, all characters are fictitious. Any resemblance to real persons, living or dead, is purely coincidental. This book is a sequel to *"The Girl Who Rocked Stars,"* beginning where that book left off.

Chapter 1

Titan

"Death be not proud"
A plea by the romantic poet John Donne
Written in the early 1600's
A time of plague, war, and starvation
Where the end was often a relief
A brief step beyond this sad existence
To something better than bloody fighting
A wolf's nighttime howl at an implacable moon
Mixing equal parts defeat and defiance
A wail as futile as it is splendid
Preening confronting dark doom!

The Rise and Fall of *Homo* *sapiens*, 1:10-13

Probably no one will ever read my diary except me. But if anyone ever stumbles upon it, this is my personal account of the *hell* you will experience if you ever dare to become an *immortal*...

"Sazz, pleas' don' go oot today. They's black brood in the scuds ye'll not be comin' back! Ye'll be nude-bared oot on a skiff plyin' the seas of Titan," Jags warned me.

I'd learned dozens of languages in my extended lifespan, but still found the Scottish clanner-accented spacer-English amusing. "Oot" and "nude-bared" and "scuds" were just funny words.

But I couldn't let myself get distracted. My immediate task was deadly serious.

"I know."

I groaned to myself, focusing on my immediate task: putting on my complex excursion "spacesuit" then making sure it was working properly. That pesky Turtle Tattoo on my left wrist itched something terrible. But I couldn't get at it through the tough fabric of my suit.

You've got a job to do, Saskia—I admonished myself. *Don't let the acid fog suffocate you. Fight on! Ignore all the itchy distractions. The evil forces that killed your mother and tried to ban music from society must be rooted out and destroyed.*

I repeated that dire mantra to myself every single day. It kept me from going completely insane. It was the only path that made sense to my warped mind. It prodded me forward through successive centuries. It helped me focus like a laser beam on the underlying obsession of all criminals, dictators, and warlords. It gave me strength to resist the seductive allure that perverted the better instincts of *any* human, including me.

Yes, to bring down my enemies I had to attack them where it hurt the most...

Follow the money—I focused my mind.

Isn't that what all the best investigators assert? The phrase was popularized by a movie from the twentieth century, back on Old Earth: "All The President's Men." That central admonition became shorthand for rooting out political conspiracies, criminal enterprises, and ruthless kingpins. It targeted naked greed underlying the heedless pursuit of glory, power, and pleasure. Yes, the Bible hit the nail square on the head when it stated: "The love of Money is the root of all evil." And here I was down on the filthy surface of Saturn's largest moon, Titan, hot on the trail of the worst human scum ever to inhabit the solar system.

"Sazz, you're goin' to yer watery grave," Jags grated. He grabbed my spacesuited arm, trying to pull me back out of the docking bay.

"Take your hands off me!" I bruskly ordered him.

He reluctantly complied. He knew I didn't let anyone touch me. He must be desperate to keep me from boarding the skiff. But I was furious at him for grabbing my arm! Yet I knew his warning was on-point. Poking around Huygens Station I was relatively safe. No one dared openly attack me there, least the Company come down hard on them. But isolated out on Ligeia Mare, anything could happen.

"I'm not intending to go swimming," I huffed, "At least not in near absolute-zero conditions."

Ligeia Mare was the second largest *liquid methane* sea on Titan. A massive amount of methane existed on Titan, in the incredible cold atmosphere falling out of the sky as a liquid. Why the methane existed at all was a mystery. It should have been broken down in the upper atmosphere over the eons by ultraviolet radiation from the sun. Some suspected a biological source continually replenished it, perhaps primitive bacterial life in a deep subterranean salty water ocean, warmed by radioactive decay from Titan's core. Regardless, methane persisted, raining down to form inland surface seas. Ligeia Mare was roughly the size of Lake Superior on Old Earth, around 300 miles in length, in places up to a thousand feet deep.

We'd only be going out about ten miles to find our breaching monsters, since the seabed dropped off rapidly. But still we'd be well away from any assistance from Huygens Station.

I was on my own "skiffing" an ocean composed of rocket fuel. What could go wrong?

"At least I should go *with* ye," Jags pleaded with me.

"No. You stay here."

"Then I kin trail yer in our sub," he persisted. "I've piloted her numbers o' times inspectin' the intake tunnels to the distillation plant. It'd be easy 'nuff to..."

"Don't be silly," I bruskly stopped his tirade. "The skiff's sonar would easily pick you up. They'd realize I wasn't there just for a routine inspection. They'd be on their best behavior, with all their dirty little secrets safely hidden away."

"Great! That would stop them from *harpooning* yer skinny little arse."

"Jags! I'm your boss, remember? Give me some respect."

"Not when ye're actin' crazy, 'Inspector Saskia Regalia'," he "respectfully" addressed his disrespect of me.

I sighed deeply, shaking my head in mock despair. Truthfully, I appreciated Jags Dougal. He was my loyal Deputy. Nobody else on Huygens Station gave a damn about my wellbeing on Titan, or cared to call me by my nickname, "Sazz." It was nice to have at least one friend amongst the horde of ruthless, money-grubbing, conniving denizens of the Station. Most of my fellow Titanites (if they could get away with it) would happily slit my throat for a week's wages.

"It's necessary. It's my job," I flatly stated. "I'll be back in an Earth-day. Keep the sub in its dock. That's an order."

"Then kin ah least let me trail the skiff with one 'o our helicopter drones?"

"That'd be even worse, Jags. They'd spot it on radar if it was distant, by noise and sight if it was close. Stop worrying about me. I'm a lot tougher than I look."

Yes, I was getting a bit irritated. I knew that outwardly I looked like a teenaged girl, which I was. But I had many lifetimes of experience burned into my brain. I'd seen it all and learned to anticipate and deal with every conceivable threat. All my limbs were lethal weapons. I didn't need a "worry wart" keeping watch over me.

"I've got a bad feelin' about this whole trip and..."

"I'll be fine."

I was now in the final steps of donning my excursion suit. It was an elaborate process, since my life depended on its seals and internal mechanisms. Titan is not forgiving. The surface temperature outside the Station that day was *minus* 179 degrees Celsius (-290° Fahrenheit, yes "subzero" to be sure!). In anybody's book, that's damn cold. Plus, the thick atmosphere was unbreathable: 95% nitrogen, 5% methane, other trace gases, and no oxygen. Outside my suit I'd suffocate and/or be frozen in seconds. And yet I was about to board an *open* skiff headed out onto a *liquid methane* ocean...*brrrrrr!*

Was I crazy? Yes! At least that's what I hoped the churning, slimy underworld of Titan's Huygens Station thought of me. If they stereotyped me as merely a young, naïve "go-getter" then they'd not suspect my plan until it was too late to stop me.

"Ye've bin stirrin' too many septic pits," Jags persisted. "The word's oot on the streets ye're marked fer death today, or even worse."

I laughed. No, I don't mean I had a good chuckle. Still holding my helmet in my hands, I tilted my head back and allowed myself a long riff of loud "guffaws". My extreme reaction wasn't just at the thick spacer-English accent I'd endured for hundreds of years (which was still funny to me: a weird mixture of Scottish and Irish accents, words, and phrases imposed upon "standard" Spacer English). No, what I found hilarious was his ironic ignorance.

Sure, they'd *kill* me—if only I were so lucky. And as for the "worse", well I was a tough girl for anyone to try to gang rape.

Dougal looked shocked at my apparent glee at his heartfelt warning.

I also saw some of the personnel on the other side of the loading bay glancing over at us predatorily. Yes, they sensed "blood in the water" from my outburst, hoping they could sneak in a quick scavenging bite.

It didn't do to show weakness down on the perverted surface of Titan.

Ah, the poor fellow—I reminded myself, trying to be patient with Jags Dougal. *He just doesn't understand. But then, how could he? None of these short-lived creatures can possibly know the hell I daily endure.*

"Pleas', Sazz—yer one 'o me few buds," he now urgently whispered. "The Guild kin protect yer tender flesh claimin' sick today and stayin' behind. Don'..."

"I'll be fine, Jags. Don't worry about me."

"But...?"

"Just make sure I'm locked down tight, will you?" I now gently redirected him to his present task. "I know I've been asking too many questions, probing into too many tender activities. But then again, that's my job, right? Am I not the Station's *one and only* 'highly esteemed' and 'rightly feared' Safety Inspector? Eh?"

"Urrrr..." he grated, obviously not knowing how to respond. Yes, it was true I was the sprawling Station's one and only Safety Inspector. But I was hardly esteemed, and definitely not feared.

Indeed, I was given "respect" like Homer Simpson got it on his classic cartoon TV show. In the ancient but still-popular animation, Homer was the Safety Inspector in his hometown's local nuclear power plant. The owner, Mr. Burns, had deliberately hired the most incompetent fool in town to oversee plant safety. Homer's position was an empty gesture aimed squarely at appeasing regulatory authorities. Meanwhile, Mr. Burns ran roughshod, breaking every safety rule conceivable, making millions cutting every corner in his operation. The

Company had done the same on Titan. Their latest atrocity was re-
placing their retiring stooge with me, a "mere girl."

But as long as they continued to bribe the governing officials, a
blind eye was turned to my appointment and many blatant violations
of plant safety. Money talks loudly.

Yes, I'd been put in charge of safety at the most lucrative industrial operation in the entire solar system. Saturn's largest moon, Titan,
was the virtually inexhaustible *fuel depot* for all commercial space
travel, the cash-cow of the Company.

Massive Helium-3 fusion-reactor drives might be ok for anticipated gigantic starships. Combining liquefied hydrogen gas, H_2, with
liquefied oxygen gas, O_2, (also called LOX) was good for selective
specialized drive systems. But the grunt work of getting from place to
place in the solar system was still done burning liquefied methane by
combining methane plus LOX into "methalox". This began with the
commercial rockets in the early 21st century and continued onward.
Also for many technical reasons, methane was still preferable as the
main routine space vehicle propellant over the other available options—especially when available in easily accessed sea-sized pools.

So Titan fueled mankind's continuing expansion out into the solar
system.

"You've gone far beyond yer Company mandate, Sazz," Jags interrupted my wandering thoughts. "The dark dealers don' brook swifted
'inspections', leastwise legit ones. I'm tellin' ye that..."

"I know I'm new here," I again stopped him with a dismissive
wave of a golden space-gloved hand, "but I'm not behaving irrational-
ly. I know what I'm doing."

"Really?" he persisted as he checked my suit joints at my neck,
gloves, and boots, making sure the connectors were secure. "Ye could
'ave fooled me," he complained.

I shrugged at him good-naturedly. Truthfully I liked Jags Dougal.
He was one of the few "good guys." Still in his early twenties, he was
one of the rare "youngsters" on Huygens Station. Most of the denizens were grizzled old hands, rugged and grim. I was pleasantly surprised to spot his cheerful grin enthusiastically greeting me upon my
descent to Titan's filthy surface, a mere three weeks previous. He was
the Deputy of my retiring predecessor. Normally I would follow his

informed directions before attempting any drastic departures from the norm. But the present situation was urgent.

Unbeknownst to him, I'd been sent here by the Company on a secret mission: to interdict a major smuggling operation. The Company officials running Huygens Station skirted or defied civil law at every opportunity. But my Company employers were ruthless in hunting down and destroying anyone endangering its profits by committing similar acts against themselves. Being assigned here as the incoming Safety Inspector was just a ruse. I was actually a hired assassin, a certified "exterminator" with a license to kill any local vermin. They didn't inform Jags because he'd been here long enough to be on the take. The station's police force was likewise suspected by the higher-ups. I liked Jags but didn't yet trust him sufficiently to reveal my true assignment.

Plus, I had my own hidden agenda. My overt and covert job assignments from the Company were just convenient covers allowing me to finally zero in on my own long-pursued goal. After centuries of chasing down false leads I was finally closing in on my objective.

The secret to the centuries-long conspiracy was here, on Titan.

So, to sum-up, I was a *triple* secret agent—yay! My life should be a holo-feed game, novel, or broadcast, huh? How amazing! But I was tired, weary to my bones, and wracked with never-ending internal pain. It just wanted to bring things to an end, get to the finish. I was much too old for the intrigue, stink, and mash of failed humans squirming about the frozen surface of Titan. They didn't just disgust me, they *bored* me.

It was an old movie played over and over in my brain, from which I couldn't escape. And it wasn't just Titan. There was a pervasive decay to mankind. It was the rot of a fish with its head banged in by a fisherman, not yet dead but still squirming.

"It's just a fishing run. It'll be fun," I insisted. I forced a reassuring smile onto my lips, both for Jags and also to reassure myself.

"Then will ye at least be takin' a gun?"

He slipped a small black pistol out of his pocket and tried to put it into my life support backpack. Where'd he get it? Weapons were strictly forbidden on the Station. Ah yes, the black market... I was too fresh, didn't know the ins-and-outs of purchasing anything I wanted if I had the creds.

"No!" I stopped him, shoving the gun away.

"But..."

"I'll be scanned before they let me board the skiff. The Captain expressly forbad bringing any recording devices, not to mention illegal weapons. You know this, Jags."

"Well then, I've also got you a wee *poison knife* that you could use to..."

"Jags, I already have hidden weapons."

"Oh?" he frowned, clearly not convinced. "Well, then..." his voice trailed off.

He was much too eager. How had he survived down here for a year in such a sensitive position? I supposed it was due to his family connections. He was the favorite son of one of the ruling matriarchs of SSS, the massive space station orbiting outside the rings and radiation belts of Saturn. Connections were everything. He'd told me that he'd originally gone down to Titan in search of "adventure." His mother, Lady Dougal, wanted him to remain on the Saturn-orbiting Megalopolis, training to take his rightful place as her heir. His "destiny" from birth was to become one of the ruling Elites. But he claimed to find that prospect immensely boring.

I understood "boring." And I understood him.

What can I say? He was an *idealistic* Elite, the most dangerous commodity in human society. Even he didn't realize the power his "righteous" convictions engendered. Of course I'd seen that "nonconformity-fever" many times previously in my long life. I was always impressed by its potential, yet inevitably disappointed by its meager results. The *Love of Money* was just too powerful for anyone in a position of high authority to resist. Yes, Dougal had potential. But in his self-exile to Titan he'd become just one more sad soul looking to escape his previous, tepid life. It wouldn't take long for Titan to crush his spirit, when he'd likely go crawling back to his Mommy. In the meantime, however, he was a breath of fresh air at a dung-drenched hog farm. And who knew? Perhaps he'd surprise me.

What's done is done—I sternly admonished myself. *You can't save everyone. You can't even save yourself.*

Three weeks previous, I could have fired him on the spot and hired a new Deputy. No one would have questioned me getting rid of the old guard and bringing in my own people. Now I regretted not having done so. I should have hired as my Deputy one of the dour slugs or drugged-out freaks that slunk about Huygens' dark subterranean corridors. One of those as my Deputy wouldn't have cared or been targeted if I was caught by my enemies. But it was just so nice to have helpful, cheerful Jags in my office. He was trim and fit, with soulful brown slanted eyes, slicked-down black hair, thick dark eyebrows, and unwrinkled dark skin. Unlike most of the other Elites, he wasn't a pure-blood clanner. No, he was a so-called mongrel: his ancestry from Old Earth likely including African, Hispanic, and Japanese genes mixed in with a touch of Russian. But he'd obviously been raised well, always impeccable in his hygiene and appearance, despite not being a Clanner.

Regardless of his pedigree, though, he was a handsome young man with an obvious crush on me. It was natural. Even though I was historically and mentally hundreds of years old (unbeknownst to anyone around me, a carefully guarded secret), I outwardly appeared to be just a kid, a cute teenager. How old really? Jeez...I'd lost count. Anyway, childish flings held little appeal for me anymore. Though physically I was a pert 5' 7" with bouncy bright green-dyed hair and fashionably yellow eyes (from my custom programmable implants which doubled as personal computer AR augmented reality projectors), inside I was dried up and hollowed-out. True, my body possessed all the throbbing hormones of youth, unavoidably drawing my attention to handsome young men like Jags. But I'd long since left behind the superficial pleasures of biological sperm transfer/receipt. Sex would be more a painful chore than a giddy adventure.

But my persistently cute outward appearance had an even worse downside than attracting handsome young men to my lithe, juicy young body. The station's gritty miners, sweaty fishermen, brutal thugs, devious criminals, and scary station-stringers visibly slobbered at the "fresh meat" paraded before them. Indeed, I saw many of them hungrily eyeing me at the moment. If they thought they could get away with it, they'd giddily gang-rape me on the spot. So I didn't blame poor Jags for getting the hots over me.

Honestly, I had tried to keep him at arm's length. But he was just so cuddly and friendly. We were quickly on a first-name basis, even though I tried to keep things professional. Truthfully, he was my one relief from the prevailing cesspool swirling about us. I just hoped having Dougal in my office hadn't condemned him by association—or that his high connections could somehow protect him. I'd feel bad if he was beaten up (or worse) because of being my Deputy.

"Just keep your head down and don't make waves, whatever happens. If the pits spew, go right to the Guild. They'll protect *you*," I advised him.

"But you said I was wrong about...?"

"Just in case," I snapped at him.

I resolutely set my helmet in place over my head, twisting it firmly to set the internal seals, then locking down the external clamps. I motioned for Jags to check for any leaks. As he did so I slowly increased the suit pressure. Being out on the surface was equivalent of being at the bottom of a swimming pool on Old Earth. I wanted the suit pressure enough so the fabric was loose against my skin but not rigid enough to impede my movement.

Ah, let's see how imposing I look in my brand new, state-of-the-art, official "inspector" excursion suit—I satisfactorily instructed myself. I turned toward a large plasteel window looking out onto the foreboding orange landscape of Titan, adjusting to see my reflection.

My excursion suit was of the type reserved for enforcement officers. I saw reflected back at me a black helmet with two yellow "racing stripes" on each side. A wide transparent faceplate allowed people to see my stern expression and set lips. My narrowed eyes glared outward. Gleaming black straps held my slender life support pack firmly onto my back. My double waist-belt held attached tools. Most impressive was the gleaming gold, skintight fabric. It was embedded with micro-circuitry and artificial vasculature, capable of doing what ordinary cumbersome excusion suits did. I looked menacingly lean while staying toasty warm. The gold gloves were deceptive, seemingly having open fingertips. If that were true, though, my digits would freeze solid in seconds. But special invisible nanofiber fabric covered my fingertips, allowing precise touch and manipulation.

"Activating yer air, Saskia," Jags informed me.

As he ran his sensor around my shoulders I felt a soothing flow of warm air wafting across my face. The VR-display on the inside of the helmet showed "green" for all life-support parameters. My battery, part of my attached backpack, was supplying abundant power. It had a full charge, enough to power the suit for a week if necessary. The intricate liquid circulation mechanism was maintaining a constant 70° Fahrenheit in the suit. Hopefully that would continue out on the frigid surface. But the life support mechanisms had their limits, such as being dunked in liquid methane. So I wouldn't be going for any voluntary swims in the sea. My water and food paste tubes read as operational. My oxygen tank-rebreather was topped-off. The waste-collection processing traps were snug at my crotch. The mike and speakers located in my helmet were working. So under ordinary operating conditions I was set for an Earth-time 24-hour expedition out onto the unforgiving surface of Titan (though it'd be easy enough to stay out too long as a "day" on Titan was nearly sixteen actual Earth-days).

I should have been excited about this new adventure. After all, it was my first voyage out onto one of Titan's famous liquid methane seas. We weren't going far, only a few miles offshore, but in the thick smog we'd quickly be out-of-sight of the Station. Fortunately our prey was growing ever more abundant in the sea's murky depths, not requiring a long journey to find and catch them. It was a fortuitous effect of the Station's pollution, from our pumping huge volumes of hydrogen gas into the atmosphere. But Titan was a gigantic toxic dump site to start with, so no one gave a thought to altering its frozen ecosystem. So what if the "monster" numbers increased? That was all to the good, right?

The "skiffers" were the equivalent of Old Earth whalers.

Overseeing the safety of the fishing fleet, both for corporate and private crafts, was part of my many official duties. But still I dreaded what awaited me out there. I'd never liked boating or fishing, even back in my ancient Old Earth days. And here "fishing" was thousands of times more dangerous. And even though I was an experienced assassin hiding under a (claimed) "plastic-surgery" disguise of being a harmless young girl (as I covertly advertised myself), I took no pleasure in fighting or killing.

But I could do it. I was expert in all martial arts. Despite having a petite body my "lethal weapon" limbs could kill effectively and mercilessly. If necessary, I wouldn't hesitate to slaughter the skiff's entire crew.

What did concern me, though, were the crew's suspicions. I wasn't part of the police, so the crew wouldn't actually fear me. But it wasn't "routine" for a skiff to be inspected during an actual fishing run. According to the records in my office, none of the recent Inspectors had ever personally gone out onto Ligeia Mare, not that I blamed them. Making sure enough *wings* and *safety lines* were present or the *nuclear engine* was working properly was a low priority when one's duties supposedly included overseeing the Safety of much more complex and significant operations. Indeed, on paper I oversaw the huge *distillation plant*, the Station's massive *fission power plant*, the industrial *manufacturing complex*, the gigantic *launch facilities*, the *commercial domes*, and all the sprawling *support-infrastructure*. A portfolio like that could easily keep busy a dozen full-time Inspectors. And here I was just one lonely lady. No one would fault me for never setting foot on a skiff. Indeed, the fleet was an important but minor part of the local economy. As far as I knew, I might be the first Inspector ever to insist on accompanying a fishing run. But then again, I knew that today wouldn't be an ordinary voyage.

Concentrate, Saskia—I admonished myself. *Don't let your mind wander. Jags is correct. One misstep and you'll be a frozen corpse at the bottom of Ligeia Mare.*

If I could complete my business peacefully, fine. But if not—even with my extensive martial arts expertise I knew I was in deadly danger. If the crew was already actively plotting against me as Jags had heard on the streets, I could be taken down by sheer numbers. Despite all classic "kung fu" movies to the contrary, even a Master can be swamped and killed by a raging mob. True to Jag's warning, I suspected that today I'd be in for the fight of my long, pathetic life!

"Please be canny with thet crew, Sazz," he entreated me as I headed for the airlock, seemingly reading my thoughts. "All of they be tough veterans. They'll show ye nae mercy."

"No problem," I cheerfully replied, though inwardly I was increasingly glum.

"Haste ye back!"

That didn't require a reply. Either I'd get back or I wouldn't. But my goal wasn't to retreat. I was determined to do whatever it took to finally unravel the mystery.

I'd been hunting this last key link for over fifty years. Now that it was finally within my grasp, could I use it to wreck my epic revenge? Or would I yet again miserably fail?

God help me.

Most of the human spacefaring diaspora regarded Titan as the *asshole* of the solar system. They were absolutely correct. Titan was a disgusting place to live or work. Even skiffing—which one might think would have a degree of sport or machismo to it ("out whaling on the deep blue sea!")—was itself an appalling prospect.

But awful or not, here am I—I sternly admonished myself. *I've got to stay focused, limber, and ready for anything.*

"Ur 'arnesses and leashes are crakin' tight. So ur we bein' safe 'nuff fer ye?" one of the "harponeers" laughed derisively at me over my suit speaker.

He was leaning out over the edge of the gigantic skiff, kept from falling into the incredibly cold liquid beneath him only by a taut, semi-intelligent safety rope. His spacer-English accent was particularly thick. I had trouble understanding his garbled words. I'd rather he just spoke French or Mandarin Chinese or Spanish. I fluently spoke those and many other languages. But I found the languages and dialects originating in Scotland varied and confusing.

"Looking good so far," I cheerfully replied, keeping up the façade of dutiful inspector.

I saw him eyeing my suit greedily. He was likely imagining dragging me below deck, stripping off my skintight golden covering, raping me, tossing my body over the side of the ship, and taking the suit for his own. Hah...not likely. He'd have to make do with his clunking gray thick fabric and filth-coated brown helmet.

We were surrounded by orange smog, our giant skiff pushed forward by steady subsea jets. The craft was remarkably steady. The muddy "water" had nary a wave. It was horribly spooky and boring.

"Wait till we find a Kraken," he leered at me. "Then it'll git pure fin."

"Ah, yes," I nodded politely. "But I'm not here for fun. I'm here to make sure your Captain is following all the safety rules. I'm just looking out for your wellbeing."

"Aye," he leered again at me, "that ye be."

We were communicating wide-broadcast over our suit radios. I was keeping everything proper and formal because our "official" conversations went straight up to the orbiting Titan Space Station (TSS), along with my video feeds. This was why the Skiffer Union could insist no surface recording devices be taken onto their boats. Supposedly there was no need, since everything was recorded directly by TSS or other intermediate satellites orbiting Titan. I knew that the "fun" wouldn't really start until this skiff's Captain deliberately switched off wide-broadcast for short-range transmission. Until then I felt relatively safe. Once his "accidental disconnect" occurred, though—effectively isolating the vessel from the wider Company—we'd be offline and I knew I'd be in big trouble.

But until then I could somewhat relax and take in the depressing "scenery": a persistent *orange smog* hiding even the surrounding low mountains, the *muddy brown slick* of the near-motionless methane sea, the *slippery snow* of frozen methane rain drifting down onto our excursion suits, the *sludge of organic muck* covering everything and bubbling up as *slimy bobbing globs* from the bottom of the sea, and the "water" itself which wasn't H_2O, rather *liquid combustible rocket fuel!*

Hell, my beautiful golden suit is getting all mussed up—I groaned mentally. *No wonder the skiffers on deck look so ugly.*

It was indeed very much like being immersed in a planet-sized toxic-waste garbage dump. Titan wasn't a little moon. No, counting its atmosphere, it was larger than the planet Mercury. I and everyone else on the huge wide surface of Titan found living within its persistent filth profoundly depressing. The exterior of my helmet was already coated with an orange sheen. The drizzling organics were generated by Saturn's huge magnetic fields constantly slamming solar radiation into the upper atmosphere of Titan. Bursts of methane "rain" didn't help with the smudge on my faceplate. Wiping off the outer surface with my spacesuited forearm just smeared things even worse. Trying to live here was as bad as attempting to survive on the now permanently nuclear winter-shrouded Earth. (Hah, that certainly took care of the 21st century existential problem of global warming: slaughtering 95% of the human population, burning off most of the habitable surfaces, and covering the once blue skies with black ash clouds. So sad!)

Again, I digress. Worse of all was the perpetual *gloom* of Titan. The thick, smoggy atmosphere kept the sun from ever illuminating the surface more than what you'd experience back on Old Earth at twilight.

Old Earth...*sigh*. I was the only person alive who'd lived in that once-magical world. In the early 21st century many of the people of Earth thought things were horrible, with the world going from bad to worse. Little did they know how well off they were and...

Your mind is wandering again. Keep your focus sharp, kiddo! You know if they attack they'll come at you from behind. You can't let them immobilize you.

Yes, I'd only been on Titan for three weeks, yet the rancid environment was already crippling my mind. My already perpetual melancholy was getting darker and darker.

And the perpetual pain in my joints and muscles was getting steadily worse. Although outwardly I looked hale and hearty, a healthy youngster, inside I was a shriveled-up corpse.

"Sonar's spotted a swarm—be lively, lads!" the Captain's gravelly voice rang inside my helmet. I hadn't met him yet. His First Mate, a whiny graying woman named Ailith MacDonald, had processed me onto the skiff. She was one of the first females I'd seen on Titan. It wasn't that women were excluded. They just didn't want to be here. The degenerate male workers had to make do with clunky sex-bots instead of regular, mid-range whores. The poor fellows! Of course the Elites, managers, and occasional tourist had their pick of live, expensive prostitutes. But you had to sink pretty low to want a job on Titan.

God, a "swarm" is approaching—I groaned to myself. *I wanted my plan completed before the skiff engaged with any of those monsters. I hope I can keep my breakfast down once the dredging starts.*

I could die from breathing in my own vomit... Jesus, I'm floundering mentally. Keep it together, Saskia!

We were now sliding rapidly along the surface of Ligeia Mare, the second largest liquid methane sea on Titan. It was eerily smooth, like we were on a train supported by a vertical track. Our football-stadium sized flat craft was pushed along by subsurface propellers set into warmed drive-tubes, providing significant thrust. Most of the inner workings of the aircraft carrier-sized skiff were situated below the "waterline." Though it was possible to access the machinery-stuffed interior through airlocks, the crew usually remained on top of the flat skiff for the entire duration of the daylong expeditions. After all, they were safely contained in their fully-stocked excursion suits. No one wanted to risk being beneath the sea's surface, even protected within the ship's below-deck interior. If the worst happened, those on deck could always don their wings and fly to safety. Under the water-line they'd be sucked down, never to emerge, frozen solid. It was a horrible prospect that...

"Everythin' ta yer approval, Inspector?" the Captain startled me, interrupting my dark thoughts.

Looking up I saw he was right beside me, openly laughing through his smeared faceplate.

Why didn't I see him come up from behind? Christ, I'm really getting rattled. He could have stuck a harpoon through me and I'd not known it until the barbed tip emerged from my chest!

He was a hulking brute, over six-feet tall. In his helmet I saw a wide, stubbly face topped by short white hair. I knew from my prior review of the skiff's crew that *Lars Fehler* was a grizzled veteran, having captained various skiffs over the last decade here on Titan. Unlike his thin, nimble crew he was disturbing stout. But I noted it wasn't just fat that made him so imposing. His barrel chest, large gut, and thick arms inside his excursion suit were powerful

I best not get in a bar fight with him—I warned myself. *My usual defense methods wouldn't put a dent in that tank.*

And to make him even more menacing, I saw he was toying with me, relishing my vulnerability. But we were still in direct contact with the orbiting TSS. He wouldn't risk attacking me until we were cut-off from the officially recorded transcript.

"I'm just doing my job," I replied neutrally. "Being here on Ligeia Mare is indeed a real...experience—but one I doubt I'll ever have to repeat."

"Ah, there we do agree, lassie. No disrespect meant, but havin' untrained officials on deck is a burden to us all, as ye'll shortly see."

The words were proper, but the threat was implicit.

Despite being toasty warm in my excursion suit, I felt a chill go through me.

"I'm not your enemy, Captain Fehler," I stoically replied, maintaining my cover. "I'm just here certifying your craft, crew, and processes. Once I've certified that you are following proper safety regulations, I'll leave you to distal monitoring. Since I'm new on Titan you're just unlucky enough to be my test case for fleet operations. You won't be bothered by me again. Just like my predecessor, I'll gladly retreat to my office Station-side. I admire the work you and your crew do out here on the sea, but it's not my cup of tea."

"Ah...ye'd be surprised, lassie," he enigmatically replied. "*Titanian* Tea kin be surprisingly addictive."

I've heard of that brew—I mused. *Perhaps I'll give it a try, if I survive this voyage.*

Whatever, a nice compliment could work wonders, lowering my opponent's guard. But he was much too experienced to be flattered by a mere slip of a "girl" like me.

His eyes narrowed as he put his gloved hands on his wide, spacesuited hips. Again I was puzzled by him being a chunky fellow, quite unlike his skinny crewmembers. Fishing was only for people quick on their feet, such as dancers or sprinters. In spite of the weak gravity, any excess fat only slowed down the crewmembers at critical moments—potentially making the difference between life and death.

"I'll stay out of your way," I added.

"Good. We dinna need yer kind out here," he bluntly stated. "I bring me crews back, safe and sound."

"Not always," I sharply replied.

I'd seen his record. Over the years he'd lost several skiffs, with associated fatalities.

"Accidents happen, lassie. Fishin's dangerous and..."

"—the more reason to be *extra* vigilant," I shot back.

He snorted derisively. "And whut do ye know of prudence, a mere slip of a lassie like ye? How be ye an Inspector, anyway? Ye should still be in trade school, not lordin' it over me crew."

He was now standing much too close to me, deliberately invading my personal space. I was tempted give him a quick kick to his ample crotch. The excursion suits were limber enough that crunching his meaty balls would nicely back him up. However—even though it sent the wrong signal—I chose instead to take my own step backward. Then I was momentarily flustered, not seeing where I'd stepped, momentarily terrified I'd trip, slide down the deck, and fall into the liquid methane sea!

But the deck was solid under my boots. The surface was corrugated to give good purchase while smooth enough to drag large structures across its wide, flat length. In addition, the deck had metal ripples set into the "planks" upon which my magnetic boots firmly locked, negating the light gravity that might have left me stumbling and tumbling.

Everyone else wore the same magnetic boots as me. At low power they clung to the deck while being easily dislodged with a slight tilt of one's foot. But when cranked up to full power they could virtually weld people to the deck. The semi-intelligent safety lines (automatically maintaining the right length and tension for the situation) were an extra measure of safety, used when working near the edge of the craft or when fishing maneuvers were particularly dangerous.

But Fehler was emboldened. By my little step backward I'd deliberately encouraged this emotion from him. It's hard to intimidate me, a person hundreds of years old who has seen everything and can read her opponent like a book. I'm much craftier than I look.

But I didn't have to hide my abilities. Instead, here I would flaunt them. And he'd taken the bait just like one of his "monsters" lurking in the frigid liquid beneath us.

"I'm older than I look," I honestly declared, staring him down. I wanted him thinking he'd intimated me...but also getting angry at my continued defiance.

The horny old fool was almost too easy to manipulate.

Fehler laughed uneasily, looking away. Behind his smudged face-plate I saw him reach out a red, wet tongue to trigger a water tube to pop into his thick lips.

He sucked on the tube for a moment, looking back at me suggestively.

"Old enough to 'ave a brew with me below deck?" he spoke softly. "I'd love talkin' with you more casual, oot of our suits, where we could take a break an' be more comfortable. My cabin's fully stocked fer long voyages. I've even got a taste of the Green in me official ship's grog! And we could 'ave a nice meal instead o' suckin' paste. I kin tell ye more about these wicked seas, educatin' your little school-girl sensitivities. Interested?"

He leered at me suggestively through his mucked-up helmet.

Truthfully, he was the *least* seductive man I'd ever met.

"Well..." I slowly replied, making it seem he'd intrigued me, "Perhaps I will take you up on a below-deck tour. I'd like to see and inspect your skiff's propulsion system. As an inspector I'm always worried about the nuclear pods that supply energy on these boats. *And* I'm always happy to get to know my constituents better. I've always been fascinated by skiffing," I added, suggestively.

Not! But I wasn't going to tell him that, particularly since I knew he had no intention of letting me return to Huygens Station alive. My superiors up on Titan Base had intercepted earlier encrypted transmission between him and his unknown collaborators. Jags' warning to me was dead on. Captain Fehler had been ordered to *murder* me, making it look like an accident. And it was 50:50 I'd get the information I needed from him before *my* having to torture *him* to death.

One way or another, someone's going to die today!

I grinned at him through my helmet. I'd much rather *he* be tortured than me.

"Well, then, it's a date, lassie," he grinned, exposing broken, yellowed teeth behind his faceplate. "After the hunt, ye and me will go inspectin' below. We will celebrate me fine 'processes' with a bit of the Green, a benefit of you being with a Master skiffer," he repeated himself. "We'll be stoatin' aboot. It'll bile yer heid. In the meantime, pleas' enjoy the view. It's pure, damn brilliant!"

Despite my command of many languages, I was still disoriented by his thick spacer accent, even thicker than Jags': Scottish and Irish slang and terms imposed upon "standard" English. I watched him "clomp" away, taking the characteristically flat and solid "skiffer" steps upon the partially metallic planks. He happily swore at a group of sailors who were leisurely opening up long hatches set-into the deck. Apparently, they weren't working fast enough for him. They were busily drawing out lines, harpoons, and other equipment in anticipation of the approaching "swarm."

Things are going well. Your plan is solid—I encouraged myself. *Below deck, away from the crew, you can ambush and safely interrogate the Captain to within an inch of his life. There'll be no need to overcome the rest of the crew to back him into a corner. So, just wait until the hunt concludes. Then you can have him all to yourself.*

Outwardly I was calm, in control of the situation. But inwardly I was trembling, plagued by self-doubt. It wasn't a new paranoia. My imposed extended lifespan had a terrible side-effect, locking my mind into a permanent black depression, made worse by my perpetual physical pain. I was certain I'd never escape the problems and uncertainties of life, forever trapped in a hell of my own making. But my present funk on the skiff *was* qualitatively different. I felt a dark fear I hadn't known for hundreds of years. It was an irrational terror that I was imminently facing a *living* death. Here so close to my objective, I was breaking down mentally.

Why did I come here?—I groaned to myself. *Why did I think I could find my answers in this shithole? Am I so desperate in my centuries-long vendetta that I've sunk to the lowest level possible? I don't want to drown in this sewer forever. God, I'm pitiful!*

But the Captain was right. The view—if not beautiful—was remarkable. But it wasn't enjoyable. Instead, it was profoundly disturbing, amplifying my inner turmoil.

It's a liquid volcano waiting to erupt—I observed, growing more and more fearful.

Though a gentle wind blew against us and a passing cloud dropped yet another dollop of fluttering methane rain, the sea was completely calm. The huge skiff floated serenely with its flat deck only a yard above the "waterline." I was still nonplussed by the fact the deck was so close to the sea. I knew it had to do with the incredibly smooth, calm surface and the extreme stability of the wide, long craft. But with first-hand memories of turbulent Old Earth water oceans, it just didn't seem right. Yet Ligeia Mare might still have been beautiful if the inland sea wasn't a *fetid brown* shrouded by the ever-present orange smog. It was a sleeping giant we were about to awaken!

Tilting my head to the side, through my transparent faceplate, I looked upward half-expecting to see the looming presence of *ringed Saturn*. By rights the sight should have been spectacular. After all, if viewed directly from the equator on the tidally locked side of Titan, Saturn with its magnificent rings would occupy a full third of the sky! But Ligeia Mare was up on the northern pole of Titan. And the putrid smog of the thick atmosphere totally *hid* Saturn. Even at the equator, on the clearest day the *grandest celestial object* in the entire solar system was only occasionally visible as a *muddy blob*.

I hated Titan even more.

Then I had a profound, disturbing insight. I suddenly truly understood why only rejects, losers, and criminals descended for prolonged periods to the surface of Titan (not counting short-term tourists here for exotic pleasures that were illegal or unavailable elsewhere). My insight was that the foul environment fit the workers' *already existing* mental deterioration. Titan was a "home" they instinctively felt that they *deserved*, where they were rightly *punished*.

Maybe this is where I also deserve to be?

But to be fair, the ultimate rewards of penance in this frozen hell could be huge. As in any of the ancient old-Earth oil-boom worksites, the Company paid excellent wages. After a few stints on Titan, even ordinary workers could theoretically retire comfortably to the Lunar Colonies. There they'd have the means to pay for expensive therapists to soothe their mental ills. Failing that, they could always pay for expensive prescriptions to get exotic legal drugs that included trace amounts of the "Green" that Captain Feller was trying to entice me to drink. (I wished those methods *would* work on me. But my unique physiology made those treatments mute. Psych and drugs couldn't touch my centuries-long emotional decline.) And for a lucky few the "gold rush" boom-city rewards were enormous: legit or illegal wealth beyond their wildest dreams.

Could those rewards also come to me?

For a moment I was hopeful I might find the perfect pearl hidden within the oozing, disgusting clam. But then reality intruded on my fever-dream. Yes, I was smack-dab in the middle of that magnificent gold rush. But I was about to be *trampled*.

"Thar she blows!" an eager cry went up from behind me. "It's a big 'un!"

And so my "final" battle begins, yet again, over and over...

I spun about and saw an awesome but totally revolting sight. It looked like Ligeia Mare was letting loose a *giant wet fart!*

Slowly rising in the weak gravity out of the glassy-smooth sea was a huge, disgusting *geyser*. The vile plume was a giant conglomeration of interlocking frothing bubbles, exploding with orange/brown solid globs. Intellectually I knew that the column was caused by massive *Azotos* rising to the surface releasing stored-up nitrogen gas. But emotionally I pictured not breaching majestic whales back during the Old Earth whaling days, but outgassing dead cetacean carcasses washed up on contaminated beaches.

Yep, I was about to come "face-to-face" with *zombie* alien whales!

"Hard-ta'-starboard! Lay th' boat on fer a full spread!" the Captain shouted.

I felt the long flat deck smoothly turning to my right along our forward path. Mesmerized, my eyes were still fixed on the giant, orange, slimy geyser. It erupted ever higher into the smog, chunks now leisurely starting to fall back in the low gravity, some headed for my faceplate!

Reflexively I put my spacesuited arms up over my helmet. I now wished we weren't totally exposed out there on the flat deck. But I knew the slowly falling debris was mostly frozen shit-foam, too fluffy to damage my suit. The true danger came from the emerging *Azotos*. Those beasts could drag even gigantic skiffs down to the depths. Along the port side of our skiff a row of deadly barbed *harpoons* flipped up out of the deck, poised for launching upward into the sky.

"It's pure dead brilliant, whut?" a squeaky high-pitched voice resonated painfully in my helmet.

I tore my eyes away from the tumbling filth and the pointed harpoons, looking to my side. The First Mate stood primly there beside
me, hands on her gray-spacesuited narrow hips. Her faceplate was
relatively clean. I could see her *red* eyes glaring at me beneath her
thin gray hair. *Uh oh*, that spelled trouble. On Huygens Station turning your eye implants red was an aggressive social challenge. It was
clear she was looking for a fight. And latched to her workbelt were
several wicked looking knives.

I wasn't yet mentally primed for a fight. I had to buy myself some
time.

"Oh, hi there," I responded neutrally, swaying on the deck as the
skiff turned even more sharply beneath me. I trusted my magnetic
boots to keep me in place. Out on the sea I now saw *giant humps*
breaking the surface beneath the depleting geyser. From the skiffing
videos I'd studied, I knew a geyser usually heralded the breaching of
up to a dozen Azotos. However, I saw them rising up all around the
skiff. We were surrounded. There must be *hundreds* of them out
there! And in the distance I saw yet other geysers erupting. Was this
normal, or had we wandered into an unusual herd of them? "Yes, it's
quite a spectacle. Are you my designated baby sitter?"

She laughed snarkily, without humor.

"Och na, ma'am. A'm yer *protector*. Hings ur aft tae git wild,
don't ye know? Best you stick ticht tae mah side, and take a lash. Th'
captain's ordered me tae keep ye safe, 'n' sae a'm doin'."

She roughly inserted a safety line through a ringlet on my suit's
external workbelt. It was the standard smart-rope, looping through
and automatically tying itself into a bowline knot. It wouldn't slip off
until I deliberately tugged on it. Simultaneously she hooked my arm
with her own, pulling me over to one of the skiff's far corners, out of
the way.

"I don't allow people to touch me," I protested, jerking my arm
from her grasp. "Tell me what to do and I'll comply. But don't grab
me! I'll not give you a second warning."

She shrugged. "Whitevur…juist follow mah leid. Ask me whitevur
yi'll want. A'm 'ere tae hulp ye."

"Fine…thanks."

God, MacDonald's accent was particularly thick. I could barely understand what she said. She must be a pure-bred Scottish clanner, versus Jags who just spoke the local prevalent dialect. Clanners were a tight bunch, hostile to any "outsiders" while being fiercely loyal to each other. In a bar fight you best get the upper hand fast or they'd gang up on you and mercilessly beat you into a bloody heap. I knew too well their prowess, having been on the receiving end several times in my younger, more garrulous days. No more. I was too experienced to let anyone easily get the upper hand on me again.

"What's happening now?" I asked her, trying to keep her engaged. Of course I knew the generalities, but I found the details of the crew's skiffing dance both fascinating and alarming.

"Ah, they've spied a smooth Azotos, 'n' ur fixin' tae bring it onboard. Best tae nae git in thair wey. Ye micht git a hook thro' yer pretty shank."

Spread out before me, the crewmembers were orchestrating a well-practiced, intricate dance. Harponeers were poised along the starboard side of the deck, swinging over their heads plasteel multi-hooks attached to secured lines. The hooks resembled the heavy yard-long iron blubber hooks of Old Earth whalers, but with four outward-set barbs. One or two of the four hooks were guaranteed to imbed in the slithery sheets bobbing up from the depths no matter the angle of impact. And behind them backups were poised to help guide then process the haul once hooked.

The main means for bringing alongside the Azotos, though, was the single-barbed harpoons poised for launch. They'd soar up high into the smog then plunge downward, using their weight and momentum to sink deep into the Azotos' membranes. The inner mechanisms of the skiff would winch the speared creature close where the human harponeers would fine-tune the capture.

"None of the harponeers are wearing their safety lines," I dryly observed, keeping up my disguise as a diligent Safety Inspector.

"Hah," she laughed, "that isnae practical. Thay hae tae be able tae *shift*, nae be stuck tae th' deck lik' ye land lubbers."

"Practical or not, it's a regulation."

"A 'regulation' lik' ye fixin' tae *screw* mah captain?"

What the hell?—I gasped to myself, alarmed.

A took another look at her. Ah yes, that's why a female was on the skiff. She must be Fehler's boat-wife, keeping him "company", particularly on longer voyages. She was jealous of the new, young, "pretty" girl invited by her man to go below-deck for an "inspection." As revolting as living out her suspicions was to me, I played along with her paranoid fantasy.

"That's ridiculous," I insisted, while giving her a smirky leer in return. "I'll be writing you up for any safety violations, not looking to interfere with your boat's established chain of command...or social activities."

My words were proper, but my expression was meant to enrage her. And, yes, her already red eyes glowed even brighter. Good! The angrier she got the more reckless and loose would be her lips.

"No need tae curb yer wurds, lubber. Th' feed's bin cut tae TSS."

I pretended to be surprised. The game was afoot.

"Ah, an accident connected to the geyser, perhaps?"

"Ye cuid say that," she growled, "And I'm nae longer wide-cast. It's jist ye and me talkin', suit-ta-suit."

"Oh, really? Should I take that as a threat?"

"Depends..." she laughed as she *lunged* at me!

I daftly slapped aside the "blubber knife" that she held firmly in a gloved hand. In the same movement I twisted the blade away from her, using her own momentum to flip her onto the deck. Then I stuck a knee firmly onto her spine, neatly pinning her down.

"*Give* it to her!" Fehler yelled as everyone else's gaze was fixated on the slick *mountain* emerging right off our starboard side. It was an "azoting" command derived from Old Earth whaling days, for the harpooner to fling his harpoon into a nearby surfacing whale. But I took it as personal encouragement to set my own "hooks" into dear, feisty Ailith.

"Ungggg..." the First Mate groaned, momentarily stunned by her helmeted head bouncing off the decking.

I saw dozens of the ship-launched harpoons spring up into the sky, trailing long silvery lines. They then lazily arched downward, gaining momentum as they plunged toward the Azotos. In just seconds they sank deeply into the "flesh" of one of the creatures, securing it to the skiff. As the mass was winched closer, the human harponeers hurled their own multi-hooks, exquisitely maneuvering the mass alongside, poised to pull it up onto the deck.

I turned my attention back to my moaning prisoner.

"You're about to have an 'accident' if you don't give me the answers I want," I spoke, still on suit-to-suit transmission. I placed her own blubber-knife at the junction where her helmet locked to her excursion suit.

One little nick and she'd suffocate in Titan's poisonous atmosphere.

"H-howfur did ye juist throw m-me?" she stammered in amazement.

"Leverage," I curtly replied.

The intricate dance of the crew pulling in an Azotos was well in play. I saw a revolting flat sheet of what looked like a solid smushed turd being winched up onto the flat deck. I could feel the deck beneath my feet slightly slant as the huge weight was hauled up and slid along the surface. But the football stadium-sized width of the skiff kept the craft stable as others in the crew scrambled out onto the top of the Azotos' slimy bulk. They sliced away useless scum, trimming off short appendages. And then specialists carrying oxygen-spitting torches leaped nimbly across the sludgy mass. They went right to the edge of the boat before sparking oxygen streams that combined with coating methane to *burn* completely through the monsters. I heard strange static from my helmet speakers. Was it from the torches? The flattened sheets on the deck remained while the off-deck bulk slipped back into the sea.

"Git aff may back, ye boot!"

"I think you mean 'bitch'," I chuckled.

"That's whit ah said. Ye'r hurting me!" she whined.

"Good."

The ship harpoons and multi-hooks snapped their barbs inward such that the devices slipped out of the sinking bulk, returning to the skiff to be reused. Simultaneously, other crewmembers snagged into place other specialized hooks for the decked mass, pulling and positioning the huge liberated sheets. As that happened yet another team scampered over the slimy top of the catch, waving what looked like Old Earth *metal-detectors* across every inch of its area. It was a bizarre scurry. I knew they weren't searching for metals in general, but were actually hunting for tiny signals from crystalline *titanium* nuggets. If even a sand-sized grain were present, they'd detect its presence and slice it out using the razor-sharp edges of the detecting loop. Any microscopic rare nuggets they missed would be refined out by the processing facilities onshore. Finally, the sheets were lifted onto the top of a growing pile that covered half of the wide aircraft carrier-sized deck.

It was fascinating, but I'd not forgotten about the First Mate.

"Why did you try to kill me?" I interrogated her, now all-business.

"How come nae?" she defiantly replied with her own question.

She twisted beneath me but failed to shake me loose from my perch on her back.

"I'm no threat to you, except to remind you to follow a few basic safety rules," I lied, trying to draw her out.

"Ye'r nae 'ere tae shag mah Captain?"

"*That's* why you tried to put a knife through my excursion suit? Are you certain you weren't *ordered* to murder me by your higher-ups?"

"Higher-ups?" she again coyly reversed my question.

Clearly she knew more than she was admitting. Perhaps I should be more direct. After all, she attacked me. Now I'd attack-back.

Maybe I don't need to torture the Captain after all. Maybe the First Mate can provide the answers I need.

"Tell me the buyer of your off-books Green."

"Whit?" she gasped. Then, more cannily, she grated: "Wha urr *ye?*"

"My pedigree beyond my official title is none of your concern," I growled. I set my knee harder down into her spine while pulling back on the knife, setting the blade deeper into the suit's fabric at her throat. "*Answer* my question."

One quick yank and she'd be flopping on the deck like those beached Azotos hunks, facing a terrible death.

"I dinnae ken! I dinnae ken! Th' Captain takes care o' a' all that business. We just git oor cut," she whined, apparently convinced I was serious.

Alright then—I congratulated myself. *I've confirmed the skiff isn't operating an honest operation, content with its large bonuses from properly reported Green. They are definitely part of the illegal smuggling operation.*

"Then *where* does he take the Green? What happens when you get back from a voyage with a hot haul? *You're* his bitch. What's your 'pillow-talk' concerning your 'extra' income?"

"I cannae ken yer wurds," she protested, again trying to wriggle out from under me and failing. "How come dae ye blether in ault Earth sassenach, anyway? Ah thought ye wur juist anither privileged aristrocrat lik' Dougal, but ah see ye'r different. Whit dae yi'll waant—*in* oan th' haul? We kin dae that! Tis nae a kinch. Ye'll git yer cut."

Though they were still engrossed in hauling in and spreading out the flat Azotos sheets, a few of the crew were glancing over at me on the far corner of the skiff apparently pinning their First Mate likewise to the deck. I only had a few moments before her crewmembers came to her aid.

"*Answer* me," I repeated, ramming the tip of the sharp knife completely *through* her suit's tough fabric.

I saw her faceplate fog up as a spurt of Titan's icy atmosphere blasted into her helmet before being stopped by the automatic sealing mechanisms in her suit. They could handle a prick, but not a *long slice* through the fabric. And the First Mate knew this better than me.

Chocking and gasping, she replied: "He does tak' frequent trips tae Doom and..."

"*Doom* Mons, the cryovolcano?" I interrupted her.

It was one of the big ice-volcanoes on Titan. It was located below the equator, towering up 5,000 feet, with calderas plunging as deep as 6,000 feet into the frozen-ice "ground". As far as I knew, only a small scientific outpost was located at Doom. Why would the Captain travel there frequently? He certainly didn't appear to be or sound like a scientist.

"Aye..."

"Why? What does he do there?" I pressed her.

"He says he haes kinfowk thare, at th' outpost," she moaned.

I saw one of the crew put aside his blades and start clomping toward us on the still-open deck area. I needed to wrap this up fast if I was to have a shot at grilling Captain Fehler for details of his "family visits." Regardless though, I'd already gotten a good lead from the First Mate. I could just kill her, claiming an "accident" happened, but I had a better idea. She might still have valuable Intel I'd want.

"Your suit's password, now!" I grated at her, thrusting the entire blade of my knife deeper into her suit's neck fabric.

"*Arbroath1320,*" she gasped.

Ah, yes. It was the date of the Scottish Declaration of Independence, signed in the year A.D. 1320, penned more than a thousand years in the past. The document was revered by Old Scotland, certifying their right to self-rule. A copy of it still existed in the New Scotland Lunar Assembly Hall, inspiring all present Scottish Clanners to be stubborn, uncooperative mavericks.

I yanked open the cover of her life support backpack, entered the password on an external keypad, brought up a list of control options, and quickly punched in some key commands.

She abruptly sprang up, her arms outstretched. I'd upped the suit's internal pressure while increasing the percentage of CO_2 to 10%. And her magnetic boots were now at full power, welding her onto the deck.

"Yes, I do think this whole operation is just spectacular!" I enthusiastically exclaimed to her after switching over to wide-broadcast such that anyone could hear me. I also spread my arms wide, as if taking in the entire skiff operation.

The approaching crewman paused and then turned away. There were too many pressing duties to be wasting time checking up on the First Mate shepherding a visiting Inspector-Tourist.

And so you just go to sleep, my helpful Scottish-Clanner lady—I smugly thought to myself as I carefully backed off the CO_2 concentration in her gas mixture. Just 1% is toxic. Jacking it to 10% had knocked her out. I didn't want to kill her, just keep her unconscious for the duration. I then decreased the air pressure so she'd stay upright but not have her arms sticking out to her sides like a scarecrow. I kept her magnetic boots charged to full power so she wouldn't move from that spot, seemingly welded onto the metallic deck.

Then I put one of my arms through hers (since I was in full control I didn't mind the contact) lest anyone else observe she wasn't behaving naturally. And so, I was back again keenly observing the ship's fishing operation beside my slumbering "protector." Hah! If the titanium-searching squad got any hits, I'd see what they did with their sliced-out catch.

And so, I stood there patiently observing for several exhausting hours. Unfortunately, the detector crew didn't find any prizes. But that was to be expected. Their query was exceedingly rare, mainly present in the sheets at a molecular level, only retrievable during processing at the Station. But I was disappointed not to see the crew discovering and handling an unexpected larger bounty.

Even in the low gravity (similar to Earth's moon's), I didn't like standing for extended periods. Fortunately, I could lean on my "protector" who was snoring distinctly over suit-to-suit reception in my helmet. None of the others could hear her since she'd already turned off her broadcast radio mode. Experiencing her nasty snorting wasn't pleasant, but the overall spectacle unfolding before me was mesmerizing.

The hard work of the choreographed "dancing" crew had succeeded magnificently. Their expert efforts resulted in a high mound of cleaned-off, packed down, well-secured Azotos sheets. The slippery mass towered up *a hundred feet* on one half of the wide aircraft carrier-sized flat skiff. The other half of the surface was still receiving more of the hooked raw Azotos, but it looked like the pace was slowing. The slower harvest wasn't due to a lack of the surrounding monsters. No, there just wasn't room left to stack many more of them.

Indeed, they'd certainly found a "swarm."

And as the pace slowed, the static in my helmet decreased. But it continued even when the torches were extinguished. There was definitely a relationship between the static ad harvesting the massive Azotos sheets.

I still found it amazing that the huge flat sheets were alive. With their metabolism slowed glacially by the super-low temperatures that they constantly endured, they certainly weren't life as we'd known it back on Old Earth. The word "Azotos" derived from the term "azotosome" invoking and paralleling the "liposome" or lipid-bilayer upon which water-based life depends. The self-assembling *acrylonitrile* azotosomal membranes were as limber and stable in liquid methane as were the phospholipid bilayer of Earth cells in liquid water. Over the eons, virus-sized primitive azotosomes on Titan had evolved into the gigantic multi-branching muddy sheets I saw now laid out before me on the deck of the skiff. The large surfaces in the low gravity facilitated their glacially slow nutrient uptake.

"So are ye ready for that below-deck inspection?" a gruff but cheerful voice rang in my helmet.

Yikes, it was Fehler! Again I'd let my musings lower my response rate. I had to stay sharp. And yes, he was "licking his chops" eager to begin devouring my tender young flesh. But looking into MacDonald's faceplate he'd instantly see she wasn't just meekly standing at my side.

"No! I exclaimed, pushing away from the "protecting" presence beside me, yanking free from my safety line, and clomping toward the high pile of Azotos. "I need to inspect how well you've secured your catch. Ms. MacDonald wouldn't let me move from beside her over there in the corner. Surely *you* can take charge of me now, Captain?"

"Aye, we're wrapping up the catch, tis true. And a nice one it tis, don't you agree? Ah'll be relievin' you, Ailith."

"Oh yes, *quite* a pile," I instantly answered, obscuring the First Mate's non-reply as I steered Fehler away from her. "It's amazing how the factory turns this giant pile of slippery sheets into space-bladders that ferry massive amounts of methane rocket fuel from Titan throughout the solar system. You and your crew are truly performing a vital service to mankind!"

He was walking beside me toward the well-secured towering mass of stacked sheets, daftly steered away from the nonresponsive First Mate. I hoped my effusive praise would divert him from thinking about the silent woman standing stiffly behind us.

"That's not me job, lassie," he laughed. "I just catch the 'fish.' Others clean and process th' carcasses."

"I hear that they cleanse the living tissue composing the convoluted super-tough membranes," I blathered on, keeping his attention centered on me. "Then they chemically alter what's left into the final space-worthy bladders. I'm looking forward to inspecting the processing plant, which I've not gotten to yet. The entire process is supposed to be analogous to what happened on Old Earth when they felled living trees to turn the linked microscopic skeletal cellulose cell coverings into 'wood.' Is that your impression as well?"

"Aye, that's about all I ken aboot..."

"But I thought you had a background in biochemistry?" I interrupted him, keeping him mentally off balance. "Aren't you an expert on Titanian alien metabolic pathways? I wanted to ask you about how nitrogen gas accumulation within the Azotos' bladders intersects biochemically with the Azotos *inhaling hydrogen* in place of oxygen, 'burning' acetylene instead of glucose, and 'breathing out' methane instead of carbon dioxide."

Yes, the alien Azotos lifeform helped replenish the methane in the atmosphere, but only partly. It was still a mystery why methane persisted on Titan.

He took my arm and guided me around a slimy patch on the deck. I grit my teeth and didn't pull away from him. I needed to keep diverting his attention from the silently standing First Mate receding behind us.

"Lassie, whut have ye been lookin' at concernin' me record? I'm nae a scientist. I'm jist a lowly fisherman, always 'ave been."

"Oh, I'm so sorry," I seemingly sincerely apologized. "I must be thinking of someone else in the crew. But still, the nitrogen gas accumulation is what causes the giant Azotos lurking in the organic muck at the bottom of the seas to rise to the surface," I engagingly continued. "Surely you know more about this than you're letting on? When the accumulated nitrogen is discharged as geysers on the surface, the Azotos sink back to the depths. So nitrogen gas byproduct is what allows you to earn your living selling giant heaps of these sliced-off sheets. And that's not even mentioning the *Green* that..."

His relaxed arm tightened around mine at my mention of the Green, yanking me closer. He looked me square in my faceplate, chest-to-chest.

"We report every microgram o' Green thet we harvest," he coldly stated. "And we find only a grain or two every few voyages. As a'm sure ye'r aware, tis the rarest commodity in th' entire solar system. It costs a fortune to purchase even a small dash o' it. We git a good bonus based on whitevur little pieces we're jammy enough tae discover durin' a cruise. As ye know, hooch tainted wi' trace amounts of it kin cost a year's wage. So we're diligent tae protect 'n' report *everything* we find tae th' Company."

His grip on my arm was *very* tight. He wasn't kidding.

"Well, of course...I wasn't suggesting anything different," I hastened to add, gently dislodging his gloved hand. It was clear to me he didn't know that Ailith had already informed me of his stopping the broadcasting feed up to TSS. He was still being somewhat "proper and official" to lull my suspicions of his coming attack on me. "I was just wondering how the microscopic nodules in the Azotos tie to internally recycling their membranes, releasing nitrogen as a byproduct and..."

"It seems ye already have a good grasp of th' biochemistry involved in these monsters," he flatly stated, "so why don't we go on below and ye can 'av a real taste of th' Green? One of our official bonuses fer this dodgy task is to keep a small percentage of our duly-reported Green discoveries, mixin' it into our ship's grog in trace amounts. Keeps our crew loyal, don't 'cha know?"

More like hopelessly addicted...

I could see through his faceplate his eyes were narrowing, cold. How much did he know of my true mission? I knew he was going to try to kill me. But did he know *why* I was so dangerous? Or, like Ailith, was he just blindly following orders?

"First the safety lines," I insisted, pulling away from him and continuing on around the giant slime-dripping brown stack. I reached out to test the web of lines that stretched up the stack's side. "But I *am* quite curious of the Green. I've never had enough money to pay for the experience, so your invitation to get a sip of your 'grog' that contains trace amounts is intriguing. I know that when diluted in ethanol the alien molecules bind tightly to a variety of neural receptors in the human brain. In addition to extreme ecstasy, it's said to cause visions birthing transcendental insights. But *how* could 'organizing nodes' from an *alien* lifeform have such a profound effect on human cells? It's been the subject of intense research at Consortium University on Mars, but still..."

"Captain!" I heard a frantic yell over my helmet speaker. "A *Krakenzota's* comin' up right beneath us!"

"Whut?" he gasped, pulling away from me, "How did we nae spot it afore this?"

"The swarm blocked it from our sonar! Tis comin' up fleet, Captain. Full thrust ahead?"

"Aye! Cut loose any hooked Azotos. Get us th' 'ell oot of 'ere!"

A Krakenzota? Oh, sweet Buddha! We were in trouble! The term derived from the legendary sea monster of Old Earth Nordic fame, a *giant squid* that could engulf an entire ship, dragging it down into the depths! On Titan the term referred to an Azotos so massive that when surfacing releasing its accumulated nitrogen gas it was the size of an *entire* island! They were first spotted by radar in the early 21st century by NASA's Cassini spacecraft: transiently present *islands* that were each up to several miles in length. This close to the shoreline on Ligeia Mare they were rare, but not unheard of...

—and one is coming up right under us!

"Crank th' propellers!" Fehler yelled, so loud his voice in my helmet hurt my ears, "Full speed ahead!"

I felt the nuclear pod-energized engines rev up beneath me, sending strong vibrations through the metallic planks at my feet. The entire deck uncharacteristically tilted backward as the combined engines thrust us forward. I noted that due to the unusual shaking, MacDonald was regaining consciousness. Her helmet was moving back and forth as she tried to grasp what was happening. It'd only take moments until she saw on her red-lined helmet monitors that her CO_2 was dangerous high. She'd ramp it down and be back in full control of her senses. Meanwhile, Fehler was clomping away to help the crew jettison their last half-harvested Azotos. Yikes! Things were rapidly spinning out of control...

—when the deck suddenly *jumped upward* under my feet, dislodging my boots from the deck and tossing me into the air like a rag doll! I grabbed at webbing zipping past me and managed to snag my arm firmly into overlapping lines. I *slammed* hard into the slimy frozen heap which was still secured to the boat, to which I clung for dear life. Then our entire giant skiff *crashed* back into the sea, causing a frigid wave of liquid methane to momentarily engulf me. Briefly I feared being flash-frozen. But we bobbed back to the surface of the sea with the icy liquid draining off rapidly. Skiffs were virtually unsinkable if their integrity wasn't breached. They had numerous air pockets built into their materials and structure. I took solace in the certainty that I was relatively safe on the skiff unless it broke into pieces...

—when I looked up and time seemed to freeze: *The Captain* like-wise caught in the webbing and calling plaintively for crewmembers that'd been washed off the deck. *The First Mate* still riveted to the deck by her full-power magnetic boots, making swimming motions with her arms. The sky was filled with *bursting orange bubbles*, frothing. And long wedges of what looked like giant "turds" were plummeting straight down at the skiff!

Oh, hell—I swore to myself, fascinated. *These hurtling hunks aren't just icy foam. No, they're rock-hard spears, up to fifty feet in length!*

One *plunged* through the deck into the inner mechanisms below deck with a deafening *"crunch"* that penetrated my helmet. Several more skewered the remaining decking, one missing me by mere yards as it smashed through the pile of Azotos sheets, ripping me from my perch on the webbing. I just managed to grab onto a busted plank to keep from being tossed into the icy sea. And a *hail* of the frozen spears continued raining down on us, repeatedly *ripping* through the ship. Yep, our skiff was being "broken up" pretty effectively...

"Abandon th' ship! Abandon th' ship! Git yer wings oan!"

It was the First Mate, having regained her senses and now wide-broadcasting to any survivors. She was clinging to a slowly rotating intact section of the deck bobbing in the now violently disturbed sea.

Where was the Captain? He was nowhere to be seen. I certainly didn't care if he got squashed by the flying giant frozen turds. The vile bastard probably deserved such an ignominious end. But before he died I needed some critical answers from him!

All around me I saw crewmembers frantically searching for and opening the few still-working hatches, dragging out and belting fold-ed structures onto their excursion suits. In a few seconds the mecha-nism self-molded securely to their arms, backs, and legs. One by one they leapt up into the thick Titan air, wide wings unfolding, and flapped slowly away. I spied one lone soul leaping from one bobbing fragment to another, frantically searching for a set of wings. But he didn't find any. And his last leap was short, causing him to splash into the sea. The inside of his helmet visibly cracked as he sank beneath the surface, screaming piteously.

Giving a nod to my supposed official role, I was glad to see that those lucky enough to retrieve intact wings had gotten off the sinking vessel. The skiff's ultimate safety mechanism was working as expected. Due to the low gravity, thick atmosphere, and permissive surface pressure, people wearing appropriate artificial wings could stay aloft under their own power. Although we were several miles offshore, to leisurely flap along, even hundreds of feet up in the air, required no more effort than walking. The men not already dragged down to the depths would survive by flying themselves home.

But no one thought to sling an extra set of wings to me. I guess pesky "safety inspectors" weren't a high priority to save in a disaster.

"Hey, ye cute little hoor, look up!" I heard a familiar squeaky voice in my helmet. It was Ailith. *She'd* been thrown a set of wings. Now she was sketching a circle in the orange sky above me, "Feck you in yer rear! Ah'm soooo sad that there's nae wings left fur ye. A'm wiry bit pure tough, enough tae gie ye a hurl back tae port. I suppose I could swoop down and grab ye, but then I'd be all tuckered out when I got to the base lugging ye'r dead weight. So I think I'll pass on flyin' ye to safety. Sae sorry aboot that, heh! Ah will report thet ye died bravely, sucked doon tae th' depths. Chap *me* doon 'n' try to murdurr me wi' CO2? Say hello tae mah good friend *Ogen* at th' bottom o' th' sea! Hah!"

If something drastic didn't happen, that might well occur.

"I could certify to the investigating officials that you didn't have anything to do with the sinking of the ship!" I yelled back up to her, desperate not to be left behind. "I can make it worth your while, Ailith. There are *elites* sponsoring me!"

She laughed merrily.

"Ye'r all-so-mighty 'Elites' kin suck my dick, if I had one!" she cackled in my helmet from on-high. "Ye were ill luck tae us fae th' foremaist. Ah don't know how ye managed it, but ye've murdurred me Captain and half the crew. Noo that th' boat is breached th' sea wull crack its inner bubbles 'n' drag the leftovers down tae th' depths, includin' yer own sorry arse. Guid riddance tae ye, ye wee wanker!

The survivin' crew is all the 'certification' I need. I'll be a hero, maybe get me own skiff ta captain meself!"

Laughing crazily, she lazily flapped away into the orange haze, disappearing.

I was left all by myself on a slowly sinking hunk of the broken ship, puzzling. So, there'd be no wings or ride for me? Well, that was to be expected. Leaving me to sink was easier than harpooning me or tossing me over the side. But then again, from her prior words, Ailith had a genuine affection for her Captain. Now that he was likely dead, she just moved on? It didn't make sense.

What didn't she tell me?—I puzzled.

Quite uncharacteristically, I was confused, uncertain of what to do next. Despite my prior arrogance thinking I'd been in every situation possible this was definitely a new pickle.

"Inspector! I need yer assistance!" a faint voice caught my attention over my helmet speakers.

Was it another survivor? Clearly his radio was broken, only sending out a very weak signal.

Plus, the *static* in my helmet was now bombarding my ears. Was it radio waves from the *Kraken?* Was that even possible? I'd never heard of this happening before. Krakenzota were just larger Azotos, which themselves were just alien frozen seaweeds. Weren't they?

Stop letting your mind wander—I firmly ordered myself. *You're minutes from becoming one of those "frozen seaweeds" yourself!*

"Where are you?" I called out, searching.

The now eerily smooth, oily sea was littered with many still-bobbing hunks of the shattered skiff. The pile of cleaned Azotos sheets was long-gone, sunk without a trace. But not far from me I saw an ominously rising hump...

—which kept rising up higher and higher out of the sea!

It was the Krakenzota, "Kraken" for short. The previously lofted hunks must have been just its coating of frozen sludge buoyed by nitrogen gas, slung up from the depths to crash into the skiff both from beneath and then again when tumbling back down from above. What was the main mass doing now, "inspecting" the damage it'd caused?

That's ridiculous—I admonished myself, trying to get my wits back together after the disaster I'd just experienced. *It's only a mas-*

sively huge Azotos. Those things can't think or see. They're just alien seaweed.

"I'm 'ere! Gimme a hand. I'm sinkin' in th' sea. Hulp me!"

Buried beneath a pile of broken planks I saw a gloved hand grasping outward. The liquid methane of the sea was creeping up the pile. I tottered along the tilted deck until I reached the heap. Then I ripped and yanked out the twisted planks, throwing them into the sea. An arm, a shoulder, and a helmet were revealed. I grabbed the arm and pulled the man up out of the pile just as the sea level rose over where he'd been. Liquid methane dripped from his legs as he clung to me, trembling.

"Ye saved me," he gasped. "Mah suit heaters wur failing, mah legs chankin'. Well done, Inspector. A guess I wuz wrong aboot havin' ye onboard, after all."

My first reaction was elation that the Captain had survived. My second reaction was wary puzzlement.

Damn! The old man has a speck of humility in him. Perhaps he isn't a total rat after all. Maybe I'll leave him alive after I wring my answers out of what's left of his big, battered body.

I pulled him up to the highest edge of the remaining corner of the slowly sinking skiff-fragment. We had only a house-sized flat area left above the "waterline" of the once carrier-sized deck.

"Thank me after we get back to land," I replied. "We'll be submerged in minutes. I don't suppose a rescue helicopter from the fleet will be along shortly?"

"Ah, sadly no, lassie," he groaned. He was visibly shivering, clutching his near-frozen legs, "Th' devastation was so sudden they won't know we're skewered until the crew flaps back ta' base. It'll be hours before a rescue skiff is launched."

"Then where do we go? There aren't any wings left."

"We've got...other resources," he weakly replied. His voice in my helmet was hard to hear above the thick ongoing static.

What the hell is it with all this static? Has my helmet been damaged? Or is it really from the Kraken?

"What?" I frantically queried him, seeing only slowly bobbing and sinking debris surrounding me in the misty brown sea. "What should we do?"

He was silent. I still had an arm around his chest, keeping him from slipping away into the sea. There were small cracks in his face-plate. Had he been hit by the frozen plummeting Kraken-ejectus? Was he dead?

I shook him, hard.

"Come on, Captain, stay with me! Are you hurt? Can you function?"

He stirred in my arms, squirming from side-to-side.

"Muh...my legs...th' feeling's comin' back in muh legs...almost frozen from their dip 'n' the sea."

"Tell me what to do. Does this happen often?"

The orange mists around me seemed to be thickening. The dim light above was fading. Oh hell, Titan's slow day was waning. It'd be dark soon. Even if a miracle occurred and a passing rescue helicopter accidently flew fly over us they might miss us.

"Not often in years past...but more often now...bigger Azotos, gigantic Krakensotas flingin' skiff-killin' spears into the air...capsized boats..." his voice trailed off.

He was obviously having trouble staying conscious. I had to have him alert and clear minded to give me the key answers I needed. And not-to-mention I needed him to tell me *how to stay alive* on a sinking ship-fragment in the middle of a liquid-methane super-cold sea.

"It's the hydrogen pollution we're generating on Titan," I insisted, knowing the assertion would anger him.

"What? No, that's just a hoax by ecofreaks to hurt our jobs that..."

"Sorry, Captain, it's all too real," I interrupted him. "The limiting factor to Azotos growth used to be the amount of breathable H_2 in Titan's atmosphere, a mere 0.1-0.2%. In the brief hundred years that mankind's been mining Titan, the amount of hydrogen has jumped to 1%, *ten times* as much as when we first got here."

"I...I don' think that matters or is..."

"It's true," I insisted as our fragment sank even lower. "Numbers don't lie. Yes, the Company says it doesn't matter, that the Azotos aren't proliferating like wildfire, and even if they are so what? But we can't continually generate billions of tons of hydrogen—when we use our nuclear reactors to split water to get the liquid oxygen for sending off with our methane rocket fuel—then just dump that hydrogen as waste into the atmosphere without consequences. It's altering the entire ecosystem of Titan. And today *we're* the casualties!"

Our house-sized above-"water" chunk of decking was getting steadily smaller as the inner material air bubbles burst open. We had only a few minutes to find a solution or die.

"That's a' load of crap, Inspector," Fehler growled. "It's jist ill luck today. And *no*...we're nae casualties, not yet."

He pushed my gloved hands away and sat up, massaging his legs through his gray suit's flexible fabric.

"We're somewhere on the aft 'n' port corner of the ship," he continued more strongly, getting his wits back around him. "So, look for hatches marked with a red 'X' and a blue 'B', if any ur left."

"Ok," I answered, shoving overboard clumps of shattered planks, frantically searching. "I found one, an 'X'."

"Good...unlatch th' handle 'n' pull out whut's inside."

I did as ordered, pulling up a long harpoon which trailed a long, thin line. Its plasteel head was solid and hefty.

"What do I do with this?"

"How far off...is the Kraken?"

I peered off into the swirling orange mists. It was getting so dark I could barely make out what was right next to us, let alone out to sea. But then I saw it—a looming small mountain!

"I think it's about a football-stadium-length distance from us."

"Then ye kin do it," he whispered from my helmet speaker, clearly weakening again, slumping back onto the tilted deck.

"Do *what?*"

"Throw...the harpoon...lodge into the Kraken...and pull us over onto it...afore we're sunk down to Ogen's locker."

I didn't like the notion of going down to the Titanium equivalent of "Davy Jones' locker." I now recalled that Ogen was another name for Oceanus who was the Greek Titan god of the sea. Long before I entered that "locker" my suit heaters would fail and I'd be frozen solid.

"What, climb onto that giant Azotos mass out there?" I gasped. That didn't seem like a preferable option at all.

"Aye...it takes a while to outgas its excess nitrogen...since it's so thick...not like a regular smaller Azotos...stable enough a platform, maybe, tae last until rescue arrives."

"I'm not a professional football quarterback or a javelin thrower. We've only one harpoon. I can't toss it that far!"

"In this...weak gravity...with your newcomer 1-G muscles not yet weakened by livin' here fer years...ye kin do it."

"But even then..."

"Jist throw it high and hard!"

"Alright then," I shrugged.

I precariously stood up on the wobbling deck, hefted the harpoon like a javelin, made sure the thin, strong line was off to the side and would flow freely, reared back, and *flung* it as hard as I could off into the darkness in the general direction of the Kraken.

The line zipped out of the opened hatch at my feet—seemingly for minutes, maybe thousands of feet in all—then suddenly stopped and went slack.

"It's gone. It stopped."

"Then pull us...forward!"

He went silent as I began rapidly yanking in the slack line...it tightened. I'd hooked something! And then I began pulling as hard and fast as I could, my boots locked onto the shrinking area of planks at my feet, happy to see our "raft" moving across the smooth sea through the mists. And just as we only had standing room remaining we bumped up onto something and were stationary, no longer sinking.

"I think I did it," I grinned, my arm muscles aching and quivering. I shook Fehler's shoulder but he didn't respond. But he was still breathing. With a hand on his arm augmenting direct suit-to-suit transmission I could hear him taking ragged, unsteady breaths.

Ok, kiddo. He said something about a hatch marked with a "B." Can I find one? Maybe...

There! Over behind me under some debris...and pulling it open I recognized within it "Azotos-beaching" supplies: a multi-hook with a thicker line attached, a spark-torch with a full canister of oxygen, and a titanium-grain tuned "magnetic metal detector."

What, did the Captain think we were going exploring? I was going to try and get us better secured onto the looming Kraken, then concentrate on reviving and interrogating the Captain. I wasn't going to get a better chance to drag the answers out of him than in our present predicament. Finally, I hoped to stay alive until rescuers arrive.

So then, where are we? How do we get more secure? The line to the harpoon gets tight then goes slack. The Kraken must be an unstable, ill-defined mass.

I grabbed the multi-hook and slung it into the darkness. Pulling back, I felt some of the long hooks lodge solidly. I pulled on the line until it was taut. Then I tied it around a protruding, broken plank. Now we were secure.

"Well done, Lassie. Now *do just as I say* 'n' ye may yet live to be rescued."

I spun about ready to kick...but stopped. Ah, that rascal. He'd been "playing dead" to get the drop on me.

Sparking briefly the welding torch he held, he forced me back with its flame. He stood firmly on both of his "nearly frozen" legs. Apparently they weren't hurt near as bad as he'd claimed.

"I kin do it myself, but it'd be difficult. Ye'll be makin' things much easier for me, lassie. Pick up that detector 'n' proceed onto th' Kraken."

"What is this, Captain? I saved you. You don't have to threaten me to get my cooperation."

"Aye, I'm grateful tae ye. But I'm also greedy. And I'm thinkin' this whole disaster may give me the means to finally leave Titan behind for a life o' wealth, luxury, 'n' power. That tis if ah kin ever escape the Monks..."

"What the hell are you talking about?" I interrupted his musings.

"A stable Kraken this big must have th' largest Green ever harvested in the history o' Titan," he now spoke with resolve. "We're goin' fer it."

Ah, I see it now. It's money. Yet again, it's money taking us to the darkest place on Titan. Why must mankind be ruled by money?

"So if you can reach it, before the Kraken plunges back to the depths..." I ventured, urging him to explain.

"Aye, we'll slice it out o' the monster's guts. So thet's our goal. We'll follow th' harpoon's line into th' interior, using it as a' safety rope. March!"

With one of his suit belt knives he whacked off the end of the thin harpoon line, leaving our wrecked deck fragment still moored by the multi-hook. He attached the severed end to his belt, starting a coil to continually take up the slack as we moved forward. Then he pointed the end of the welding torch at me menacingly.

Even under normal circumstances I'd have a hard time winning a head-to-head fight against an alert whaler as large as him. And now he can set me on fire with a flick of a finger.

Reluctantly I lifted the four-foot long detector, making sure the horizontal grate at its end was above the muck level. I considered whirling around and slicing the Captain's head off using the razor edge of the detecting loop. Yes, I could do it. But I still needed to question him. For the moment I had no choice but to follow his orders. However, I hesitated, not knowing where to step.

He let off another *burst* of the terrifying red flame just to my side, which momentarily blinded me.

"Ok! Alright! I'm going!"

Blinking to get my sight back, with the detector cradled in my arms, I stepped off the broken deck into what felt like deep swamp mud. I knew it was nitrogen gas-foamed organic sludge covering many unseen layers of tough Azotos membranes, but it seemed like my worst nightmare: wading blindly into a dark, gigantic, oozing septic tank.

"Step lively, lassie," he growled at me. "We don't ken whin th' Kraken wull dive. If that happens we'll git na reward. Bit don't worry. Ah hae a feeling everything's comin' up Green. Hah!"

I was literally up to my hips in shit, captive to a maniacal pirate, wading into the interior of a giant alien beast that could plunge to the depths at any moment taking us with it. What could go wrong?

We were climbing ever higher. It seemed we'd been slogging along forever, but it was probably less than an hour after the skiff was destroyed. Regardless of how brief or long, this expedition had become a total nightmare.

I'd not yet gotten to question my captor. Surviving on the Kraken required every bit of our attention. We could barely see where we were going in a slimy, gooey, dark quagmire. Our helmet lights helped some, illuminating overhanging nearby shapes. But what helped most were periodic flashes of flame from the oxygen torch, revealing drippy vistas of looming mounds. Fehler however used the glaring torch only occasionally and briefly. He was obviously conserving the oxygen canister for burning down to a hoped-for treasure.

And it didn't help that a mere fifteen minutes into our slog we found our deeply lodged harpoon. With a knife from his workbelt Fehler cut loose the attached line and ordered me to free the harpoon's tip, which I did. He cut a short length and used that to sling the harpoon up over his back. Then, brandishing the oxygen torch at me, he ordered me to tie the end of his thick loop of coiled line to my suit's workbelt.

And so we proceeded onward, with me forced to lead the way.

"Watch yer step, lassie!" his harsh voice reverberated in my helmet. "Keep th' detector loop up oot o' th' muck. Fouling it will compromise its sensitivity. We don't know how deep the Green will be lurkin'!"

Even though we were close to each other, it was still difficult to hear him over the continuing loud *crackling* and *hissing* in my helmet. If anything, the static was getting fiercer as we proceeded up the Kraken's mushy slope. Were we nearing the source of the radiofrequency emissions?

"I'm doing my best," I protested, knee-deep in foamy, organic "mud." Even in the weak Titanian gravity, keeping the long detector up was straining my shoulder muscles.

"Do better! I don't want ye fallin' into another hole or gettin' sucked down a stank channel."

We're definitely proceeding faster, getting our bearings. Soon we'll be expert Kraken-climbers, hah! But now's my chance to get the bastard talking.

"Ah, so you really love me? You're concerned for my wellbeing?" I sarcastically replied.

"Ye'r me only crewmate left. All the rest abandoned me, leaving me here to die. So I've a bit of fondness fer ye, Lassie. But I'll not hesitate ta torch ye. So clam up 'n' keep climbing."

Yes, twice I'd almost been swept away by a flash-flood of pooled liquid methane higher up above us breaking loose. And then the "ground" gave way beneath me, almost tumbling me into a deep black crevasse. Only Fehler's grabbing my suit's slim backpack to yank me to the side saved me.

And not only was the "ground" untrustworthy, the landscape kept shifting...rising and falling and drifting this way or that. It was obvious the Kraken wouldn't be staying on the surface much longer.

"So your buyer is at Doom Mons?" I defied his order to keep silent, desperate to get the information I needed. What, was he going to harpoon me and lose his only pack-mule? I knew he'd try to kill me once he didn't need an extra set of arms, but not now. So maybe he'd be comfortable telling his secrets to his (not so subtly reminded by me) "doomed" prisoner?

For a moment he was quiet behind me.

"How'd ye hear of the cryovolcano?"

"Your First Mate mentioned you had relatives there. I know you've been moving contraband Green. I put two and two together."

"Ye'r a smart lassie. Did the Company send you to spy on me?"

"So it's true?" I evaded his question. "That's where you sell your stolen goods?"

The darkness pressed down on us. He prodded my back with the tip of the oxygen torch, keeping me stumbling forward.

"Stolen? Have ye been out here fur a day and not seen what we 'av ta do to make a bare livin'? We risk our lives every single time we set out from th' port after th' sea-monsters. It used to be easy, slicin' hunks off isolated Azotos. But now we 'ave to fight swarms guarded by freakin' giant Krakens! The wee bits of Green we snag to the side are jist part of our due pay."

Right—and so also has claimed every thief out there who ever stole from his boss or company.

"Ailith said you'd let me in on the take."

That quieted him for a moment as we continued to slog upward.

"Sure, why not? If ye protect our operation then ye kin have a fair cut, identical as th' rest o' th' crew."

Ah, his greed has overcome his common sense—I triumphantly congratulated myself. *Now to press my advantage...*

"To be most helpful to you, I need to be cognizant of the next level up. You've got to take me to meet your buyers."

"Hah! The Monks don't talk to anyone, even me."

Ah! Here was that reference again to some religious group...

"Monks? Do you mean the...?"

He prodded my back with the tip of his unslung, sharp harpoon.

"Jist keep movin'!" he growled. "Let's jist say...I'll consider your request, once we get back to port."

Ok, then. He's not buying my claim of wanting to get in on the take—I coolly observed. *He's just stringing me along. He's got his orders from his superiors. He's never going to allow me to make it back to the base.*

"I need another flare, Captain. The ground is shifting. It seems really loose, different from anything we've gone across yet and..."

"No, we don't," he snapped, though jerking the line to bring me to a stop in front of him. "Look ahead."

We were now on a relatively flat stretch, some sort of plateau. And in the deep darkness I now saw a faint glow—a *green* light.

"Is that...?" I gasped.

"Th' grains we've harvested to-date are all crystalline, like wee jewels. They're all green, which gives them their name. But that light ahead can't come from a wee nugget. Th' source has to be *huge*."

"You're right," I added, trying to keep him overly excited until I could strike back at him. "I researched this before I took this job. The concentrated titanium compounds in the crystals act as catalysts for various exotic biochemical reactions feeding the Azotos' alien metabolism. The molecular structure is much more complex than simple Old Earth calcium titanium silicates, which are rare crystals found in titanium ore. On Old Earth they glowed yellow-green when light was shone through them and..."

"I don't need a lecture, 'professor'," he snapped at me. "Jist march on forward an' start diggin'!"

We carefully stepped around towering frozen "turds" onto a frilly surface that felt like long grass beneath my boots. The green glow was much brighter, seemingly emanating from the ground itself. Looking down I saw the "grass" was actually tightly packed foot-long tendrils. It must be some sort of gas-exchange mechanism feeding the Kraken's central controlling nodule.

"I see it," I gasped.

Yes, there in the center of the bizarre landscape was a *pulsing bright green beacon* emanating from a deep pit.

A large valve of some sort comprised the lip of the pit, which regularly widened then narrowed.

"Holy Senhora!" Fehler gasped from behind me, referring to the patron saint of Old Earth whalers. "Th' crystal at th' bottom of thet pit, generating that light, must be *gigantic.* Th' largest one found to-date was the size of a walnut, which fetched a king's ransom at auction. This will make me th' *richest* man in the *entire* solar system!"

"You mean you, your crew, and *I* will be filthy rich and...?"

"Shut up an' get down there," he cut me off. "Take the detector. It'll confirm th' nodule is near. Then you can use its sharp edges ta' whack through any overlyin' membranes."

Membranes...membranes...the tendrils beneath my feet were like pubic hair, the edge of the pit like a sphincter valve...and all around the "plateau" were the "frozen turds" that'd decimated our skiff...?

Christ! This is the true anus of Titan. That "pit" leads down into the reeking "rectum" of the Kraken—I groaned in revulsion. *Oh, God, I'm about to be a proctologist probing a gigantic alien beast!*

"Hurry up! Get in there," Fehler ordered me. "This whole thing's gonna dive any minute now."

I promise to be gentle—I mentally pleaded, stepping up to the wet-looking edge of the green-glowing pit.

"But we've no idea how deep it is," I tried to protest. "There's no way I'm going down there before we..."

BONG!

Oh, Christ! That greed-crazy skiffer whacked my helmet from behind with the heavy harpoon!—I dizzily noted as I tumbled forward into the wide pit, momentarily stunned.

Then I was dangling precariously from the long line, with Fehler slowly lowering me ever deeper. The green glow was so bright I couldn't see to the bottom. But I did note the disgusting thick layer of bubbly slime oozing from all the walls around me. The hole was a dozen feet across, causing me to scrape along one wall or the other. The putrid brown organic slime was coating my legs and hips as I tried to kick off the walls and stay in the center. My golden excursion suit was being further defiled. I saw the loose foam bunching and coalescing in the air around me, turning from a vile fog to little globules. I now knew where the fifty-foot "turd" spears originated from. Somehow the hardening slime came from reprocessing membranes outgassing excess nitrogen gas. That in turn produced buoyant, hardened cast-off "spears" which were periodically ejected from the pit. I'd already descended more than a hundred feet deep. I was without a doubt in the deep "rectum" of the Kraken.

And the radius narrowed as I descended, such that there was only room for one person toward the bottom.

Then my feet hit a soft, mushy membrane. The green light flared up *blindingly*. The generating crystal had to be very close. My detector sent a "brrrrrrmmmm" into my helmet, the gauge on its top surface snapping up to "max." Simultaneously, the slack line coiled around my feet.

"Dig th' damn thing up!" I heard Fehler yell down at me. His angry shout cut through the now-deafening static in my helmet. "Tis richt under ye!"

Knowing if I refused he'd just torch me from above then descend himself, I jammed the sharp edge of the detection loop hard into the mushy surface at the bottom of the pit.

I felt the entire gigantic Kraken *convulse* around me. And over my helmet speaker, through the continuing blasting static, I now heard a high-pitched *whining*.

"I'm hurting it!" I yelled up in confusion. "It's screaming out in pain!"

"Don' be ridiculous!" he shouted back, now on his knees peering down from the distant top of the pit. "It's jist a giant freakin' hunk of seaweed. Whut ye're seein' and hearin' is jist some automatic reaction. All Azotos contract 'n' twist whin we slice intae them."

"Not like this!" I protested. Horrified, I saw what looked like *red blood* oozing up from the cut I'd made.

"Ye weak-kneed, yellow-livered eejit!" his voice cut through the spiking static in my helmet. "You're boggin' useless to me!"

A *wall of red-yellow flame* engulfed me as a blasted-down oxygen stream plus incendiary sparks ignited the loose liquid methane down in the pit. I beat at rocket-fuel fed *explosions* enveloping my faceplate and suit, trying to keep them from penetrating to the inner fabric. Already I could feel the heat *scorching* my skin.

"Nooooo!" I howled, anticipating the agony of burning to death.

Suddenly I felt the tough, fire-resistant line tighten and *yank* me up and out of the pit. He hauled me up so fast I was lofted upward in the weak gravity, tumbling through the air, before falling down hard upon the surrounding frozen-solid turd spears. The impact plus the previous blow to my head immobilized me. The continuing high-pitched agonized *screech* in my helmet deafened me. I could only watch in horror, knowing Fehler had secured his line and was climbing down into the deep pit. I pictured him ruthlessly hacking into the "ground" at the bottom of the burnt-out pit. All around me the green light flickered and glared as convulsions wracked the giant Kraken. At any moment I expected it to outgas its remaining nitrogen and plunge back to the bottom of Ligeia Mare.

I struggled to get my wits back, to push my bruised body back up to my boots. But I fell back, helplessly waiting.

"I got it!" Fehler laughed gleefully, clambering up out of the pit. "*You* are going to lay there and die. *I'm* going to find somethin' still floatin' to escape the Kraken and await rescue. Whoever shows up will be glad to spirit me 'n' me prize away in exchange fur a slice of th' world-bustin' fortune *this'll* bring!"

In his gloved hands he triumphantly held up a *basketball-sized* green, multifaceted crystal. Shockingly, it was dripping what looked like red blood. He'd truly cut the heart out of the Kraken.

"I think not," I grimaced, finally getting my boots under me. "I may get beat down—but I always rise!"

Before he could react I leaped over and grabbed the oxygen welding-torch which he'd dropped before descending into the pit. I pointed its nozzle right at him, flicking its trigger. *Roiling red flame* caused him to stagger backward, almost falling into the pit behind him. Even with the violent convulsions still rippling through the Kraken I was now steady on my feet. I had the drop on him and he knew it.

Through his faceplate I saw a mixture of rage, fear, and defeat. I had him right where I wanted him. Now I'd finally get my answers!

"Tell me everything you know about the Monks and maybe I'll..."

A *violent pain* shot through my stomach, doubling me over.

I gasped in disbelief. Looking down I saw the blood-smeared tip of our barbed harpoon *protruding* through the suit's fabric at my stomach level. The agony was incredible. I writhed in agony from being skewered, my right gloved hand tightly clutching the plasteel head sticking out of my guts. Fortunately, the sealing mechanism in my suit had stopped air leakage from occurring around the shaft at the entry and exit wounds. But I knew I was fatally wounded. The harpoon had done terrible internal damage, causing profuse bleeding inside my abdomen.

But I still have the oxygen torch in my left hand—I managed to remember.

Dropping to my knees and turning my helmeted head to look behind me I saw a furled-wing-wearing *Ailith* standing there haughtily. Her gloved hands grasped the end of our harpoon which she'd thrust through my guts. And with a disdainful sneer she kicked the torch out of my hand.

"Did ye really think I'd abandon mah Captain?" she sneered at me through her faceplate. "Lars knew I'd find ye both!"

The yellow light in her helmet lit up her narrow, gray head. The green glow from the Kraken was fading, dying. The crystal-lump held by Fehler glowed sporadically, sending out bursts of yellow-green. Other than that, we were again engulfed in darkness.

"You...speared...me," I groaned, barely able to stay conscious against the fierce pain. "You'll regret..."

"Nae likely! I'm carryin' me jimmy away, baith him 'n' his glorious prize. We'll bide lik' kings and queens while ye'll be frozen solid oan the bahookie o' th' sea, a skewered deid fish."

"Ailith! Me love!" the Captain exclaimed, quickly recovering his arrogant swagger, "Ye'r late. I expected ye sooner than this."

"Ah'm so sorry," she apologized. "Ah heard ye'r meager signal thro' th' static o' th' Kraken 'n' turned back. Ah've bin circling up heich tryin' tae git a bearin' oan ye. Whin the arse-hole o' th' monster unfolded 'n' revealed itself the glowing Green led me 'ere. Sae then, shall we gang?"

"Aye," Fehler acknowledged, climbing up onto her strong back. He made a big lump on her scrawny form, like a slug on a butterfly's back. He tightly clutched the giant green crystal as she unfurled her mechanical wings. "Well done, me love. Now off with ye!"

She struggled to get aloft, but the weak Titanian gravity helped her bear her burden. After a few strokes she was on her way. Together they flapped higher as the Kraken went through another massive convulsion. I groped over to the torch, jerking the trigger down tightly, sending a continuous stream of flames up into the sky. I hoped to set the fleeing skiffers on fire, but they were long gone, lost in the pervasive orange smog. Then I felt like I was on a plunging, free-falling elevator. By the light of the still-glaring torch I saw a *massive high wall* of liquid methane thrown up around the plunging beast, now crashing down at my still-flaring torch!

Oh sweet Jesus, I'm going to ignite an ocean of rocket fuel for my funeral pyre—I wryly laughed to myself. *It's actually not a bad ending, though. It's very dramatic, considering how it all started.*

Yes, it's correct what they say. Your entire life flashes before your eyes as you die. And that sad movie starts from the moment you were born—or, as in my case, *re*born...

Chapter 2

OLD EARTH

From "sea to shining sea"
From the "mountains to the prairies"
And in the "oceans white with foam"
Verdant Old Earth teemed with life
Of every form, type, and variation
Seemingly robust, eternal, and impervious
Revealed as frail, transitory, and vulnerable
Where mass extinctions regularly inflicted
Horrible confusion, destruction, and death
From hurtling asteroids, belching volcanic chains,
Smothering ice ages, crushing ecological upheaval,
Strangling sea changes, suffocating gases,
Or man-made global atmospheric warming
Only the lucky and clever survived
But none continue unscathed...

The Rise and Fall of *Homo sapiens*, 2:25-29

The first time I resurrected I had no idea what was happening to me. I was terrified, thrashing about, trapped in a tight, cold box, and writhing in pain in utter darkness—panicking!

I'm in a coffin! Jesus Christ, somehow I've been buried alive!

"Help me! Please help me! Get me out of here!" I yelled, to no avail.

My head pounded with a splitting headache, worse than I'd ever thought possible. It was like my skull was being broken into pieces. Plus I could hardly breathe from the agony in my chest and ribs: like a sledgehammer had shattered all the enclosing bones.

53

And then I mentally tried to calm myself down. I was hyperventilating, suffocating, gasping for breath. I knew that I had to slow my breathing, figure out exactly my present situation. With a huge conscious effort I pushed the anguish in my head and chest to the side. The torment was still there, but muted enough I could start thinking.

What's happening to me?—I tried to focus my chaotic thoughts. *The last thing I remembered was being marched into a large square and securely tied to a post...*

On the other side of the square was a long line of military officers holding rifles "at ready"—my firing squad! There were two dozen sharpshooters. They weren't taking any chances I'd somehow survive. On a long balcony above and around me I saw a crowd of gathered witnesses. They peered down at me with expressions that ranged from disgust to outright hatred, loudly heckling me.

Standing primly beside me, a stern white-haired official cleared her throat. She spoke authoritatively into a handheld microphone, reading from an ornate-looking scroll.

Her amplified voice boomed, drowning out the shouting witnesses: "Susan Hollie King—a.k.a. Suzette Kingly—it's by order of the *International Court of Justice* that you are hereby condemned to death for high crimes against humanity," she solemnly read. "Due to the unprecedented nature of your offences, life-imprisonment was ruled inappropriate. Your execution today is directly witnessed by gathered dignitaries sent here from all governments of the United Nations. Indirectly witnessing your execution, by world-side simulcast, are billions of your fellow citizens. Immediately after your sentence is carried out by firing squad, three court-appointed physicians will certify your heart no longer beats. A subsequent, duly recorded autopsy will confirm brain death. Before your remains are remanded to surviving relatives, cellular death in all of your tissues will be confirmed by definitive laboratory tests. This execution is being conducted beneath a warp-field constructed by designated Time Keepers to prevent any temporal tampering. Your execution will thus be authoritatively certified as complete and final. May God have mercy on your soul."

She paused before continuing. The jeering crowd spread out above me on the long balcony hushed.

"Any last words?" she asked, placing the microphone against my tight-pressed lips.

I shook my head in the negative. I stared straight ahead, stoically awaiting my death.

Assistants slid a black hood over my head. It wasn't for my benefit. It was so that the viewing audience didn't have to see the awful results of their vengeance, other than spreading red stains. I didn't blame them for brutality executing me by bullets rather than lethal injection. I deserved my punishment. Even more, for the good of humanity's continued freedom from extraterrestrial (seemingly benign) enslavement, I *needed* to die.

Though no one knew it, as long as I was alive a theoretical official protest from Earth could still be launched to my having thrown the musical contest at the Galactic Core. With me dead, there was no longer any possibility that mankind could petition the alien *Lords of the Galaxy* for redress. My vile conduct on the Concert Planet would stand forever unchallenged, as would its consequences.

Yes, the witnesses hated me for so filthily and shockingly throwing away humanity's one chance at winning the incredible global prize that the Lords granted to the Contest's winning world. If not for my actions all of Earth's citizens might have gained personal wealth, unlimited power, perpetual health, and virtual immortality. But I hoped that someday the distant descendants of the gathered dignitaries would appreciate my bizarre historic performance. They would realize that my sacrifice allowed humanity's continued struggle onward, bravely defying the brutal forces of nature to travel to the stars!

But today they did not understand. Today I had to die. There was no other option.

It'll be quick—I stoically reminded myself. *With that many rifles fired simultaneously you won't feel a thing, Suzette. The hail of bullets will instantly shatter your head and chest. So stay strong. Don't let a peep come out of your mouth!*

"Ready! Aim! F..."

Everything blanked out.

And then—seemingly an instant later with no intervening time—I woke up confused and disoriented inside a *dark metal drawer*. Drawer? Yes! I could see a sliver of dim red light down at my feet.

When I thrashed about I could feel the metal around me slightly yielding. I could hear a "clinking" of metal-on-metal. This wasn't a coffin buried deep underground. This was a container from which I could maybe escape!

But all my memories were jumbled and incomplete, scrambled by the still-throbbing intense pain. I vividly recalled the firing squad and what I'd done to deserve my execution, but exactly how and why all that had occurred was foggy. Everything that led up to that terrible end was a swirling fog of disjointed pictures, shards of a mirror recently smashed to pieces.

"Ok, Suzette," I tried to calm myself, whispering to myself. "Forget about everything that came before. Focus on the task at hand. Push hard with your hands behind your head while you jostle for all you're worth!"

I bounced and rattled, trying to get the drawer to move outward.

"Success!" I happily gasped, out of breath, seeing more light at my feet. I jostled harder, hearing a latch of some kind "clink" open as the drawer jerked outward.

"Out! Out! Out!" I urged myself, squirming downward, up over a lip, and dropping heavily onto a hard cement floor.

I lay there for a minute, looking around, trying to get my bearings. The incredible pain of my head and chest was subsiding. It was still there, but lessening to the level of a manageable migraine headache. The lights were off except for a small red emergency light which dimly illuminated the room. Beside my half-slid-outward drawer I saw three other closed drawers set-into a metallic wall. Off to my right I saw two mobile metal examination tables. Hanging on one wall above a long steel sink were what looked like medical tools, saws, and various meat hooks. High up on another wall was a digital clock which read 1:15 AM. No wonder the lights were off, it was the middle of the night. And turning my head to the left I saw what looked like the slightly ajar heavy metal door of an *oven*. The gray metal was coated with a thick black layer which I assumed to be soot. What was this place? And then it dawned on me...

I'm in a crematorium!

"Oh Christ," I whispered. "I was executed and my remains must have been sent to my hometown of Sulphur Oklahoma for my distant relatives to deal with. They're going to burn up my body!"

Wait, what? I certainly *wasn't* dead. Did the International Court of Justice at The Hague somehow botch the execution? How was that even possible, given all the extreme means my executioner claimed would be taken to certify to the world that I was good and dead?

I levered myself up into a sitting position—realizing I was totally naked in an icy room, shivering uncontrollably—then stood up shakily. I spied a full-length mirror and wobbled weakly over to it. In the dim red light I got a glimpse of myself: a natural blond with hair to my shoulders, athletic body, small breasts with perky nipples, a small bush of pubic hair at my crotch, and bright green eyes matching the glaring green tattoo on my left wrist. But that perfect teenage body was to be expected—if not a few days prior I'd been *shot to death* by a firing squad!

"Where are the bullet holes?" I marveled, moving close to the mirror and frantically searching my chest and face.

My skin was unbroken, except for some faint discolorations. They were bruises! The darkened areas were readily apparent, scattered across my forehead, face, neck, and chest.

"What the hell? Did they shoot me with rubber bullets?"

If so, there must have been a high-level conspiracy to keep me alive despite the verdict of the High Court and hatred of my fellow humans. They must have fired dummy bullets that contained red ink of some sort, so that when I was knocked unconscious it'd look like I was killed. Somehow they must know my secret, that as long as I was alive a petition for reconsideration could be launched with the alien Lords. It seemed that a few of my fellow humans weren't ready to give up on the incredible riches given to the Galactic Core concert winner.

My memories were flooding back at me. There were still big gaps and foggy sections, but the history of "the girl with the turtle tattoo" was congealing together inside my battered brain.

But if some conspiracy to thwart the execution really happened, then the attending physicians, pathologists, and lab techs "certifying" me dead would all have to be in on the charade—I puzzled, unable to believe such a vast conspiracy actually happened. *And why would they then send my unconscious body halfway around the world back to Sulphur?*

"This just doesn't make any sense," I groaned, staggering away from the mirror over to one of the autopsy tables. Neatly laid out on the table were some dissection tools, including a sharp scalpel. "Am I a conked-out regular person or some sort of undead zombie?"

I snatched up the razor-sharp scalpel with my right hand, pressing it into the left side of my neck. Wincing from the new pain, I was nevertheless relieved to see red blood flowing from the shallow cut, dribbling across my fingers.

"Ok, I'm not an undead zombie. I'm alive. But whatever the hell is going on, it *can't* continue. There's too much on the line. All the sacrifice I made to end up a corpse in a funeral parlor would be for nothing. I've *got* to finish the job!"

With the blade still at my neck, I took a deep breath, swallowing. I didn't want to have to do this. All my childhood Christian training told me it was wrong to commit suicide. I could have killed myself many times while awaiting my sentence in The Hague, instead waiting on the State to do the job.

Oh, well, perhaps it's part of my punishment that I be damned to hell for the ultimate personal crime...

With a grimace I jerked the scalpel all the way across and through the entire front of my neck, from left to right.

Choking on my own gushing blood, gagging, in extreme pain from the lethal slash through muscles, tendons, and blood vessels, losing consciousness from the sudden lack of blood flowing into and out of my brain, I sagged back to the cement floor.

The second time I resurrected I was calmer, more contemplative. Though my memories were again jumbled-up, I retained the overall history of what had just happened to me.

I awoke face-down in a wide pool of congealed blood. My throat hurt worse than the most horrible sore throat I'd ever experienced. But feebly groping at my neck I realized there was no gash.

"This...isn't...right," I lamely observed.

I pushed myself up and wobbled back to the mirror. Although my chest and neck was completely coated with freshly clotted blood, the ragged slash was gone. My wound had healed. And I didn't feel weak at all from massive blood loss. Instead, I felt rather invigorated.

I looked up at the digital wall clock. It read 4:07 am. In less than two hours my body had recovered from a lethal wound: healing my sliced-open flesh while replenishing my internal store of blood.

"I guess one knife-cut is a lot less damage than a fusillade of bullets slamming into my head and chest," I gulped to myself.

And then, with sinking horror, I realized the *root cause* of what was happening to me. After my foul "performance" at the Concert which destroyed Earth's chances to become a "blessed" occupied planet of the Lords of the Galaxy, I now vividly recalled the cryptic message that appeared on the public scoreboard: "*Suzette is hereby cursed.*"

They *did* something to me! The alien Lords made it so I could never escape the guilt and shame of my despicable performance at the Galactic Core. They'd insured that I'd forever have to live in the shadows lest my defiance against them be undone. They made certain I'd suffer on and on, miserably dying...time after time after time!

That which should have been an incredible reward for all mankind they made into my own personal damnation. They locked me into a hell of my own making!

If I ever doubted I'd done the right thing in freeing humanity from the grasp of those Galactic aliens, I was now certain of my course of action. Intelligent Beings capable of such exquisitely targeted revenge were *monsters* that humanity should never encounter again—and definitely not have to live under their rule! They were *psychic vampires* who would have sucked the creativity and drive from mankind. But to pay for humanity's freedom I'd condemned myself to a *living* death.

"Alright then," I muttered angrily. "You 'got me back.' I insulted you and your 'blessed' worlds in the worst possible way and now you've gotten your twisted revenge. But I'll find some way to make you and or your witting-or-unwitting human collaborators pay. You'll rue the day you didn't let my soul pass peacefully onward!"

Chocking down my rage and again pushing down my perpetual pain I focused on the task at hand. The clock was ticking. Soon the workers at this crematorium/funeral home would arrive for their workday. I had to escape. And before that I had to leave an *unmistakable* message.

I could enlist my own "collaborators," whether voluntary or not.

"First of all, I *didn't* resurrect. That's not possible. I came here as a cold, dead corpse and I left as *ashes*."

Deliberately not switching on the normal lights, leaving the dim red nightlight on in case there were internal cameras triggered by regular light, I went over to the oven. Pulling open the heavy circular hatch I saw a pull-out metal grill upon which a body would lie, with rows of gas vents underneath. Between the gas vents I saw leftover ashes. I grabbed a nearby narrow shovel and scooped out as much as I could. Going over to my half-opened drawer I dropped in the ashes.

I heard a glass-like "clink."

Curious, I reached into the drawer and stirred the pile of ashes. I felt something round and smooth, pulling out a *blue marble*. What the hell?

It stirred a deep anger inside me...like someone did me a terrible wrong. But the memory was fuzzy, just out of my reach.

Try as I might I couldn't grab the memory. Ah well, it'd come back to me. I popped the blue marble in mouth, sucking on it like candy, since I was still naked without pockets to hold any cryptic "souvenirs."

Briefly I wondered if I could kill myself permanently dead by turning on the gas, lighting the hot flames, and jumping in as I slammed the hatch closed behind me.

"No way!" I shuddered. "It was agonizing enough just cutting my own throat. I don't want to experience *burning* to death."

When the proprietor came in the morning and found my body missing, he'd also see the pile of ashes left in my place. He'd get the hint. Rather than be responsible for having carelessly lost the most notorious corpse in history to thieves, he could just claim I'd already been cremated. Reporting a break-in to the very unforgiving local police, plus to the brutal second-dimension Peace Keepers, and finally to the intolerant locally ruling Phoenix council was much preferable to having lost custody of my infamously dead corpse.

"Now what about my congealed blood?" I mumbled around my mouth-marble. "Ah, yes..."

This was a crematorium that dealt with dead bodies, many of them in bad shape to start with. It was a messy, dirty environment. There had to be cleaning supplies somewhere. And in a closet I found a bucket, mop, and lots of liquid ammonia cleaner. I could saturate the place, dump everything I mopped up into the large sink, wash clean the mop, and trust that the ammonia degraded any remaining traces rendering any lab tests on them inconclusive.

The air vents seemed to be working well. The smell of my liberal use of ammonia would be rapidly sucked out.

I set to my tasks, got the place cleaned up, and looked up at the clock.

It read 5:13 am.

"Rats! I've got to get out of here," I urged myself around my sucking-marble.

I exited the main cremation chamber, found a shower room, quickly washed dried blood off me without bothering to adjust the cold stream, liberally splashed myself and the shower surfaces with more ammonia cleaner, showered off again, and found a towel to dry off with. In a half-opened locker I found what looked like a set of janitor clothes: a long-sleeved red flannel shirt, blue coveralls, socks and black boots, and a light black hoodie. I threw them onto my naked, shivering body, absently transferring my marble from my mouth to a pocket.

I glanced at another digital wall clock. Now it read 5:37 am. I ran from the shower room, up some basement stairs, and found other linked rooms. There were office spaces, other preparation rooms, displays of lined up ornate coffins, viewing rooms, and a medium-sized auditorium conservatively adorned for solemn ceremonies. All of the exits I tried were locked tight. Through small windows I saw overlapping bars protecting the glass and doors. Even worse, the darkness outside was starting to lighten. Sunrise was imminent. If I didn't get out soon, despite all my heroic efforts to leave no certifiable trace of me they'd find me alive and well, cowering in a corner.

"Jesus, this is why there's no guard on duty," I gasped, starting to panic again. In frustration, I stopped whispering and *shouted* at the top of my lungs: "There's no way to get in or out of here. This God-damned place is a *fortress*. I'm trapped!"

A "thump" resonated loudly in the auditorium, startling me.

"What the hell?" I moaned, trying to duck beneath a chair and failing. There was no place to hide in the large, open room.

Another large "BOOM" happened and I saw the main double-door to the auditorium *buckling inward*. I dashed to it and tried to wrench it fully open so I could sprint into the darkness past who or whatever was bashing the doorway inward. But as hard as I tried it wouldn't budge beyond a slit in the center of the twisted double door.

"Come on, come on!" I yelled in frustration, straining backward with all my strength...

BOOM!

—as the doorway was *smashed* fully inward, trailing broken iron grates behind! A cloud of broken fragments and dust obscured the entrance.

I was flat on my back, helpless, cringing, when a *long, wet tongue* slathered my cheek.

"Arf!"

Stunned, I looked up into a long narrow snout framed by shaggy gray hair. It was a Scottish deerhound. More memories flooded back. It was *my* Scottish deerhound.

"Scotty?" I whispered, pushing his head to the side as I reached up my arms to hug him around his neck. "Is it really you?"

He was warm and fluffy, excitedly trying to hop around me as I clung to him. Tears dripped from my eyes. It was yet another impossible occurrence in a miraculous morning. The only thing different about him from what I remembered was that other than on the top of his head his fur over the rest of his body was cut raggedly short. It made him look distinctly different than previous, but it was definitely him.

"But I *killed* you!" I cried. "I stuck a *sword* through you, *beat* you to a bloody pulp, and *smashed* your android mechanisms into broken pieces!"

"Arf! Arf!" he playfully answered me, tugging at the sleeve of my hoodie jacket.

"Alright," I shrugged in acceptance. "I guess if a flesh-and-blood human can be resurrected this morning, then so also can a blended flesh-and-robot, android dog. But how you got fixed can wait. You heard me inside, used your super-dog strength to break down the door, and now are trying to lead me off somewhere. Should I follow you?"

"Arf!"

"Good enough for me," I smiled, getting wobbly to my feet. I grabbed a fistful of the hair on his neck, letting him pull me along.

I flipped the hood up over my head lest any security cameras catch a shot of me. Then together we staggered out into the dwindling darkness of early morning Sulphur, Oklahoma.

I dizzily recognized where we were. Though it was still dark, by the faint hints of the imminent sunrise I could see looming shapes around me. Scotty was leading me down a series of town streets and back roads, on the north-west side of Sulphur. Everything was still eerily silent, with no cars yet on the road. It wouldn't remain that way for long. Around me in the gloom I saw shabby, older homes. Soon we'd be beyond the town limits, in the countryside. I saw we were jogging down West 14th Street, headed in the direction of Oaklawn Cemetery...where they'd likely want to bury my body or ashes!

Plus, it wasn't far beyond there to the "Suzette Kingly Animal Shelter" where my mother and I had launched the failed world-wide conspiracy to overthrow the strict religious rule of Phoenix. Surely that was now an armed encampment as the government sought to stamp out any remnant of my rebel organization. It was the *last* place I'd be able to find safe haven.

"Scotty, we've got to head toward the other side of town, maybe into the Park where we can..." I tried to slow him down, turn us back...

"*Grrrrrr!*" he growled at me, barring his long teeth as I slowed him.

"Look, I'm sure you mean the best for me. But the animal shelter you remember just isn't like that anymore!"

"Arf! Arf! Arf!" he insisted, again grabbing the sleeve of my jacket, yanking me forward.

"Alright! Alright!" I laughed in resignation, continuing to trot along beside him. "I guess I just have to trust you. But please don't bark. You'll wake up the whole neighborhood. They'll turn us into the Peace Keepers and the both of us will get blasted by their energy weapons! Hah, let the alien Lords' resurrection process try to bring me back after I'm blasted into little cooked chunks. But...?"

Scotty suddenly stopped, his long nose turned to the side, pointing directly at the run-down house next to us. The house certainly had seen better days. By the dim dawn's light, I made out a leaning, low wood fence. Behind it was a yard with tall uncut grass filled with junk and trash. At the back of the overgrown lawn was a shabby, set-back small house. Its roof was a patchwork of old tiles and plywood sheets. Its once-white paint was muddied and flaking. It had rotting planks nailed across broken windows.

And everywhere there were *cats*...lots and lots of felines.

"What? What is it, Scotty? Why are you stopping here?"

Extremely reluctant but apparently still determined to proceed, the dog edged across a busted-down gate. Since I was latched onto his long neck hair, he pulled me along behind him.

All around us in the brightening twilight, *cat-eyes* gleamed.

Some spat and *hissed* at Scotty, baring fangs and brandishing extended claws.

"Uh...this is kinda spooky," I said, edging along behind the dog as he pulled me up onto a low, creaky, covered porch. A screen door hung askew in front of the main, solid, wooden door. "But I suppose I shouldn't get too finicky, huh? After all, I'm a zombie human being directed by a ghost dog. Hah!"

I was glad to see that despite my aching body I was getting back my sense of humor.

Obviously, Scotty wanted us to go inside.

But I didn't want to go in. I wanted to find somewhere secluded, private, like off in the wilderness area of the Park. But in my haste to get away from the funeral home in the darkness, I'd gone in exactly the opposite direction needed to get to the extensive *Chickasaw National Recreation Area* on the south side of Sulphur. And the sun was now poised to leap above the horizon, people getting up and out, cars zipping down the roads—with us walking along totally exposed to discovery!

There was no time to go elsewhere.

"So...I wonder if anyone's home?" I gulped, pausing at the front door.

"Urf!" Scotty urged me as he glanced nervously at the overgrown lawn and its tribe of seemingly hostile felines.

"Hello! I'm sorry to bother you so early in the morning," I called out as I reached out my fist and timidly "thumped" on the door. "But I wonder if you could help me and my dog?"

Nothing.

I knocked louder.

"Hello? Is anybody here?"

The knocked-on door creaked inward a bit. It was unlocked. We could go straight in, but...?

Scotty stuck his nose through the opening then dashed inside.

"Scotty! You shouldn't just..."

I stepped inside to try to snatch him back when the *smell* hit me. It was the overpowering, sweet-rotten odor of well-marinated death.

"Oh, my God," I gasped, holding my nose and taking a step back. "Scotty, we should leave. Something bad happened in here."

"Urf!" he seemingly agreed, but still slunk past me.

Then he dashed deeper into the dark house, rounding a corner into an adjoining room.

"Arf! Arf! Arf!" he excitedly barked.

"Alright, alright," I answered, getting somewhat used to the cloying stink. "I'm coming."

My eyes were adjusting to the deeper darkness in the house, helped by a faint glow coming from the other room. I saw stacks upon stacks of stuff surrounding me, reaching up to the ceiling. There were magazines, newspapers, old clothes, containers, photographs, toys, household goods, broken equipment, dishes, and everything else imaginable. It was all jumbled together in no obvious order.

And peeking out from beneath, behind, and on top of the tottering piles were more cats, seemingly tamer than the ones out in the overgrown yard. I heard a few hopeful "meows" and "purrs." Flavoring the stink of death was yet another smell: that of overused, filled cat boxes. It was a toxic brew, one I knew I wouldn't be able to bear for much longer.

Plus there was a huge pile of dry cat food boxes in a corner, many of them ripped open with their contents spread around the base of the stack. Somewhere I heard the "drip-drip-drip" of a leaking faucet. Whatever happened in here, the cats were still eating and drinking well.

"This must be a hoarding cat-person's house," I mused to myself, steadfastly refusing to gag or throw up. I turned the corner into a similarly cluttered room, "—and there she is, dead as a doornail."

Slumped in a chair at a low table crammed into the corner of a similarly overly stack-filled room was an old woman. She sat hunched over in front of a still-glowing flat screen of a desktop computer. A motionless, bloated hand was on a computer mouse. Her bald head lay to the side, flat on the desk. Her half-opened, glazed eyes looked past earthly concerns to eternity. On her well-wrinkled face was a frozen, big smile.

"Whatever she was doing, she died happy," I comforted Scotty. He sat whining at her house-slipper clad, bloated feet.

She must have died days ago, probably of a heart attack since she is slumped over her computer, as her body is well into the decay process—I observed to myself. *Her skin is discolored, the flesh bloated, and foul odors are coming from her. She's probably been dead for a week or more.*

"Just what were you looking at?" I mused, gently moving her limp arm to the side and tapping on the computer mouse. The computer that had long since gone into "sleep" mode (though the screen stayed active) came back to life, its internal fan whirring. And on the screen sprang up the last website she'd accessed in her browser: "humongousgiganticdicks.com"!

Several well-endowed, muscular, aroused naked male models appeared on the screen.

"Ah, porn for refined ladies," I laughed. "I guess you had a heart attack. At least you died happy!"

Then I sobered, quickly clicking through a list of "favorites" on the open browser. Although her house was in total chaos, she must have been an introvert stickler for computer-generated organization. Everything you'd need to have available at your fingertips for conducting one's life in total seclusion—banking, utilities, retirement income, credit cards, taxes, medical providers, key contacts, grocery store food selection and delivery, amazon purchase account, last will and testament, etc.—were all computerized with stored passwords for each already in her browser.

I saw that all of her regular bills were automatically paid from her bank account, which was automatically replenished each month from a generous retirement source. Apparently she'd been a mathematics instructor at an out-of-state college before retiring to Sulphur some years in the past. Plus I even saw in her documents a recently updated file labelled "passwords to-date." So I could get at all her passwords. Whatever hoarding compulsions or mental deterioration occurred in her later life, she'd nicely automated her day-to-day existence. And then I saw past videos and trolling hate-email directed against the "crazy cat lady." They were vicious. No wonder she'd walled herself off inside her house. She too was a victim of the outside world, labelled and persecuted as being bizarrely "different."

But perhaps her torment could be my immediate salvation?

Jesus, this is the answer to my present dilemma. I can just take over her life!

But to do so I'd have to know everything about her...

Who was she? Well, I took a quick look at a "personal achievements" file. In it I saw documents detailing the life, interests, and achievements of "Ms. Delilah K. Murtz." One entry struck me as particularly relevant: "obituary." I clicked on it and brought it up on the screen. She'd written her own press release for the local paper to print for her "obit" at her death. The date she put at the head of the document was seventeen years previous. Apparently she'd been ill with cancer for some time. It said she was an only child, never married, and was locally survived by only a distant second cousin. But in a later addendum she'd typed "no survivors, cousin passed away." She was all alone. And in her "last will and testament" I saw that she'd blithely left everything to her cats. Well, they would need an administrator to provide them with their inheritance, right?

Wait...the amount listed in stocks and bonds was huge! Plus, she'd purchased a significant amount of the initial issue of bitcoins. God! That alone would be worth a fortune. Why was she living by herself in a rundown small house in a small town when she was wealthy?

Ah, here's the answer—I concluded as I studied the links in her last-used browser.

She inherited much of her money. But instead of living a life of luxury chose to pursue her love of teaching and cats. Regular large donations were made anonymously to wild life preservation projects for big cats. It was very noble of her, using the principle of her wealth to generate interest which supported worthy causes—all as she lived on a modest pension in a rundown house.

So she was a rich recluse, in love with a menagerie of felines. It happens!

And it was perfect. I was about her size. There were numerous video files she'd made of her playing and chatting with her cats that I could use to imitate her movement and speech patterns. Of course I'd be defrauding the university retirement system and bank posing as her, but tough. The "system" sure did enough bad stuff to me!

And I was already thinking of the right spots to steer her online fortune into that could withstand the worst imaginable societal up-heavals in the future, socked away and accruing interest, just in case I needed it.

"I'm so sorry for what happened to you," I sincerely addressed the swollen, reeking corpse. "But you've given me a great gift. Scotty, did she take you in also? Was she your mistress?"

Still with his head buried in her floppy slippers he thumped his tail several times on the dusty floor. Apparently her generous cat-loving heart had opened up for the "stray" dog. I still had no idea how *he'd* "resurrected." But Delilah helped him and I was grateful

"Then we'll do right by her," I stated, patting her tenderly on her house robe-clad mushy shoulder. "What's the backyard look like?" I asked my android dog.

He hopped up and led me through a crammed utility room to the back door. Cracking it open and peering out cautiously lest neighbors spot me, I saw a large yard secluded behind a high wood fence. The backyard was in the same condition as the front, totally overgrown with bushes and weeds. Plus, there were high trees that sheltered the entire volume. I heard a few birds twittering in its branches. I didn't have to worry about neighbors seeing me. But it wouldn't hurt to be extra cautious. It was sunrise. Light was now streaming through the overhanging branches. We'd found this hideaway just in time.

"Before we can get things squared away here and decide what to do next, we've got to take care of our benefactor," I told Scotty. "If that awful stench continues, even a person passing by on the street will smell it. Is there a shovel around?"

He dashed over to a dilapidated shed, nosing at the thin metal door. I made my way through the thick undergrowth to it, pulling it open slowly so as not to make any screeching noises. Yes, neatly hanging inside, rusting from lack of use, I found a full suite of gardening tools, including a sturdy shovel.

"Let's dig," I grinned at Scotty.

I stood there with a scraggly blond wig on, my teenaged body hidden within a floppy house robe. Before quietly digging the grave I'd gone back inside and found a closet with an assortment of the woman's old clothes. Also, I grabbed one of her tattered wigs which apparently she'd used to hide her cancer-shorn head. In case anyone happened to see me out in the yard they'd assume I was her.

We stood at the head of the well-concealed, bush-shrouded fresh grave. It held our benefactor's sheet-covered corpse. The dead body was patiently awaiting the final few feet of dirt that would embrace it back into the earth.

It wouldn't be as formal or permanent as a grave at Oaklawn Cemetery, but I suspected Delilah would have preferred being interred here surrounded by her pets. Peeking out from behind every bush and tree, hanging from the branches, and milling unhappy through the high grass was an army of cats. They were clearly grieving. They knew that their beloved mistress was disappearing from their lives. Or, they were just worried about who'd keep ordering their food. Cats were notoriously selfish and regal.

"I envy you, Ms. Murtz," I softly stated for the gathered grave-side cat audience. I was careful to hopefully not be heard beyond the encircling high wooden fence. The grieving cats wouldn't understand my words, but they'd feel my genuine emotion. "Your struggle is over. From what I know of you from your computer records, you were a woman dedicated to your particular interests. You were kind to your fellow creatures, hardworking throughout your life. Maybe you were a bit messy and obsessed at the end. But who isn't? You hung in there to the last, doing your duty as you saw it. Now you've moved on to whatever is next in the vast scheme of things. Me, I'm trapped here. I'd actually rather be with you—hopefully as an angel floating on dreamy clouds in some heavenly paradise—but I'm stuck here daily having to eat, piss, and poop. I'm tired of it all, but cursed to live-on beyond my allotted time. So I honor your example. Screw everybody else! If I want to pile-high and horde my 'treasures' then I'll do so! If I want to collect measly, ungrateful cats I'll start my own zoo! Actually, I've officially done that not far from here...but I digress. My point is that you lived your life to your own standards and your own values. Good for you! Maybe no one else ever knew about or honored your heroic struggles and your own peculiar accomplishments, but you persisted nonetheless. You never sought or wanted personal glory, even for your large donations to worthy causes. Instead, you built your own home-shelter for a bunch of stray cats. Sure, a few people have three or four cats, maybe a dozen, but you collected a whole *army* of them! Yes, you died unsung and unappreciated, getting your final jollies at a porn site. But I extend to your memory *congratulations* on a life well-lived. Both me and my faithful sidekick Scotty salute you!"

I slung the shovel up over my left shoulder like a rifle and actually saluted her with my free right hand. I held the pose, giving her a full minute of silence. Sitting silently beside me, Scotty did the same, mournfully looking down at her sheet-covered corpse, his long red tongue hanging out sadly.

"Amen," I concluded, bending to push my shovel into the mound of dirt beside the open grave.

"That was a nice speech," a gravelly voice sounded from behind me. "I never revealed myself to her, but from afar she seemed like a fine person. She certainly took good care of her measly, flea-ridden animals."

I whirled around, the shovel held in both hands horizontally—ready to use it as a fighting staff!

"You," I grated in disgust.

"Well, who else did you expect?" he shrugged, disdainfully kicking aside three cats to stand right in front of me. "Did you find the present I left for you?"

Repressed memories came flooding back into my mind. I instantly recognized the hulking, brooding man. It was *Arthur Anderson*, an Agent of the FBI before that organization was disbanded. Plus he was a God-damned *time-traveler*, a rogue so-called "Time Keeper". Of course that was before he was totally defeated and corralled by the Commissioner. And yes, I now remembered the origin of the blue marble I'd found in the crematorium, which I still had in my pocket. I'd given him that blue "clearie" marble when I time-traveled back to the iconic folk-rock Woodstock concert, in 1969. Caught up in a toxic mix of idealism, romance, and throbbing music I'd fallen head-over-heels in love with him. Of course at that time he'd been a young, sexy hunk. Now he was a beaten-down, disfigured, old man. He was a shell of his younger self: crippled on the right side of his body where half his face was burnt and scarred. A poorly healed slash exposed his teeth, making him look like a modern-day ogre. He was dressed well, though, clad in an expensive brown Italian suit, sporting his ever-present, black dark-glasses.

"You mean this?" I asked. I pulled out of my pocket and held up my sparkling blue marble. It was seemingly lit by an internal fire.

The audience of cats tensed, entranced by the glowing orb.

"It...meant a lot to me, over the years," he sighed, dropping his mutilated head downward in apparent shame. "I hoped that when I left it in the furnace ashes you'd find it and be heartened by it, triggering your memories. I figured when you resurrected you'd need something tangible to grab onto and connect you to your past, which if discovered by others they'd not know its significance, so..."

I dropped the shovel, stepped up to him, and *slapped* him as hard as I could across the intact left side of his face!

He staggered back a step from the force of my blow.

At my feet, Scotty growled menacingly. The cats hanging all around us seemed poised to attack, claws displayed. I heard scary "hissing" all around me.

"Ok...I deserved that," his garbled voice admitted. "Can we please just get beyond our past troubles? Surely you can see this is an extraordinary circumstance, obviating whatever disagreements we've had. And I can't stay here for long. I'm on my way back from giving my weekly report to the local Phoenix Council. If the authorities find out I'm making an unscheduled stop returning to the Colony they'll surely investigate. And then..."

"*How* did you know I'd come back to life?" I spat at him, interrupting his monologue, shaking with fury. "Even *I* didn't know it!"

He glanced around nervously at the lurking, agitated felines. Obviously he wasn't a cat lover.

"Well...I brought your mother's body back here from the Galactic Core for burial, and I..."

"—a death that *you* caused because of *your* incompetence!"

"I...I'm so sorry, but..."

"You were her bodyguard!" I yelled at him, not caring if the neighbors heard us. "You let her get captured by those murderous counter-revolutionaries! If you'd done your job she'd still be alive. God, Anderson, you're nothing but a miserable failure, in everything you've ever done!"

I was trembling with anger, ready to rip him to pieces!

And the reality was even worse than my cutting accusations. Anderson was high on my list of conspirators not just for allowing but *causing* my mother's death. He was a devious, extremely experienced, well-connected secret operative. There was no way he could have been caught off guard by a ragged band of discontents. No, despite the savage beating he'd supposedly endured, I was convinced he was a *crucial* part of the conspiracy that brought down my sweet Mom.

"I've changed," he whispered, his garbled voice breaking.

"You just told me *right now* that you are *collaborating* with the Phoenix Council. You're a damn opportunist! What other atrocities are you planning?"

"Nothing! I'm just trying to help," he snapped, actual tears glittering in his eyes. "You've got to believe me that I'm…"

"No, I don't!" I coldly replied, bending to threateningly lift up the heavy metal shovel again. "And stop yelling! I don't want the neighbors to get curious about what's happening in this backyard. I admit I don't know how the hell you're here, but I don't care. Leave! *Now!*"

"Just give me a minute," he pleaded. "There are things you need to know about. There's…"

"I hate you!" I stopped him.

"Please!" he again begged me.

"Get out and never come back!"

He sagged down onto his knees, his grotesque head buried in his big hands. He sobbed uncontrollably, his shoulders heaving. Yes, I'd hurt him deeply with my biting words. But he deserved it. And I wasn't moved by his supposed show of contrition.

Scotty however relented, ceasing his growling to whine in sympathy. His doggy instincts were to comfort the grieving. Even the horde of cats seemed affected, drawing back. But I knew better. Anderson was an inveterate liar and traitor. In the second human Dimension he'd betrayed his boss and mentor, The High Commissioner. Before that he'd directly caused Woodstock's incineration by an atomic bomb, ending the "love generation's" defiant jubilee with fiery destruction. And worse of all, he'd betrayed my affections. Now, true-to-type, it seemed he was betraying the townsfolks by collaborating with the local Phoenix Council. Sure he wanted redemption, for me to "put behind us" his evil betrayal—but he'd *never* get my forgiveness.

Anderson's humiliation was a welcome part of the sweet *revenge* I longed for…but not as sweet as I'd anticipated.

For the moment, his show of emotions seemed real. He said he had information I needed. Well, that was probably true. Before I kicked him out forever I should get from him whatever would help me.

"Alright then," I relented, lowering the shovel. "Tell me what you want. But be quick about it. I'm a busy girl. Start with how you knew I wasn't going to stay dead."

Stifling his sobs, he slowly got back to his feet. He brushed dirt off the knees of the fine fabric of his otherwise impeccable suit. His voice was now carefully controlled, cold. I saw again the calculating, conniving traitor that I despised.

My mild pity for him evaporated.

"I was the only 'relative' that would accept your body here in Sulphur," he explained. "So the authorities insisted I identify your remains when they arrived here at the funeral home. It was part of their elaborate 'chain-of-custody' certification of your execution."

"So?"

"When I briefly glanced into your coffin I saw that the terrible wounds weren't as large as when you were killed. I watched your execution along with billions of others on the worldwide broadcast. I also saw your extensive wounds on the simulcast autopsy video. And then I remembered the cryptic public message left by the Lords after you threw the Contest. I put two-and-two together. As a disgraced, fired Time Keeper I saw the cosmic justice of you not getting off easily for betraying mankind by insulting the Lords of the Galaxy. So before I left the crematorium, I managed to slip my prized marble you'd given me into the furnace ashes. It wasn't easy. There was an official delegation all around me, plus armed Peace Keepers and..."

"You think sitting on *death row* and then facing a *firing squad* was 'getting off easily'?" I growled at him, arrogantly cutting him off yet again.

"Yes I do," he replied, his gravelly voice trembling. Angrily, he turned away from me. I could see that his shoulders were shaking from his effort to stay reasonable, rather than breaking down again begging for my forgiveness. "*I'm* mutilated for life, never to see redemption no matter how hard I try. I understand what's happening to you, how horrible it is to become a self-made pariah! I know you'll always hate me, Suzy, but..."

"*Never* call me that!" I snapped at him. "You can either refer to me as 'Susan' or 'Suzette.' I'm *not* your cute little 'Suzy'! I'm *much* different from the sweet girl you wooed and betrayed at Woodstock."

"I know...I'm sorry...you've got to trust me," he whimpered, still not daring to look me straight in my eyes.

Yes, his story did make a twisted sort of sense. But it was still hard for me to believe he'd accomplished all of that from mere suspicions I might not stay dead. He wasn't telling me everything.

"You did all this just because my wounds seemed smaller? Couldn't that just be due to the normal decomposition process?"

He was quiet for a moment, as if mentally searching for a fresh argument.

"I *had* to do it, Suzy...I mean, Susan. I just couldn't conceive of a Universe in which you no longer existed. It just didn't 'compute.' I know a lot about the Universe, about how different timelines progress. You *couldn't* be gone! If you were truly dead and gone then there'd be no more 'girl with the turtle tattoo' to stir the temporal pot. With you alive there's still hope that mankind isn't trapped in a hell of its own making, that *I* can still stop the Commissioner! So I made preparations for..."

I knew what he was doing. It was classic "cliff-hanging": going right up the edge but not revealing the full truth. He was playing me.

"I'll *never* trust you, you lying son-of-a-bitch!" I stopped him. "I bet you're lying to me right now. Putting 'two-and-two' together is fine for routine things but *not* for knowing I'd be *resurrected* from the dead. Tell me what *really* happened!"

His voice was sheepish, as if caught in a web of his own making: "Well...before the Commissioner cut me off from my resources, I did have glimpses of possible timelines beyond the Galactic Core concert...where you were inexplicably still alive despite your execution."

"If that's true then *why* didn't you *tell* me?" I demanded.

"Would you have believed me? And none of it was certain. Thousands of different timeline-possibilities splintered out beyond the chaotic events of the Concert. My instrumental glimpses of your continued existence were only in some of the fainter prospects where..."

"You're claiming you were already primed for 'putting two-and-two together'," I again cut him off. "Ok, I get it. But keeping that future possibility from me *then* only makes me trust you even less *now.*"

"I fixed your dog," he whispered, his broad back still turned to me.

Scotty looked up to him in seeming gratitude, wagging his tail.

"You...repaired him?" I asked, a bit less angrily. Perhaps there was some good in him after all. But it still didn't make up for his repeated betrayals. He was correct: I would always hate him!

With a moment of clarity, I realized I despised him so intensely because I saw in him disturbing traits from my *own* obsessive character. But that was beside the point. He was a wily sleaze-bag, who'd betrayed his own Dimension and government. He was an inveterate schemer plotting to achieve his own twisted objectives. Over his "career" he'd even worked to facilitate the incineration of Earth just to "bring mankind closer to God". He was even worse than the religious fundamentalist Phoenix coalition now ruling Earth. They at least were working for their own collective, time-honored, publically proclaimed doctrinal objectives. Anderson was dancing to his *own* music while trying to trick others into doing the same.

"The overlying android cellular remnants regenerated once I got the busted mechanics and circuitry back together," he stoically continued, his back still turned to me. "You see, his 'heroic' remains—lauded because of him publically trying to stop your disgusting betrayal of humanity—were also remanded to me. As instructed by the local Peace Keepers I dutifully had them buried at the Oaklawn Cemetery next to your mother's grave. The Cemetery made an exception of not burying animals there because of his fame. But then I snuck back that night and dug up his remains. I used my future-tech expertise to get him working again. Then I covertly placed him here with our dear deceased hostess as a local 'stray' so he could keep a close eye on the funeral home at night. She did the terrible job at grooming him, but it assured that no one would recognize him."

Ok. I had a decision to make. But I was in no shape to do so. I was physically exhausted, trembling with fatigue and hunger. My head was still pounding from having my brains blown out then regrown. It was still hard for me to draw in a breath due to my sternum and ribs having been pulverized then reconstructed. My throat still hurt from being sliced open then stitched back together at the cellular level. My regenerated previously dead muscles were trembling with exhaustion from cleaning up the mess I made, then escaping the funeral home, then jogging through the streets, and then digging a deep grave. The pit of my stomach seemed bottomless. I was starving. I quickly needed to find some food, cram it down, then crawl into a bed for a week—not get into a possibly savage fight to the death!

Yes, I knew that I should *kill* Anderson right where he stood. He should die not just because he was a rat but also because there could be *no one* who knew I was still alive.

One swift swing with the edge of my shovel aimed at the back of his neck—and his obscene head would topple from his body.

If I was quick enough there wouldn't have to be a tough fight, just another body to roll into the grave on top of Delilah.

But something—perhaps a premonition—made me hesitate...

"I never want to see you again," I concluded, losing my resolve. "Leave!"

God, I'm such a pussy. I can't do it. And it's not just because I might need him in the future. I'm not a killer. I never was. I'm trying to save mankind from its own worst instincts. How can I do that if I become a cold-blooded assassin? When I'm rested I'll just have to figure out some other solution concerning Anderson's forbidden knowledge.

"But I can help you to...?" he said as he turned back to face me.

"I don't need your help," I shot back at him, cutting short any further arguments. "I appreciate your fixing Scotty. Thanks. But unlike you, *he* knows what *true* loyalty means. I'm not and never have been a means for you to achieve your own selfish objections, Arthur. I'll never be able to trust you. Now *get out* of my life. And take your damn blue marble with you!"

I threw it in his face, which he deftly snatched out of the air in a big fist.

He stood there, looming over me, his disfigured face a mix of conflicting emotions.

"For Sally and Dave's daughter, you're really a stupid little girl," he snorted.

That shocked me.

"You should read more," he now sadly shrugged, shaking his big head. "I could recommend a local writer with. He's accumulated a fascinating library, kindly allowing me to borrow..."

"Get the *hell* out of here!" I screamed at him, not caring if the whole neighborhood heard me.

How *dare* he insult my intelligence?

"If we don't meet again in this life, Suzy, we'll meet on Saturn."

With that strange comment he turned away. Perhaps my "premonition" was correct, but in a bad way!

As he slowly walked back to the house he seemed to shrink before my eyes, hunching further over, walking heavily with a more pronounced limp. All around him cats darted out of the shadows, slashing at his legs with their claws, hissing and spitting. Then he disappeared inside the back doorway, his hasty retreat hidden from my sight behind high stacks of hoarded junk and trash.

I heard the heavy front door slam shut behind him.

Good riddance to bad rubbish—I groaned to myself. *Hopefully I'll never have to see him again, whether "on Saturn" or not!*

All around me the cats began pitifully wailing and "mewing." They'd seemingly forgotten the momentary interruption. They'd returned to their mournful goodbye. They were all packed together around the grave, cats of every size, shape, and color—looking down at the remains of their beloved human mother.

"Put some paws to it, Scotty," I said, now stoically shoveling dirt onto the white-sheeted corpse below us. Obediently, he began digging with his front paws at the dirt pile, raining it through his hind legs down into the grave.

What did Anderson mean by "Colony"?—I groaned to myself. *Rats, I should have questioned him further before giving his sorry ass the boot. But it's too late now for regrets. I have a good disguise from which to wreck my terrible revenge. I don't need him!*

All those, including Anderson, who contributed to the death of my innocent, beautiful mother, Sally King, the original "girl with the turtle tattoo" would pay in full. Once I stabilized my present situation in Sulphur, I'd search for and find all my hidden enemies. They'd rue the day they ever tried to put *me* in the dirt. Unlike the dearly departed Delilah Murtz, I wouldn't stay buried.

I'd take my sweet revenge out of their hides.

Chapter 3

THE MOBY DICK

All across human history one thing was certain
The utter depravity and evil of Homo sapiens
A latent bomb never thrown away or defused
Waiting for permissive conditions to explode
Hidden in good times by pious good will
Constrained by societal norms, laws
But under stress seeking immediate release
In drugs, sex, violence, gambling, and thievery
From which many happily earned livelihoods
Taking pleasure causing pain to innocents
A noxious brew of vomit, piss, shit, and blood
The definition of evil made horrifically manifest
Money reaped providing temporary pleasures
Rotting bodies and souls in heedless reveling
All in the name of "good, clean fun"...

The Rise and Fall of *Homo* sapiens, 3:68-72

I resurrected inside a tight tube, instantly triggering terrible memories, thinking I was back at my first resurrection in the crematorium!

But no, this was different, even worse. My body was wracked by a brand new pain. It felt like my skin and flesh were made out of brittle *glass* that was repeatedly *shattering* into slivers then *fusing* back together under the fierce blast of a hot welding torch.

Waves upon waves of *excruciating agony* rolled from my toes to my head then back again, time after time...

"No! No! No!" I screamed.

After what seemed like an eternity, the surging waves of torture subsided enough for me to realize I was still in my excursion suit, sort of. Yep, my suit was still on me, but not exactly intact. I could feel that the golden fabric all over my body was hanging in tattered shreds. My life support backpack was entirely missing. The supposedly unbreakable faceplate on my helmet was shattered, with only a few shards left to obscure my shaky gaze. The helmet itself was dented far inward, pressed painfully into the back of my skull.

Oh, man, my beautiful excursion suit is totally ruined—I groaned to myself.

"What...what's left?" I gasped out loud, fumbling about.

Groping at my double workbelt I found it ripped in half, dangling to the side, all its attached tools gone. A faint, blinking red light shone on me from somewhere behind and above my head. Peering downward I saw that my right boot was split down its middle, exposing gray-smeared flesh. My left boot was completely gone, my foot covered in gunk. Only protruding baby-pink toes suggested I wasn't a stinking corpse.

What was left of my excursion suit was *burnt black* in places. Apparently I'd ignited a nice firestorm before being sucked below the surface with the diving Kraken. Black soot layers encrusted my face and torso, mixed grotesquely with oozing brown muck.

My flesh looked like I'd been dipped in shit, fried in hot oil, and then mashed into a putridly crinkled French fry.

Jesus, Saskia, that was a rough one!—I groaned to myself as my agony slowly subsided to a manageable level. *Now how the hell do you get yourself out here?*

I recognized my prison. It was the floodable airlock within my department's small submersible. We used the torpedo-adapted launch tube to release or retrieve AUV's (autonomous underwater vehicles) when wanting to closely inspect or manipulate submerged cables or structures. Indeed, I realized that I was attached to a torpedo-shaped device. Above me in the tube I saw a cylinder with a propeller on its far end. Close to me at the nearest end, large mechanical claws protruded. The blinking red light was coming from a rectangular black object magnetically held on the AUV's topside. I recognized a "black box" likely from the shattered skiff, retrieved from the bottom of Ligeia Mare.

One of the AUV's claws tightly held the end of the harpoon that had protruding from my survival suit. I fumbled at my abdomen and found that the shaft sticking out of me had cleanly sheared off. Apparently the remotely operated AUV had gotten hold of the dangling harpoon's end while it still skewered me, using it to stuff me into the airlock as it followed in behind.

A loud "clang" sounded and a hatch opened down at my squirming feet.

"Sazz?" I heard an incredulous cry. "How kin ye possibly be alive? I heard the noise and came to investigate...sweet Buddha, it's a freakin', bloody miracle!"

I tried to twist around but couldn't. The circumference of the tube was too small. I grit my teeth and pushed with my hands against the cold metal of the SUV above me, slowly exiting the tube feet-first.

Again, this was much too similar to my first resurrection when I'd squirmed free of the refrigerated corpse-drawer. Still wracked with pain I flopped onto the floor of the sub like a caught-but-dying fish.

"You...defied my orders...and followed the skiff?" I gasped, weakly turning onto my side and looking up accusingly at my freaked-out deputy.

"Of course nae!" he exclaimed, still looking at me in astonishment, his eyes stretched wide. His high, strained, rapid-shot voice sounded like he was talking to a ghost. "After I was notified o' the sinkin' o' th' skiff, I filed papers to come keekin' fer its black box. After all, that's mah job, right? With you dead I am...was...th' acting safety officer. The surviving crew who flapped back to the Station all testified ye wur dead, sucked down to the depths. So when I finally got out here ah kept an eye on muh AUV video feeds, hopin' tae find your body—which ah did. I discovered yer burnt, speared, suit-ripped-off corpse!"

*Yes, he's definitely freaked out—*I almost laughed. *But what am I going to do about it?*

He didn't even reach a hand down to help me stand up. He just stared at me, his eyes stretched wide.

"*No,* you didn't," I instructed him. I groaned as I weakly sat up on the cold floor. I started pulling patches of adhered, frayed fabric off my slime-coated skin. "You found me battered but still very much alive on a floating hunk of debris. I congratulate you on your timely rescue. Well done, Deputy Dougal. I'll make sure you'll get a nice bonus in your pay for..."

"Sazz, whut th' *hell* 'ur ye sayin'? Ye've been *frozen solid* at the bottom of Ligeia Mare fur over *three months!*" he now yelled at me. "And after I got your body back onboard, yer scorched, icicled flesh has been an additional day thawin' out in th' evacuated torpedo tube! I had ta let the black box circuitry slowly reach temperature equilibrium so as not to damage it further. Plus yer stiff corpse was blockin' the tube until it got thawed. And what th' hell happened to that *harpoon* I saw on my monitors that impaled ye? There are just a couple sticks left of it! How did it git out o' yer body? And how come ye don't have any entry or exit wounds?"

He was babbling, the words gushing out of his mouth.

Now he paused, pointing with a shaking hand at my fully revealed tummy. Behind scorch marks and sticky muck my flesh was the image of youthful firmness and health. There wasn't even a bruise left to suggest recent penetration by a harpoon.

"Oh, rats," I groaned, realizing I couldn't just make slick excuses. There was no denying what he'd seen with his own eyes. His remote-controlled submersible had snagged a stone-cold frozen corpse that turned back into a living girl. "I guess I owe you an explanation."

"Ye think?" he laughed hysterically.

"But first, could I maybe get what's left of my suit off, get cleaned up, and then have something to eat? I'm famished."

Indeed, my recently punctured, reinvigorated guts were making loud gurgling noises.

He seemed to gather himself before carefully replying, reaching down to grab my hand and help me to my feet.

"Oh, sure, sorry...but then ye've got to tell me th' truth—the whole truth n' nothin' but the truth. Do ye swear to me?"

"Fair enough," I wearily shrugged.

"Swear!"

"Alright! I 'swear' I'll tell you the whole truth and nothing but the truth."

As far as I can—I mentally added.

"And I've no bloody idea how I'm gonna explain this to headquarters," he shook his head in resignation, firmly holding my arm as I stumbled along. "This is impossible."

"Have you told them you found my body?"

"Not yet—it's hard transmittin' through the organic mush down here and..."

"Well then hold off contacting them again until after we talk."

"But I've finally snagged th' black box, Sazz. They're expectin' my report and..."

"Tell them you've found its location but are having trouble retrieving it," I stopped him.

"What, ah'm to lie to them?"

I glared at him. His handsome, olive-skinned face paled. When I want to, I can be quite intimidating, even when coated in black-brown gunk half-naked in a shredded excursion suit.

"Ok, then," he gulped, sighing deeply.

He sat across the small tabletop just *glaring* at me.

We were in the tight galley section of the sub, its curved walls pressing in on us. I ignored him, shoveling simulated maple syrup-slathered pancakes into my face. They were just prepackaged, hydratable food, part of the small stock always kept in the sub's pantry. But they were delicious. I was on my third helping. Resurrection always left me with a raging appetite. Filling the "hole" in my gut did double duty: replenishing depleted energy-stores while soothing my ever-present, throbbing pain.

"Ah...that was good," I smiled contentedly, pushing the plate to the side. "Now we can talk."

"Finally!"

Unfortunately there was no shower on the small sub, but I'd splashed myself down as best I could at a sink, toweled off the gunk, and then donned fresh clothes. I'd put on a spare set of underwear, work overalls, and soft boots. Most of the organic muck, black soot, and flaking outer dermal layers were gone, revealing baby-smooth skin beneath. Resurrection is great for one's complexion. Even my cute little green *Turtle Tattoo* on my wrist survived, intact and seemingly undaunted. I ejected the remnants of my destroyed excursion suit plus the blackened filthy towels out the waste chute. I didn't want any questionable evidence left behind on the sub. But that imperative also applied to *Dougal*. What was I going to do with him? Leaving people alive who witnessed one of my actual resurrections was a big mistake.

"I know that you're an honest, decent young man," I softly began, "quite unusual for the typical Titanian..."

He winced, furrowing his dark eyebrows during my long pause, anticipating the worse.

"—so I'd be a real shame if you were lost in an additional tragedy: the *implosion* of this fragile inspection sub."

He gulped, his eyes going wide. Yep, the "worse" had arrived.

I sat looking at him for a few seconds more, letting my statement sink in.

"What do ye...?" he gulped, his voice trembling in disbelief.

"Just shut your pie-hole and listen, *acting* Inspector Dougal!" I rudely yelled, cutting him off, "And by 'listen' I mean *hear me* better than you've ever heard anyone else in your sad, short life. Your whole future—or lack thereof—depends on your next few words."

He just nodded, his brown eyes stretched wide, this time in fear.

"You *didn't* locate my body because it *never* sank beneath the surface in the first place. What *really* happened was I sent you a distress signal on a secure tight beam when I first knew I was in trouble. You immediately sent out our helicopter drone to flutter slowly to us. As the Kraken dove, our slow-but-powerful drone fortuitously arrived, swooped down, and plucked me to safety. I've been back at Huygens Station this whole time. For the past three months I've been covertly investigating an illegal Green smuggling operation. Since everyone thought me dead, including our superiors, I was free to investigate the dives and criminal underworld in minimal disguise. You went along with the deception because I ordered you to do so. This is what you'll report to our superiors up on TSS once we return. Tell them I've made significant process, am wrapping things up, and will soon return to my duties. This is what you'll *forever* say concerning this skiffing misadventure to *anyone* who *ever* asks you *anything* about it. *Got* it?"

He nervously wet his lips with his tongue, frowning. I could see him coming to a difficult decision. I knew he wanted to shout his incredible discovery to the top of Huygens Station's Domes, but he was a smart kid. He'd "heard" me loud and clear. There was a chance he'd be able to tame his wagging tongue.

"Got it," he reluctantly nodded.

"Good, then we can move on. We have to deal with..."

"Ye'r *her*, aren't ye?" he eagerly interjected.

Was I still going to have to kill the kid? It'd take just a second for me to reach out, grab, and snap his neck. I'd then covertly return to port and set the sub on automatic to go back into the depths, timed to implode once it arrived back at to the skiff-sinking site. It'd be easy. And as to the guilt of my deed, well...Jag's murder would be just one more tick on a long list of terrible transgressions. In a few years—just a blink of an eye to me—he'd be old and gray anyway, one step from the grave. I'd just be giving him a "gentle" nudge forward.

"I don't know what you're talking about," I shrugged, leaning toward him.

He hastened to explain himself, his words running together.

"My family's long held a fascination w' auld earth history. We've collected many a' ancient, rare artifact. Ah meself am particularly fascinated by its 21st century legends 'n' myths, from before the Extinction. Ah always suspected that some of th' wild stories had a grain o' truth behind them. Ah was particularly interested in th' results of th' fabled 'Concert at the Galactic Core.' Th' infamous *Suzette Kingly* was rumored to have survived her execution. Th' officials called the stories a 'persistent urban legend.' The very idea wuz ridiculous of course. What with the extensive documentation of her death n' cremation, she couldn't still be alive. But supposed 'sightings' wur frequent. The officials always dismissed those to th' same nonsense as Elvis-sightings, UFO's, and Sasquatch. But thar wur so many reports on and off world down thro' th' decades, then centuries, that..."

"—and not one of them true!" I emphatically lied, hating to do what now seemed inevitable. I didn't enjoy killing people. I only did it when it was unavoidable. I particularly didn't enjoy killing friends. "This is a very dangerous and ultimately useless line of speculation, Jags. Keep it up and you'll be yanked off to a slave-farm raving about modern-day mythical zombies. Are you sure you want to pursue this line of addled thinking?"

The sub swayed to the side as I sat unblinkingly staring at him.

He yanked his hands up, palms-out, trying to soothe me, seeing the *icy resolve* in my eyes.

"Ah won't tell anyone!" he hastened to assure me, his accent thickening along with his panic. "Jist like ye said, ye were ne'er here on the sub to 'ave to come back to life. It'll be easy 'nuff to sneak ye off unseen, once we dock back at th' port. But surely having a completely discrete, understandin' ally is better fur ye than a boggin', dead colleague? Ah'm jist privileged to work with ye, Sazz. It's a lifelong fascination that ah'd be satisfyin'! Ah'm not lookin' to cause ye any trouble at all. But I kin *help* ye, don't ye think?" He weakly concluded. He relaxed his defensive posture, his hands slowly dropping to the small tabletop in front of me.

I leaned back in my seat, considering. This interview was disturbing on a profound level. It was so hauntingly similar to my initial "vampire" origin, arising from the crypt with yet another transient, frail human asserting he could "help" me. I refused Anderson then and I'd refuse Jags now. But I was angry on yet an even deeper level. Despite my outward appearance I *wasn't* some weak little girl needing "big strong men" to run interference for me. God—that always *enraged* me!

Feeling that all-consuming, righteous *rage* building up in me, driving me to do something reflexively which I might later regret, I instead bit my tongue and forced myself to lean back in my seat. For the moment I would behave rationally.

"I *do* value you, Jags."

"It's just..." he paused again, looking relieved. "If ye ever wanted to *really* talk with me, well I'm 'ere for you, Sazz."

I reached across the small table and patted his soft brown hand. It was like a tigress caressing a choice piece of meat. To his credit he didn't cringe away from me.

"I know."

All around was the hustle and rumble of surly, packed, sweaty humanity. Miserably jammed in amongst them was me...at least, the *new* "me".

I was riding one of the wide, enclosed rollways between the major Domes of Huygens Station. The main passengers were early morning commuters going to their jobs, crushed into the cylinder like sardines on their way to being canned. Other travelers like me were interspersed, of every stripe and shape. I recognized sophisticated Elites, wearing fine, silvery clothes. Likely they were rich executives briefly here to oversee their prized operations. Some were filthy beggars plaintively holding out their i.d. cards, trying to snag a few stray credits. Slaves were obvious by their irremovable black neck collars. Overtly religious people were scattered throughout. Hell apparently attracts the pious: Hindu men with elaborate turbans, an occasional Islamic woman in a fully concealing black burca, bald-headed Hari Krishnas, Jewish men with skullcaps, Christians with dangling golden crosses, Martian Originalists with red mud face-streaks, hooded Transcendentalist Monks, and other even more-exotic faith practitioners. If I weren't so old, seen so much, the bizarre mixture would have been fascinating. However, I was bored sick, wanting this slow transit to finish so I could get on with my quest!

Next to me a hooded Monk in an orange robe smiled at me. She was female, with a shaved bald head. I smiled back. I liked them. They were an offshoot of the Buddhist religion, so-called "transcendentalists." Striving for "Nirvana" they sought the means to elevate their consciousness to a higher level. They were somewhat crazy but harmless. They gently but relentlessly focused on their other-worldly objectives.

We were all jammed together within a transparent plasteel tunnel. Periodically the walkway shook as a deep RUMBLE announced the distant launch of a fuel tanker or arrival of a transit liner. Behind us was the Port Dome where my office was located. Through the ever-present orange smog ahead I saw the towering Rendering Dome where freshly harvested Azotos membranes were processed. The Commercial Launch Dome, the Space Port Dome, the Agriculture Dome, and other facilities were out of sight in the pervasive smog. But there beside the Rendering Dome I saw my immediate destination, the *Recreation* Dome. Through thick orange swirls I saw it was festooned with glaring, flashing neon signs. It wouldn't be crowded at this hour. Instead, it'd be ripe for some covert inspection and...

"Don' ah knows ye?"

It was a thickly whiskered middle-aged man glaring down at me, check-to-jowl. He was mashed up against my side in the crush of the commuters. His black beard was filthy, brushing my forehead. His bulging eyeballs were bloodshot. He reeked of sweat-drenched clothes worn for a week then "washed" with spilled cheap grog. The greasy black hair on top of his head was mused up. Likely he'd been up the entire night, drinking at the Port Dome bars, just now getting back to his job duties.

"No," I shrugged, trying to shut down any further conversation.

But he was undeterred. "What's yer name, honey?"

"What's yours?" I shot back at him. For the moment I was trapped next to him. I didn't want to talk to him but couldn't afford to piss him off either. I surely didn't want to draw attention to myself getting into some stupid argument. Casual conversation would get me through the walkway transit.

"People call me Big Grendie. *Ye* can call me *Big!*" he chuckled drunkenly, splattering my cheek with his spittle.

Oh, how hilarious. The last thing that I needed at the moment was to cuddle up to a drunken knee-slouching, knuckle-dragging factory slogger. I was gearing up mentally to tease strategic nuggets from my next targets of conversation, not random nonsense.

"So what's yours?" he repeated obnoxiously. "I'm *sure* thet ah remembers you. Yer face is strikin'!"

I considered lying. But I had to build and thicken my new identity. It wouldn't do to be incongruent, just in case anyone investigating me in the near future looked at my recent past.

"I am *Sister* Lakeisha Penda, Sir," I aloofly replied, hoping my arrogant attitude would put him off. "And I *don't* believe we've met before."

I was wearing one of my favorite disguises: that of a vaguely religious Shirazi woman, a full-blood Swahili-clanner. My body sported deep brown skin from a transiently active pill, a short curly black wig skillfully placed over a skullcap hiding my natural hair, and eye color switched to black using the AR-implants in my eyeballs. My skin itched terribly from the alteration in its melanin pigment concentration. My scalp was particularly sensitive under the scratchy wig. But I couldn't appear uncomfortable, attracting unwanted attention. Prominently on the right sleeve of my modest, finely threaded black jilbaab robe was a yellow armband. It signified that I was a freed slave of some authority, an "uber"-supervisor. My social status was thus rated at a "low-medium," high enough to keep people from taking advantage of my ex-slave status but low enough such that the ordinary laborer wouldn't be intimidated by my presence.

The more refined denizens of Titan would, however, recognize my regal bearing and robe. They'd assume that in addition to being a proud freed slave I was also a minor female cleric, a "sister", or some other notable. One's social status in the Solar System could be complex.

But this "gentleman" had no such discernment.

"Nae, ahm certain ah've seen yer face somewhere..." he pondered, frowning. "Say, were ye on the skiff that tanked a few months ago? Th' crew's bin livin' high with their comp' payments. Maybe we could tak' a break to get a brew or two twixt business hours, jist you 'n' me?"

Rats. I was between two identities. I still could revert to "undercover" Saskia if it suited my purposes. If I'd done a full conversion I would have surgically altered the dimensions of key face features, such as the tilt of my nose or cheeks. Instead, I'd done a minimal job, just altering my skin color and hair.

I smiled nicely up at the hulking brute, revealing sparkling white veneers augmenting my teeth, magnifying my grin. Sometimes the best disguise was minor changes. Despite the same face profile, I was every inch a different person than Saskia Regalia, the Russian ancestry-derived Inspector. But a keen-eyed pursuer might still recognize my resemblance. This fool had likely seen at some point Saskia's image, talked about in reference to the skiffing disaster. Likely it was a discussion of why the Safety Office hadn't somehow prevented the accident. Certainly the omnipresent AI monitors, if actively searching for me, wouldn't be fooled. Again, for a full conversion, I would have deployed "cryptic crawlers" that would have infiltrated the physical hardware of the local AI net, spraying undetectable microwebs altering key data. I'd only had time to dispatch a few to the spaceport. They'd insert video feeds documenting my "arrival" yesterday. But any deep search would show they were fakes.

Hopefully, however, everyone still thought I'd perished three months ago. Arriving back to Port, Jags had dutifully spirited me off the sub in a priority crate containing and protecting the recovered black box and other wreck artifacts, exempt from any inspection procedures. At the first opportunity I slipped out, flipped up the hood of my jacket, and made my way covertly to one of my safe-sites. Whenever I went to a new location such as Titan, the first thing I did was establish several secure drops containing everything I'd need to change my identity. After all, you never know when you were going to be killed and have to come back as someone else entirely, right?

Christ, I'm getting a bit giddy—I warned myself. *I shouldn't be out here in the toxic mix of Titan Station, where anything can happen at a moment's notice and I have to be sharp as a tack. I should be back in my safe-room sleeping off my latest excruciatingly painful resurrection. But I've already lost three months in my pursuit of Ailith and Captain Fehler. They could be anywhere, their trail long gone cold. I can't waste even a minute sleeping it off in some hidey hole. I have to be out there on their trail, whether I'm exhausted, wracked with pain, or whatever!*

"Skiff tanked?" I forced myself to neutrally address the reeking thug plastered up against me. "Don' know 'bout that. Just came in on the SSS shuttle yesterday, don' you know. What is this then that happened to some poor skiff? Should I be prayin' for their souls?"

He leered down at me, clearly enjoying being pressed up against me in the crush of the crowd, where I had no ready escape. I wished the rollway were a commuter train, traveling quickly to its designation with semi-private, separate seats. But it wasn't. We were traveling at about twice a leisurely walking pace, a slow jog. It was a lot faster than going in and out airlocks, boarding shuttles. But the walkway got people directly where they wanted to go, albeit slowly. It would be a whole fifteen minutes until we reached the next cluster of domes. By his leering expression he was likely thinking I might be persuaded or blackmailed into giving him a quick hand job. Though I wore traditional Islamic garb, his smirk said my lack of a head covering was evidence I might be a rare human prostitute, newly arrived.

Rats, my disguise putting me at a low-to-medium social state is working too well—I groaned to myself. *Perhaps I should have worn the scarf. I have it at-ready in one of my robe's big pockets. Otherwise I just might be forced to give him a "hand job" he wouldn't like.*

"That skiff got ate by a big, bad monster," his grog-soaked breath swept disgustingly into my nose as he lowered his grizzled head down against mine. "But don' worry, sweet cakes," he whispered, "*Big Grendle Harlock will protect ye.*"

He slid a large, muscular arm over my neck and down my back. Simultaneously, a meaty hand fumbled at the Velcro holding my robe together in front, squirming its way inside. Sweaty fingers crawled toward the nipple of my left breast.

In response I slipped my small right hand inside after his, finding his slippery fingers, and yanked one back until I heard a "snap".

"You friggin' *whore*, I'll...!" he barked in pain. But instead of pulling away as I'd hoped he tightened his strong arm around my back, threatening to crush me...

—as I instinctively shot upward my left arm such that (hidden by my own head from those around us) my hand grasped his Adam's apple. In one smooth movement my stiffened fingers drove into the surrounding soft flesh, twisted violently to the left, and held that position until his panicked gurgling stopped.

"And you have a nice day too, don' you know," I spoke distinctly enough for those nearby to hear, but not overly loud. Simultaneously, I squirmed away through small openings between the packed people which opened as we rounded a curve in the track. I wiped blood off my fingers on the inside of my robe as I cinched it back shut. Glancing backward I saw that "Big's" perverted, glazed eyes now looked out on nothing, his bushy beard covering the blood oozing from his mangled throat. His dead body was still held in place by the crush of mashed-together humanity surrounding him.

I slipped out of the packed walkway at the first exit, jogging briefly to get back to a slow walk on the stationary arrival platform. I then pulled out my headscarf and covered my head, hunching even lower than my normally petite height, as I slunk away with the departing crowd.

What the hell is wrong with you, Lakeisha?—I reprimanded myself. *Assuming a new, discrete identify, which you want to keep low-key, the first thing you do is murder some drunken slob? You could just as easily have immobilized him by batting his sweaty balls. Instead you crushed his windpipe! You've got to be more careful. Hopefully no one will recall what happened to him once the walk-way gets to its end and his body is discovered. But the ubiquitous security cameras don't lie. Likely the police won't care what happened to some low-level slogger. But should they trace back his journey they'll see what happened. Should you return to the Port and assume a new identity?*

But there wasn't time. I was almost where I needed to go. I'd get what info I could and then decide on my next move.

Everything a person could want for "fun" was to be found in the Recreation Dome. It was place for workers to blow off steam. It also catered to the needs of the rare tourist, pilgrims, executives out to do deals at lavish client dinners, and every cred-bearing pervert in the Solar System.

Yes, expensive gymnasiums, soccer fields, museums, dance studios, tennis courts, holo-theaters, fine restaurants, public pools and the like were all there for any personal-development nut or casual tourist to enjoy. But for those of wider "tastes," all sinful pursuits were garishly on display for a fee. One way or the other, the Company took back the salary and souls of most of the workers on Titan Station. Though the careful, intelligent worker theoretically could make a fortune after a few years, most chose to plow their generous salaries and bonuses back into prostitution, gambling, liquor, gluttony, lethal-contact sports fighting and betting, plus hard drug usage. Those that went into debt were indentured by the casinos, even sold into slavery. And I saw the most *infamous* of Titan's dens looming right before me...

It was aptly named the *Moby Dick*.

"Come in! Come in! We got whatcha' want!" a bald-headed midget grinned up at me, tugging at my robe. He was rather cute, like a prematurely wrinkled-up little kid, clad in a bright green jumpsuit.

"Leave 'er be, Squatch," a very fat man with buzz-cut orange hair bellowed, driving off the little man. "She obviously be a sophisticated righteous lady, not wantin' your ugly mess. I bet she wishes a taste of the Green, don't ya, Sister? It's transcendent, takin' your noble spiritual essence to the highest peak! The Monks crave it but can only afford the cheapest dilutions. Now for a fine, righteous lady like you, Sister...we've got the best in the Solar System. What do ye say?"

He bowed deeply to me across his bulging belly, holding out a white-gloved hand. He was dressed in a formal black-tie suit. He cut an impressive though bulbous figure. And he'd nailed me. The best Barkers could read their "marks" like a book.

The local, system-wide infamous "whaler" dive was obscenely impressive. The Moby Dick towered up in all its "glory" in front of me. The entrance was beneath a giant, swaying, erect, simulated penis. It was a "mobile dick" complete with a neon-glowing smile etched into its tip. Hah! I wasn't such a dedicated assassin that I couldn't admire attempts at crude humor. At street level a double-door sized gap beckoned between two huge, hairy balls. *That* wasn't so funny. It disgusted me. I was yet again reminded that Titan was a disgusting, perverted, hell-hole.

Oh, Christ...am I to go down yet another exposed alien anus?—I groaned to myself. *The last one ended up getting me killed!*

The Barkers outside on the street were rounding up their morning customers, luring and tempting them into the dark depths of the obscene opening. They offered coupons for fabulous "deals", promising fantastically slashed prices. More-specialized Barkers handed out free tokens to select customers, for use at gambling units or to get endless free drinks. Pimps paraded their latest sex-bot models: half-clad human-looking female figures with lusciously red smacking lips, enticingly bulging breasts, and incongruously tiny rear-ends (a nod to current sexual standards).

"Yes, I've heard of your famous but illegal pure Titanium Green," I nodded primly to the fat Barker. "And you are quite perceptive, Sir. I *am* here seeking a transcendental spiritual experience, don' you know. I'm no 'tall satisfied with weak hallucinations engendered by the watered down, legal trace-Green that's available elsewhere. For the full experience I've pilgrimaged across the entire Solar System. I desire *pure* unadulterated Green...and fresh! I fully understand that such a formulation is illegally potent and prohibitively expensive. So, can you do this for me? Or should I go to 'nother of the Titanian establishments?" I sniffed haughtily.

"Oh, no! Stay here, Sister! There's no need to go elsewhere!" he hastened to loudly assure me. "We be the finest entertainment establishment on Titan," he nodded briskly, his three extra chins flopping obscenely at his neck.

"I don't know..." I pretended to demure.

"Our latest batch of Green is wonderful. It was purified from a marvelous crystal obtained by us recently. I promise you, Sister, it'll take ye up to heaven!"

Through my robe he gently took hold of my left arm and steered me toward the dark opening through which other customers were streaming inward. Interestingly, none were emerging. I hoped that was because the exits were located elsewhere, not that the customers were being consumed within. Titan was indeed a mecca for all illicit tastes, including human flesh.

"Well...perhaps," I pretended to reluctantly agree.

"You are very fortunate, Sister," he continued in a hushed voice, conspiratorially. "Our newest batch has exceptional purity, just what you're requesting. By all reports, it is sublime for those who kin afford its pleasures. In its purified form it is *most* precious and *very* expense. And should you also wish to enjoy companionship while you partake we could also..."

He gestured discretely toward several nearby garishly endowed male sex-bots. Though their genitals weren't revealed (not out of prudence but to gin up a bit of "mystery"), their overly muscled bodies sported large long bulges beneath tight pants. Their square-jawed faces glimmered with male seductive power. They each radiated intense love and adoration for me and only me. Very realistic! I could see why spacers became addicted to the allures of artificial companions, whether male, female, or other.

"Just the Green, please," I sniffed again with just enough distain to fit my new identify, "And price is no object."

"Ah! Then you will have a wonderful..."

"—though an accompanying concert by a *taarab* orchestra would make the experience absolutely perfect," I added, enhancing my "sophisticate" disguise.

"Yes, my Lady, we *will* do this for you," he grinned enthusiastically. Then, more cautiously, he added: "...and what kind of music is this?"

"It is time-honored Tanzanian music from Old Earth, of course," I haughtily replied, making it seem he was an utter dummy not to know. "It began in the late 1800's," I patiently explained, "started by the Sultan Seyyid Barghash bin Saidi. It features bongos, violinists, and accordionists. It was very popular in 19th century all-female clubs, often accompanying spoken poetry, and was revived recently at the *Lunar Classical Conservatory*. I am one of its most generous patrons. Surely a refined establishment as this knows of the beauty and power of taarab for its Islamic female customers?"

A crowd of orange-smeared Azotos workers streamed past me and my fat Barker, likely from the nightshift getting out at the Processing Dome. Their feverish "whoops" and animalistic "barks" contrasted sharply with my delicate ruse. They reeked of Titanian filth. The marked contrast with my refined manner and robe, though, lent even more credibility to my disguise.

"On such short notice," he demurred, "we may not have a live group to perform for you. Would recorded taarab be sufficient?" he hopefully asked as we neared the dark, foreboding entrance.

"No, that won't do," I sniffed delicately, cringing back, making it seem I was again having second thoughts of entering. "I prefer a live orchestra, though an ensemble will do if that's all you have. But keep your recordings. I have them aplenty. Rest assured, I can pay whatever is necessary for a full orchestra to accompany my pure Green," I added. "This is the experience of a lifetime for me."

At least the money part of my story was true. I had many accounts and assets built up over the centuries, scattered strategically throughout the solar system. As to the "taarab" music, it was just a detailed part of the backstory to my present elaborate disguise.

Taarab was indeed a passion for many Islamic Swahili-derived spacers, though I'd never actually heard it performed live before. If they managed to cobble an ensemble together that would indeed be a real treat for me, particularly if they performed in Swahili. I enjoyed the influence of Arabic in the flow of the words, how it danced over one's tongue. Swahili was one of many languages I'd mastered over my long-extended life. I always tried to find ways to incorporate creative endeavors into or during my work.

Despite everything, I was still a musician at heart: the "Girl Who Rocked Stars"!

The man's orange-topped head was bobbing quickly in agreement.

"Yes, Sister, whatever you desire! We will provide it," he grinned even more broadly, now massively bowing his entire upper body repeatedly as he ushered me inside...

BLARING "*SKRACK*" MUSIC! STROBBING RAINBOW COLORS BLINDINGLY PUNCTURING UTTER BLACKNESS! OVERWHELMINGLY RICH FOOD SMELLS! REEKING HUMAN ODORS! MASSIVE CROWDS DANCING AND SWIRLING!

I was surrounded and immersed in a torrent of *sensory-overload* as my Barker whispered urgently with a Hostess to the side. Clearly, he was anticipating a big bonus for snagging and bringing in such a "whale" to the Moby Dick. I was pleased to see that the woman was real, not an AI sub. I must have done a good job in my act outside. This had to be one of the human owners. I recognized her humanity by her imperfections: the small mole above her lip peeking out from beneath thick makeup, the touch of gray at her impeccably coifed blond hair roots, and a slight limp as she walked. Just the person I wanted to talk to and...

"I'm looking for the real thing, not a fake!" I abruptly yelled at her over the pounding music, staying in character. "And this circus of animal orgy and noise I find quite repulsive! Have I come to the wrong establishment?"

She just smiled at me, taking my arm.

"Yes, the central atrium is for the masses!" she yelled back at me. "Our special guests get a different experience, one that's fine-tuned to their exact wishes and sensibilities!"

We walked into a side room where the door closed behind us and the booming music instantly vanished. The soundproofing of the walls was impressive. This was proof that *The Moby Dick* wasn't just a local dive. They had an easy sophistication that confirmed I was on the right track. This was more like what I needed: professionalism and criminal knowledge equal to the fabled Old Earth's big-roller Vegas casinos.

Though outwardly I was reserved, inwardly I was getting more and more excited. As I've mentioned here in my diary previously, the direct path to my objective lay through *money*—and this place screamed obscene "wealth!"

Now I just had to continue credibly playing my part.

"My name is Madam Challax," the woman introduced herself to me in perfect Standard English. "I will personally be overseeing your experience today."

"Thank you," I sniffed a bit haughtily. "I was no muchly impressed by the vulgarity of your street people and foyer that..."

"We serve many clients of varying tastes," Challax smoothly interjected. "Rest assured your more refined sensibilities can also be fully satisfied."

"I'm not here for any fakes," I sniffed. "I've come across the Solar System to find your establishment."

"You need have no fear of fraudulent products," she assured me. "First, though, there are a few formalities. Please be seated while I certify your accounts. I apologize for the inconvenience. But since this is your first time with us, we must establish your credentials. You understand, of course?"

"It's no problem," I shrugged, nonchalantly extending my dark-skinned hand palm-up for a DNA scan.

Pressing a small disc to my skin she waited until it "beeped."

"This will take just a few minutes," she smiled at me. "In the meantime, please refresh yourself. The restroom is through the door in the corner. A buffet is accessed through the opposite wall-panel. The System-Wide News Feed, SWN, or any other vis-aud entertainment you'd like is on-call in full-wall holo-projection. Just say what you want and the AI will accommodate your wishes. We are pleased to have you with us today and will fulfill your every need. You have only to ask and it will be provided. I recommend having some hot TT while you're waiting. You will find it very relaxing and..."

"What is that?" I rudely interrupted her. It was a nice speech, slickly delivered. She must have said it a thousand times to other "high rollers." I needed to keep her off balance, not allow her to set the agenda.

"It's a local product, called 'Titanian Tea,'" she smoothly replied. "It's not near as precious as the Green but still quite rare. The tea plant is fertilized by fossil remnants of Green. Titanian Tea does not produce visions like the Green, but *is* uniquely soothing. We hold it in great regard here on Titan."

"I've heard of it," I nodded. "But I don't know much about it. If it's so great, why is it so obscure?"

She smiled politely. Clearly she'd heard this question many times before.

"It degrades rapidly. After only a day or two following delivery it turns toxic. We only serve fresh leaves obtained from a trusted source. It is highly prized by Titan's aristocracy."

"I wasn't aware Titan had an aristocracy," I sniffed contemptuously, getting her to open up even more. "Frankly, Titan's reputation is as the *anus* of the Solar System, populated by shit-muckers, criminals, and the losers of human society."

She laughed politely. "Yes, we cultivate that unflattering image."

"Why?"

"It protects us," she mysteriously replied, bowing slightly to me. "I will return shortly. You and I are very much alike, *Sister*."

I frowned at her as she departed, broadcasting my irritation. But it was just an act. In truth I was immensely excited.

Where better to hide a vast, history-transgressing, society-altering conspiracy than at the bottom of one's garbage can?—I nodded to myself. *I'm on the right track! She literally just admitted a covert aristocracy exists here. But for the moment I've got to wait patiently. Maybe I will try out that TT brew. If it can soothe my interminable pain, even for just a bit, it'll be well worth it.*

I normally didn't drink tea, coffee, or take any drugs. My radically souped-up metabolism instantly detoxified any external stimulants or depressants. It seemed that part of my resurrection punishment was not to be able to enjoy my extended lifespan. I was cursed to carry around all my prior pains, each adding onto the prior sufferings.

*Yes, I can push it off to a short distance, still function, do what's necessary, but never escape the throbbing "toothache" of my resurrections—*I winced mentally. *But I'd better get back to my "job" and survey my present jail.*

The waiting room was nothing but understated luxury. The real-wool carpet beneath my thin shoes was soft and thick. The walls were mahogany panels, likely imported from New Earth excavations, incredibly expensive. The ceiling was high and seemingly nonexistent. A realistic blue sky hovered in its place, complete with fluffy white clouds. They'd spared no expense to make their "whales" feel comfortable spreading-open their cred-cards.

As to her "certification" of me I knew it would be thorough but not extensive enough to detect my deception. A place like this took no chances on their biggest customers but had no patience for true forensic investigation. They wanted me swiftly participating and paying for my particular illegal product or activity. Fortunately, my extensive preparations should be sufficient. Indeed—according to implanted video feeds and other documentation—yesterday I apparently rocketed in from "triple-S," the Saturn Space Station (a hooded figure on the cams, all records correct). My cred balance in the account linked to my present DNA profile was astronomical. My history was well established, a seldom-seen but quite real Saudi-fortune heir, my family having thrown off servitude a century ago to usurp our masters. My travels, masked as a "low-medium" socialite, were well document. My heritage extended back through time to Old Earth. The one thing I never cut corners on was the documentation of my many alternate disguises. In the age of omnipresent AI one could not create a new identity "on-call." It had to be verifiably maintained down throughout the centuries, with a previously established detailed prehistory. And who could do that as well as an immortal?

"Titanian Tea!" I snapped imperiously, sitting on an exquisitely comfortable real-leather sofa.

A mechanical arm instantly extended from the wall with my drink. Smoothly settled down onto a side table beside the sofa, was a

beautiful, antique crystalline cup. In it was a small quantity of a rather vile-looking muddy brew.

She wants me to drink that crap?—I laughed to myself. *Ah well, it
surely can't hurt me. "Toxic" means nothing to my metabolism. I
might as well keep up my "regal" act and taste it.*

I raised the cup to my lips, mentally reviewing my preparations...

As to the DNA scan, part of my conversion to each of my new
identities included a retroviral infection soup that reversibly altered
non-critical regions of my genome throughout all the cells of my
body. Yep, I truly "transformed" into a new person, both externally
and internally. It's amazing what you can do when you accumulate a
vast covert fortune over centuries. Unspeakable wealth can break
down any regulatory norms, hire the best professionals, and facilitate
"mad scientist" miracles.

Originating from Old Earth where people rightly feared genetic
manipulation, though, I was still hesitant every time I took the little
white pill. I didn't casually subject my body to a convection of DNA-
altering viruses. But in the present world where one's DNA code
could be read in seconds it was a necessary and critical procedure.
Fortunately, my whole-genome DNA alteration didn't work on ordinary humans because you'd never get 100% integration of the retroviral vectors into all one's cells, leaving a "red-flag" mixture of old and
new genomes. But my unique physiology allowed me to open up all
my cells and "suck-in" the viruses, very cool. Of course prior to this
date I'd always given the process at least 24 hours to work before having to submit to a DNA scan. But I should be fine. A few hours
should be sufficient for the viral vectors to be taken up by my intesti-
nal-lining cells, translocated across the cellular membranes into my
bloodstream, and from thence populate throughout my entire body.

So I've nothing to worry about—I mentally patted myself on the
back as the foul-looking tea hit my lips.

But I was still nervous. I was in a constrained space, with few options if my deception was discovered. So to be extra safe I was covertly surveying the waiting room in exacting detail. I used my AR eye
implants, specially adapted by my pet scientists and engineers, to do a
full EM spectral analysis of all the surfaces. Thusly I located all the
hidden conduits, junctures, surveillance-devices, and lethal-force

weapons. I saw it was no accident that new members were kept here before being allowed to go further into the private areas of *The Moby Dick*. Identified enemies could be locked out by titanium shields slamming down behind the walls, or outright killed. An establishment like this would be ripe for every thief and competitor to come in and ravish it for its hidden treasures. Thus the waiting room was, if needed, an execution trap.

Wait! Something's happening—I gasped to myself, feeling the tea-sludge sliding down my throat.

A warm, comfortable blanket spread over my body, covering up all my pain-points. For the first time in hundreds of years I felt at peace, like I was floating on a soft cloud.

Jesus Christ!—I exclaimed to myself in amazement. *If this is what a degraded, plant-derived version of the Green does then I can't wait for the real stuff!*

Satisfied I'd located all of the room's secrets, I chose to relax and fully enjoy this rare respite from my continuing, barely-suppressed agony. So I settled in, leaning back on the real-leather sofa (from actual cows!) while watching the local SWN channel. The uprising on Ganymede, Jupiter's largest moon, was nearing an end, put-down by MEF, the "Martian Expeditionary Forces." Damn rebels, I hated them. They kept stirring the pot of my neatly constructed solar system's social order, scrambling my leads. As I continued flipping through the channels, I leisurely sipped the addictively soothing TT. I was still amazed that my metabolism was accepting its alien Titanian chemicals. I drained the cup, thoroughly mellowed-out. I was starting to dose off in the super-comfortable sofa when the back door suddenly opened and Challax returned.

I was instantly on guard. By her puzzled frown I knew I was in deep trouble.

"Sister 'Penda', I'm afraid we have further questions for you," she began as I warily stood up from the sofa, "or should I say Inspector Regalia?"

Oh, crap!—I mentally winced. *I didn't allow enough time for the viral vectors to propagate into all my cells. Their AI's found me out! In my eagerness to get back on the trail I walked right into a trap that even I might not survive. And that damn TT has slowed down my normally razor-sharp reflexes!*

As if to confirm my fears, my implants detected pinhole ports snapping open all around me, behind which hid powerful laser weapons.

I could try to grab and smash the antique glass beside me, whip the cut shards into Challax's throat, and then maybe escape before laser beams chopped me into bloody chunks...but the odds of success were slim. The AI could react far quicker than human muscle, even my uber-human tissue. And I knew that the tea in muting my protracted agony had dulled my reflexes. However...perhaps I could still get out of this mess if I was *verbally* clever and quick? The dreaded "self-awareness" awakening of AI had never occurred. A human mind was still sneakier than any artificial intelligence for analyzing and re-adjusting reality.

"And what is this, you say? Inspector who?" I indignantly demanded, pretending I had no idea what she was talking about.

She looked momentarily uncertain. "Your DNA affirming your claimed identity shows traces of another person, someone who was supposedly killed in a skiffing accident and..."

I can't give her even a moment to stay on the offensive!

"Oh yes," I cut-into her statement," I heard of this incidence on my way here this morning on the walkway," I forged ahead, concocting a counter-story on the fly. Wow! I was sure good at making up stories. I should have been a science fiction author! "Someone thought that they recognized me from some old News Feeds of the accident. I suppose there could be a distant relationship. My enslaved purebred Swahili family was forcibly interbred for centuries with various masters, particular Russians," I lied. "That *is* a Russian name you mentioned, is it not?"

"I..."

"Or, now that I think of it," I hurried on, keeping a keen eye on the fully-opened pinhole ducts through which lethal laser blasts could instantly blast at any moment from both the ceiling and walls, "I have a more likely explanation. There *was* another odd encounter at the spaceport when I arrived here on Titan yesterday. Another person unexpectedly claimed to know me, shaking my hand vigorously as she went past, presumably to board a departing liner. The voice was fe-male, so I assumed her to be some past acquaintance. She wore a full burqa, an Islamic comrade don't ya know? Perhaps this was the per-son to whom you refer, obscuring her identify while pretending to recognize a fellow believer, leaving some loose skin cells on my hand? I fasted and prayed the whole night, so haven't washed up yet from yesterday. You are welcome to thoroughly cleanse my skin and draw blood for a more accurate reading."

It was a shaky explanation, but the best I could make up on the spot. Hopefully it sounded valid since it was based on my cover story. I didn't doubt that stolen versions of Jag's report to headquarters were already being circulation through the security nets of Titan Sta-tion. They'd believe Saskia could be out there in disguise, as I was indeed!

I cooperatively slid the sleeve of my black robe up on my right arm. Grasping my upper arm tightly with my other hand I caused a vein to bulge up through my dark brown skin.

I hoped the viral vector had finished its job inside my body. Skin cells were the toughest for it to transform, because many of those were just dead remnants of my prior identity waiting to be shed and cast aside. I should have anticipated the Moby Dick's DNA profiler would be the most accurate and precise available, not just the gross aggregator of normal scanners, and offered blood upfront. But my larger fear was that the AI they used would scan the spaceport records and find no burqa-wearing females there yesterday. Then again, maybe I'd get lucky. I'd already seen at least three in the crush of the morning walkway commute, so they weren't unknown here on Titan. Islam was a very persistent religion, in all its various forms.

"Well?" I impatiently asked as she paused.

I gambled that they wouldn't want to kill a hooked whale before gutting it of its precious fat, likewise the Inspector. No, they'd rather send in skilled armed guards to capture her rather than just chop her into pieces with laser beams. Since I was already listed as dead, un-der their "expert" interrogation I'd surely be forced to reveal all my supposedly valuable Company secrets to their casino interests. Sup-posedly owned by the Company, on Titan everyone's selfish interests were pitted against everyone else's. The many cliques and businesses were always seeking an edge, an advantage. But if they dragged those secrets out of me then they'd surely find out my *real* identify. I was as susceptible to physical torture as anyone else, maybe more-so since I was hypersensitive to pain. And that just wouldn't do!

"Yes, if you don't mind," she answered, clearly hoping that I *was* a rich fat "whale" instead of a pesky, not-dead, of-little-means Inspector.

"No, not at all," I shrugged nonchalantly, still holding out my arm. "I didn't come all this distance across the Solar System seeking transcendental spiritual ascendance only to be stopped by a few stray cells picked up along the way from some total stranger! I'll keep the vein nice and pumped-up, don' 'cha know?"

She smiled politely as she opened a drawer in the side-table, taking out a phlebotomy kit. She set the tourniquet to the side, not needing it. Then she cracked open a sterile syringe-needle, swabbed my arm thoroughly with an alcohol wipe, and skillfully inserted the attached needle.

As she popped in a vacuum tube I watched my red blood spurt up into it. She patiently waited until the tube completely filled up. I realized they were planning on conducting extensive tests. That was bad. My cells were different than normal human cells. Not only was my old identity in danger of being discovered, but my *real* identity. She cleanly slid out the needle as she simultaneously pushed a cotton wad onto the puncture.

She expertly placed a bandage over the cotton wad. Yep, she'd done this procedure many times before.

"How long will this take?" I sniffed as with a finger I placed firm pressure on the bandage to prevent any internal bleeding.

"It shouldn't take longer than an hour to produce an in-depth profile," she carefully replied, inverting the tube of blood gently to allow the contained anticoagulant to disperse throughout. "But I assure you the wait will be worth your inconvenience...that is if everything checks out."

"And if not?" I asked as I heavily sat down again upon the sofa, still putting pressure on my pierced vein.

"I'm sure everything will be fine," she coldly asserted. "Meanwhile, feel free to have more TT."

She was exiting...

"Just one more thing!" I snapped, stopping her halfway through the doorway.

"Yes?" she politely turned back, holding her tube of fresh blood.

"After all these indignities, I'll *not* be paying a king's ransom for a taste of Green without *my* certification of *its* freshness and purity!" I snapped at her.

"And...how do you propose to do so?"

"How do *you* determine its purity and freshness?" I sniffed, deflecting the details of my spur-of-the moment new wrinkle to my false identity.

"Well, Sister Penda, we can provide a full chemical analysis. However, the exact configuration of some of its shifting molecules is still not completely understood, so the spectrum changes from evaluation to evaluation. I'd suggest judging it by its effects. If your experience is anything less than spectacular then we will happily provide a partial refund or even..."

"Not good enough!" I again snapped. "I'm not a chemist and could be easily fooled. Even trace amounts of the Green can provoke potent hallucinations, don' cha' know. I don't want a 'good trip.' I'm willing to pay the price of purchasing an *entire moon* for the *full* effect of saturating my *entire* brain with *pure* Green. I'm not looking to see God, Madam Challax. I'm looking to *actually* touch the Face of God!"

She gasped at my arrogance, but reluctantly nodded.

*Hah! That set her back on her pricy heels—*I congratulated myself. *Part of convincing people of one's authenticity, in the face of "iffy" evidence, is overwhelming their personal doubts. I have to convince her I'm indeed a regal heiress, regardless of whatever minor anomalies her tests reveal.*

"I will find a way to satisfy your valid questions," she stated. "It may take me a bit longer, though..."

"That's no problem," I bruskly interrupted her. "I'm comfortable here, thank you. And I *will* have some more of that delicious TT. So take as long as you need."

She exited, softly closing the door behind her. I heard a large locking mechanism "snap" shut. She was making sure I was safely contained. That was ok. I'd planted the seeds that could sprout into extremely useful information. They thought they had me in a box. But I'd used their doubts to set the stage for bringing me what I *really* wanted. That is, if they wanted my bio-verbal authorization for transferring a massive amount of credits into the Moby Dick.

But they're not taking any chances...

My trained ears heard the faint but unmistakable "thump" of titanium barriers slipping down into place behind all four walls and beneath the floor. My only escape was the ceiling. Looking up, I saw it'd changed from a happy blue to a neutral white. At least it wasn't fiery red! Judgment was suspended, awaiting the outcome of intricate clinical tests of my lifeblood. Traces of all my previously assumed identities lingered in my oft-altered genome. If they concluded I was too dangerous to capture, the laser beams would instantly slice me into a zillion pieces.

And then I feared an even worse prospect. My body had always been left intact in my past deaths. Could I resurrect from being chopped into sushi? And if so, would I be doomed to live as a hunk of raw hamburger?

Oh, Christ—I sighed to myself. *My overactive imagination is taking me down culinary nightmares. I must be hungry.*

I sighed deeply, picking up my empty teacup. Ah well, I'd often in the past "rolled the dice" and won. Then again, I'd also ended up stone cold *dead*...and maybe this would be the final toss. Whatever!

"More TT!" I loudly ordered, "And maybe a tray of cookies."

The mechanical arm zipped out of the wall, snatching away the empty cup from my hands while plopping an identically filled one in its place. The opposite wall opened and an entire rack of every type of desert imaginable sat there enticingly.

I took a sip of the hot, putrid-looking brown fluid. God, it was tasty! I could already feel its mellow tendrils spreading through my body.

If this is my last drink, I'm going to enjoy it. Even in the worst of circumstances, the "show must go on!"

Chapter 4

THE COLONY

"The show must go on"
A grand sentiment always conditional
Rain, riots, no audience, withdrawn backers
Disapproval by prevailing society or officials
Crushing even the finest performances
That which might have been exquisite art
Left in dismantled sets in the mud or just undone
Worst yet, shoved off to the side and ignored
A last enclave struggling to sing its sad songs
To strum thin chords on shredding guitar strings
Growing old, shrinking, its glory days gone
Still hoping for a miraculous revival
All our beloved friends reborn...

The Rise and Fall of *Homo sapiens*, 4:6-10

"Goin' to the jig ta-night, hee, hee?"

I glared from under my floppy brown hoodie at Zeke, an old be-whiskered geezer sitting on a bench to the side of the trail. He was nodding his head back and forth to silent music, tapping his crumbling boot into the concrete, while slapping on a crinkled paper bag. His somewhat demented mind made for loose lips. Cackling-on about illegal musical gatherings could get him snatched up by Phoenix-sanctioned fanatical enforcement gangs, then turned over to the Peace Keepers for summary punishment.

I looked about nervously. The black-helmeted, black-uniformed, energy weapon-totting grim enforcers lately seemed to pop up on every corner. Luckily there were none within earshot as we were way out in the more secluded area of the "Chickasaw National Recreation Area" or Park, as the Sulphur, Oklahoma locals called it.

"Maybe," I grunted, wearily plopping down next to him. I felt an urge to calm him as I rested my weary bones. "Where's it at?"

Usually I ignored his babblings, trudging on past him. But today I needed some human company. I was out walking Scotty, with two attending cats regally peering out of my coat's big side-pockets. I was lumbering along in my "old crazy cat lady" disguise, getting much needed physical exercise using the two lazy cats as weights. It was a good trek from Delilah's house on the North side of Sulphur. I'd gone across Broadway, then south down 12th street, to the Park's main entrance. Presently I was slogging through the extensive Rock Creek camping grounds. From there I'd go onward to Veterans Lake, jogging around its three-mile circumference sidewalk path. I enjoyed the exercise, particularly in the early morning when the gangs, park rangers, local police, and Peace Keepers weren't yet out in force. But today I was exhausted, both in body and mind.

I'd been diligently searching the dark web and local power structure for six months now as to who or what organization ordered my mother killed at the Galactic Core, but with little success. Evading the online sensors was a constant game of cat-and-mice computer tricks. But as long as I never left traces or took the same intricate route, I had access to an underworld of violent perversions and rage. The same was true locally and (I assumed) in every other community across the planet. The whole Earth was now stuck under the righteous thumb of Phoenix, whose absolute rule was enforced by the all-powerful extradimensional Peace Keepers.

Yes, I know this all sounds unbelievable. Truthfully, if you'd told me all this would happen a few years previous when I was on the top of the world as its most popular teenage rock star "Suzette Kingly"...well, I would have laughed at you. But it all happened!

The present awful state of the world—where superficial calm and order barely contained an underlying volcano of discontent and anger—was all too real.

Superficially there was an obvious "upside." The world was, for the first time in its long sordid history, at peace. All societies now lived in apparent harmony, without war or crime. It seemed a modern-day paradise: *Homo sapiens* having at last conquered its vilest perversions. But just beneath the placid surface bubbled a toxic brew of all humanity's worst failings. The "seven deadly sins" were alive and well: "pride, greed, lust, envy, gluttony, wrath, and sloth." Globally online, anything was available for the right amount of untraceable, illegal bitcoins. Addictive-drugs, alcohol, tobacco, prostitution, slaves, porn of every type, forbidden weapons, hired thieves and murderers were just a dark-click away. Locally, all the regular "evils" also still existed, just pushed into dark corners. Somewhat akin to the old fashioned "rave" gatherings, "jigs" offered illegal drugs, smoking, alcohol, dancing, and loud music. But you had to have an "in" to find it: the banned gathering moved nightly from barn to glade to abandoned building to two-car garage.

I attended several just to see what they did. It was rather amusing: a small group of people writhing and groping together in the dark. If you walked past on the street, you'd not know anything was happening. The "jiggers" all wore headphones and augmented-reality (AR) helmets. The feeds were activated by shielded wifi-routers transmitting music and visuals generated by instantly self-wiping, illegal flash drives. Drugs, alcohol, and tobacco were dispensed by internally-coated edible balloons activated upon inflation. Sampling could be done by eating them or deflating them into one's closed helmet. If you drove past a barn out in the sticks you'd never guess a combination orgy, rock-concert, and drug den was in process. There'd be no sound, light, or smells to give it away. On my few visits it was easy enough for me to make a hasty retreat before being sucked into any of the addictions. I just layered scratchy cats over my padded shoulders and pretended to have a fit. "Crazy Cat Ladies" have many unique powers!

But the vagrant locals I met on the streets didn't have any such constraints or defenses. For them and many other "respectable" citizens, their only relief from relentless oppression was the sporadically held nighttime "jigs." Zeke was a regular who had a long-established friendship with Delilah, my secret identity. Fortunately for me he was deteriorating mentally, lucky to recognize that I was lumbering past, let along detect my subterfuge. I knew he wouldn't be around much longer. Either he'd die of pneumonia some cold night curled up on a bench or be swept up by periodic "cleansing" gang-grabs.

"Gonna be at the senior-center tonight," he snickered, as if he'd said something funny. "I'm playin' live!"

Oh, that was bad. The one cardinal rule for jiggers was "no noise." Everything had to be externally muted by repressive sound-cancelling speakers or funneled through headphones. The authorities and fanatical gangs hated the jigger movement and did periodic nighttime sweeps through suspected neighborhoods. I knew that Zeke had been a talented banjo player and country-western singer in his earlier pre-Phoenix days. Now he was just a sad bum recalling his happier youth. But addled or not, even he should know not to brag out loud.

"I'd love to hear you," I sincerely said, maintaining my scratchy "old lady" voice. "But if anyone else hears you then..."

"Don' give a damn 'bout them," he snarled. "Yer cat's *yowl* an' *they* don' get hauled away to jail," he argued loudly. "I wanna do what I wanna do when I wanna do it and I'm a-gonna! So there!"

I looked about worriedly. The wintery early morning sky was gloomy, dark clouds hovering above us threatening rain. A cold wind was stirring the leafless branches of the surrounding trees. I was warm in my thick brown coat which I wore over a hoodie, but only from my exercising. If I stopped too long I'd get chilled. The dark water out on the lake, normally placid, was choppy. It wasn't a day for locals or tourists to be out in the Park. But just then a happy couple in matching red jogging suits bounced past us. I noted with alarm that they looked at us angrily.

Oh Christ, let them not report us—I gulped to myself, starting to panic. *Zeke was just being loud and stupid!*

Normally Zeke's muttering wouldn't cause much of a reaction from the occasional passing jogger. But I saw the woman raise her wristphone to her lips...?

Why was she so upset? Sure, it was the law that anyone "seeing anything must report it." But most of the locals knew well enough to just ignore any odd behavior. That'd gotten me out of potential trouble several times. Why was she so bothered by Zeke to risk drawing attention of the religious zealots to herself and her partner?

"Come on, Zeke," I urged him, grabbing his arm and trying to get him to his feet. Scotty looked at me uncertainly, his ears flattened to the sides of his narrow head. "Let's go there right now. You kin make sweet music for me only to hear. You can 'yowl' with me cats. Heh?"

It was then I spied what he'd stashed right *beneath* him under the bench for anyone passing to see: a beat up, cracked banjo!

What the hell is he doing?—I groaned to myself. *Having a musical instrument out in the open is like waving a flag saying "come arrest me or worse."*

"Leggo my arm!" he barked at me, yanking backward to the bench. Something popped out of his brown paper bag and "clanked" on the sidewalk. Oh, rats, that was why he was being so careless—the damn old fool was drunk. He'd had an ancient glass liqueur bottle hidden in that paper bag. He must have had it squirreled away for months, waiting for the "right" time to flaunt it. Or, more likely, it was some of his backup hooch he'd hidden away previously and only recently discovered. Whatever, the couple stopped and pointed, the man looking like he was going to come back to confront us...

No need. A park ranger car suddenly braked to a stop beside us. Out of it stepped *Losa Yanash*, a thick-bodied, full-blood Chickasaw Park Ranger who I knew from my past life as Suzy King. He was dressed in his official brown uniform with flat-brimmed hat and holstered pistol. And he certainly was well acquainted with the crazy cat lady and the vagrant Zeke. He'd surely realize I wasn't the real Delilah!

But, then again, he'd probably just take the illegal alcohol and banjo away from Zeke and send him on his way. Losa Yanash was one of the few "friendly" officials who'd not been intimidated or co-opted by Phoenix.

Zeke would be ok.

"Arrggghhh," I sputtered, turning away from Zeke with my head tucked down under my floppy hoodie. I brandished a cat at Losa who jerked back from its extended claws. "Ain't got time fer no foolishness! Keep away from me, you old drunk," I spat back at Zeke, as if he'd just disgustingly propositioned me.

I lumbered quickly away, tucking my free cat back into its pocket, Scotty close to my side.

Glancing back I saw that Losa was standing with his big hands on his hips, sadly shaking his head back and forth as Zeke groped for his lost liquor flask, on hands and knees, pitifully latching onto it like a baby grabs his milk bottle...

VRRRRREEEEEEMMMM!

I instinctively ducked as I hurried away. I knew that sound, as did everyone else. It was a Peace Keeper *hopper*, a levitating platform powered by an unknown energy source. It dropped from the sky onto the sidewalk beside Losa and the yelling old man. They'd clearly been monitoring the local channels, hearing the joggers' call to the Park Rangers. Two black-helmeted Peace Keepers in black uniforms stepped out.

"Hey, I'm handling this and..." Losa attempted to protest...

—as one of the officers pulled out his black energy-gun, pointed it at Zeke, and pulled the trigger!

BLAM!

I should have just kept on going, but I stopped and looked behind me. Horrified, I saw Zeke was now a burnt, smoking corpse. His extended, motionless hand was still holding the flask, which had fused into a featureless red-glowing glass blob.

The officers yanked out the banjo from under the bench, quickly stomping it into pieces. Then they turned to the stunned jogging couple who were still standing there, staring.

"We were just running past and we immediately reported..." they began, clearly terrified of what might happen to *them* next.

I didn't wait to see what happened to them, the "good citizens." They deserved whatever the Peace Keepers had in store for them. I ducked into the outer edge of the extensive forest which safely hid the Rock Creek encampment. I kept on breathlessly stumbling along the tree-shrouded trails then small-town streets until I got back to my across-town borrowed house.

It was only then that I let myself break down and cry. I knew I'd not be going out on my regular morning walks ever again. Perhaps I'd do a few night-obscured sorties. But trying to blend into the small-town landscape was over. It was just too dangerous.

A couple months later I was lying on my stomach atop a low hill, spying from afar into an extensive compound. I was using a powerful set of binoculars. It seems that my benefactor Delilah was not just a closet pervert, but enjoyed voyeurism as well. I'd found the binoculars in the computer desk and it had come in handy.

The vista around me was beautiful. It was now springtime. In the low-hill ranching country everything was green. The trees were bursting with fresh leaves. Grassy knolls sat above small ponds. The sky stretched out blue and wide. The landscape was dotted with occasional barns and ranch houses. Cattle placidly grazed on rolling fields. Fences were few and low.

Everything seemed peaceful. But I knew terrible currents were running hidden beneath the placid facade, threatening to explode out and destroy the entire world!

I was well-hidden on the secluded hilltop, intently scrutinizing a distant facility. It was a cool morning. The sun was just coming up, starting to warm the chilly air. I had on my gray hoodie, one of Ms. Murtz' many hoarded clothes. It was several sizes too large, so hid most of my body. I had the hood up over my scraggly blond wig, peering from beneath. If discovered I could instantly revert to my disguise of being "the crazy cat lady." I even had a kitten sleeping in one of the large pockets so I could snatch it out to brandish, further confirming my stolen identity.

"I don't believe it," I marveled to Scotty who crouched beside me, panting with his long red tongue hanging out, "They're here!"

"Woof!" Scotty happily replied.

I was excited, getting careless. This was my first expedition to find out what had happened to the "Suzette Kingly Animal Shelter" and the *scientific complex* that was hidden beneath its stately acres. I'd been safely masquerading as the "crazy cat lady" for almost a year now. Traveling outside the house, though, was increasingly dangerous. The religious-zealot enforcer gangs, local police, military, and extra-dimensional Peace Keepers prowled the streets. They were markedly nervous, agitated, eagerly arresting or executing people for the slightest of offenses. Something was up. Something big was about to happen. So I knew I had to proceed with my oft postponed expedition to the compound.

To be fair to myself, it had taken me a long time to scout out a safe path. Traveling out of town on foot I'd be glaringly revealed for any observers or cops to stop and question. But I found a route offering enough concealment through backroads and across fields to safely reach the hilltop. Getting closer was impossible. I saw not only prowling guards but razor wire fences and even minefields. They clearly didn't want anyone knowing what was happening in the compound.

But I felt relatively secure on the scrubby hilltop. Scotty was keeping guard. I knew he'd warn me if any patrolling soldiers approached. The low hill was shrouded by thick brush, low trees, and waist-high weeds. I was confident it was impossible for anyone to sneak up on us.

Would that I'd been less confident and more fearful...*sigh*. If I'd gone back to my house and been there when the end came, maybe I'd finally have suffered a death from which I couldn't resurrect, finding peace.

But what had happened just a week ago could not be ignored.

What finally brought me out of hiding, prompting me to make such a dramatic expedition, was the recent *disappearance* of all the Peace Keepers across the world! It was a total shock when we awoke to find no "hoppers" floating down from above at any reported deviation from Phoenix-imposed local Rules. At first people rejoiced. Even the local police and religious Council smugly asserted: "We no longer need a chaperone. Earth is ours to govern as we wish!"

But it soon dawned on people that the lid had been removed from a world-wide, volcanic, seething, boiling pot...

All the suppressed *anger, disagreements*, and *differences* that before were tamped down now sprang up into the open. Worst of all, the incomprehensible alliance of the radical religious fringes—so dramatically different, even diametrically opposed to each other—fractured! Across the world, every fundamentalist "we know the Truth" religious or other discipline was at each other's throats.

And, even worse, the world's already limping *economy* was tanking. In sad shape before, financial systems were now crumbling. In Sulphur, the tourist establishments had always brought in much needed revenue for local jobs. Replacement by pious Pilgrims celebrating my "martyred" dead mother before going camping in the Park helped some but not much. Now even the Pilgrims were at each other's throats. Paper money was worthless. Online credits were losing their value at an alarming rate. The world was sinking into a deep depression. The surrounding rural economy of self-sufficient ranches was back to preindustrial bartering. Early on, Phoenix had outlawed eating meat. Cows and pigs had been slaughtered by the fundamentalist gangs by the millions, their corpses left to rot. The thin rocky Oklahoma soil wasn't much good for farming. Weed-clogged fields—with no grazing cattle to convert the plants into tasty hamburgers—were worthless for human consumption.

So in Sulphur things were going from bad to worse. Transportation of goods to local markets ground to a stop. Store shelves emptied. Those who had jobs were fearful of being fired. Those without jobs survived on meager bread and water handouts from the government. The few with independent means blockaded their homes in closed communities. Everyone lived in fear, without even religious unity to soothe over the suffering. The draconic religious Rules imposed upon our small town were universally opposed by virtually everyone of whatever sect, religion, or belief system. Before Phoenix we'd all gotten along with "you do your thing and I'll do mine" type of religious viewpoint or lack thereof. But the local Council was still mandated by higher Councils to continue its Edicts. Even the council members were at each other's throats, with no Peace Keepers to keep them in line.

Did I mention there was no longer any resupply to the local Megamart? I heard that the shelves there were mostly bare. The townsfolks were in real danger of starvation.

*Well, if worse comes to worse I suppose I can eat from the mountain of horded dry cat food that's still hidden inside Delilah's heaps of trash in her house—*I sadly concluded. *At least the cats are set until the Apocalypse arrives.*

I wasn't exaggerating. Something very bad was brewing. We all realized the End—whatever that might be—was drawing near. The official news feeds were ominously quiet. Rumors of uprisings and rebellions across the world were rife. And what made everything even worse was that nobody knew *why* the Peace Keepers had withdrawn to the alternate Earth dimension. One day everything was normal and the next they were gone. Did the Enforcers tire of policing us, disband, or were they just waiting for us to destroy ourselves before returning to pick over the spoils?

Whatever, I knew I'd better risk going back out into the open to find out what happened to my past comrades. Search as I might online and locally, I still couldn't figure out who or what was behind my mother's murder at the Galactic Core. There were many possibilities but no hard evidence. And access was spotty on the web, even the dark net, as supportive systems broke down. Maybe if I could somehow contact the others who'd been there with me at the Galactic Core, might they have discovered some answers on their own? Perhaps I'd put aside my hatred of him and even seek out Author Anderson. That is if he hadn't vanished also. After all, he was the most notorious ex-Time-Keeper of them all.

Ok, Suzette, focus!—I mentally admonished myself. *You've got to find a way into that compound. It's your final option for pursuing the Conspiracy.*

I began searching for any possible path below to sneak into the facility.

"I thought the authorities were going to relocate all the musically talented attendees at the Galactic Core Contest to some remote island or mountain monastery or deep-jungle retreat," I muttered to my faithful robot-dog Scotty. "But I guess this does make more sense. Why go to all that trouble that when you already have their secret 'lair' right here? It's actually ideal, a secluded compound in the small-town ranching countryside of southern Oklahoma. Just keep 'em there and add extra guards."

"Urf!" Scotty politely agreed with me.

Yep, there they were below me. Through my binoculars I recognized many of the Galactic contestants, workers, and audience members who I'd known and worked with. They were just walking about, freely moving between military-style barracks, pausing to play with many of the free-ranging animals of the "Suzette Kingly Animal Shelter." The dogs, house cats, horses, other critters, and even occasional big cats seemed tame and well cared for. But they and the humans weren't free. Razor wire-tipped high cyclone fences contained everything. At strategic corners were guard towers. I noted that the soldiers manning those towers carried high powered rifles. But other than that, it looked like a *resort* down below.

"Well, at least Phoenix didn't just execute my friends," I continued softly reporting to Scotty. "I guess religious fundamentalist roots have some moderating effect on Phoenix's 'righteous' rule of the Nation, unlike the Peace Keepers who just execute people at a whim."

Still, all music was still strictly banned from the world's population. The world-wide religious fundamentalist loose coalition called "Phoenix" had imposed strict moralistic laws upon all societies. However, they catered and tweaked to the preferences of whichever religion dominated the local landscape. In all my disguised sorties into downtown Sulphur I found the same thing: a dour, fearful population where cars no longer had radios or disc players, pedestrians no longer sported earbuds or mp3 players, and "background" entertainment "music" in stores was *sermons* delivered by members of the local Phoenix Council. Ugghh...so boring!

Even churches couldn't sing or play instruments any longer. The official services "music" was now mind-numbing repetitive monotone chants. All sources of online music had been shut down. Even flash drives capable of carrying mp3 files were banned. Worse yet, anyone *hearing* whistling, singing, or the playing of forbidden musical recordings was required to promptly report it. To be labelled a "good" citizen you had to turn in "evil-doers." Then, like poor Zeke, those "criminals" were either summarily executed on the spot or taken into custody to be "reeducated," or just disappeared, their fate unknown. Phoenix knew that it had to hold the line on banning music. If that prohibition crumbled, then all their other repressive rules would fail as well.

Just a few years earlier such repression would be unthinkable, even laughable. But as the world's resources were drained or destroyed, the population became increasingly jealous and fearful. The "conservative" mindset of protectionist fear dominated. Governments became increasingly authoritative, nationalistic, and then outright dictatorial: setting the stage for the birth of Phoenix.

That which once was unthinkable was now commonplace!

The blanket ban on "Satanic" music of all types was just the most odious of the new repressive rules that blanketed society. Women in the USA had to wear long dresses and keep their heads "modestly" covered in public. Most billboards and advertisements were gone, torn down or replaced by religious slogans and jingoistic admonitions. Communication vehicles—from News channels to books and magazines—were strictly censored. All stores and businesses were now closed on Sundays, adhering to Christian fundamentalist dictates. Social media platforms such as Facebook, Twitter, and YouTube were limited to State-approved topics. Independent reporters were a thing of the past, replaced by official Spokesmen. Women were mostly banned from the workplace, relegated to their homes and kitchens under the strictly imposed "oversight" of husbands or male relatives. Birth control devices, pills, and procedures were no longer available. The penalty for abortion was death by beheading, both to the practitioner and the woman. Thieves were punished by having their hands cut off. Alcohol and smoking were strictly forbidden. Drug dealers were burned at the stake. Was I forgetting some other awful trait of "holy" dictatorships? It seemed I *was* forgetting something important, but I couldn't recall... Oh yes, even the mere accusation of being a "liberal" was enough to get you "disappeared."

Lately the only cheerful folks I saw on my brief trips onto Broadway, the main street of Sulphur that previously was lined with fast food joints (now converted to Bible stores and prayer centers), were the many pilgrims. The Park behind the town had been officially designated as a family friendly, "nurturing" vacation spot by Phoenix. The Cemetery was a sanctioned international pilgrimage site. Presumably that was for visiting my "hero" mother's grave: the woman (so the official story went) who died fighting trying to stop me from disgracing mankind at the Galactic Core. But the local townsfolks were condemned to special repression as "denizens" of the *birthplace* of the much-vilified and hated Suzette Kingly. My beautiful bronzed statue, previously sitting grandly beside the Broadway artesian fountain was toppled by the townsfolk. It was then cut up into pieces, melted, and used to make tourist Phoenix figurines. But despite their show of revulsion for their infamous daughter, the citizens of Sulphur, Oklahoma were still subject to constant suspicion and scrutiny.

They were forced to constantly prove their loyalty or be snatched away by the authorities.

One way that criminals vanished was to be put into *work camps* similar to what I thought I now saw down below me. It was a horror inflicted by every authoritarian government in mankind's sordid history: mass-isolation and torture of dissidents.

"But they don't actually look that miserable," I puzzled as Scotty nestled up against my prone body, trying to stay warm. "What's going on here?"

I was excited to recognize some of the people walking about in the big compound below. Through my binocular lenses I spied the distinctive hairstyles, walk, and getups of several of my past key colleagues and "partners in crime": *Eun Jung*, my hairdresser and key assistant, sporting his Mohawk of wavy brown-gray hair; *Darlene M'hamba*, my African-American manager, with her ramrod bearing and white buzz-cut; *Sam Greene*, my overweight stage manager, once chubby and now even fatter, wobbling along; and *Maurice Chevalier*, a dreamy young French pop star who'd schemed to be my singing partner when I'd been on top of the music scene, strutting with his short trimmed beard and iconic golden dark-glasses.

That rat Anderson wasn't jerking me around. There was indeed a "Colony" of exiled musicians and it was right before me! Likely he was slinking around somewhere in the throng below, like the snake he was...

Alright, stop obsessing on Anderson! And you might as well add "skunk" to your reviled animal-characterizations of the ex-Time-traveler—I snickered to myself. *God, my head's spinning...*

Yet again, for the umpteenth time, I pushed back the throbbing pain that wracked my resurrected body. Would my constant agony never lessen? Was my new life to be a constant migraine headache times a thousand? Did the Aliens do this on purpose? They gave me eternal life but made sure I'd live it in hell?

Agghhh—I groaned to myself. *Get your act together, Delilah. You've a job to do!*

"But where are the others?" I mused, focusing back on the distant crowd. I ignored the buzzing flies and itching stiff grass tickling my tummy. "All those wonderful historical icons that I rescued from the past, where are *they?*"

And then I heard it: the distant "thrumming" of a deep, booming base guitar. It sent shudders of fear through me, recalling poor Zeke and his shattered lone banjo. I cringed, waiting for bombs from the sky to rain down on the camp. But instead, wafted on the breeze, I now detected the sweet strains of a soaring *violin*. And behind the leading strings came the intricate dance of a full *orchestra*. They were enthusiastically playing a classical piece joined and enhanced by a rock group, a beautiful arrangement that sounded hauntingly familiar but different...?

It was so wonderful to hear out-in-the-open, powerful, expertly executed, soaring music. I didn't dare have any such music in my commandeered house, not even earphones least the online sensors detect my questionable downloads. Not that there was that much to download anymore. All the overt music platforms had been shut down or destroyed, including access to optical discs and movies. I didn't even sing to myself least any neighbors hear it and report the crazy cat-lady for breaking a cardinal religious law. But how was it those below could get away with such "heresy"? And why was the distant music so familiar?

I knew I had to get down there, sneak into the Colony. How I'd do it, I had no idea. But my quest led there. I'd already set up another new identity in case I got caught, that of *Jeanie Jones*, the "grand-daughter" of my present disguise. I'd backfilled all the online documentation, established a history, plus bio-signatures such that I could access all of the now sadly deceased Delilah Murz' well-placed accounts as her duly designated heir.

But hopefully I could sneak in, get whatever information I needed, and escape undetected using my present "crazy cat lady" disguise.

"Ah, I think I know part of what's going on," I nodded to myself, laying down the binoculars and reaching over to stroke Scotty's long head. He happily thumped his tail into the ground beneath us. "*Mozart* has written a brand new piece. His style is unmistakable. But he's incorporating modern instruments and styles, incredible! But how is he allowed to do this?"

The distant music brought me back to happier times, when I was the world's most celebrated musical heroine, performing at the Galactic Core to bring back to Earth a stupendous prize. Of course that was before I blew it all, "throwing the contest" in the most disgusting manner possible. I instantly went from being the world's most celebrated pop superstar to Earth's most reviled villain.

"Times change, huh Scotty?" I sighed to my robot dog.

"Urf!" he agreed.

"What are you doing here?"

I leapt up, spinning around in midair, my floppy sweater ballooning around me. I landed hard on my hands and knees, caught up in its folds, momentarily helpless, fearing a bullet from a soldier's gun...

"Hey, I'm not going to hurt you, Delilah!"

Indeed, my "guard" dog wasn't afraid or defensive at all. He was hopping around giddily, "woofing" at the person who'd come up behind me. I vividly saw standing right there in front of me, illuminated by a shaft of early morning sunlight, a *tall, sexy* young man. He had *broad shoulders* and *slender waist*. He wore a *leather vest* over a *brown plaid shirt*, threadbare *blue jeans*, and *moccasins*. His hair was long and brown, braided into a thick *ponytail* at his back. His tanned face had *high cheekbones* framing a *prominent nose*. He was every inch a young Chickasaw modern-day warrior!

But I knew he wasn't going to attack or scalp me. Nope, this was a prior good friend of mine, Scott Yanash, the *son* of Losa Yanash. Unfortunately, though, he was a young man that I now fervently hated! He'd *failed* to rescue my mother, as he'd promised, allowing her to be *murdered*. The sight of his handsome face made me sick to my stomach. Wow...I sure despised a lot of previous love-interests, huh? Was I *really* crazy, not only twisted and tortured by my physical resurrection but *mentally* deranged as well?

Jesus Christ, I'm going off the deep end—I groaned to myself, forcing my extreme thoughts to quiet. *I've got to stop thinking in exclamation points and italics. I can't accomplish anything if I don't think rationally and clearly.*

Now *that* was a sobering thought.

"Wait!" he gasped. "Your dog, it can't be...and you're not Delilah, you're...?"

"Auuugghhh!" I shouted, pulling my hood up over my head and sputtering incoherently. I grabbed the startled kitten from my pocket and held it out like a talisman as I stuffed the binoculars into another big side-pocket. The cat "yowled" in protest. "I ain't hurtin' nobody!" I yelled. "I was jist lookin' is all! I come here to admire all th' big cats inside the yard down there. I likes cats. Arrgghh!"

Scott Yanash just stood there grinning at me, his hands on his slender hips.

"You can drop the act," he laughed. "I've known Delilah for years. I bought and delivered cat food to her from the local Megastore before they instituted their own online ordering and delivery. And—though it's absolutely impossible for you to be here alive and well—I know *you*, Suzy King. So why don't you just tell me what's going on? Is Delilah ok?"

I sighed deeply, slumping. I returned the scared kitten to my sweater pocket where she immediately curled up and went back to sleep. Scotty sat down his rump, looking expectantly up at me, then at Scott, then back again at me.

"Did you trail me here?" I peevishly whispered, sidestepping his incisive questions.

"Trail you?" he snorted. "You're practically standing on one of my secret tunnels into the Colony. The entrance is hidden beneath a boulder here on this mostly inaccessible strategic hilltop. Since they buried your ashes at the Cemetery—not to mention your revered mother and heroic dead dog, who's also inexplicably here—my concealed crypt entrance at the cemetery is inaccessible due to all the tourists there making the officially sanctioned pilgrimage."

"To see my final resting place?" I facetiously laughed in return.

He good-naturedly shrugged.

"Your dog is a media-friendly world hero and you're blamed for everything bad. The Pilgrims take pictures at his dog-shaped tombstone while cursing your vile memory. I'm told doing so is cathartic, considering everything you snatch away from each of the Pilgrims."

"Huh..." I dejectedly agreed, moving over a few feet to sit heavily down upon a moss-covered boulder. "So is your hidden entranceway beneath my sorry butt?"

"As a matter of fact, it is," he kindly nodded, not having moved from his spot, "Not that your ass is so sorry. I imagine beneath that awful robe it's just as pert and cute as it's always been."

"It's a sweater!" I insisted, trying to stay mad at him despite his off-handed "compliment."

Awwww—I groaned to myself. Despite my still-raging anger against him for his abysmal failure to protect my mom, he sure had a winning manner. *The kid's always had a way with words.*

"I'm your prior inner group's secret conduit to get stuff from the outside world," he continued. "I used to be a part of your merry band of idealistic rebels fighting Phoenix, remember? Now I'm just a common criminal, a smuggler. But we 'lower classes' have to make a living just like the Elites, right?"

"Lower class?" I frowned, not following his logic.

"Native-American?" he smiled, pointing to himself with one hand. "All those with land claims older than those of our latest oppressors, in this case Phoenix, have been officially branded as 'deficient.'"

Yep, that was what I was forgetting before—I realized, *not because it was insignificant but because such an attitude is so utterly stupid. You control large swaths of the population only by first dehumanizing them.*

I looked up at the brightening blue sky. It was getting time for me to make my way back to my "safe house" cat-haven. I couldn't risk being out in the open least I catch the eye of any of the authorities. Especially with the present uncertainty, all beggars or mentally challenged individuals were being arrested without cause. Previously they were just too disorderly for the new "perfect" society, harassed. Now they were deemed dangerous, total wastes of precious scarce resources, fit only to be eliminated. The Perfect's first impulse following labelling their enemies as "infidels" is to purge them as defined "inferiors."

"I'm making a delivery, *pizza* actually," Scott laughed, revealing his perfect set of pearly white teeth. He lifted up a large, square, heavily sealed package tied securely with thick string. "It's banned but still precious inside the Colony. They're only allowed 'healthy' food. We Native-Americans are adept at taking money from the 'white man' providing them with addictive pursuits."

This is just getting more and more confusing!

"Addictive pursuits?"

"First of all, the illusion of riches, gambling, giving them a little to get back a lot."

"Well, sure, gambling casinos—but *pizza*?"

"It tastes great but is loaded with clogging fat, particularly saturated fat, and blood vessel-hardening cholesterol—all major contributors to cardiovascular disease, heart attacks, strokes, and early death. We still have an official 'other nation' status where we can cook things that others would be jailed for baking."

"Ok, ok! So you're a pizza delivery boy," I acknowledged. "But what do the Elites and Rulers care about my musicians down below? And why do they let them play concerts? That's the most illegal activity in the entire world. Is it perhaps like when smallpox was eradicated but a few highly protected stocks were kept just in case they might be useful to science in the future?"

He wryly laughed. "No, it's nothing like that. It's a lot more mundane than Phoenix being super-clever masterminds."

"But then...?" I frowned, still not understanding.

"It's just a matter of control," he shrugged, evading my question.

"Well, that makes sense, I guess," I replied. "They've isolated the supposed societal 'virus,' and now are maintaining it in strict containment in case it's ever needed in the future. I have to disagree with you on Phoenix's lack of cleverness, based on their track record. The fundamentalist World Council is anything if not devious. In fact, Phoenix is one of my chief suspects for having ordered my Mom's murder. They'd do anything to stay in power. But so far I haven't found any solid proof that..."

"Suzy, that's all in the past," he bruskly interrupted me. "I feel real bad about what happened at the Galactic Core, but we have to find ways to survive here in the present. And, speaking of survival, I don't know how in the world *you're* still alive! You don't have to tell me, though I'm guessing it has to do with those mysterious Aliens who sponsored the Contest. But if you're looking to get into the Colony, I can take you with me...if you'd like, that is."

I previously believed that Phoenix and even the Commissioner welcomed the imposition of ultimate order and health from the Lords of the Galaxy. Therefore, they wouldn't try to throw a monkey wrench into the proceedings by murdering my mother. Now, though, I saw that they were relieved not to have to deal with yet another, even stricter dictator. The powers-that-be were happy being left as the ultimate authority on Earth, thank-you-very-much. Despite what our present rulers lost they must have all breathed a collective sigh of relief when I blew off our chance at Earth's gaining "protected" status. Dictators don't like to share power, no matter the possible benefits.

"I'd certainly like to visit the Colony," I slowly began, "but I can't have anyone recognize me. It's bad enough that you saw through my disguise. But I guess you're unique in closely knowing both the cat lady and me. She's dead, by the way, of a heart attack...or stroke, I dunno, one or the other. Anyway, Scotty led me to her house where I assumed her identity. Others don't question my being the 'crazy cat lady.' I've gotten pretty adapt at mumbling incoherently and waving around half-tame cats."

He held out a strong, youthful hand to me.

"Sorry to hear about Ms. Murz," he frowned. "She was a sweet old lady. I'm sure she'd be happy that you've taken her place, living in her house and taking care of her cats. So please come with me, my lady," he gallantly invited, brightening. Then, again more seriously, he continued: "I know I may never be able to atone for my failure at the Galactic Core with your Mom. But I really want to try, Suzy...that is if you'll let me?"

God, he was so smooth! At the same time my anger came rearing up in my throat at his reminder of the tragic murder of my mother, I still felt a warm glow in my heart from his sweet words. Well, that was a conflict to be addressed some another day. To continue my hunt for the true assassin(s) behind my mother's demise, I desperately needed information. I'd gotten all I could from Sulphur (not much) and the dark web (even less) so the only way forward was into the Colony.

Plus, I had a terrible feeling that time was running out. Whatever I was going to do, it had to be done fast.

"Won't I just be voluntarily imprisoning myself?" I frowned, rejecting his helping hand. I rose up from the boulder on my own, moving aside into the brush to get out of his way.

Shrugging diplomatically at my not needing his helping hand, he leaned down and began tilting and rocking the heavy boulder back and forth.

"They have many lethal barriers to keep people from getting out," he explained, "huffing" and "puffing" as he manhandled the large boulder from its hole. "But there are fewer for keeping people from getting inside. And once into the prison, you just become another face in the crowd. Don't draw the attention of the guards and you can do pretty much whatever you want to do."

"Good to know," I nodded. "And...thank you for your understanding and help, Scott," I forced myself to politely acknowledge his effort. "It's...good to see you again. But it'll be confusing keeping you two *identical twins* straight."

He looked confused at my feeble attempt at a joke. I wasn't that good a relieving tension. I needed his help even though each time I looked at him I saw my dead mother. Then he laughed, reaching over a strong hand to scratch the dog behind his ears.

"Oh, right...'Scott and Scotty'..." he laughed. "Yep, I definitely see the resemblance. We're both hairy and handsome."

"Woof!" Scotty acknowledged the attention, thumping his tail happily.

Then the young Native-American returned to his boulder, giving it a final shove over to the side. He straightened up, brushing dirt off his jeans. He pointed at a dark damp hole leading deep into the hillside. He placed an old, dried-up bush over its top, temporarily concealing the entrance we'd take from any casual discovery.

"Ok, then. I'll go first and you follow at my heels," he directed me, now not so cheerful. I understood by his tone that though escaping was tough, getting into the prison wasn't all that easy either. "Crawl under the shrub and let it fall back into place behind you. The dog can follow you. No one will even notice Scotty inside, since there are so many of your older dogs and cats still scampering around in there."

"That's a long distance to crawl," I gulped.

"Yes, I'm afraid much of the stretch is a tight haul, Suzy. So I hope you didn't wear your Sunday church clothes," he laughed. "I certainly didn't wear mine. Anyway, in places we can stand up. But we still have to do a lot of crawling. Many teams of my tribal members helped me dig this long tunnel, in addition to several others. We didn't have any construction equipment so it's narrow and dangerous. It's not even lighted. All I've got is a small penlight. Sections could collapse at any moment. So if you'd rather not...?"

"Lead on."

He wriggled in, pushing his well-sealed pizza package before him. I cautiously oozed myself after him, head first. Scotty, whimpering pitifully, stuck his nose beneath the shrub and followed along behind me. It was moist, stinking, dirty, and gloomy.

Uggghhh! I had a terrible premonition that this wasn't the last time I'd be entering a dark, filthy tunnel...

Thoroughly disgusted and coated with a thick layer of dirt, after a couple hours we emerged from a drainage duct set into the floor of a *public latrine.* My lungs were clogged with dust. I was trying not to cough too loud. And now I was assaulted with the stink of raw sewage!

Scott carefully put the slotted metal cover back over our tunnel exit. I saw we were hidden behind a screen where a pile of cleaning supplies was stashed, a sort of closet. On the other side I could hear the "tinkling" of several men relieving themselves, talking excitedly as they did.

From their chatter I caught something about..."feed being disrupted"..."guards deserting"...say what?

I was exhausted, filthy, and trembling. My poor pooch wasn't in much better shape. He flopped onto the concrete floor, rolled onto his back, and tried to squirm-away caked-on dirt.

"Well, that was fun, right?" Scott cheerfully whispered. He stood up, vigorously brushing grime and clods off his jeans, leather vest, and pizza package.

Still on my hands and knees I just glowered at him, trying to get my breath back without coughing my lungs out.

"You exited us into an open *pissing* trench?"

"It's not open. We're inside a long shed. The wastes flow down into a septic tank. This drain is just for water used washing the concrete floor. I'm sorry if it's not up to your refined tastes," Scott casually replied as he carefully cleaned off his still-sealed pizza package.

"Things have gone to hell here, especially lately. The crowds need places to relieve themselves while attending the mandated concerts. There's not much time between shifts for them to go back to their regular quarters. The shifts are getting longer and longer. And the arena bathrooms aren't working any more. The whole infrastructure here is breaking down. Everyone's on edge."

"Concerts? Shifts?" I groaned, my head spinning, leaning back against an unfinished wood wall.

"The live performances go twenty-four hours a day now, seven days a week," he quietly continued explaining. "The crowds have designated shifts for attending and providing enthusiastic, real-time audience responses. Here's a brush if you want to clean up."

He handed me the broken end of an old broom. I glowered at him but began swatting thick layers of dirt off me and Scotty.

"I need a shower plus clean clothes."

"Sorry, Suzy, that would definitely expose you in more ways than one. And, if it helps, I've got the same problem of not drawing attention to myself. If I'm caught smuggling contraband, the soldiers will kill me. They started out as friendly jailors. Now they've gotten more brutal than the Peace Keepers."

I wrinkled my nose at the stench, eager to get out of the latrine.

"Then why do you risk it? Surely it's not worth a big tip for delivering a few, measly pizzas?"

He quietly laughed. "These are worth more than your weight in gold, Suzy. These and similar 'portables' have kept my local tribe from starving this past year."

"Starving?"

"As the economy crumbled, those of us on the bottom are crushed by the wealthy hording their possessions. My marginalized people barter with the rich for our very survival."

What he said made sense but was still appalling.

"So you're saying that the people here inside the Colony are rich?" I grimaced in confusion. I had a very hard time believing that a prison population could actually pay Scott my "weight in gold" for a pile of cold pizzas. "Are you saying the prisoners have access to bitcoins? Regular Credits are virtually worthless now."

"You'll see..." he mysteriously answered, pulling back a couple loose planks in the wooden wall behind the screen. "Stay close beside me and keep up your 'crazy cat-lady' disguise—but not so much that you draw attention to us. There are, maybe, ten thousand people imprisoned here, enough for us to remain anonymous in the crowds. But distinctive personalities stand out and are widely known. Draw attention to yourself and we may not get out of here alive."

"You don't have to tell me how to blend in," I huffed at him. "And I'm not here to help you deliver pizzas. I need to get in contact with..."

"No disrespect meant, Suzy," he soothed me, peeking out through his crack in the wall. "I'll help you if you help me. Alone, lugging a large package, I stand out. But helping my 'girlfriend' move something I'm less conspicuous. So get ready to quickly follow me and..."

"I'm *not* going to be your...!"

He bent back the planks and was through the gap in a flash, holding it open for me from the outside. I shoved Scotty through first and then stumbled after him, hearing the boards "snap" shut behind me.

I hoped the urinating men inside didn't notice. It'd be easy enough for them to discover our exit point then report it to the guards. Even if we weren't executed on the spot we still might be trapped in the Colony. And as enticing as the thought was to become Scott's girlfriend, I couldn't "settle" for him. My mission was much larger than finding some sexy guy to shack up with while the Earth's society crumbled around us. I was now doubly convinced that a huge *conspiracy* was behind the murder of my Mom. It had almost stopped me from protecting the world from the alien psychic vampires—a *vast* conspiracy that might still be playing out!

"Take my hand."

"What?"

Without waiting to explain, Scott grabbed my arm, swung me into his strong arms, and planted a wet, lingering kiss on my lips.

Scotty the dog coiled himself around our legs, whining. I was afraid he'd dash off to play with the many loose cats and dogs I spied around us. But he stuck to us like glue. Good robot-dog!

"Meow?"

Oh, Christ! The kitten's woken up and hungry for some milk. Surely the soldiers will hear her and investigate?

I stuck a hand in my big side-pocket, stroking the cat while jiggling some of the dry cat food I'd put in there for her.

"Get to the Arena! Get to the Arena! Your shift's on-deck! Hurry up!"

The kitten settled back down as a squad of heavily armed soldiers pressed through the crowd around us, "thumping" people with their rifle butts. Seemingly out of amused politeness—or perhaps just exhausted neglect—they ignored the two young "lovers" plastered up against the latrine's back wall.

As they moved on past us, Scott slowly drew back from me.

"Whew, that was close," he gasped. He was still holding my arm tightly. "They came right around the corner just after I emerged. We beat them out of the latrine by only a second."

My legs felt wobbly and it wasn't just from the exhaustingly long crawl it'd taken to get into the Colony.

The handsome, young, Chickasaw warrior was getting to me.

"Leggo my arm!" I snapped, jerking it away from him.

Keep your focus! Keep your focus!—I sternly admonished myself. *You've a mission to complete!*

"Sorry..."

"Let's deliver your pizza," I angrily ordered him. "And then you're going to help me locate and anonymously question *Darlene.* I have to find out who *really* orchestrated the death of my mother. *Got* it?"

"Got it," he meekly replied, now gently taking me by the hand and leading me into the surging crowd. The large package dangled by its strings from his other strong hand.

I flung my hood up over my head, hunching down. I *wasn't* a perpetually spry teenaged girl. Nope, if questioned I was a stooped-over, tattered, old crazy cat lady being helped along by my "nephew". I had to stay in character.

I grabbed out the kitten and waved her at a group in the crowd that looked puzzled by my hunched appearance. I *cackled* under my hood.

They looked away, clearly embarrassed by my pitiful performance. Great! I jammed the cat back into my pocket.

This expedition is going to be very dangerous. Be careful, Delilah—I admonished my assumed character.

But it was *so* wonderful to be back inside the "Suzette Kingly Animal Shelter" complex. The large facility was beautifully landscaped within the surrounding lush farmlands. Tall trees, big bushes, neatly laid out flower beds, and gravel-covered walking paths were all around us. Compounds in the distance held larger animals in wooded glades complete with flowing streams. In the main public area smaller critters mingled with the walking crowds: dogs, cats, goats, many brightly colored birds, and other "petting" animals. The air was clean and fresh, the sky bright and blue, and the sunlight gentle and warm.

If I didn't know the people here were captives in a prison compound, apparently forced to continually "sing for their dinner" I'd think it was a beautiful paradise.

"So just where are we going?" I demanded, despite my aversion snuggling up close to Scott's warm side. People were all around us, griping and groaning about having to go "on duty" yet again, bumping into us. We got into the densest section, trying to blend in. Scotty the dog kept close to my legs. I appreciated him not dashing off after a squirrel or cat. Though he had all the "doggy" instincts he was unusually loyal, at least for a robot.

"To the main Arena."

"Why?"

"Don't you know that the best place to make an illegal exchange is in the most public, crowded space available?"

That didn't seem right to me, especially if the price of the pizza delivery was *my* "weight in gold". But he certainly knew more about smuggling than me. I'd just have to trust him.

"Besides," he continued talking in a normal voice since the noise of the swirling crowd protected us. "One of your favorite musicians is on next. You'll definitely want to be there for her act."

"Who is it?" I asked, intrigued.

"You!"

Oh, sure. That was a laugh. He was kidding me. A resurrected but hiding pop superstar was certainly *not* going to appear on that stage before thousands of previous fans who now viscerally hated her. He was just pulling my leg, wasn't he?

But glancing up at his handsome bronzed face I saw a serious, focused expression. What was he up to?

I guess I'll just have to wait and see.

The Arena was much as I remembered it. While flush with unlimited cash preparing for the Contest at the Galactic Core, we'd outfitted the Compound with every conceivable facility, including a variety of "smaller" stadiums. This was one of my favorites, the size of a large high school football stadium, built to hold up to 18,000 people. We'd commissioned it to be "multi-use": with an open field suitable for baseball, football, track, or rock concerts. I noted the long dugouts along each side of the arena field for opposing teams. They served double duty as prep areas for the various performers.

The high bleachers were only a quarter filled, with many sections roped off. My expert eye spotted the live-feed cameras set at strategic points. Most were aimed to capture jammed seats and dance areas in front and back of the large stage situated there in the middle of the field. So the illusion of a jam-packed sold-out performance was maintained with a (for the size of the stadium) meager crowd.

There finishing up onstage, I was delighted to see *Joan Baez*. Well, she certainly wasn't *me*, as Scot had joked, but it was marvelous to see and hear her. She hadn't figured prominently in the Concert at the Galactic Core, but she did contribute as one of the many backup singers. She'd not taken kindly to being snatched from the past, refusing to take a leading role on my organizing team, not at all overjoyed the doctors had restored the marvelous singing voice from her youth. Now she seemed just as dispirited as before, listlessly strumming a guitar while softly singing solo: "*Let me Wrap You in My Warm and Tender love.*" She sounded tired. The exiting audience looked likewise dispirited, largely ignoring her fabulously warbling, iconic folk-singing.

I could have stopped in my tracks and just drank in her exquisite voice and guitar-playing. It'd been *so* long since I'd heard her even on a recording. Her voice was a breath of fresh air.

Indeed, the morning breeze, warm sunshine, and stadium open to the deep blue sky made it a perfect moment for uplifting folk songs and...

"Keep moving, Suzy," Scott warned me, interrupting my drifting thoughts.

He was pulling on my hand. Yep, he was right. As the old, exhausted audience was moving out we were trudging with the fresher "volunteers" inward. If we blocked the isle the soldiers with rifles, standing around the perimeter, would instantly focus on us. I saw other guards down at the dugouts. There'd be no riots at this facility.

But it's so nice to be at a concert once more, no matter how perverse or supposedly illegal!

I particularly liked this stadium for its "open" central stage with its own giant speakers. Amplification here didn't rely on "house" speakers. We weren't inside an enclosed dome. Instead, the blue sky soared grandly above us, marred only by a few fluffy white clouds. Also, there were no giant projection screens. The concert was mostly driven by the actual music, not stagecraft or additional images. In fact, the whole arena reminded me very much of the crude setup in place way back at the original 1969 Woodstock, which I'd time-traveled to right before it was destroyed by an atomic blast. Now *that* was a real "bummer." Trying to protect the future from the insidious Phoenix movement, I instead caused its "peace-and-love" antithesis to be destroyed. *Sigh!*

I had a terrible feeling in the pit of my stomach that history was about to repeat itself...

Calm down, Delilah—I mentally ordered and reaffirmed my assumed identity. *You're just a crazy cat lady sneaking into a concert without paying for a ticket, that's all. Stay "under the radar." Keep your head down and your cat in your pocket!*

"We should get down on the field," Scott said as we moved along with the surge of the entering crowd. Many around us were leaving the central isle, moving out to fill designated stadium seats.

"Why?"

"That's where I usually make the exchange. We're all supposed to dance and writhe-about while all mashed together down there. My contacts can approach us without suspicion."

"Exchange for what?"

He hesitated a moment then seemed to make a decision.

"Flash drives."

"Say what?"

"THANK YOU JOAN BAEZ!" I heard an announcer thunder over the speakers. "SHE'S A LIVING LEGEND! SHOW HER YOUR AP-PRECIATION..."

There was a smattering of polite applause.

"—AND WELCOME ONTO THE STAGE OUR PREMIER IN-TERMISSION ACT, READY TO TURN YOUR EARS INSIDE OUT AS EVERYONE FINDS THEIR SEATS OR PLACE!"

This was interesting. The offstage announcer didn't give a name. Probably it was a member of one of the bands, doing a solo on his-or-her particular instrument.

We were descending the main isle toward the open area of the football field, which was filling up rapidly in front of the stage. Walk-ing past a dugout, from which peered a nervous-looking guard, we joined a thick crowd of standing fans. A lone performer walked onto the stage, sitting down at a synthesizer keyboard. He began slowly playing a simple melody with odd additions. I found it strangely mesmerizing. I'd had many synth players in my bands and concerts, but this was somehow different...?

"It's a closely guarded secret, but that's the point of this whole thing," Scott spoke in my ear, jerking my attention back to him as we worked our way closer to the elevated central stage. Clearly, he was agitated now that the critical swap was nearing. "This highly illegal 24/7 concert we're being forced to attend is *musical porn* for Phoenix and the other Elites. In public they oppress the masses with right-eous indignation at the 'evils' of music. But in the privacy of their walled mansions they feast on continuous live streams of your time-rescued performing geniuses."

I was dumbfounded. I'd always assumed that the Phoenix fun-damentalists were religious zealots single-mindedly forcing everyone else to "do God's will." As such—though I totally disagreed with them—I still respected them for their twisted religious dedication. The idea that they were subject to the same lusts and sins as all the rest of us was disturbing on a gut-wrenching level.

The synth music from the stage, amplified manifold by the giant speakers, was constantly changing. I recognized the instrument. It was an older Yamaha full-keyboard workstation model, top-of-the-line in the 1990's, with hundreds of different internal programs. The player onstage had gold glasses, long brown hair, and a full beard. He was skillfully improvising an escalating theme that was now pounding out brilliant instrumental combinations and blazing special effects.

"You're saying..." I mused, pausing, again having to drag my attention away from the fascinating music, "that they are keeping my concert team together in order to generate musical 'porn' for their own enjoyment—all the while banning it from the masses?"

He shrugged. "Sure, they're hypocrites. What's surprising about that? Some of the most powerful religious rulers in history were only seeking the power it gave them. They hid behind their outward 'holiness' while in secret doing the most-evil deeds imaginable. Sure, I suppose there are some totally sincere, unselfish Phoenix rulers. Many of their followers are certainly totally devoted fanatics, committed to their 'God-given' rules and regulations. But most are just thugs that found a way to legally harass and steal from us 'undesirables.' However, under the direction of your musical geniuses, some of the trusted technicians make covert recordings. That's what they exchange with the outside world for their lusted-after contraband."

"Pizza?"

"*Suzette Kingly, listen to me!*" was suddenly pasted on top of the continuing dazzling rhythms and mixed synthesizer instrumentals, sung more as a chant than a melody.

Startled, I fearfully ducked lower, yanking the hood down to cover my face...

—as the growing audience shouted back: "SUZETTE KINGLY, LISTEN TO ME!"

"What?" I gasped, afraid I'd been discovered. "What's going on?" I whispered to Scott, jammed up against his side.

"It's just one of the acts," Scott whispered back, reassuring me. He roughly shoved aside some lingerers in our way. "Suzette is used as a punching bag. Everyone tries to bring her into their performance. That's just some local guy from Sulphur that got swept up in one of the purges. He'd been hording some musical instruments instead of turning them in to be destroyed. They preserved his classic synthesizer. He was good enough at playing it that the police brought him here instead of putting him in jail. He's totally unpredictable. Each of his performances is radically different from his last one."

Wow! He's not just performing a well-practiced set, but impro-vising new compositions "on the fly." Amazing!

"I like him," I replied into Scott's ear, "but what are the odds he'd focus on me during my one and only visit here?"

"Hah...yes, that's odd, isn't it? But it's not unusual. Like I said, they all beat up on you. The audience loves him because he never gives the same performance twice, unlike the pros that mostly give the same tired old sets over and over. His music is always impro-vised, interesting and new. And his lyrics are simple but intriguing, co-opting the audience by getting them to repeat what he says. It's a clever act."

"It's not what it seems!"

"IT'S NOT WHAT IT SEEMS!" the audience shouted back.

Jesus! That's an appropriately mysterious message for me. What is this guy, some sort of prophet?

A crackling series of *chimes* and *bells* erupted around us, radically different from the jazz combo the performer had just been brilliantly executing. Yes, his abrupt shift in genre was jarring but dazzling. I now realized what he was doing. His rampant, random improvisation was a form of "electronica" in which synth instruments produced wonderful noises on a compelling beat garnished with simple words enthusiastically repeated by the audience. I'd used synth keyboard players of course, but mostly as fill-in and supplementation to tradi-tional sounds and progressions. This guy was using his synth as a master-instrument altering his mixed "voices" in marvelous, unpre-dictable combinations.

"But how can pizza be so important?" I marveled. I was trying to get back on our immediate topic instead of being swept up in the in-creasingly amazing synth music reverberating all around me.

The acoustics in the stadium were marvelous. The performer's single keyboard executing complex computer programs in unexpected sequences simulated a full orchestra plus jazz band plus rock-and-roll group. It was amazing!

"Darn right it's important, Suzy," he spoke back into my ear so no one else could hear us. "Pizza is prized over almost anything else in the Colony. The people here now subsist mostly on potatoes, carrots, onions, and water. Throw in a covertly 'harvested' dead cat or two and I hear it makes a nourishing stew. That's actually not bad considering what's happening outside, where millions are starving to death just here in Oklahoma. But the musicians think they're being tortured, so trade their 'forbidden fruits' for 'luxury' items."

"But still...recordings on flash-drives? Don't you quickly saturate the outside market? Sulphur's just a small town that..."

An incredible soaring series of electronically simulated violins, oboes, and pounding grand piano burst from the giant speakers. On top of that were weird distortions and fluctuations. It was beyond just mimicking a larger group. It was astonishingly original and good!

"The filled flash-drives are too dangerous to keep, Suzy," he hurriedly explained as we stopped walking and started dancing. "The local jiggers have to wipe the flash drives any time there's a hint of discovery. Most of them just set them on self-wipe as they're played one single time. I bring a bag of empties along with the pizza or whatever else the performers want from me and..."

"—they give you filled-up ones, which you then barter for all sorts of goodies on the outside. I get it. Clever," I nodded. I was no longer surprised by the hypocrisy of the world's oppressive leaders or the desperation of my previous colleagues. There was nothing new under the sun. The perversion and selfishness of *Homo sapiens* was a constant. It wasn't my concern. My one and only goal in my unlikely elongated life was *sweet revenge.*

After that, humanity could all go straight to hell.

"*It's all just a dream!*" the synth player concluded grandly, seemingly admonishing me. His last chords rang out, vibrating throughout the stadium, shaking my bones!

"IT'S ALL JUST A DREAM!" the audience roared back.

Wow! That was some amazing "opener" act. I was truly impressed. It wasn't regular "music." It was the guy seemingly directing *several* orchestras mixing in amazing special effects from his one single keyboard! Who was this local guy, anyway?

"THANK YOU *DANIEL LYLE!*" the loudspeakers squealed as the Master of Ceremonies walked up on the stage, grandly gesturing at the departing man. "ISN'T HE GREAT?"

This time the jaded audience erupted in a thunderous ovation at this "fresh" music, which I enthusiastically joined.

And I was pleased to see who was conducting the concert shifts: *Swami Satchidananda.* He was an Indian mystic famous back during the "flower child" generation of the 1960's, who'd given an opening speech at Woodstock in 1969. And here he was snatched by me from that time period into the far distant future, still in all his glory: a dark-skinned gentleman in a long pink robe. He had gray-brown hair falling past his shoulders, a huge bushy gray-white full beard and mustache, a gleaming smile, and warm brown eyes.

I was a sucker for warm brown eyes. Come to think of it, that's what I liked most about Scott...his dreamy, warm eyes.

Of course Satchidananda was still a long distance from us up on the stage, but I felt warmed to my heart by his enthusiastic embrace of all true spiritual Essence.

Around me I now spied some hooded figures who weren't dancing, just applauding the Guru on the stage. Were they governmental operatives? They didn't look like typical military. Instead, they had the serious but rapturous look of "true believers"...what?

One of them, a woman, looked at me and nodded. Did she recognize me? She held out a glass to me, pouring a sparkling brown liquid into it from a jug. Was it iced tea? That would be welcome. I was thirsty after all my exertions.

*Wait, at a rock concert it's probably laced with LSD or something worse—*I concluded, shaking my head "no." *I best stay thirsty rather than idle my brain with poison.*

She shrugged and took a long drink from the glass, seemingly taunting me.

"...AND WELCOME TO THE STAGE THE ONE-AND-ONLY, THE WORLD RENOWN, THE UNDISPUTABLE CHAMPION OF DEVASTATION, THE QUEEN OF DISASTER, THE HORRIBLE PHENOMENON YOU'VE JUST ADMONISHED IN THE WAY OF TRUTH—*SUZETTE KINGLY HERSELF!*"

I stood stock-still, stunned. My jaw hung down, no words coming out. I was speechless. There, strolling nonchalantly onto the far stage was...*me!* I had on my iconic torn blue jeans, a white tank top, a blue-brown plaid long-sleeved shirt, and a broach of fake amber jewels above my breast pocket. The broach exactly set off my natural blond hair which swirled freely around my head. And in my hands was my iconic red electric guitar.

I was the picture of an eager, young, teenage popstar!

A huge cry of *rage* went up from the entire crowd of nearly 10,000 people: "GET OFF! GET OFF! GET OFF!"

Others "booed" and "hissed" their contempt.

"It's a hologram," Scott whispered in my ear. "It always juices up the crowd. They really hate you. They blame all their problems on you. As far as they're concerned, it's you that's brought the world to the brink of ruin."

Ok, then—I sighed to myself, relaxing a bit. *This is like fake professional wrestling, where you always need a villain to jeer while you simultaneously cheer the hero. Of course I'm the villain. So who's the hero?*

"WHO DO YOU WANT?" Satchidananda yelled.

"HENDRIX! HENDRIX! HENDRIX!" the audience screamed back at him, getting into the clearly oft-repeated, well-practiced act.

Onto the stage ran a jumping, air-swatting *Jimi Hendrix*. He slashed his iconic *white* electric guitar back and forth through my hologram until I faded away, seemingly defeated.

"I gotta song for you that I ain't sung for quite a while," he softly spoke into the standing mike. "It ain't been political to do it. But it's one of my grooviest numbers. It's my take on the state of the nation and the world. It's as true today as when I played it back during the Vietnam War at Woodstock in 1969. I don't know what's going to happen to me for performing it for you today, but my band and I talked it over. People hated me for doing it then but I hope you'll like it now. It puts new beauty into an old, taken-for-granted national anthem. I hope our masters around the world will see the beauty of what I'm doin' and not the badass. Maybe they'll pull back from any freaky stuff they're planning. I'm callin' for the fuzz and our guards to peace-out. Maybe they can smoke some grass? We don't need no heavy bummers today, right? So let's just hang loose and cut some sweet gas. Can you dig it? Are you with me? Is that far out?"

Excited and energized, the audience roared its approval.

Grinning widely, Hendrix and his band *Gypsy Sun and the Rainbows* took up their instruments. Then he launched into his famous, distortion-rich version of "The Star-Spangled Banner."

I was mesmerized. I stuck up my arms and twisted with the crowd to the teeth-rattling, soul-stroking vibrations. It was just incredible to see Jimi up there in all his past glory. His "banned" tune was magical. The stunning vibrations filled the beautiful stadium. His bright blue jeans contrasted dazzlingly in the morning sun with his red bandana. His white electric guitar flashed like a weapon as his fingers caressed it, seducing it with expert ease. The long blue tassels on his white shirt flopped and flowed around him as he twisted and gyrated, lost in the magic of his squealing chords, notes, progressions, and distortions.

"No," Scott said next to me, bringing me back to my mission. He held the package close, refusing to release it.

"But we agreed..." a frowning short man insisted, looking about furtively as the crowd swirled and pranced around us.

"The deal's changed. I'll give it to Darlene, no one else!"

Oh, my. Scott was standing tall for me. He was bringing Darlene to me. What a nice guy...who I still hated!

It's getting harder and harder to stay mad at him—I groaned to myself. *He's just too sweet, helpful...and handsome!*

The audience was invigorated by Hendrix, dancing at their seats and prancing on the field. He certainly wasn't dully playing an oft-repeated, boring number. The guards up on the crosswalks of the stadium looked uncertain how to respond. He was "going for broke" doing a famous piece he'd apparently not done for years. The audience was entranced and enthused. And I was right there with them, reveling in the incredible music.

And then Darlene was there, plastered against Scott's side, making token dance motions. I was startled. She looked extremely nervous. This wasn't like her. She was always ice-cold, in-control, and focused. Something was up, something *big*...

I noticed that the hooded religious figures had vanished. Where had they gone?

"Well?" she yelled in Scott's ear. "I'm here! What's wrong? I've got to get below."

Her black eyes were hard. She obviously didn't like being brought out in the open to accept the contraband. Her dark skin glowed in the morning sunlight. She looked healthy but thin. She'd worked tirelessly for me when I was on top of the music scene. She was the ultimate organizer who was in charge of everything. If anyone knew anything about who actually ordered the death of my mother, she would. She had her ear to the ground, a finger to the wind, and an eye on the soul of all those who crossed her path. But I was pleased she didn't even glance at me hunched over in my long sweater, doing a weird gyration beside her and Scott, my hoodie over my head. To her I was just another dancer in the crowd.

"I can't live with the guilt," he yelled back. "I've got to have answers!"

"What guilt? What answers?"

"When Suzette needed me the most, I couldn't save her mother. I have to know who killed Sally King!" he yelled at her.

"You know the results of the official investigation as well as me!" she yelled back, her voice barely audible to me over Hendrix's screeching, squealing guitar. "It was a *criminal syndicate* on Earth. The military raided their mountain compound, destroying their operation. The leaders were all killed. Corroborating evidence discovered in the raid confirmed their role!"

"And you believe the official version?" Scott responded, the pizza-package swinging on its strings in an arc around him as he twirled and pranced.

"I've heard...rumors," she said more quietly, speaking directly into his ear such that I could barely hear her. "The criminal syndicate may have been a patsy, commissioned by another entity."

"What entity?"

Hendrix and his band reached the joyous climax of the Star-Spangled Banner," immediately launching into his hit "Purple Haze."

It was Woodstock all over again!

"I don't know, but..."

"Yes?"

"I think it might have been a rival mega-religious group, working to dethrone Phoenix."

Oh, wow! That was a great lead. Scotty had just advanced my search by a quantum leap!

Wait, a reclusive largely unknown religious movement? Could this tie to those mysterious hooded figures?

"That's helpful, Darlene. Here's your package. Enjoy!"

"My courier will take it in a few minutes. I've urgent business below. You should get out of here as soon as possible, Yanash. Get back to your family."

"What's wrong?" Scott demanded, stopping her by grabbing her arm.

Her look would have killed him if her eyes were laser beams. Instead, he hastily released her as dancers swirled and leaped all around us.

For a moment we were in a strange closed bubble inside the ecstatically writhing mob.

"We've lost touch with the rest of the world. All our transmission and receiving feeds are down. Even Hendrix's present performance isn't being broadcast by the usual tight satellite beams. We're just recording it for subsequent release."

"Then...?"

"It's probably just a glitch on our end. But I've got to go get it worked out. Our survival depends on the users getting our products live!"

"Ok, but...?"

She was gone. The crashing, clanging, exploding music continued. Hendrix was on a tear, *shredding* his guitar! I was afraid it was going to burst into flames!

Then after a few minutes the short man reappeared beside Scott, grabbed the package and dashed off. He left behind a small leather pouch that Scott immediately secured inside his leather vest.

"Ok, we can go," Scott said to me, still dancing spritely a few inches from me. "Satisfied?"

"I..."

Scotty the dog darted into my feet, almost tripping me. He began barking frantically.

"See? My 'identical twin' is agreeing with me. It's time to leave and..."

"Wait, what's that?" I gasped.

A giant FLASH had just eclipsed the blue of the sky. Everyone froze in place. Jimi and the band stopped in mid-stroke. In an instant we'd gone from mind-bending, shrieking rock-and-roll music to utter silence. We all looked at each other, not knowing what was happening.

"RUN!" the Swami shouted from the stage over the giant speakers. "*RUN!*"

But it was too late, much too late. The ROAR—far deeper and more bone-shattering than even Jimi's electric guitar—deafened us.

And then the BLAST WAVE *slammed* into the stadium walls, smashing them inward!

I was aware of a raging INFERNO engulfing thousands of people who caught fire where they stood, screaming and writhing. The lucky were crushed beneath tumbling debris from the blown-inward stadium walls. The unlucky were buried beneath heaps of dead bodies, suffocating in place.

I reached out for Scotty and Scott but they were gone, blown away.

My last thought was: *Damn! Why didn't I drink that tea? I'm dying parched!*

Chapter 5

<u>TITANIAN GREEN</u>

Some called it the "spice of life"
A magic elixir dissolving away pain
Electrifying pleasure centers of the brain
Instant Nirvana erasing all nagging Questions
For which wise men surrendered their very minds
Frightened individuals gave up their precious defenses
Kings clashed, empires crumbled, and armies fought
All for control of a rare chemical mixture
Bringing or costing heaps of money
All to untie the "Gordian Knot"
To claim ultimate victory
Whatever the cost...

The Rise and Fall of *Homo sapiens*, 5:4-8

I was sound asleep on the sofa, stretched out flat along its soft surface. Instead of waiting an hour, I'd been there all morning. After a couple hours I figured I might as well get some much-needed rest. But then I suddenly jerked awake. I'd heard the faint "swish" of the titanium plate behind one wall sliding upward.

The other plates stayed in place. The exit door opened. Pretending to still be asleep, I analyzed the first footsteps of the person entering. It *wasn't* Madam Challax...

I was ready to spring into action, *kill* the person and try to escape deeper into the Moby Dick—or, more likely, take whoever it was hostage as possible protection against the lasers.

"Excuse me, Sister Penda? A'm sorry tae disturb ye, bit thay said yi'll need certification o' thair newest batch o' th' Green? I'm happy tae answer ony quaistion ye hae concerning it. I haid tae fly in fae mah private dome. Sae I'm sorry ye hud tae hauld yer horses."

I'd know that thick Scottish-clanner accented high-pitched voice anywhere. It was the "first mate" Ailith. I was just hoping to get a lead as to where I could continue hunting her. The "fresh batch" of Green had to be from the huge crystal that I and Captain Fehler cut out of the Kraken. And here they delivered her right to me. Yippee!

But I couldn't let my enthusiasm show. I had to maintain my aloof, woman-of-means illusion. If she knew it was me she'd clam up, warn the others, and cheer them on as they used their laser beams to slice me into sushi.

"Oh...hello," I yawned, stretching my arms as I leisurely sat up on the sofa. "I was just taking a nap, don' 'cha know. And just who are you, please?"

I kept the scarf on, obscuring my head. The lines of my face were hid by my left hand held beside my cheek. Staying hunched over I hoped she wouldn't suspect that the dark-skinned wealthy woman before her was actually the Inspector she'd recently viciously harpooned!

She sat down on a lushly padded chair facing the sofa. I barely recognized her. Her gray stringy hair was now fluffy, tinted with stylish golden highlights. In just three months she'd transformed. She was no longer a thin, muscular, old-lady skiffer. Now she looked like a pudgy Elite. Clearly, she was eating well. Her blotchy skin which I remembered so well through her smeared faceplate was now delicately made up, powdered and highlighted. And she wore a silk robe dyed purple and blue, the clothes of the upper class. Plus only someone of considerable wealth could afford a private Dome on Titan. If I could trick her into telling me where her home was—or, better yet, get her to take me there—I was certain I'd find Captain Fehler.

Then I'd teach them both not to strand a speared Inspector on a diving Kraken.

"A'm th' gaffer o' th' skiff that recently harvested th' Green ye'r interested in purchasing."

"Gaffer? Are you saying you're the *owner* of the entire fleet?"

"Aye, a'm," she proudly asserted.

I didn't doubt it. In just a few months she'd gone from being First Mate on one single skiff to owning the whole shebang. And she'd certainly only gotten *part* of the vast "take" from the huge crystal we'd found. This correlated with the claim by that slob on the walkway: that the sunken skiff's crew was living high. But the Captain would still have the lion's share. Supposedly that's why the First Mate agreed to come over to the Moby Dick to soothe the doubts of a rich "whale." She still needed money, and would likely get a nice kickback from my purchase. All of them needed more money, no matter how wealthy they became. It was their greatest weakness: follow the money!

"That is so interesting. And it's so kind of you to come reassure me, don' 'cha know," I said in a soft voice, stroking her ego. From our prior "interaction" I knew she was a needy person unsure of her own worth. I'd seen many like her along the way, minor officials angry they weren't taken seriously or hadn't risen higher in their careers, overreacting in moments of crisis. It didn't absolve her guilt but did explain her bitter attack upon me.

"A'm happy tae dae sae. Whit speirins dae yi'll need fae me?"

I smiled shyly from behind my obscuring dark-skinned hand, batting long eyelashes adorning my deeply black eyes. "Please just tell me the story of this batch of Green. It's so fascinating to me what you do here on Titan, skiffing the methane sea like whalers of Old Earth. That's what attracted me to the 'Moby Dick' versus other dealers here in the Pleasure Dome. Your marvelous occupation and brave fleet are so romantic. I'm privileged to hear your account, don' 'cha know?"

She visibly blushed. Though Captain Fehler was her "man" it was clear she was susceptible to flattery from powerful women. It was easy to turn her now that I wasn't perceived as an obvious threat. No longer a dangerous "Inspector", I was just an admiring, easy mark. Plus I was engaging with her personal fantasy of dominance. I fixed a happy smile on my lips, knowing I was going to have a hard slog making it through her deep-Scottish wordage. But I was sure the nuggets of information I'd get would be worth the slog.

"Och, certainly," she smiled, clearly flattered. "It 'twas only three munths ago. Mah flagship wis oan Ligeia Mare, harvesting th' sheets that haud th' fuel that runs th' solar system. We cam upon a giant monster that threatened tae drag us doun tae th' depths. Mah Captain battled bravely bit wis taken whin th' skiff wis destroyed. Ah wuz lucky to be along fer thet voyage. Ah donned wings 'n' flew tae save him. Ah clocked a chance tae strike tae th' hert o' th' monster wi' mah harpoon, whaur the Green is accumulated. So ah murdurred th' monster, slicing oot its hert, while saving mah Captain. The Green wis remarkable, pure 'n' potent. I've tested it oan masell. A'm a changed wifie due tae tis power. Afore, ah wis fearful. Bit noo I'm duin tae dae whitevur ah mist. Mah mind's flown beyond Titan, by-gane Pluto, oot tae th' stars! Ye wull fin' th' remarkable experience you're seeking wi' this batch, ah assure ye."

Wow, that was hard to follow. But I just nodded repeatedly, making small adoring noises throughout.

Realizing she'd been rambling, she paused, clearly embarrassed by her long speech. Great! Her lies were evident to me since I'd been there myself, including being the recipient of her cowardly harpoon stab from behind. She was making herself into a heroine. I doubted her self-inflation was just due to the intoxicating effects of pure Green, but came from her pre-existing psychic defects. Whatever, she was ripe for the plucking.

"Oh, how marvelous!" I gushed, pretending I'd understood everything she'd said in her garbled Scottish accent. "I dressed modestly to come here in person, not to attract attention. But as I'm sure our host has already certified I'm also a woman of considerable wealth. It is so wonderful to meet a fellow female adventurer with the will to *take* what she wants."

Ailith's ageing eyes went misty at my praise.

"Weel then, ah hawp a've..." she said, beginning to stand up.

"But I fear I've another request of you," I interrupted in a meek small voice. "I don't want to presume upon your generosity but..."

"Please, ask whitevur yi'll waant," she grinned as she sat back down.

"I am now happy to purchase and partake of the Green. But I fear doing so in a helpless state, even here in this sophisticated establishment. They mean well, I'm sure, but I'll be totally vulnerable while under the Green's influence to any outside authorities. To travel here 'incognito' I had to leave behind my usual large staff, including my bodyguards. Plus I'm uneasy 'using' in a place under the thumb of the State. I understand that both possessing and partaking of purified Green is highly illegal and...?"

"Aye, lassie, it's," she firmly interrupted. "Appropriate officials git thair cut o' the' tak', of course, bit mah capture o' th' green fae th' Kraken wasn't reported ta th' Company. They seenle prizes ur kept fur mah crew 'n' ah alone. A've a special relation wi' th' Moby. We wirk th'gither quietly 'n' effectively tae shift th' product. The Green is unstable whin separated fae tis natural matrix, sae th' process o' purification is lang 'n' complicated tae hae a stable product. Ah vouch fur thair trustworthiness. Bit separate fae thaim, a've git th' personal netwurk tae bade safe 'n' secure, if you'd lik'?"

"Yes!" I eagerly agreed. "I *so* value your kind help in this matter. I'm happy to pay the house for my Green, but to actually consume it...?"

"That's na kinch. It wid be mah honor tae hae ye fur may guest in mah private Dome. Pay fur th' amount yi'll waant 'n' we kin depairt immediately. Ah hae mah 'copter thet's waitin' outside th' Moby. We wilnae hae tae don excursion suits. Mah craft exits oot a private heavy equipment airlock fae th' Buzz Dome."

Buzz Dome? Ah, that must be local slang for Pleasure Dome. How'd I miss that in my research prior to descending down onto Titan's surface? Ah well, no sense kicking myself. There are some things you only pick up by actually being there.

"Oh, you are so kind," I seemingly shyly agreed. "I gladly accept your kind hospitality. How much of the Green should I purchase to have the maximum effect?"

"Oh...a milligram shuid dae. Bit that wull be gey dear tae yer purse so..."

"Then I'll buy a gram!" I grinned broadly, clapping my hands together in apparent glee. "That will give me enough to experience the full effect both now and later. I assume you can advise me on how to properly smuggle the remainder off Titan?"

Through her heavy makeup, Ailith's face visibly blanched. Her cut of the astronomical amount I'd have to pay to the Moby Dick would satisfy her money lust for decades. Certainly she'd gotten a good wad handing over the raw Crystal, but the markup to customers was where real money appeared. Yes, it would deplete one of my main accounts I'd built up over hundreds of years, but what the heck?

Unlike these fools, I wasn't the servant of money. And Green in hand, my path forward would be *so* much easier.

"O' coorse," she gasped.

"Then call back Madam Challax. Let's make this deal!"

I was pleased to hear the faint "shush" of titanium panels being hastily withdrawn. The pinhole laser beam-exits quietly "snapped" closed. I was now their certifiably hooked whale-of-a-century. And I had *them* right where I wanted them: ripe for *my* "harpoon" to penetrate *their* slimy guts!

"So will I get to meet your Captain?" I innocently asked.

In the few minutes since we'd launched out of "Buzz Dome" I'd covertly mapped out all the circuitry of our cabin. I'd located every security bug and weapon hidden behind the inner wall.

Good, just audio is active. The crew isn't looking in on us. So I only have to be careful with my words, least they hear anything questionable.

"How come wid ye wantae catch up wi' him?" Ailith suspiciously replied.

I leaned back in my incredibly comfortable flight chair. The First Mate's ill-gotten, newfound wealth had been well spent on the large helicopter. The passenger cabin was equivalent to flying first class on a luxury airline on Old Earth. I spied a bathroom door, a galley section with a sink, and a holo-casting wall unit beyond the six passenger seats. Aft was a closed door, leading to the cockpit. Likely it was a luxurious as the passenger cabin.

"Why, to thank him of course," I replied, smiling shyly behind an uplifted hand. "If it weren't for you needin' to rescue him, I wouldn't have this marvelous treasure, correct?"

I pulled out from beneath my robe the sealed, clear vial which contained a smidge of glittering, green powder. The vial hung at the end of a solid gold chain which tightly circled my neck. It wasn't going to accidently drop from a pocket or get misplaced! Madam Challax had assured me that once locked in place only my fingers could remove it from my neck. The golden chain was virtually unbreakable. It better be...that 1/6th teaspoon of purified Green had cost me half my vast fortune. News of the mammoth sell was likely reverberating throughout Titan Station's criminal underworld. It instantly made "Sister Pena" a hot target for assassination, kidnapping, or mugging. Even my "benefactor" might be plotting to retrieve her precious grains off my dead body after removing my impeding head.

I slid the vial carefully back beneath the collar of my robe.

Three pairs of greedy eyes followed its path. Ailith had two burly bodyguards with her, sitting alertly beside us. I was somewhat surprised they weren't armed with guns. A person as obviously paranoid and wary as Ailith would only travel with a well-armed crew. But then I saw they had concealed knives.

Great! I've stirred the stinking "road-kill" pot and who knows what noxious leads might bubble up?

"He's nae at me Dome, guid riddance tae him," she snidely replied. "Ah fired him fae my fleet. He'll ne'er captain anither skiff on Titan!"

"Fired him? Why?"

We were slowly "whumping" away from Titan Station. The noise of the rotors was muted by the double-walled, airtight cabin. Through several oval portholes I saw thick orange smog swirling. Regularly puncturing the gloom outside were vivid ascending *yellow glows* of fuel pod rockets being continuously launched. The pods were joining orbital clusters, about to begin their slow transit of the solar system. The Domes were completely obscured. The seashore was undetectable. It was like we were all alone in a foul soup, a meaty morsel about to be consumed by some hungry Entity.

Ailith leaned back in her form-fitting flight chair, pursing her lips before replying. She cut a discordant figure. Wrapped up in silky luxury her squinty eyes and angry frown betrayed a petty, scheming rodent. Although I doubted she had actually "fired" Captain Fehler, he'd obviously fallen out of her favor.

She seemed to be thinking about how much to reveal to her new "friend." Then she shrugged and launched into a diatribe.

"He tried tae double-cross me, tak' a' th' Green for his-sel. Ah insisted oan a fair cut fur me 'n' th' crew, hauf o' th' crystal. He shored a token scrapping tae us. Sae ah *throttled* him 'n' teuk th' hail thing fur masell!"

Wow. She was being very open with me now. That had to mean that she didn't expect me to ever repeat this conversation. I was in extreme danger.

"So he's dead?" I asked in apparent fascination.

I was keeping up my act of being the adventure-seeking, romantic-but-naïve sophisticate. It wouldn't do, yet, to reveal I knew her intent. Sitting silently in the small but comfortable cabin with me and the First Mate, the two beefy bodyguards were ready for anything. They definitely weren't there just for show. Narrowed eyes and cool demeanors bespoke "trained assassins." Despite their pristine black suits and refined manner, at a nod from Ailith I knew they'd slit my throat. As a fellow certified assassin, I admired their stance while detecting faults in their technique. Problematic to their craft was positioning slender knives under their suitcoats. Yes, it provided instant access but also produced slight rippled patterns in the overlying fabric. That was sloppy of them. And they didn't have the neutral stance of trained assassins. One of them wasn't even looking at me, his eyes glazed, his lips silently quivering. Was he *praying?*

"Unfortunately, na," she sighed, jerking my attention back to her. "He recovered, stole another helicopter, 'n' escaped wi' hauf th' crystal. He aye wis a sly bas."

Ah, yes. She means "he always was a sly bastard." Well, that's true enough.

The cabin swayed, rocking me backward then forward. Ailith and I wore seatbelts that kept us tucked into our form-fitting, cushioned seats. The bodyguards had no such constraints, poised on the edge of their flight chairs. I admired their exquisite balance. One of them would be no problem for me to dispatch. Two of them, though, made things more uncertain. In a fight, either of them might slip a knife into me while I was fending the other off. And then there was the wild-card First Mate. I wouldn't put it past her to happily torture me for my accounts-access information before personally killing me. I knew from sad experience that she was a beast, even worse than her trained gorillas.

And it was time to gently agitate her.

"But where could he go that you, the owner of Titan Station's skiffing fleet could not find him? Surely with all your resources, you could...?"

"Juist fly tae th' volcano 'n' grab him? Hah!" she bitterly laughed, revealing to me his present location. "That's juist whit he'd waant me tae tuv a go. He haes military pals there who'd nae hesitate tae launch missiles against mah 'copter. Th' main buyers ur mair powerful than ye kin jalouse. Wur safe enough 'ere at th' station, bit exposed in th' dune-fields we'd be sittin' ducks ripe fur th' clocking. Sure, oor energy cell cuid tak' us there in a day flyin' at tap speed. But flying wee enough tae evade their radar wid be gey dangerous ower the dune fields. Sae, na, wur nae worried about him. We've git enough tae bade pie-eater 'n' fat and happy fur a lang time richt 'ere."

I had all the information I presently needed. So Fehler had escaped from Titan Station to the "volcano." It was time to end this charade. I needed to move onward to Titan's main cryovolcano, *Doom Mons*, where I was certain something much more than an illegal Green-smuggling operation lurked. A military presence with advanced defenses against air attack bespoke a high-level conspiracy. It was just what I'd hoped to find.

Hidden under a strategically placed fold of my robe, my hands unhitched my seatbelt.

Now all I need is...ah!

The helicopter took another unexpected lurch to the side as I flopped forward into one of the bodyguards. In the split instant before he realized I'd not just accidently been thrown loose I had his knife out from under his jacket and jammed it through one of his eyeballs into his brain. I twisted it side-to-side before yanking it back out. In the next instant I rolled over onto the other bodyguard and in one surgically precise slash decapitated him.

Hah! Secretly lust to chop off my head to get my gold chain with its incredible treasure? Take a dose of your own medicine!

"Whuh...?" Ailith gasped as I now held the bloody knife tight to *her* throat.

Now *that* was a professional job. There'd not been a peep from my victims to betray what happened to the security bugs. But the knife in my hand was *shaking*. What the hell?

Nice weapon—I nodded my approval. *Somehow it enhances its own cutting power by vibrating. No wonder it went through those neck bones so smoothly!*

"Don't speak, just listen," I whispered in her ear. "Nod if you understand me."

She feebly nodded, her squinty eyes now stretched wide in terror, fixated on the still-twitching, brain-scrambled guard.

Blood spurted briefly from the other guard's beheaded neck as his heart kept beating a time or two. The gory fountain sprang up unexpectedly high in the cabin due to the low gravity. Drops from the red fountain spattered both me and Ailith. But I ignored the mess. There'd be plenty of time for cleaning up later.

"Order the flight crew to alter course. Tell them to carry out your just-stated plan," I hissed in her ear.

"P-plan?" she gasped.

"Yes, that's a brilliant plan!" I loudly proclaimed. "Why not do it? I can help you if you'd like. I have agents of my own at Doom Mons who will help protect us. I'd love to assist you in taking revenge on that nasty Captain, maybe even get back *all* of your crystal. And then you could perhaps kindly give me a small reward, adding some to my vial of refined powder?"

I knew that our conversation was being carefully monitored in the attached crew cabin. The "helicopters" on Titan were actually small spaceships capable of rotor-mode travel through the thick atmosphere. For slow, precise travel rotors were best. When necessary, though, the choppers could switch to their rockets and blast up into orbit. So my present transportation was ideal: a "luxury" covert transit on to my next target.

"*Say* it!" I whispered again in her ear, pressing the slender blade into her flesh.

"Aye, that's a braw idea," she gulped, shaking with fear. "We'll dae juist that. Pilot Shiela, change coorse richt noo! Tak' us tae Doom Mons, stealth mode. We'll sneak in oan Fehler 'n' tak' back whit's rightly ours."

"And put our cabin into 'privacy' mode, please?" I whispered yet again.

"And...and...switch us tae privacy. Stay oot and don' interrupt ainlie whin wur nearing th' volcano."

I saw with the aid of my AR implants that the circuitry in the wall switched, cutting off the auditory bugs. The crew was complying. The door to the cockpit snapped into "locked" position. Excellent!

"Now we can have a nice chat," I grinned. With relief I removed my itchy headscarf and wig.

"You!" she gasped, cringing back.

"Yes...me!"

I balled my fist and *smashed* it into her chin. Her head whipped to the side from the force of the blow. Lucky the audio bugs were turned off. She slumped, unconscious. She'd have a terrible jaw-ache when she awoke, but would still be able to talk. Meanwhile, I had a mess to clean up.

Ligeia Mare was over a thousand miles from Doom Mons. Even flying at top speed through the thick atmosphere it'd take us most of the day to get there. I knew the flight crew wouldn't risk going into jet-mode or ascending to where the atmosphere was thinner. If they did that then we'd stand out on everyone's radar like a sore thumb. We'd have to fly right above the dunes, rotoring along relatively slowly.

"Plenty of time to clean up this mess," I sighed, now regretting slaughtering the bodyguards. Blood was everywhere. "But first let's make sure my 'dear friend' is snug and tight," I grinned to myself.

I went to the galley and found towels. Ripping some of them into long strips, I used them to gag and hogtie the groaning but still-unconscious Ailith. I jammed her twitching body beneath her seat where luggage might have gone, making sure she was totally immobilized, out of my way.

"Ah, now what about...?"

I saw what I wanted. It was a neatly folded, black, large plastic sheet, secreted beneath the seat of one of the dead bodyguards. Good. They'd come prepared to neatly wrap my dead body for subsequent disposal. That was a chalk mark on the "professional" side of their records. Unfortunately for them, though, the sheet would nicely wrap up *them* instead of me.

"You *fail*," I grinned happily, laying their corpses side-by-side on the spread-out plastic.

Being a professional assassin is fun when you win. Sucks when you don't!

It'd taken me a couple hours to leisurely clean up the cabin. If you didn't look too closely at a scattering of faint stains, you wouldn't know that two men had recently died there, or that Ailith had her jaw busted. My neatly taped black plastic package was out of the way in the back of the cabin, on the floor in the galley section.

Excellent! I was always compulsive about being neat, clean, and orderly. Having the cabin littered with dead bodies and blood stains would be creepy. I felt much better, able to interrogate my captive further without distractions.

Ailith was moaning pitifully, still jammed beneath her seat. It must have been very uncomfortable for her. Good! Maybe it gave her a slight taste of what it felt like to have a *harpoon* shoved through one's guts!

But—I sternly reminded myself—*this isn't about petty revenge. It's about information. I need to know everything she knows about Fehler and Doom Mons.*

Her off-the-cuff statement that we'd "sneak up" on the Captain and "take" what was ours was ridiculous. From public records I'd researched, I knew that a sizable group of scientists and engineers occupied a Research Dome which was buried at the volcano. Much of their work was classified, which explained the presence of military. And if the conspiracy I was after was located there, they'd be on the alert for anything.

I'll have to plan our approach carefully—I mused to myself.

I yanked the old woman out from under the seat, simultaneously tearing off her blood-stained silk dress. She shivered in her underwear, fully exposed to the relative cool of the passenger cabin. I wadded up her dress and stuffed it into a garbage bag. As I mentioned, I always liked things neat, clean, and orderly. Plus, putting her in her underwear was as intimidating as threatening her with further violence. I glanced out the nearest porthole. All I could see was smoggy haze whipping past. The pilot was skillful. I barely felt the rise and fall of the ship as she hugged the high dunes which were flashing past unseen right below us.

One "zig" when we should "zag" and we'd be a field of debris on Titan's frozen surface. Since this was an unofficial, spur-of-the-moment, stealth-mode flight there'd likely not even be an investigation. Even if there were, they'd likely find nothing in the wastelands of Titan. By the length of time and speed we'd been flying, I reckoned we were somewhere over Shangri-La. It was a large, desolate, dark region on Titan's southern hemisphere. The dark plain was an ancient dry seabed where a methane ocean had long since evaporated. If we crashed there our corpses would likely be lost forever.

Hey, that might not be so bad—I grinned to myself. *Then I'd never again have to reanimate. I'd finally be free of my curse!*

No such luck.

"I'm going to let you drink some water and go to the bathroom," I quietly explained as I undid her tight gag. "Try anything funny and I'll pop your eyeballs out, understand?"

She hastily shook her head up and down.

"How'd ye survive? And wha ur you really?" she gasped, wincing from her broken jaw. "Ye'r nae juist some pesky bureaucrat."

"Someone you never should have screwed with," I calmly replied as I helped her to her feet.

And then the cockpit door *slammed* inward and a uniformed man with short black hair stumbled in.

"Somehow they knew we were coming! They just launched *missiles* against us and...?" he stopped in midsentence, startled to see his boss tied up, with me holding a gag in my hand.

He blinked in confusion, looking for the two burly bodyguards. Realizing they'd mysteriously vanished, he yanked out his holstered pistol...too late. I had his arm jammed up into his back, his gun in my other hand, forcing him back into the flight crew's cabin.

Behind me, Ailith was shouting: "Stoap her! A milligram o' Green tae a'body wha kills th' boot!"

A navigator to the side sprang up from his radar screen yanking out his gun as I calmly *fired* a bullet through his skull. They'd not expected me to fire the weapon inside an airtight vessel. But I knew the caliber, the velocity, the density of the target, and had perfect aim. The bullet was safely contained within his braincase.

He dropped to the side.

Up ahead I saw the instrument dial-laden cockpit with a uniformed, plump lady turning toward me.

"What defenses do we have?" I barked at her as I felt the speeding 'copter tilt dangerously to the left. "Get a grip! Don't crash us before the missiles hit!"

She turned back to her instruments as I tossed my captive over into the empty navigator chair. He'd do well enough. On Titan, with a limited workforce pool, cross-training was the norm.

"We've disruptive radar and tinfoil," she now spoke crisply and matter-of-factly, noting the smoking gun in my hand. "Or, we could just turn back and hope that whoever launched the missiles will disarm them."

"There's no chance of that," I informed her, gripping the headrest on her seat in order to stay steady as the craft swerved dangerously. "Those missiles are too sophisticated for your weak crap. How long until they arrive?"

"Thirty seconds," the man to the side replied, having regained his equilibrium. "We just spotted them on radar, coming in low like us, head-on!"

"How many?"

"Maybe a dozen blips," he gulped.

"Take us lower," I ordered the pilot.

"What? That's suicide! And who are you to...?"

"I'm an *official Inspector* on a high priority mission. Do as I say. Take us *between* the dunes!"

"No! Turn back! Turn back!" Ailith yelled through the open door behind us, still trussed up on the floor.

"You heard what I said," I ordered the frantic pilot.

"Are you bloody insane?" the man at the navigator station cried-out, now leaping at me.

I "conked" him sharply on his forehead, putting him to sleep. I couldn't kill everyone. I'd need them to fly me back out of Doom Mons once I did whatever was needed there.

"It's our only chance," I told the woman, placing my faith in her. From the few seconds I'd seen her I was impressed with her cool demeanor under stress.

"Yes, Inspector," she acknowledged.

"No! No! No!" Ailith screamed, her already high-pitched voice going up an octave.

We sickeningly *dropped*. I saw out the forward viewscreen foggy dune-peaks *above* our level of flight. Fortunately for us, most of the dunes were set into fairly regular lines across the Shangri-La dry seabed, allowing us to flash along through deep furrows.

She's doing it—I thought in amazement. *That pilot is damn good! We're going to...*

—when EXPLOSIONS suddenly ripped-apart the dunes around us, blinding us in a hail of "sand" that coated our craft in clogging filth!

"We're going down!" the pilot shouted as the rotors jammed and we spun-about in midair. "Brace yourself!"

"Ye god-damned, glaikit *numpty!*" Aialith screeched in Scottish profanity...

—as with a horrific "shriek" of torn metal, we *smashed* through the top of one giant dune, bounced high upward, and saw a *multi-finned missile* seemingly poised motionless in front of us on the viewscreen: which *tore* through inches away from us, *exploding* at the rear of the craft as it exited.

The inrush of frigid, toxic air grabbed me by the throat.

God, Fehler's "buyers" are even better killers than me—I marveled to myself as I, my companions, and a cloud of broken 'copter parts *slammed* through the next series of dunes.

Naked, I resurrected inside a smelly, cluttered, airtight *salvage truck*. I recognized it from the research I'd done prior to accepting my covert assignment to Titan.

Although it seemed impossible, scattered groups of humans lived away from the established outposts. They were thought to be mostly ragged nomads, just barely surviving. I now recalled they were tolerated for their unique, mildly addictive tea which they grew in subterranean caverns. They bartered their "Titanian Tea", which I'd so enjoyed at the Moby Dick, with the official settlements for supplies they couldn't scrounge, make, or grow themselves.

But I also knew that the nomads, who called themselves the "Yuan", happily stole whatever they could lay their hands upon, rooted through any "trash" discarded by the colonies, and eagerly scavenged any abandoned equipment or crash sites.

I'm now a one-person crash site.

And I was wracked by a brand new pain. It felt like I was being repeatedly torn into pieces then frozen back together into a slimy mush. My guts were being twisted into knots, snapped, and then rammed together over and over.

I'm helpless—I groaned to myself, not yet able to move or speak through the intense agony I was suffering. *I need some more of their soothing tea!*

But there wasn't much chance my captors were going to bring in a tea tray and politely offer me a cup.

There was no doubt of my intended fate, why the nomads had brought my body inside the truck. Next to me was the half-thawed body of the female pilot. Most of her flesh was missing or inextricably smushed with stinking Titanian filth. I recognized her by the remnants of her uniform. Her head was cracked open with half her brain scooped out.

God! These nomads are as vicious as the Fijian natives I encountered back in the 1800's—was my first emotional reaction.

But my more rational mind reminded me that where edibles, particularly meat, are scarce or missing, humans quickly descend into cannibalism. So the one edible, preserved part of the pilot was her fortuitously skull-protected brain. Hey, I didn't blame my captors! Protein is protein, so why not consume a big hunk of thawed flesh that would otherwise just decay?

But still, I didn't want to be the next culinary item in any scavenger's meal.

"Garee yago!" a gurgling voice happily chortled as I felt a hand roughly grab my naked leg.

In the gloom of the salvage truck I vaguely made out an eager crowd of shuffling figures. I heard an airlock hissing back shut, more scavengers returning. They were clearly amazed to find a whole fresh feast waiting for them, where before was just a frozen carcass.

"Gahnay! Gahnay! Donge me prado!" another voice angrily yelled, knocking the first hand away.

I saw a small shadowy figure in a ramshackle excursion suit excitedly thumping on the firm, uncorrupted muscle of my newly resurrected leg. Then the person flung back its helmet's cracked faceplate and sank yellowed teeth deep into the tender calf of my leg!

"*Stop* that!" I yelled.

Despite my continuing agony I surged upward and grabbed him by his greasy long hair.

Amid a burst of *shrieking* and *howling*, I swung him around like a baseball bat, *swatting* the crowd away from me. He *screeched* like a wounded cat as I tossed him into a heap of sharp crash fragments.

"You...are...alive?" a voice to my side chirped.

Panting, grimacing, and snarling I turned to kick away yet another vile pest—when the little person grinned, hopping around my bare legs in apparent glee.

It was a midget lady, with big eyes and pudgy cheeks. She wore a ragged, one-piece woven sack that enveloped her body. On her bald head was some sort of copper crown. I was startled to see that her skin had a distinct *gree*n hue to it. And her eyes were *bright* green. I also noted that she didn't have any *arms*...say what?

"Alive! Alive! Alive!" she chortled. "You, the 'black lady who fell from the sky, turned white, and would save the Yuan'? I find you? Me? I, *Momma Glenda* of the Yuan, find you? I doubted, but no more. It's all true!"

I was totally confused. White? But my new identity was that of a Swahili descendant with deep brown, even black skin...oh, right. I wasn't of that genetic phenotype any longer. They'd dug up a black-skinned corpse but my latest resurrection had "reset" me back to being the eternally white-skinned, teenaged, *Caucasian* Suzy. And how could this tiny green lady with no arms be a mother? She looked like a child, young and innocent.

Just how long was my corpse buried in the frozen dunes of Titan?

The others hushed, looking at me uncertainly, awaiting confirmation of my "deity." They clustered around me, patting at my white skin in apparent confusion. They all had greenish skin, just like "Momma Glenda." Grateful for the reprieve from their overt attack, I sank back down onto a pile of recovered shredded cables and plastic. I was still wracked by the excruciating pain of reanimation. I didn't need a savage fight with feral humans. And, after all, they'd just saved my frozen ass.

Maybe I can barter with them. After all, my fortune in pure Green is safely secured to my neck by an "unbreakable" gold chain, right?

I fumbled at my throat, dismayed to find the vial and chain was gone. The explosion and subsequent crash had shorn my mangled body of clothes while snatching away my one and only bargaining chip.

All well, if not that then another—I sighed to myself regretfully. *Get your quick-reflex, super-imaginative, story-telling brain into action!*

"Sure—why not?" I shrugged, agreeing with them. Then, since they didn't seem convinced that I was some supernatural manifestation from "above", I croaked loudly: "I *will* save you! I will save *all* of you! I am the *Messiah* of Titan!"

As little Glenda giddily translated my response into their gibberish, my vision blurred and I sank back into my awful pain. For the moment I could let my guard down. I knew I was far from being their prophesized "savior." But until I figured a way to trick them into taking me to Doom Mons, I'd play my part as best I could.

I wouldn't let a "little" thing like crashing into the wilderness of Titan keep me from my quest and ultimate revenge.

I'll delight and amaze their simple minds with my regal "holiness". Hah!

But as the jabbering mob of shabby little-people clustered above me, pointing hungrily down at my giant naked body and arguing loudly with Glenda, I was chastened.

Who am I kidding? I'll be lucky not to be their next meal's main course. I'm in a different world now.

Chapter 6
<u>**TRANQUILITY BASE**</u>

A noble sentiment enshrined in history
"We came in peace for all mankind"
Engraved on a plaque left behind on the moon
By Neil Armstrong and Buzz Aldrin in July 1969
The grand fulfillment of an epic challenge
Humanity's initial tiny reach up to the stars
First footprints of people on another celestial body
That noble instinct to discover and explore
Men and women colonizing the solar system
Leaving behind all the problems of Earth
A united, worthy, "Star Trek" vision
Of mutual respect, pulling together
Reaching down to offer a helpful hand up
Cruelly slapped aside in territorial national pride
In every failure looking for someone else to blame
Focusing on the negatives, "everything sucks"
Corporate greed, tribal fears, and selfishness
The same old animal instincts inflamed
When Homo sapiens could not leave behind itself...
The Rise and Fall of *Homo sapiens*, 6:91-96

I resurrected to a changed world...

A hot, dry wind was howling ominously above me. It was difficult to breathe. It was like lying near a blast furnace. My skin itched terribly. My throat was raw and inflamed. Weights were pushing down on me, keeping me prone.

I can't stay here. Get up, girl!—I ordered myself.

Blinking away grit from my eyes, I tried to figure out what had happened, where I could go. At first I couldn't see anything. I thought maybe it was nighttime. Then I detected granularity to the gloom. I saw what looked like snowflakes close to my face, drifting leisurely down to settle on my naked flesh. But they weren't white, cold, or "melty." No, instead they were solid, hot, and gray.

It was *ash flakes*, falling in a steady stream down from the dark sky.

"Help!" I yelled, pushing aside a crushing pile of burnt limbs and seared torsos. "Is anyone alive? Can anyone hear me?"

A half-melted, still steaming iron girder lay on debris across my legs, pinning me down. I grabbed its edge in both my hands and flung it off me. Then I crawled out from under the heap.

Wincing, I looked at my palms and fingers. That'd been seared by the hot metal. I smelled cooked flesh.

That's going to leave a mark—I winced, shaking my hands to ease the pain.

I managed to stand upright and look around. My eyes were adjusting to the perpetual gloom. I could now make out large objects around me.

I saw that the stadium was gone. In its place were piles of still-smoking rubble. Looking upward I saw *not* blue sky but roiling black clouds. Sheets of lightning lit up the undersides of the suffocating horizon-to-horizon blanket. Looking around I saw *not* lush ranchland but a blackened, flattened landscape where nothing moved. The friendly pet animals of "Suzette Kingly's Animal Shelter" were long gone. Here and there I spotted what might be stiff animal legs thrust up from beneath the thick layer of ash. Those paws would never pounce or prowl ever again.

"You there! Don't move, we'll come to you!" a deep, male voice boomed out.

I slowly turned around, my bare feet smarting from stepping on sharp objects under the ash layer.

What looked like a group of spacemen was plodding toward me. They had on thick contamination suits, boots, and gloves. Their closed helmets were hosed to air canisters. On their backs were heavy life support packs. Some held what looked like radiation meters, on which lights were rapidly blinking. The leader had spoken to me over a hand-held megaphone wired into his helmet.

It's like I'm on the moon's surface, surrounded by ancient craters and desolation—I marveled to myself.

I weakly waved at them before collapsing back down into the smoking debris. Having gotten my bearings, the searing PAIN of resurrection which I'd previously pushed off now enveloped me. Not just my recently burned hands and fingers ached, but my *entire body* felt like *every cell* was on fire!

Christ...this must be how it feels to be cremated—I moaned to myself, writhing in agony. *At the funeral parlor I didn't escape that terrible fate after all. I just delayed it by a few months...hell!*

But strong arms were lifting my limbs, spraying something onto my exposed skin. It was soothing. The anesthetic liquid took the edge off my torment, particularly my seared hands. And a loud voice assured me they'd have me "below" shortly. They said I'd be "out of the radiation." They assured me they could treat my burns. And then they seemed confused to discover that under all the ash coating my bald head and body there were no burns except on my hands.

"I...I...was protected, inside one of the dugouts," I gasped unevenly, "I just now managed to dig myself out. Thanks...for your help."

That was the best lie I could come up with on the spur of the moment to hide my secret: that I was the now-immortal, universally hated *Suzette Kingly*. I hoped my improvised story would be sufficient. I knew I should try to escape, find a secluded haven until I figured out my next move. So I tried to jump up and dash off into the gloom, but I didn't have the strength. All I managed to do was jerk grotesquely on the ground. Yep, recovering from near-incineration would take some time.

"Don' worry, we have you," a soft, female voice now spoke from a second hand-held megaphone, trying to calm me.

She succeeded. I immediately relaxed, letting them lift me onto a stretcher. I recognized that voice. Squinting at the nearest dark-tinted faceplate I saw behind it a familiar face. For a moment I thought it was Darlene. The face had deeply black skin. But instead of a white buzz-cut I saw curly, fluffy-black hair. The skin wasn't wrinkled but smooth. The face wasn't lean but round and plump. And the eyes weren't squinted and calculating but wide and welcoming. Her *big brown eyes* looked down at me sadly.

She likely thought I was as good as dead, exposed as I was out on the surface to what I now suspected was a massive amount of ionizing radiation. But they were still willing to try and help me. Why?

Ah, I see—I nodded to myself. *It's because it's the right thing to do. There are still good people in the world.*

The kind-hearted person I recognized behind the faceplate was *Lelea*, the young girl I'd befriended on the Fijian islands in 1867. I'd snagged her out-of-time along with my other historical musical geniuses. She'd brought along her entire tribe of cannibals. *That* was interesting. It turned out they were excellent drummers and backup dancers.

But the important thing now was I had a friend, someone I could trust. Hopefully she'd not connect this seared "miracle-survivor" with her disgraced, executed mentor. With my hair not yet regenerated, covered with grime, I hoped I'd unrecognizable. Regardless, I knew I was in good hands.

I smiled at her and slipped back into blessed unconsciousness.

I woke up in a triage area. It was within a large room, possibly a converted cafeteria. I saw what looked like a buffet table, a long serving counter, and booths. The rest of the area was filled up with stretchers upon which bodies lay. Most of the injured weren't moving. A few twitched or weakly jerked, moaning in pain. Doctors were clustered around a few survivors, anointing and wrapping up terrible burns. Helping them were women wearing hooded gowns. I recognized them, the mysterious figures I'd spotted in the stadium crowd.

Ah—I nodded absently to myself. *They must be some sort of Buddhist monks. Sure, they're into all that "transcendentalist" stuff. Now I'm remembering. Many of them are trained in first aid, loving to help other people. Well, there's sure a need for them now.*

I saw one person whose arm was being amputated. The discarded limb looked like squashed hamburger.

I realized that my hands were bandaged. I'd done serious damage to the flesh on my fingers and palms, but at least I still had my arms!

Flexing my hands I realized they worked well enough. They'd heal and...

"You were lucky to be in the dugout," Lelea spoke softly to me, startling me.

She was out of her containment getup, wearing a gray jumpsuit, sitting beside my stretcher. She was gently holding my bandaged hand. Beside her sat a tablet upon which data concerning my case was displayed. I hoped that their tests so far had been cursory. A deep study would reveal I was different from normal humans.

"The only lasting damage was to your hands," she continued. "Some of the burns are deep."

My hands will repair themselves, but it'll take time.

"If that's all the permanent damage I sustained...then I'm grateful it wasn't worse," I gulped, having trouble speaking. My throat was raw, my lips cracked. "Were there other survivors? I was with a friend, a young man. And we had a dog that..."

"I'm sorry," she sighed deeply. "Most everyone else in the Arena, human or animal, was killed outright. But don't worry. We decontaminated you thoroughly in the shower before bringing you inside. There's no more radiation on your skin. You don't appear to be injured except for your burned-off hair and badly seared hands. I'm sorry about your friend and dog," she glumly concluded. "We've all lost many friends. Unfortunately we'll likely never identify their bodies. Except for a few like you who were fortuitously protected up on the surface, they were shredded."

Wait..."on my skin?" Did that mean I was fatally irradiated internally? Can my remarkable metabolism protect me from ionizing radiation ripping my DNA to shreds?

"What...what happened?" I gasped. "I...can't remember anything before some sort of explosion," I lied, trying to buy some time. "Who am I?"

I groped with my free hand at a floppy white hospital robe that Lelea and her fellow rescuers had kindly put onto my naked body. Then I fumbled with my bandaged hands at my head, unused to being bald. It was unnerving to be without my long, beautiful hair but helpful. Lelea didn't seem to recognize me. Good! I was in enough trouble without people discovering my secret identity. They'd probably blame *me* for whatever terrible thing had happened up on the surface.

"It was one of those awful God-weapons," Lelea sighed. "Just rest and recover. I'm sure your memory will return."

"Who are you?" I asked, keeping up my new disguise as an unidentified survivor who'd lost her memory.

"I'm Lelea," she confirmed. "I was working below with the next group of performers, helping them get their makeup and costumes on before proceeding to the stadium. There aren't many of us left, just those who happened to be below when the bomb exploded, plus the scientists and such in the deeper research cavern. Thankfully, hundreds of feet of rock protected us. Our generator down here is still working. So we're ok for now and..."

"I'll take over from here," a deep, guttural voice interrupted her. "You can go back out to find more survivors."

I recognized that voice. Peering to the side I saw *Arthur Anderson*. He looked as bad as I felt. In the months since I'd last seen him he'd aged considerably. The gash on the side of his face which revealed broken teeth was wider. His preexisting burns were cracked and oozing. His burly body was now hollowed-out and hunched-over. His dignified, well-combed gray hair was now white and scraggly. Even his ever-present black sunglasses were cracked and askew.

"Yes, I should do that," Lelea agreed. "I'll be back shortly if you need me, miss. I'm sure once you get your memory back you'll remember us. I suspect we're good friends. In a few days we'll probably laugh about not recognizing each other," she hopefully sighed.

"Yes, I hope so too. Thank you, Lelea."

She hesitated, enduring Anderson's glare at her lingering. "We're about to stop our surface searches. We're switching from rescue to recovery mode. There's not much left up there," she sadly concluded. "Well...back to work."

Then she got up and walked away.

All the others in the triage area were occupied with their duties, at a distance from us. So I turned my attention to Anderson. He was a shadow of his former imposing self. There was nothing left of the handsome young soldier-of-fortune I'd fallen in love with in 1969 at Woodstock. Likewise, he was no longer the proud FBI Agent he'd been disguised as in our Prime-Earth dimension. Plus there wasn't even a trace of the arrogant Time Keeper who'd eventually rebelled against The Commissioner of the other human parallel dimension. But then again, he'd lost that time-war, lost me, lost his FBI job, and finally lost his dignity. That's what I saw sitting next to me now: a broken-down old man. I almost pitied him. But I knew he'd had a choice when he betrayed me at Woodstock and every other time he'd turned traitor. At each step he chose wrong. So in my eyes he deserved everything which had subsequently shattered him.

"How are you feeling, Suzy?"

"What do you want?" I whispered, ignoring his question.

Yes, he recognized me. I wearily closed my eyes. My head was still throbbing, my whole body seemingly on fire.

"Are you here to gloat?" I continued. "I'm just like you now, a stinking *failure*."

"So you found nothing in the last year concerning who was behind killing your mother?"

I clutched the white hospital gown closer to me, trying to hide in its floppy folds. I felt a belt at my waist and tightened it. I wished I had shoes on. I felt naked in my bare feet, my pink toes dangling out in the open. I didn't even have on underwear. I hated Anderson seeing me "exposed" like this. I felt helpless.

"What, are you going to rat me out to the survivors in this bunker of lost musicians and geeky scientists?" I quietly spat at him. "I just got a hot clue at the Arena when everything went to hell."

"So you...?"

"What happened outside, anyway?" I moaned in frustration, again deflecting his question. "I thought Phoenix and The Commissioner had our world completely controlled and pacified. That had to be a *nuclear bomb* that went off, *close* to the compound! As far as I know we don't have any such weapons in Oklahoma. It must have been a *missile*, fired at us from afar. How could such an attack even happen? All the governments and militaries of the world were coopted by Phoenix. It just doesn't make any sense," I sighed, my voice trailing off in confusion and defeat.

"It makes perfect sense," he grated annoyingly.

I opened my eyes to stare unblinkingly over into his mutilated face.

To his credit, he turned away, ashamed to meet my accusing gaze. Good!

"Well, *tell* me!" I demanded. "You could have stopped all of this. But instead you sat back and did nothing. You're a *collaborator*, Arthur. Were you ratting out my colleagues down here? Were you a spy for Phoenix?"

I now remembered him saying he was reporting to the local Council about the "colony" when he found me at the Crazy Cat Lady's house. *Of course* he was a spy!

He glowered at me, visibly grinding his broken teeth together before replying.

"I did what I had to do," he whispered. "I tried to help your friends. I kept them from being summarily executed, making excuses for their continuing defiance. I didn't know about the coming bombardment. But it didn't surprise me."

"Why not?" I demanded, still furious at him.

He was silent a moment, as if considering what to reveal to me. Why did Anderson have to keep secrets? What was there left to hide? What wasn't he telling me?

"When the Peace Keepers withdrew, that lifted the lid," he seemingly reluctantly admitted.

"The 'lid'?"

"After a revolution there's always a counter-revolution," he sourly observed.

"What?"

"I've seen it time and again throughout history, across timelines, and in every type of movement, particularly religion-driven ones."

My head was pounding terribly. My skin still felt like it was on fire. My throat ached. My scalp felt like it'd been torn from my skull. And, most of all, I'd lost my "identical twins" of Scotty and Scott. Except for when he'd been coopted to turn against me at the Galactic Core, the robot-dog was my faithful, best friend. And I was just warming up again to the handsome young Native-American. So my physical ongoing torture was magnified by my equally brutal mental anguish.

"Would you...*please*...just tell me what happened?" I moaned.

He sighed deeply, lowering his hideous head closer to mine. He whispered to me so that none of the others could hear: "Without the Peace Keepers enforcing rules of conduct with their energy weapons— against which we've no defense in this Dimension—Phoenix's loose coalition of religious fanatics, radicals, and extremists fell to pieces. Each faction went for each other's throat. And since they'd taken over all Earth governments, the military was co-opted by conflicting factions. Before, relatively sane people controlled the vast arsenals of nuclear weapons that *Homo sapiens* had amassed across the planet. With rigid extremists in command, all the slightly different 'heretical' enemies had to be exterminated, regardless of the cost."

"But...'mutually assured destruction'...really?" I gasped. "Surely even fanatical religious leaders wouldn't want their own movement to be destroyed?"

"Most of them fervently believed that the world would end in fire. It's a common doctrine for fundamentalists. It was their central religious vision. They were convinced that God would cleanse the planet such that the 'true' faithful could emerge to establish a New Earth. Even *I* once believed this to be true...when I was younger and somewhat innocent."

I was shocked and appalled. Even the screams of the fatally burned and dying in the triage area failed to distract me from a sense of utter futility.

"So mankind is inherently insane," I sighed, reluctantly accepting his explanation. "What else is new? But how...widespread...has been the destruction?"

He ran trembling fingers through his ragged white hair. "As far as we can tell, it's been a world-wide conflagration."

I was dumfounded. The *entire* Earth was gone?

"How...did...it start?"

"No one knows, exactly. We had limited reports right before the launches. It could have begun at any of a dozen flashpoints around the world. Then, once the first missiles began dropping, counterstrikes were triggered. Mutual-defense treaties snapped into place. Within minutes most or all the world's atomic, hydrogen, and neutron-bomb missiles were launched. As best we can tell, World War

III lasted only a few hours. Bombers, land-based missile nests, and nuclear subs all released their payloads and..."

"Get me some more plasma!" a frantic doctor yelled to his nurses, drowning out Anderson. A new batch of surface victims had just arrived. I sadly noted that only a couple of them were breathing. The rest were just relatively intact corpses.

"I suppose I should help them," Anderson sighed in his garbled voice. "I can donate blood and maybe..."

"Wait!" I yelled at him, grabbing his thin arm to keep him in his seat beside my stretcher. "Are you saying that humanity is totally screwed?"

He shrugged. "There are other deep bunkers like ours scattered around the globe, initially built for military or governmental usage. Then they were coopted to feed the perversions of Phoenix leaders. It seems that the Elites in each country were all diligent at establishing and hiding sophisticated musical-porn sites, coincidentally protecting some of Earth's best artists, thinkers, and scientists. We're getting back in contact with our fellow outcasts. Fortunately, most of the communication satellites were untouched by the carnage on Earth's surface. Plus the moon colonies and space stations were also spared. Since they're still small, they are populated, like us, mainly with engineers, scientists, and highly qualified workers. Phoenix, of course, sent political operatives and administrators to the moon and space stations. But these overseers were overruled and isolated when the momentum to this senseless, final World War III built up and reached critical mass. So it looks like space is now truly mankind's 'last frontier.'"

"So the Earth is...?" I whispered again, shocked.

"The entire globe is one continuous nuclear wasteland," he flatly stated, his gravelly voice trembling. "Sufficient nuclear missiles were launched to destroy the world many times over. So it's nuclear winter out there, Suzy. The skies won't clear of soot and ash for centuries. Except at a few deep sites like ours, everyone is dead. They were incinerated in the fireballs, suffocated in the propagating heat waves, or buried by soot. It's ancient 'Pompeii' all over again, but this time not at an isolated volcano but everywhere. Any surviving chlorophyll-dependent plants and microbes will die without sunlight. The few remaining plant-dependent animals will go extinct. Earth as we knew it is gone."

I lay there on my stretcher in silence for a few minutes, trying to block out the curses of the medical personnel trying to save a few more lives. The lights above us flickered. It seemed we were doomed as well.

"The infrastructure's been in disrepair for some time now," Anderson explained, also looking up at the flickering ceiling lights. "But we'll get that fixed. Our nuclear reactor down below in the research cavern is fairly new. Phoenix gave it to us to power access nodes reaching into the second Dimension, safely isolated and protected within our underground research facility."

"Can we escape to the parallel Dimension?" I asked, perking up. "Maybe there's still hope to...?"

"All the nodes on our side went dead when the Peace Keepers abruptly withdrew. We're totally cut off from the second human Dimension. Even my previous colleagues the Time Keepers are gone. They probably foresaw what was happening and left the 'sinking ship' before it was too late."

"But can't you...?"

"—use my own 'Time Keeper' skills? Don't you remember, Susan? I'm disgraced, defeated, cut-off, exiled, without my equipment, and left here to live a normal lifespan and die with the rest of you pitiful first-Earthers," he sighed deeply. "I've got no resources or contacts. I'm stranded here...except perhaps for..." his voice trailed off.

"Except?"

"I've got you."

Despite my burning pain I levered myself up onto my elbows, *glaring* at him.

"What do you mean?" I coldly asked him.

"You've still got it."

"I've still got *what?*"

He ripped off the concealing bandages on my lower arms and hands, pointing a shaking finger at my left wrist.

Glancing down I saw what he meant: looking as fresh and bright as the first day I'd gotten it as a young girl—was my Turtle Tattoo.

Ok, but that's no excuse for tearing off my bandages. My fingers still hurt, damn it!—I groaned to myself, flexing my seared digits.

"It has access to the 2ⁿᵈ Dimension."

"You mean that my *Mom*, Sally King, could use it to...?"

"It's the same for you, Suzy. She used it to cross the divide, to connect with a suitable target on the other side. You can also."

"You mean like Mom 'resonating' with my Dad?"

"Yes, exactly."

I took several deep breaths, trying to control my spinning mind. What was Anderson telling me? Did he mean I could somehow time-travel on my own—perhaps go back into the past, to see my Dad before he died?

"But when I time-traveled...when I was gathering together the historical musical geniuses which ended up here—that was powered by the Sphere through its wormhole ends located inside the marbles my brother gave me that...?"

He held up his "clearie" marble. It was a beautiful, sky-blue. It was a dazzling piece. I'd given it to him back at Woodstock, a small gesture to repay his generosity in paying for lunch when I was famished and had no suitable money. He'd subsequently placed it in the ashes of the cremation oven for me to find. But then I'd thrown it back into his lying face. Was he now taunting me for rejecting him?

"The Sphere imploded after I lost the Contest at the Galactic Core," I protested. "Now that marble's just a worthless hunk of glass."

"Give me your arm."

"I'm *not* going to..."

He impatiently grabbed my arm in a surprisingly tight grip. Then he pressed the marble to the Turtle Tattoo on my left wrist. I was surprised to see something actually happen. The small orb was now *glowing* a bright green-blue!

"This will anchor you here. It will be your focal point of return. You can travel to the other Dimension by another link, see what's happening there. If possible, you can build a bridge that others might travel across as well. Trust me, Suzy, I know about these things. I may no longer have the equipment or tools to time-travel myself, but my knowledge is intact. We have to know why the Keepers withdrew.

Was it to escape our inevitable destruction or for some deeper purpose? You're the only one who can find out the truth."

The "truth"...right...what a strange concept. But wasn't that what I was pursuing trying to get revenge for the death of my mother? If my tragedy was just random cruelty from the Unholy Trinity (Mother Nature, Human Frailty, and Lady Luck) then my quest was senseless. Bad stuff just happens. If that was "the truth" then I could forget my quest and concentrate on finding a way to end my pain, die once-and-for-all, permanently. But if it weren't, then that would validate my "crazy" obsession for *sweet revenge.*

"Ok, assuming that could somehow happen, then what would be my other 'point of contact' in the second human Dimension? My Dad's not there. My Mom's not there. Whatever mysterious forces that initially gave me and my Mom our Turtle Tattoos don't seem to be working anymore to...?"

Lelea and her crew were back, lugging in cleansed still-intact bodies. She wearily smiled over at me and I smiled back at her.

"The *Commissioner* is there," Anderson flatly stated.

"So? She's..." I stopped speaking, stunned.

She was an evil genius, who'd turned her brilliance and attention to infiltrating and co-opting the governments of the "other" (our) human Dimension. In her own Dimension she'd risen to the position of global High Commissioner. She was in charge of her worldwide Peace Keeper forces, not-to-mention founding and directing the *Time* Keepers using time-travel technology that she herself invented. She was a mathematical prodigy who'd never married: my duplicate "mother" from another timeline.

"You mean that she...?"

"Yes, Suzy, she also has a Turtle Tattoo. Theoretically the link between the two of you is unbreakable, a "quantum-entangled" pathway you can use to travel across time, space, and Dimensions in order to reach each other."

"Did she...could she...?"

"—kill your mother?" he shrugged again. "I don't know, Suzy. She certainly hated her doppelganger. But I see no purpose to The Commissioner murdering your mother at the Galactic Core."

Yes, that's what I'd also concluded, scratching her off my list of possible villains. But perhaps I was too hasty? Whatever, it seemed I had yet another "hot lead" to pursue. Great!

"But then again," he continued, seemingly having his own doubts, "she *is* incredibly devious and manipulative. What higher plan she was hatching, might even still have in motion...could be anything."

"Alright, then," I groaned, pushing myself up to wobbly sit on the edge of the stretcher. "What must I do, Agent Anderson, to cross over? Do I click my 'ruby red slippers' together three times and say 'there's no place like the 2nd dimension'?"

He laughed at my "wizard of Oz" reference. For a moment I saw the entrancing, cheerful young man I'd fallen in love with so many years ago. But then he sobered, rubbing at his burned face with a shaking, liver-spotted fist.

"Lie back, visualize your mother's Turtle Tattoo, and rub your own."

I sighed, sinking back down upon the stiff stretcher. I grabbed my left wrist in my right hand. The tattoo felt unusually warm, even hot!

"That sounds rather naughty," I half-joked.

Then I gently rubbed my burnt palm over my wrist. I didn't expect anything to happen.

"You look like you're doing better and..." Lelea's soft voice intruded.

"Get away!" Anderson bruskly ordered her. "She's going into shock, dying! I'm getting what I can before having to eject her body."

"I'm sorry, Mr. Anderson," she gasped, sounding hurt. "I didn't mean to interrupt your interrogation of..."

Interrogation? Do they know I'm not one of the regular audience members from the Colony? Do the leaders here already know my secret? Is Lelea just pretending to be my friend? Or, perhaps, are they just trying to figure out which of their thousands of "extras" have survived the decimating blast?

As Lelea hastily departed, Anderson pulled a sheet up on me, hiding me.

"Keep your focus!" Anderson yelled at me, grabbing my hand and wrist, plastering them tightly together. "Remember, Suzie—I'm your anchor. When you find out the truth, *return* to the Blue Marble!"

My head hurt from him yelling at me.

"But I don't think it's..." I protested.

I fell about two feet, landing hard on an uncarpeted floor. All around me were ornate statues. Was I in a museum? Was I off course? Did I somehow "key-in" to the huge amount of white *marble* all around me in the looming statues?

I don't recall a museum with this many statues all in one room— I frowned, trying to get my bearings.

"Who are you? Where did you come from?"

A shadowy figure hid behind one of the nearest statues. I recognized that particular statue. It was the infamous Roman Emperor *Nero Claudius Caesar*, who allegedly fiddled giddily as his precious capital city, Rome, burned down around him. The other statues were of other infamous leaders of notoriously evil, authoritarian empires. I saw scattered about me—most still standing but some toppled and even shattered—the motionless forms of Joseph Stalin, Mao Zedong, Benito Mussolini, Kim il-sung, Genghis Khan, Adolf Hitler, King Leopold II, Qin Shi Huang, Caligula, and many other vicious world leaders vilified by history...plus others I didn't recognize at all. Some weren't even human, obvious aliens.

Ignoring the questioner, probably just a museum guard, I picked myself up off the floor and tottered over to a half broken-out, full-wall window.

A *cold wind* was howling through the broken sections, but the view was stunning...

In the gathering twilight, with lights coming on here and there, I saw far below me a winding blue river filled with ships, docks, and spanning bridges. A forest of smaller skyscrapers reached up from below. By its profile, I recognized I was in New York City. I was on one of the top floors of a gigantic skyscraper. Yep, it had to be the World Trade Center. But it wasn't the One World Trade Center built after the 2001 terrorist attacks that brought down the Twin Towers. No, I was on one of the two main towers of the *original* World Trade

Center complex. Had I gone back in time? Or was this truly the *other* Dimension, where "9/11" never happened because dueling Empires still existed which brutally banned all religions?

But all was not well below. I saw raging fires. I heard the distant chatter and "boom" of guns and artillery. On the city streets I saw what looked like military units battling huge crowds of people. And I was stunned to see a *bright yellow energy beam* suddenly *slice* through the nearest skyscraper beside me. I was both fascinated and horrified as I watched the other Twin Tower topple with a horrendous "screech" to the side, *crushing* several smaller skyscrapers below it. Then *jets* zoomed past the broken-out window, sending me staggering away from their hot backwashes.

"How did you get in here?" an intense voice lashed out at me from behind.

That was a *very* annoying museum guard. I turned to confront...
—*her!*

Except for the icy stare and haughty twitch to her lips, she was the spitting image of my dead mother, Sally King. She had dyed red-brown hair graying at its roots, looked spry and fit, was dressed in a black pantsuit outfit, and had piercing green eyes. The last time I'd seen my mother—following a knock-down, drag-them-out fight between us that I still regretted—she was a corpse on a medical examination slab. Now, seemingly, she was standing right in front of me!

I shook my head sharply, trying to focus on my task. This doppelganger was *not* my sweet, loyal mother. "The Commissioner" was a weak simulation, a brutal dictator, and an imposter.

"I used *this*," I said, holding up my left arm. The white hospital robe's sleeve fell back, exposing my wrist. Glowing brightly, the Turtle Tattoo undeniably proved who I was.

Her eyes narrowed as she felt at her own left wrist. It saw her replica Tattoo was also glowing.

"*Why* did you come here?" she asked, seemingly accepting my identity.

"Why did *you* destroy my world?" I shot back.

Another squad of jets zipped past our shattered wall-window, their "ZOOM" reverberating throughout the hall of statues. A few moments later I heard loud "BOOMS" as missiles rained down on the city.

"Destroy?" she indignantly replied. "I *released* your world from my control, withdrawing all my Peace Keepers. I left you to your own devices. Whatever subsequently happened there was *your* fault, not mine."

Wow, what a bitch. It was obvious she wasn't used to being questioned. It was hard to believe she was a time-shifted clone of my mother who was a sweet and compassionate soul.

Then again, Mom did have a hard, tough side to her—I reluctantly acknowledged to myself. *Maybe this disagreeable version of "the girl with the turtle tattoo" just stresses the negatives?*

"Why did you withdraw your troops?" I asked, trying to strike to the heart of the matter.

"Why do you care, Susan? Your world was a thorn in my side for ages, a cesspool of 'freedom' and 'creativity' with resultant perversions. I gave your people a *gift* to help them bring forth their best angels. And what did I get back in return?"

"Well, what?" I spat back at her as we slowly circled each other.

An *explosion* rocked our remaining Twin Tower, almost throwing us to the floor. Several statues toppled over.

"My Peace Keepers caught your infection!" she seethed at me. "When they rotated back here, they brought a lust for permissive 'music', for 'self-expression', and for political backstabbing. Worst of all, in policing the radical religious leaders, some of the Peace Keepers were brainwashed by the 'conservative' religious mindset. Here they *already* had peace, order, and safety. They *didn't* need to invoke some inflexible, mean-tempered God in order to live a happy life! But all those ills spread like wildfire through my *nice* society. So I cut off all contact with your twisted Dimension. I ordered my Peace Keepers to return and put down the unrest they'd already caused here."

"And it didn't work, did it?" I sneered back at her.

"For a young person, my virtual niece, you're very stupid," she laughed bitterly. "Don't you know who you're talking to? I'm the *High Commissioner* in charge of all this Earth's police. *I* finally stopped the perpetual wars between my world's competing Empires. *I* imposed total world order. *I* taught the people on the street how to be nice to each other, under penalty of summary execution. Why couldn't they be satisfied with their beautiful world? Why?"

I was stunned to see her fall to her knees, her face buried in her hands, tears streaming from her eyes.

My anger evaporated. In her own way she just wanted to do good stuff. But I saw that her brilliant scientific mind treated society like a giant equation to be solved. Having gained the power to manipulate and direct the entire world, she lay down "reasonable" dictates assuming her people would see the wisdom and happily agree. But, sadly enough, *Homo sapiens* just isn't a reasonable species.

I slumped down beside her, putting my arms around her and letting her sob on my shoulder.

This was an unexpected turn of events, which left me confused and tongue-tied.

"I...I g-guess...people just d-don't want others telling them what to do," I stammered, trying to order my own jumbled thoughts. I was still disoriented, confused, and wracked with the pain of my recent resurrection. "They want to l-learn on their own, make their own m-mistakes."

"They're *not* children," she sobbed loudly. "They have to take responsibility for themselves and their effects on the people around them! Even the idiotic religious zealots they find so appealing agree on that principle."

She had a point. Why couldn't *Homo sapiens* just grow up?

"Maybe we're too complex?" I asked, starting to get my swirling emotions under control. "There's just too much stuff banging around in our heads, both environmentally and genetically. Maybe if we had more time as individuals—rather than in a virtual instant being born then living then dying—then society could maybe...?"

"You're right, Susan," she nodded, clearly getting her own emotions back under control. I was startled at how alike we were. Truly we were close relatives! "Human societies *are* like little children. If we put them in too tight a protective box they'll just fight to get out. And there *are* too many variables. Try as I might I could never reduce humanity to a definable mathematical equation. Just when I thought I'd pinned down all the bad things more would pop up. I failed!"

Wow! She's admitting mistakes. She's evolving before my eyes. She really does share the brilliance of my mother.

As if again reading my mind, she nodded and hugged me tightly.

"You are indeed my duplicate's daughter," she whispered in my ear, stroking my still-bald head. "If I'd had someone like you beside me, advising and challenging me, then perhaps I'd not gone so wrong."

She gently pushed me back and looked up into the glowering marble face of Nero.

"You know," she sighed, "he was my hero. I patterned my life after his example of authoritarian rule both here and in your Dimension. I celebrated all of the tough-minded rulers here in my 'Hall of Heroes', both from this Dimension, yours, and other worlds. They all had *ruthless aggression* to *impose* their will upon their people. I emulated them. But almost all of them met terrible ends. I thought I was smarter than they, could avoid their fates. But I guess I wasn't as smart as I thought. The *One World Order* centered in this headquarters of mine is crumbling down around me. Yes, I heard the Economic Tower fall down just now, sliced in half by a captured Peace Keeper laser canon. It's a total disaster! Everywhere, insurrections are toppling the local governments and stripping my Peace Keepers of their overwhelmingly powerful weapons. I now regret having banned and destroyed all nuclear weapons. I no longer have that ultimate threat to hold over my rebelling populace."

*If only we'd done that on our side of the dimensional divide—*I lamented to myself. *Perhaps we could have avoided total world destruction.*

"Now," she continued, "the energy weapons I invented are in the hands of the common people. And they're using them to level my world, driving it back into stone-age superstitions and bestiality. If I stay here I'll be lynched by the unwashed masses. Even now they're 'pounding at the gates.' If I somehow manage to escape the howling mob, then I'll be a pariah, living in constant fear. Everything I tried to do has come to nothing."

I stood up. My Turtle Tattoo was still glowing brightly, even pulsing. I saw there was no sanctuary here on Earth Two for the remnants of Earth One. I now knew that my planet's only hope lay in abandoning our radiation-soaked, burned-off, nuclear winter-shrouded world and move out into the solar system. My only path forward was to rub my pulsating Tattoo, think of the "blue marble," and make my way back home.

I have to leave behind The Commissioner—I sternly ordered myself. *I have to let her wallow in her regrets. I feel sad for her. But she brought it all on herself. And...wait! I almost forgot!*

"Did you orchestrate the murder of my mother?" I sternly questioned her.

As acrid black smoke drifted in through the broken wall-window, she sadly shook her head in the negative. There wasn't much time left to get the answers I needed. Her "One World Order" New York City headquarters was on fire! It was already getting hot there in the "Hall of the Heroes" as flames crept up from below, smoke now bellowing in through the broken wall-window.

"I heard what happened at the Galactic Core," she sighed, her previously imperial voice quaking with grief. "It hit me hard. My future self that you dealt with in regards to your musical contest—at least a *possible* timeline version of me—may have done it. I just don't know. I always admired your mother. She took a radically different path than me. And I'm jealous of her. As I already admitted, I think if I'd had a child like you it would have made up for my personal failures. I suspect she died happy, Susan, proud of you. *I'd* be proud of you."

Now it was me spontaneously crying my eyeballs out. I sank back down to the floor and again hugged my mother's doppelganger tightly.

It wasn't as easy to leave her behind as I'd thought.

"I'm so sorry for everything," I whispered to her. "I love you."

I came ready to do battle with an evil genius. But she unexpectedly gave me a priceless gift: the chance to have a final "goodbye" with my mother. Yes, I knew she wasn't really my dead Mom, but *The Commissioner* was a powerfully realistic representation. She was tough and relentless but endearingly vulnerable.

Despite the tearful "reunion" it was time to go.

I resolutely stood up, turned my back on her, rubbed my Turtle Tattoo, and said the magic words: "Blue marble! Blue marble! Blue marble!"

Nothing happened. The smoke was getting thicker. I was coughing, finding it hard to take a breath. I heard shouts and gunshots right outside the "Hall of Heroes." In a few moments a mob would be break into the museum, be upon us, and slaughter us!

"Come with *me*, Susan," The Commissioner invited, now all-business as she stood ramrod straight. "I can teach you many things. Just like me, where you came from there's nothing left. Your world is lost, just like mine. Together we can have a fresh start, forge a new and better life."

"What, on some other planet elsewhere in the Universe?"

"Sadly, no," she grimaced. "Your sick stunt at the Galactic Core caused the Alien Lords to curse not just you but mankind. We're blocked from subspace, unable to travel beyond our own timelines and Dimensions. Except for conventional, slow rocketry they've isolated our 'contagion' to our solar system."

"Then where...?"

A "bub" suddenly materialized beside her, knocking over Nero and Caligula. It looked like a classic 1960's VW beetle "bug" but with a transparent bubble top, from which its name derived. Dethroned from being *The Commissioner* she was still the absolute Master of time-travel. I realized she was escaping into the future!

A loud "banging" sounded as a *battering ram* beat relentlessly at the locked doors leading into the Hall of Heroes.

"Come with me!" she ordered me.

"I can't," I said, turning away.

"Why not?"

"I still have a job to do."

She sighed deeply, shaking her head in defeat.

"Then I hope we meet again," she replied as she lifted the dome of the time machine, stepping resolutely inside. "Good luck to you."

"And to you," I sincerely replied as she slammed down the lid and faded away.

With a loud CRASH a raging mob swept in...

—as I ran toward and *launched* myself through the empty portion of the broken window! Then I was tossed-about by fierce winds at the top of the skyscraper as I *plummeted* toward the street far below.

"This probably wasn't my best idea!" I yelled as I saw the crowded street zooming up at me...

"BLUE MARBLE!" I screamed, in a last desperate plea, as my hurtling body spun wildly through the air...

—and *slammed* into the pavement!

I resurrected feeling like every bone in my body had been smashed into little bloody fragments and now was being pounded back together. The pain was indescribable, completely immobilizing me where I lay.

I saw above me an utterly black sky studded with glaring pinpoint stars. Through the haze of red-hot pain from the resurrection process I was in awe. But then I saw, set against that stunning cosmic backdrop, that which should have been the miraculous "blue marble" of our precious planet Earth...

—now just a *muddy-black* smudge.

"Mommy! That lady just fell out of the air!"

Oh, Christ, wherever I am I've got to get moving!

Pushing away my agony, I weakly picked myself up from the floor. I saw a lady hushing a small child. Both were dressed in matching pink plastic-looking outfits. Dangling from their necks were badges on short chains.

"Oh, I'm so sorry," the lady apologized to me. "My daughter has a vivid imagination. Did you trip and fall? Can we help you?"

"I...yes! And n-no, I'm f-fine," I stammered in confusion, trying to reorient myself yet again. I suppressed the urge to *scream* from the torture I was enduring as my body rebuilt itself from the inside out. But I knew from past experience that the agony would gradually subside to a bearable level. I shakily gathered my floppy hospital gown about me, tightening the belt at my waist.

Rats, I'm still barefoot. What the hell's going on? Where am I? This isn't the research facility beneath my animal shelter outside Sulphur. I must look like a freak to these plastic-wearing people!

"Thank you so much," I continued, trying to back away. "I was in a rush and my feet went out from under me on this slick floor and..."

The little girl in her mother's arms frowned suspiciously at my garbled story. "No, you didn't!" she loudly insisted for everyone to hear her. "I *saw* you pop right out of the air!"

Yes, others were looking over at us, curious as to the commotion.

You can't be discovered before you get your bearings—I desperately ordered myself. *You have to figure out where you are, come up with a new game plan. This whole new situation is spinning out of control!*

Then time seemed to stop. For an instant everything froze around me. I was able to look about and try to get my bearings. I saw that I was inside what looked like a curved exhibition hall. On the outer wall were regularly spaced display cases, to which I was strangely drawn. I had the feeling they were pulling me toward them. What? I forced myself to widen my viewpoint...

The roof and inner wall of the tunnel was one continuous, transparent viewing-window. And through that curved window I saw a stunning sight. I saw before me a flat gray field, about the size of a football stadium's playing field, completely surrounded by our viewing tunnel. In the center of the gravelly, dusty field I recognized a squatting Lunar Module *descent stage*. Various equipment and gear were scattered about, including a toppled-over *American flag*. Beyond the enclosed field I saw several high white Domes, all connected to the viewing area by a straight walkway tunnel.

This is a historical preservation of the actual Tranquility Base—I marveled to myself. *It's where Neil Armstrong and Buzz Aldrin first walked on the moon. Oh, Christ...I'm on the freakin' Moon!*

Yes, I was on the moon, marked on a nearby display-map at the south-western corner of the Sea of Tranquility. Also, I was in the future! There'd only been a small struggling outpost there when Anderson sent me to the alternate dimension. Now I was within a complex moonbase large enough to host a museum.

What's this about museums, anyway?—I hysterically laughed to myself. *Do I have some weird fixation with historical displays? And just how did I travel into the future? How far ahead have I jumped?*

Time unfroze and I saw a uniformed guard approaching me. He had a friendly smile on his face and carried no weapons. But I was certain he would question me closely.

"Hah!" I laughed, grinning broadly. But my eyes were squinted almost shut against the still-blazing pain roiling through my bones. "I just came in on the shuttle from Earth...don't have my 'moon-legs' yet. Hey, I'm wobbly on my pegs. It's my first time here and I'm tripping all over myself, so sorry. I'm moving on quickly so I just had to run over here to see Neil's landing site before departing. I didn't have time to change from my flight clothes and..."

"That's ok, Ma'am. Can I guide you to a roller?" the guard, a pleasant-seeming, black-haired young man said, offering me his arm. He pointed at wheelchair-looking fold-ups set against the outer wall between the display cases. Apparently other visitors had similar problems.

I'm sure good at making up plausible stories—I congratulated myself for my quick thinking.

"Well, maybe that would..." I started to agree as I took a step and flew up to the ceiling! I banged my head sharply before fluttering back downward, my arms flailing in the air.

"Oh, the poor dear!" the pink-clad lady exclaimed to her daughter. "You saw her float down from hopping-about. The attendant will help her into a roller. It has heavy weights so she won't go flying through the air anymore."

"But mommy...?" the little girl whined.

"I'll be fine! Thank you so much!" I waved to everyone as I flopped down onto the floor, bounced up three feet, and finally settled down uncertainly upon my bare feet.

I took the kind guard's arm and let him help me shuffle slowly along.

"Could you just point me to the restroom?" I grinned sheepishly at him. I realized I'd not had a piss since before the world turned into a radioactive blob. My distended bladder was throbbing. "I'm sorry to be so much trouble."

"It's not a problem, miss," he kindly replied, steering me to an opening in the inner wall with a sign above proclaiming "Lady's Restroom." "But could I please have your ID number? I see you haven't gotten your official visitor's badge yet and…"

"I'm going to burst if I don't get in there!" I groaned, only half-pretending. "Please! I'll be right out and…"

"Of course, no problem," he said, releasing my arm. "I'll be at the guard desk by the exit when you're ready to register properly. Take your time, no rush."

What a nice guy.

I skidded and bounced into the restroom and found everything much as expected. A line of private stalls awaited tourists. For the moment I was the only person in the restroom. The toilets in the stalls were a bit wider than I was used to, plus had alternate modes to trigger vacuum-assisted collection of urine versus feces, but it was all intuitive.

In a few minutes I was much relieved, standing at a sink, trying to get cleaned up and better configured. A few tucks and extra folds to my hospital gown and it looked more like a regular dress. Spotting a cleaning closet I found some pull-over booties and put them on. They were large for my small feet, but had strings that secured them nicely. They were rough on their bottoms, allowing me to get a better purchase on the slick floor.

Why the hell do they have slick floors here?—I complained to myself. *Ah, I'll bet they're imbedded with metal strips so that magnetic boots help people maneuver and…*

"Ok, Susan, that's enough aimless observation. Focus!" I verbally ordered myself, squinting into the mirror. The raging pain of resurrection was finally abating. "So what's your new secret identity? And how are you going to escape this closed historical loop without an 'ID number'?

I looked better. I was pleased to see baby-blond fuzz slowly sprouting on the top of my head. My hair was growing out. In a day or two I'd have my regular long blond locks back. But how could I on the spur of the moment come up with a *new* identity?

Maybe I'll get an inspiration from the display cases outside which seemed to be drawing me to them—I forced myself to focus. *At least I can figure out what happened between my leaving Earth One and returning to the future-Moon.*

A group of giggling young girls swept in. They were all in green uniforms. It looked like a fieldtrip from a school. Great! It was a distraction. I shuffled out into a now filled-up viewing tunnel. The attendants and guards were busily explaining things to the eager kids. One of them mentioned today's date in relation to the initial lunar landing...say what?

Oh, Christ, I'm more than a hundred years in the future—I gasped, my job of "fitting in" made infinitely more difficult. How could I blend into a society that I didn't know?

Then the nearest display case snagged my attention: "Artifacts from Old Earth." A wave of nostalgia swept over me, urging me to connect with a lost past.

Inside the case I saw ordinary items like a battered cell phone, a torn newspaper from 2019, and a cracked SpongeBob Squarepants doll. And next to them, encased in a clear plastic square, was a *blue marble.*

"What the heck?" I marveled, bending in close.

As the laughing, jumping kids swarmed by—hopping up impossibly high then drifting down around me—I examined an attached placard. The words were tiny, hard to make out.

I read softly to myself: "A reminder of what once hung in our sky, a *lucky blue marble* once used on Old Earth in a child's game. It is also a loving gesture, memorializing an ancient romance. The anonymous donor described it poetically thusly..."

"A reminder of my dear friend,
With whom I enjoyed many a throw-down,
She never came back from a long voyage,
To whom I apologize for all my wrongs,
All the times I cheated and tricked her,
I'll not see her again in this present life,
But I hope she'll still think well of me,
Your turned-around, backward buddy,
Our last games scored 25-to-13 and 17-to-21,
Converting all our hurtful words to numbers
We never beat each other permanently, tying overall
Let it be the new foundation to your dreams,

Returning your stolen youthful innocence...”

“Let this beautiful poem fragment inspire you,” I slowly read the concluding statement. “Even though it may require a thousand years of global mitigation, humanity will someday return to once again re-populate the precious ‘blue marble’ which two brave astronauts first viewed from this spot on July 20, 1969.”

Oh my god! There’s no doubt. This is from Arthur—I marveled. It’s his message to me from the past! It must be how my Turtle Tat-too brought me here after I was smashed flat from jumping out of that skyscraper. And, come to think of it, I’ll bet that The Commis-sioner’s time-bub somehow dragged my corpse along in its wake. My resurrecting body was tossed into the future and then drawn to this very spot by the Blue Marble!

“Oh, are you better now?”

I jerked up from where I was bent-over the display case. It was the same guard as before. He was now looking at me suspiciously. In his hand was a flat tablet upon which I spied the words: “passenger manifest.”

Oh, rats...he’s found me out—I groaned to myself. He knows I wasn’t one of the “just arrived” passengers on the last Earth Shuttle. I’m about to be arrested and detained. They’d do a genetic analysis on me and discover I’m a freak, requiring dissection in a research lab!

“Oh, hi,” I lamely grinned back at him, wondering where I could run and hide. But there wasn’t any refuge within reach. Even if I managed to sneak out of the viewing tunnel, where could I hide on an isolated, self-contained moonbase? “Yes, I’m much better, thanks. But I’d better get back to my quarters and prepare for...”

“First I’ll have to have your ID number, please?” he insisted.

I saw other guards now backing him up. I was cornered, trapped!

“I...I...” I gulped.

Numbers! I need a valid ID identification number. It must be something like Old Earth’s USA “social security” number, establish-ing your identity. I don’t even know the new ID’s format, let alone any valid sequences. Hell!

I tried to spy numbers on the dangling visitor badges of the kids and adults around me. Maybe I could figure out a common sequence and guess at a valid number? But they didn't have any numbers...just face-photos on the small display-screens on each badge. I was royally screwed.

But then again...?

"Ok, my ID number. Yes, of course...here it is...my personal identification number is..."

I paused, my mind racing.

"Yes, Ma'am?" he insisted, his finger poised to punch it into his tablet's keypad.

Could it be? Did Arthur set it up for me?—I desperately forced my mind to recall the sequence I'd just read.

"Uhm...it's...2-5-1-3, and then..."

"What?" the guard frowned, not typing anything. Clearly I wasn't even in the ball park.

Oh, hell. I got it totally wrong. But wait! The poem said "turned-around, backward" and "convert words into numbers" so...

"Oh, I'm sorry," I grimaced as I shook my head to seemingly clear it. "I guess my brain is still a bit scrambled what with all the extra g's during acceleration, then deceleration, and the weak gravity here. It's my first time on the Moon, you see. Wow! I'm all turned around. Anyway, my actual number is..."

"Yes?"

If Anderson had set up a new identify for me, one that would last into the future, he'd have to hide the ID number within his publically displayed poem. The actual sequence for me couldn't be recognizable. That'd be too suspicious. So he put the number backward, plus hiding extra "2's" as the word "to"...maybe.

Well, here goes nothing!

"1-2-2-7-1-3-1-2-5-2..."

I paused, hoping my "gamble" with the present "game of marbles" was successful.

"And the last two numbers?" he prompted me.

Last two? What the hell? That was all the numbers there were in the poem, starting at the last then reading them backwards, inserting extra "2's" for the two "to" words. There weren't any more numbers!

"Oh, sure, it's..." I desperately searched for another clue from Arthur.

Wait! He said "we never beat each other permanently, tying overall"...both of the "game scores" were the same when added up: 38!

"Thirty eight," I nonchalantly finished, pretending to be interested in another item in the display case.

I looked up to see his face blanched, his eyes stretched wide.

"Can we p-please have your thumbprint for c-confirmation?" he stammered, looking fearful. The other guards seemed similarly affected, pulling back from us. "Or, we c-could take a DNA scan if y-you'd prefer? But then we'd have to go to one of the clinical labs for..."

"No, a thumbprint's fine," I said, placing my thumb on his screen. "Is there some problem?"

Yep, there could be a *huge* problem. Resurrection reset me back to "zero" biologically, re-establishing the full phenotype of the supposedly long-dead Suzette Kingly. There was no way I could give them a futuristic "DNA scan." That would totally reveal my impossible true identify. But my thumbprint was just as bad because...

Wait! What about the radioactive burns on my hands and fingers that I suffered back in Sulphur, Oklahoma following my last resurrection?—I frantically reminded myself. *For me, that was less than a day ago. Those alterations may still be present on my hands and digits if I've not yet been fully rebuilt by the resurrection process. The last thing to get "fixed" seems to be my outer skin cells. And Arthur had access to the altered prints from my triage clinical test records.*

Looking at the results, the young man visibly shuddered, snapping stiffly to attention.

"No problem, General! We're sorry for any inconvenience. We were just doing our duty, checking out all unidentified visitors. We're on high alert because of the ongoing troubles. Would you like an escort to your quarters?"

General? What the hell? How did I get to be a soldier?

Hiding my relief and confusion, I nonchalantly nodded. "Yes, that would be appreciated. And, no, there's no inconvenience. I was just testing your procedures and vigilance in these...'troubling'...times. You all did fine. At ease, soldiers!"

Man, I'm glad I have quick reflexes.

He and the other guards looked visibly relieved, eager to please the unexpectedly visiting "General."

I still hated the vile memory of Arthur Anderson. But that rat sure did come through for me a century beyond my departure. I had to give him his due: a grudging respect. He provided me with a secure, authoritative identity. What else had he given me? I had to get to a computer terminal to dig out the truth. As the guard's tablet visibly certified, they still had computers a hundred years in the future.

"Lead on!" I grandly gestured.

I took the arm of the still-fearful young man, letting him help me shuffle toward the exit tunnel.

It was time to face the future. As Anderson had prophetically written in his "love poem," I and mankind could lay new foundations for a fresh dream. Humanity had survived its "trial by fire." Perhaps now a "youthful innocence" could spring forth as *Homo sapiens* moved out into the solar system.

Hah! Not likely. When I finally step out on this beautiful moonscape someone's just gonna kick sand in my face.

Chapter 7

<u>DUNE</u>

A world made out of sand
Where the rarest thing is water
And giant worms guard precious Spice
Fought over, harvested, and horded by the Elites
A grand science-fiction odyssey by Frank Herbert
Published in 1965 during the psychedelic revolution
"Flower children" reveling in their pot and LSD
Thinking they'd discovered the "fountain of youth"
A new awakening of peace, harmony, and wisdom
They instead walked through a wicked gateway
Into the horrors of meth, horse, and coke
Addicted to receding spurts of delight
They "lived in hell for a taste of heaven"
Where the drugs created their own need
Devouring the very concept of hope
Promising light but bringing darkness
Instead of vaulting to the stars
They sank into their own depravity...
The Rise and Fall of *Homo sapiens*, 7:34-39

I awoke feeling better, though my eyes were encrusted shut. The new pain of my latest resurrection was fading into the general agony I continuously endured. Before forcing my eyes open, I felt about gingerly. I realized I was lying on a pile of small sacks, each filled with something lumpy and smelly. Rough blankets covered me up to my chin. Someone had put scratchy, woven clothes onto my body. I had on loose pants and a separate, short-sleeved shirt. Feeling at them I

193

noted they weren't single pieces but crudely sewn-together segments. The little people had kindly accommodated my "giant" body. On my feet were sandals. Once again they weren't intact, but tied-together pieces. And I felt the vehicle bouncing under my body as it simultaneously swayed far to the left then to the right. We were traveling over rough terrain.

At least they hadn't eaten me! And I wasn't tied up. That was encouraging.

Dare I let them know I'm awake?—I pondered silently. *Oh, why the hell not. Where else can I go?*

I slowly squinted opened my eyes, painfully getting my eyelids unglued from each other. Then, not detecting anyone around me, I opened them wide. I spied only the gloomy interior of the same salvage truck. Piles of cables, broken panels, and smashed equipment surrounded me. Past the heaps, however, I saw a brighter light: in a "cockpit" of sorts.

Well—I stoically concluded. *I might as well go forward and meet my captors.*

I pushed myself up and stumbled through the salvaged trash into the vehicle's cab. There I saw three of the green little-people working frantically at creaky controls. I had to bend over to get into the "cockpit", slumping to sit in an unoccupied corner. The pilots ignored me. I was fascinated by their movements. Any airtight, Titan-worthy vehicle had to be, by definition, a sophisticated marvel of engineering. The vehicles had to protect their human crew while functioning within a poisonous thick atmosphere, unforgiving mushy landscape, and incredibly cold temperatures. But this truck was a jumble of ancient parts seemingly haphazardly melded together around a salvaged frame. I marveled that it could move at all, let alone provide a viable interior environment. Plus it was a jumbled antique. Instead of display panels, digital readouts, keyboards, and holo-interfaces I saw ancient buttons, knobs, levers, and an actual steering wheel.

But it was the vista I saw through the scratched and warped plasteel windshield that fascinated me the most. I saw *gigantic dark dunes* on both sides of us towering up three hundred feet into a glaring orange sky. We were creeping along in a furrow between two parallel dune-columns, much as I'd tried to fly in my doomed helicopter.

It was an unusually clear day for Titan because I could see for miles into the distance. But the "coffee grain"-looking brown sand was periodically "rattling" into the windshield, distracting me.

There must be a stiff wind out there. We're still in the vast dune fields of the dried-up methane ocean of Shangri-La—I concluded. That's a hell of a long ways from Doom Mons, especially creeping along at a snail's pace on the surface. Hmmm, I wonder what it'd be like to try sand-surfing out on those marvelous slopes. That might be fun to...

"You're awake!" I heard a squeaky voice cheerfully proclaim, interrupting my meandering thoughts.

Pushing with her copper-crowned, green head out of a small bathroom cubicle's door behind the cockpit was Glenda. Her wide grin was infectious. After a moment of surprise, I totally disregarded her having no arms. In fact, I belatedly realized that one of the three pilots lacked both his legs. Hey, they'd make a cute couple!

Sick—I admonished myself as she skipped happily into the cockpit. Don't get freaky. And don't make fun of the little people. Sure they look like "little green men" aliens, but they're as human as you. This is a deadly serious situation. They could turn on you at any moment. You could bat away a single piranha, but a school of them could devour you in seconds. Don't be lulled by how diminutive and "elfish" they look. Stay on their good side!

I saw that another of the pilots had only one eye. The other eye wasn't damaged or plucked out. It was just absent. And the third pilot had a large tumor growing from his neck, which looked inoperable. It seemed that these little people had a high incidence of genetic mutations. Why was that? But I didn't have time to speculate.

"Hi there," I smiled wanly at her. "Thanks for not eating me."

She giggled endearingly. "We don't consume our gods, at least not until they tell us to do so."

That was a strange statement. It triggered something in my foggy memories...was it a reference to Jesus saying people should eat his flesh and drink his blood in the communion ceremony? Damn! I was still confused, my head spinning, trying to force my thoughts through a wall of shimmering pain.

"You speak very good Standard English," I mildly observed.

"Yes, I'm a Holy Momma," she said, padding the couple steps to me and sharply "bopping" my bare arm with her copper crown. "One of my tasks is to communicate with the Domers. I'm not so good with the spacer dialects, but everyone understands Standard."

Little did she know I spoke many languages fluently and could easily converse in any space dialect.

Wait, that little lady cut my arm with her sharp metal crown.

"Ouch!" I complained. It was a delayed-reaction. My response-time was still much too slow. I saw blood dribbling from a scratch on my arm. The three pilots looked over in apparent awe, speaking in their "gibberish" into a large microphone, some sort of ancient radio transmitter. They must be talking to the crowd that I encountered when I first resurrected. Where were all those other little people I'd seen before anyway? They certainly weren't in this stuffed salvage truck anymore.

I guess I'm big news?—I marveled.

"Oh, I'm so sorry I hurt you," she laughed, clearly *not* sorry. "But now we're 'blood-bonded'. None will dare touch you after this. You are safe, under my protection."

"Well, thanks...I think," I mumbled as I dabbed at the blood with the loose bottom of my roughly woven shirt. "So what religion do you represent? I'm grateful for..."

"We're COG-C," she happily interrupted me. "Have you heard of us?"

"Uh...I don't think so...'cog-see', did you say? Is that a religion unique to Titan?"

"No, silly!" she laughed. "It comes from Old Earth. But it's different from the established Great Religions. Instead of forcing set doctrines, traditions, and rituals on people it's an enabling framework for helping people *best* get to where *they* want to go. It expertly facilitates exercising God's greatest Gift to us: Godly Creativity."

"Ok...so it's a fringe cult that...?"

"It's the *Church of Godly Creativity*," she distinctly enunciated, bobbing her head in affirmation. I had the feeling she would have slapped her hands gleefully together, that is if she had hands, which she didn't.

"Well, I'd like to hear more about it," I politely lied. I didn't need to hear about yet another fringe religion. I figured if anyone wanted to be part of a structured spiritual group, there already were plenty history-validated movements from which to choose. "So where are we going?" I said, changing the subject.

"To a big deposit!" she giddily exclaimed, spryly hopping up into an empty seat at the controls to peer eagerly forward through the windshield. "The recent increase in titan-quakes has broken open many dunes, spilling their contents. One of our scouts just discovered the vein. And it's a rich one! But we've got to get to it fast before the trackers find us."

"Sounds great," I listlessly replied. "Let me know if I can help. Say, how did you find me in this wasteland, anyway? And what's that about an uptick in quakes?"

She grinned cheerfully at me.

"You ask a lot of questions! One of our scouts spotted debris from your crash. You were on our general path to the residue fields so we swung by to grab whatever looked useful. We hoped to get a good meal out of your carcass, but ended up with far more. We discovered the long-prophesized Goddess! Isn't that *glorious?* The titan-quakes ae part of the prophesy foretelling your wonderful arrival. Everything is coming together now, to finally save the Yuan!"

"Uhm, sure...very glorious," I yawned, not impressed with my supposed holiness.

I knew I should be trying to get them to contact Jags back at Huygens Station. I was probably too far away for our drone to come pick me up. But maybe he could commandeer or rent another helicopter? After all, as the temporary "Acting Inspector" it'd be part of his duties. Maybe he was already on his way to the site?

Hah!—I laughed to myself through my pounding super-migraine headache. *He's going to get real tired of doing disaster inspections of crashes that I caused. Maybe he'll just leave me here in Shangri-La to rot?*

Well, there wasn't any rush. Perhaps these prospecting Yuan could help me make it to Doom Mons. I had to get there before these little people discovered that not only wasn't I a "goddess", I certainly wasn't the fulfillment of whatever religion they followed. Plus the trail to the conspiracy that Captain Fehler was part of was already going cold. I'd lost three months since I'd sunk to the bottom of Legei Mare. So I *should* be in a rush to move onward...

—but I was bone-weary tired. The gentle "sway-and-roll" of the ponderous vehicle was like being in a comfortable rocking chair. I closed my eyes, leaning back against the cold, plasteel wall behind me. I yet again surrendered to my interminable pain, allowing the "patter-patter" of hurtling sand hitting the windshield to lull me back to sleep.

"Wake me when we get there."

"Goddess, we need your mighty muscles!"

"Huh? W-what?" I stammered, jerking wide awake, disoriented and floundering.

My back hurt from lying against the hard wall. My limbs were stiff. My lips were cracked and dry. *I* needed a drink of water. And I was famished, starving for calories.

But the prior "patter-patter" of the whipping sand wasn't a soothing background rattle anymore, rather a pounding "thud-thud-thud". Outside the windshield I now saw what looked like a raging hurricane. Our heavy vehicle was rocking far over onto each of its sides, like it was about to be blown over, immobilized, and buried.

"But...?"

"We have a facemask big enough for you. We found it in the wreckage of the ship you fell from the sky within. Put it on! I'll connect it to an oxygen canister."

"Uh, ok?"

The mask was old and corroded, but fit airtight over my larger face. Plus self-adhering flaps covered the rest of my head. And then a gentle flow of pure oxygen energized me as I dazedly looked about the cockpit. A swarm of little green-people was affixing thick layers of garments around my arms, chest, and legs. Jury-rigged "extra-large" gloves and boots were crammed over my extremities.

"We must move fast, before the storm weakens!"

"Weakens?"

"The trackers are nearby. They're waiting for the winds to abate to attack us!"

"What the hell?"

Before I knew exactly what was happening, I was crammed into a tight airlock and unceremoniously ejected out onto the surface of Titan. An icy blast slammed into me, cutting through many small cracks in my protective clothing. A swirling wall of coffee-grain "sand" blocked my vision, sneaking through the edge of my mask, chocking me with their foul taste.

This isn't a proper excursion suit—I mentally groaned. *They're supposed to totally protect you. This doesn't even have a heating unit. I'll be frozen solid in minutes out here. God, this is the exact opposite of my skintight golden enforcer suit!*

Small gloved hands grabbed my arms, pulling and pushing me forward through the raging storm.

And then I fell into an opening and found myself in a dimly lit cave. A group of (similar-to-me) poorly suited and ill-masked little people were frantically digging at one of the walls with small picks and shovels. They were stuffing into a sack whatever flakes they managed to chip out.

"Holy crap!" I gasped, looking at the wall closely.

The vein was *glowing* blue-green—seemingly an entire *slab* of the precious Green. If my tiny sample of the pure stuff cost me half a king's ransom, this must be worth the entire "GDP" of the whole solar system! No wonder "trackers" were after the little people. A discovery this large would set brother against brother, sister against sister, and one's own right hand against one's left.

"It's too thick for our hand tools!" Glenda yelled up at me over the outside roar of the continuing storm. "If we had more time and the cyclone hadn't hit, we'd bring in cabled power tools. But we only have a few more minutes to mine it before the wind-blown sand covers the entranceway forever. Can you help us?"

What to do? What to do? Maybe if they had a sledge hammer or...?

I spied an ice-rock boulder lying by the opening. I grabbed it around its circumference, hefting it up. Even in the low Titanian gravity it was heavy, something the little people wouldn't be able to lift off the surface. I hoisted it high. At -300 ºF, it wasn't just a hunk of breakable frozen ice. No, it was a steel-hard *battering ram*.

"Get out of my way!" I hollered through my mask, Glenda frantically translating for me.

"Take this!" I screeched as I ran at the green-glowing vein. I smashed the boulder time and again into the frozen sand-wall. I pounded out hunk after hunk of the green "ore", bashing my way deeper and deeper into the cave wall until I saw no more remaining Green.

I collapsed down onto the cave's frozen rocky floor, gasping for oxygen in my mask, trying to get my breath back. I was exhausted. I saw all the sacks were now filled, the gang of little people dashing out of the cave's mouth laden down with bulging bounty.

"You are wonderful!" Glenda cried-out in glee, dancing a jig around me, clicking her booted heels together.

It was hard to hear her over the escalating ROAR of the storm outside and through our thick facemasks and head-flaps. But I didn't have time to bask in her praise. I saw that the dim light from outside was rapidly fading. I heard an ominous *rumbling* noise. A sand *avalanche* was sweeping down over the cave's entrance. In seconds we'd be trapped forever inside!

I grabbed Glenda up in my arms and raced with the last of the little people through the thudding waterfall of tumbling sand. Then the brutal winds threatened to lift me off my feet. I staggered forward. Finally, I saw the long salvage-truck emerge from the storm. Behind our vehicle I glimpsed several others. They were tied together by thick chains reaching from the back of each to the front of the trailing vehicle. It was a nomadic train!

In a brief lull in the sand-blasts I caught a glimpse of our entire "salvage truck." I saw it was more a huge *tank* than a transport truck. Through the swirling sand I spied four sets of wheels powering two lengths of wide treads. What looked like hydraulic pistons held the vehicle-proper elevated above the treads. On top of the long, blunt vehicle was a movable turret from which thrust out a cannon. And atop the turret was a clear bubble where a little person sat visually aiming an external machine gun. The armor of the giant tank was painted a patchwork of deep brown, purple, and orange. It was perfect camouflage to hide amongst the Shangri-La sand dunes of Titan. I also spied large cylinders beneath the undercarriage, plus other big hunks of impressive hardware. That made sense if this was a long expedition, requiring plenty of fuel.

Christ, this is a military vehicle armed to the teeth—I thought, amazed. *How could they possibly be afraid of these "tracker" enemies?*

"I've got to get inside!" I plaintively yelled, putting Glenda down on the slippery ground, my arms trembling and numb. "I'm freezing!"

Glenda staggered, caught in a particularly ferocious blast. In an instant she was lofted and spun away.

"Oh, no you don't!" I yelled, sprinting for her.

In the weak Titanian gravity I shot into the air, grabbed one of her flailing legs, and dragged her down into the side of the nearest towering sand dune. We slid down its slippery slope, tumbling and flopping, trying to get our feet under us.

Several little people emerged from the sandstorm, now with ropes tied around their waists anchoring them to the unseen salvage truck. They grabbed us and dragged us along with them.

They shoved me and Glenda into an airlock. Before, it'd been cramped with just me inside. Now we were like two sardines in a small tin can. But it didn't last long. We were ejected inward, flopping down onto the floor.

Holy crap!—I gasped, feeling violent jerks as the hurricane outside rocked the vehicle. *I don't think I like sand-surfing on Titan.*

Attending Yuan peeled the various layers of insulation off me. I knocked off my facemask with a stiff fist, greedily sucking in warm cabin air. My little friends gasped at seeing my revealed hands and legs. Unbeknownst to me outside, one glove had torn completely free. One boot was dangling by a strand. Both my hand and foot were frozen solid.

"Not to worry," I weakly grinned at them, "I heal fast."

And then I collapsed, yet again, into blessed unconsciousness.

I awoke shivering and gasping for air. Something was terribly wrong. The internal atmosphere in the transport was foul, much colder and smellier than I remembered. I heard loud "thuds" and felt violent shudders as something outside impacted the vehicle. Answering "bangs" and sharp jerks told me someone was firing the main cannon above me. And a persistent "chittering" bespoke the machine gun on top of our tank being continuously triggered, which seemed strange to me. That would waste a lot of precious ammo!

My military background snapped to the fore and I once again became "The General."

"What's happening?" I asked of the little people huddled up against me in the gloom, "Report!"

But they didn't speak English, just their garbled language that I didn't understand.

Damn!—I growled to myself. *I can fluently speak dozens of languages and when I need to do so a new one pops up. Did it independently evolve here on Titan? It must have done so.*

One thing I did understand: we weren't moving. I shoved through the group around me and crawled up into the cockpit. Through the scarred windshield I saw the storm had abated. The orange skies were clearing. But pinning us down outside was a group of armed marauders. They darted out from behind and over the top of the surrounding brown dunes on what looked like big-wheeled dirt bikes. And amongst them were scampering, long-legged, spider-like robots, which were tossing *grenades* at us! The black-suited, black-helmeted petite riders were firing stubby rifles, pinning down our responding little people. I saw spurts of sand kicking up where our machine gun was missing the speeding attackers by a mile and...

BLANG!

The entire vehicle rocked, new cracks appearing in the tough windshield.

Yikes! Someone's firing artillery shells at us!—I concluded, hoping the armor of the giant tank could hold. That explained the foul, cold atmosphere inside. *Holy crap, we've already suffered breaches.*

Ominously, the "chittering" of our machine gun above us fell silent. The outside attackers zoomed back and forth like a pack of wolves on wheels, approaching ever closer to pounce on their prey, coordinating with their spider-robots. Now the riders were firing close-range energy weapons as they zipped past, which did little damage to the tank but set afire our troops out on the surface.

It was a bad way for anyone to die.

"You should get back with the others," Glenda firmly told me. She was sitting at the controls, peering intently out at the ongoing battle. Clearly, she was in charge, directing our counterattack through the large microphone set before her face.

"I assume those are the 'trackers' that you were worried about before?" I asked, ignoring her order.

"Yes," she nodded. She was intent on what was happening outside. "They're a rival group, who don't respect us Holy Mommas. They're thieves and murderers. They raid our encampments, hijack our tea shipments, and slaughter our people. We're short on experienced soldiers. They ambushed us just now and we're losing!"

In a few seconds of silent observation I analyzed the tactical layout of our people. Our defense was pitiful. The defenders out on the sand weren't behaving like experienced soldiers at all.

My combat experience kicked-in. The pain in my body retreated. I was cool and collected, focused.

"Your enemy is well-armed and equipped," I clinically observed. "Their dirt bikes are sophisticated machines. The grenade robots are nimble. Their energy-guns are cutting edge. They have high tech!"

She nodded in grim agreement.

"Yes, they have a powerful sponsor who craves the precious ore we found. They'll stop at nothing to take it from us."

"So how can I help?" I asked, acknowledging her authority. Bullets "spattered" the windshield, causing the armless Glenda to duck down. She tottered precariously on her stool, now looking anything but in command.

"You're hurt," she insisted. "Get back with the others."

"No, I'm fine," I responded, showing her both my hands. My previously frozen fist was completely healed. Likewise, my naked frozen foot had all toes wriggling freely on the floor. "Should I suit up and go outside to join your forces? I'm skilled in all forms of armed combat. Just give me a gun and I can fight."

I smelled smoke. There was a *fire* in the main cabin or storage compartment. Apparently those energy blasts weren't as harmless to the tank as I'd thought.

"Can you shoot a machine gun?" she asked hopefully. "I fear our sister who was manning it just died in that last artillery strike. We're tracking their trajectories for their over-horizon artillery emplacement to respond with our main cannon, but we need more time to..."

"Say no more," I answered, whirling around and making for where I figured there should be a hatch leading up into the gun turret.

Yep, there it is—I thought as another artillery shell exploding nearby, rocking the tank. *Now where's that damn leaky mask of mine?*

I saw it lying beside a heap of my prior outer insulating garments.

"Help me!" I yelled at the workers who were trying to beat out several fires. Clearly, the "soldiers" of our expeditionary force out on the surface were fighting a losing battle.

Not understanding my words but seeing what was needed, the little people swarmed around me, fitting the insulation layers expertly onto my body parts, including better-constructed large gloves and boots.

"Good enough," I said, screwing a dangling hose from my full-face mask onto a canister. Hopefully it was oxygen.

I sealed my insulated head-flaps as the others now dashed away from me. They crammed into the small cockpit, slamming shut the forward hatch. Then I cranked open the above hatch. It dropped down with an inward rush of incredibly cold Titanian air. I pulled myself through the hatch than yanked it shut behind me. Crawling through the cannon mechanism then up into the external bubble, I surveyed the immediate situation.

Wow. I'm totally exposed in this busted canopy. But it's a great strategic spot. I can see everything around the tank.

The transparent dome I'd spied previously was shattered. Orange fog swirled through it unimpeded. The prior occupant was gone, blown out of it when the artillery shell hit. Most importantly, I recognized the weapon, an ancient *Browning M2 heavy machine gun*. Excellent! The little people must have gotten it from some museum. It dated way back to the end of WWI on Old Earth. Subsequently, it was used in all armed conflicts up to the Incineration. I saw minor enhancements had been done to it for operating on Titan, including electrical heating tapes to keep it warm enough not to freeze solid when inactive. The 0.50 cartridge it fired was a formidable projective as a continuous stream or singly in sniper mode. The big bullet was capable of penetrating and destroying other armored vehicles, both surface and aerial, in addition to taking out individual combatants.

"Attack my little buddies, will you?" I muttered as I tore off the distal activator mechanisms, reset all the controls properly for manual usage, and reached out of the shattered canopy to grip the "spade handle" with both my gloved fists.

The enhanced M2 had an effective range of over 2,000 yards, putting all the dune-skimming attackers within its reach. It was a formidable weapon.

Sighting carefully, I tightened my thumbs to trigger short bursts aimed just in front of the speeding attackers. That precise, anticipatory targeting sent the zipping "dirt bikes" exploding and tumbling in all directions. The slower spider robots were easy to hit. I blasted them to shreds. My defending little people jumped up and down, waving their rifles triumphantly in the air.

But the attackers weren't defeated. One in particular zoomed in on his dirt bike beneath my field of fire, close to the tank. Triggering a seat catapult of some sort he launched himself up into the air, firing pointblank at me as he fell onto the side of the broken canopy!

I ducked away, just avoiding his rifle shots. Then I swiped at him with one fist, knocking the rifle out of his small hands.

"Keeg daga!" he shrieked at me through the facemask of his biker's helmet. He yanked a long, slender, "stiletto"-type knife from off his belt.

"Get off, you little pest!" I yelled back, still trying to aim at the darting attackers with one hand on my machine gun, swatting at him with the other.

"Keiga!" he shouted gleefully as he plunged the blade past my defending arm. I felt the knife penetrate my armpit, plunge past my ribs, and lodge in the right side of my body. It had lanced my lungs, stopping just short of my beating heart.

"Auugghh!" I grimaced. The new pain threatened to double me over, preventing me from firing the machine gun.

And then he savagely *twisted* the blade in place, *breaking* off the end of the blade against bone as he yanked out what was left to take yet another stab at me!

There's no time to feel pain or deal with the wound, he's a trained assassin—the thought flashed through my brain.

Time seemed to slow down around me as it often did when I was under extreme stress.

This isn't just some ordinary soldier—I coolly observed. *Their so-called "sponsor" sent a crack troop after this tank. Did they know the Yuan rescued me? Am I the real target here?*

All that zipped through my mind as I released the grip of the machine gun to block his next blow, using my other hand to grab his air hose and yank it out of his helmet.

"Suck that!" I yelled as I slammed his knife arm repeatedly into the ragged plasteel of the broken canopy top.

"Aiiieeee!" he screamed, dropping the broken knife-haft.

Hah! Not much of an assassin after all. That was an amateur defense, letting me get to his facemask. I guess I misread him.

I saw his face twisting up. Titan's poisonous air was flooding his helmet. He was done for, no longer a threat. Contemptuously I swatted him away.

Simultaneously, the tank under me *rocked* as a shell BLASTED out of our cannon, impacting somewhere beyond the nearest towering dune. I saw a *sheet of flame* leap up beyond the dune's peak, indicating a direct hit on the enemy emplacement.

Ignoring the spreading agony in my side from the broken-off, still-embedded knife blade, I grabbed the handle of my machine gun and renewed my precise peppering of the squads of bike riders. The swarm of attackers was now hastily retreating. I gave them no mercy, mowing them down until only a few stragglers escaped behind the nearest dunes.

Securing the gun and remaining ammunition strips, I slipped back into the torrent, *banging* loudly on the hatch with my now again nearly frozen fists. With a great deal of fumbling I could probably open it myself. But I didn't want to risk depressurizing the cabin from the shattered canopy if others had already come back into the main cabin.

As the hatch swung down inward, a fully suited little person gestured through white smoke for me to come back inside.

Securing the hatch, I was happy to hear the "hiss" of the Titanium poisonous air being ejected as breathable air was pumped in. That would help stop any internal cabin fires, damping them if not putting them out completely. I happily tore off my ill-fitting facemask as the forward hatch opened. Hunched over, clutching my bleeding side, I went forward and entered the cockpit. I kept my left hand tight to my right side, staunching the blood flow.

"Goddess, you're hurt!" Glenda gasped.

"It's nothing. Don't worry about it. What's our situation?" I demanded. Glenda sat ashen-faced at the controls. She was so pale that her normal green-sheen was gone from her skin. I saw this battle had taken a toll on her. I sympathized with her but knew from my many past battles that the time to freak out is after you're back safe to your base, not before.

I knew I was bleeding badly internally, the broken-off knife blade continually challenging my super-healing talents. But with proper medical care I'd likely survive. I just needed to stay still, avoid mashing my damaged organs and broken ribs repeatedly into the embedded blade.

"There are...many dead," she said in a small voice. "We're...the only crawler left intact. Our other vehicles are completely destroyed. Fortunately, though, the precious residue we harvested is safe in our external cargo bin so..."

"Can we take on the survivors?"

"They're boarding as we speak. We'll have them all inside within a few minutes and..."

"So what's next?"

I was still in my "General" mode, anticipating a counter-attack.

She gulped, looking fearfully up at me with her big green eyes.

"We can't stay here. Now that the trackers know our location and how badly we're damaged, they return shortly in greater numbers. We have to launch."

"Eh?"

"We were headed for hidden entrances leading to a series of natural caverns," she explained. "Normally we'd sneak through that circuitous route, safely inside long, dark ravines and canyons. Now we've no time, so..."

"We 'launch'?" I repeated. "This tank has *flight* capabilities?"

"Well...only in an emergency...we've not tried it before in this one...and..."

She paused, gulping, fearful.

"Yes?" I prompted her.

"It takes all our fuel, so it's one shot or nothing. And the sponsors of the trackers will surely see and track our trajectory. If we land off-target, exposed for too long at our destination, they'll know the location of one of our main entrances. We'll risk all our secret settlements. But there's no other way for us to make it to Xanadu. And our cargo is critical. Our people desperately need the ore we dug out of that dune. Our stocks are nearly depleted!"

I knew from my pre-investigation research that "Xanadu" was a vast, raised territory of Titan located right next to sunken Shangri-La. Xanadu was a huge ice plain the size of Old Earth's Australia, versus the dried-up ocean bed of Shangri-La. That'd be quite a jump to make in one burn. Glenda must be really desperate to risk attempting it. But it'd put me that much closer to Doom Mons. And I desperately needed medical care if I was to stay in my present reincarnation!

"Then it's obvious we have to try," I encouraged her. I saw I had some sway. To them I was the "Titanian Messiah." Of course that didn't really help much except for morale. But I was also in addition to being a licensed assassin a trained military officer. You like things to go "to plan" but war often scrambles your best intentions. Sometimes you just have to take a "leap of faith" to complete your mission.

"Yes, of course...we'll start charging the rocket," she said to me as she spoke rapidly in "gibberish" to the three pilots. "And we'll sacrifice one sack of the residue for the thrust chamber."

Huh? That stuff has explosive potential? It's some sort of "super-charger"?

But I didn't have time to query Glenda on the interesting rocketry chemistry. All around me, the surviving little people were coughing and gasping. The cabin air was a noxious blend of retained Titanian atmosphere and acrid smoke.

"I'll go back and help put out the remaining fires," I groaned, clutching my side. "What's your main fuel, anyway? Are you using methane? For a vehicle this heavy, you won't get much altitude with..."

"It's compressed hydrogen and oxygen gases," she said in a low voice. "But the added residue will help, a lot!"

Ah...I understood her reluctance. Although she'd get a good burst of energy from her rocket, an undefined mixture would surely be hard to control, especially in a ramshackle vehicle like this.

"How long until you can launch?" I called back as I moved into the main cabin, with one arm helping the little people beat out flames with wet cloths.

"Soon, very soon!"

Having put out the fires, I stumbled back to the cockpit and was dismayed to see artillery snouts peeking out over the peaks of the surrounding dunes.

"How about *now?*" I asked.

She yelled out a burst of little-people gibberish. Everyone ducked down, held on tight, or snapped shut their seatbelt buckles.

I felt the entire tank tipping upward as the rear lowered and the front wheel-pistons extended. A fierce "rumbling" beneath us hurt my ears. Then a teeth-jarring VIBRATION swept through the junky, already badly damaged vehicle.

The pilots slapped a big belt around Glenda, attaching her securely to her seat.

"Hold on!" she yelled at me as we EXPLODED upward into the sky, tossing me brutally about the cabin. My already damaged side was battered mercilessly.

Stabilizing myself by grabbing onto an equipment bank, I barely stayed conscious from the flaring pain in my torso. The high g-forces were terrible after having lived a while in Titan's low gravity. We seemed to be zooming up much higher than necessary. I saw through the windshield we were swooping upward through thick layers of orange clouds. I expected us to slow then drop precipitously.

Finally we stopped accelerating to *float* serenely along. Through the windshield I now saw a sea of *stars* glaring unblinkingly at us, set upon utter blackness. We'd zoomed up *above* the thick smoggy atmosphere of Titan!

Jesus, that "residue" has a real kick to it—I marveled, once again mentally wincing at having lost my pure vial of the stuff. *Ah well, what's gone is gone.*

How much time had passed? It seemed just seconds, but it had to be longer. And why did we go all the way up into orbit? I thought we were only doing a "small" hop across Titan's icy surface? Had the residue's "kick" thrown us to some unknown destination?

"Is this where you wanted to end up?" I gasped.

"Oops," Glenda gulped, her big eyes stretched wide in awe. "At least we're still in one piece. Lucky this tank was constructed from a decommissioned orbital shuttle."

I'd always traveled on commercial spaceships, safely isolated from the vastness of outer space. Now it seemed I was thrust into the Universe itself.

Oh, God, there it is—I sighed in amazement to myself. I'd forgotten how magnificent the view was above the ever-present orange smog of filthy Titan...the *spectacular rings* of Saturn glimmering in pinks, grays, blues, and yellows. And behind the hovering, circular disk was the giant gas planet itself, a dazzling yellowish-brown sphere of alternating, massive, roiling cloud banks.

One of the pilots jabbered excitedly.

"We're descending," Glenda now calmly reported. "Hold on tight, Goddess!"

We dived back into the swirling orange clouds below us, leaving behind the magnificent near-orbital view of Saturn. But we were going much too fast. It looked like my quest would end in a rapid *splatter* all over the ice plains of Xanadu. And this time I'd likely have no intact body left to get resurrected!

"Are we going to crash?" I grated-out. The savage vibrations were about to tear me loose from the equipment panel. It was very hard to hold on with one hand. It was getting difficult to breath. My punctured lung was likely filling up with blood. But that probably wouldn't matter much longer as our jury-rigged rocket was threatening to rip itself to pieces. We might not even make it to the surface to crash. We'd tear apart or be consumed in a fireball!

"Wings!" she happily laughed, seemingly recovering her congenital cheerfulness.

With a violent jerk I felt our ramshackle vehicle slowing. The plunge changed into a smooth glide-path. Out the now frosted-over window I just made out the jutting edges of snap-out wings.

These nomads aren't just simple Titanian peasants—I marveled to myself. *They built a sophisticated vehicle, by any standards.*

We tilted precipitously as the pilots struggled to guide our ponderous, fuel-depleted glider to the desired landing area. I was reminded of the "dead-stick" landings of the Space Shuttles back on Old Earth in the 1990's. I saw below me a fast-approaching plateau. The gigantic glacier below us was festooned with deep "criss-crossing" cracks and ridges. Then we were zipping over an area dotted with dunes and low hills. I saw what looked like wide rivers and valleys, carved out of the ice glacier by methane rainstorms. Then we were over another flat glacial area, swooping lower and lower. I saw a rapidly approaching high cliff wall beside a precipitous drop a thousand feet down from the ice plateau.

Even worse, I saw the surface below suddenly *heaving*. Large crevasses suddenly opened up along our landing path.

It must be those "up-ticked" damn titan-quakes—I groaned to myself. *Just when it looks like we might actually survive our jaunt up into orbit, Titan is looking to gulp us down.*

We bounced heavily on a slick surface. I felt a strong "jerk" as a parachute deployed behind us, slowing us. We spun slowly in a circle as we tacked against a strong wind. I saw the thousand-foot drop approaching rapidly, there at the edge of the plateau. On the other side of us cliffs loomed. We sped just feet away from a deep crevasse in the flat plateau.

Oh, Christ—I gasped to myself. *Either we're going to fall off the edge, drop into a crevice, or smash headlong into that ice mountain!*

The pilots slammed down their brakes on the tank's treads and we skidded to a stop, mere yards from the edge of the precipitous drop.

A small army of suited little people ran out from a dark opening in the mountain cliff, attaching ropes. In minutes they dragged our vehicle beneath a sheltering ledge.

"We made it," Glenda beamed at me, "right on target."

I smiled back at her, speechless with relief, giving a shaky salute to the likewise relieved pilots.

Welcome to Xanadu—I giddily congratulate myself before passing out.

Xanadu far exceeded my expectations. Of course that was after we arrived at the main settlement, after a long journey through an underground labyrinth cut by natural forces (crustal cracking plus liquid methane flows) into the massive ice glacier above us.

I wasn't much aware of the trip. I was in and out of consciousness. My body was struggling to replenish a continual massive internal loss of blood from the still-lodged, broken-off knife blade. I could feel my lung being freshly sliced each time I took a breath. I couldn't walk. A squad of little people kindly stretchered me through a bewildering maze of many long dark tunnels, either natural or melted out of the surrounding rock-hard ice. Some were so narrow we could only go through in single file. We were all in our excursion suits, either on foot or riding on narrow, wheeled wagons. It seemed our group trudged along through the maze for a week, but it may have been only two or three days. In various small, airlocked caves we took off our gear and got some food and drink. But for the most part it was a depressing trudge through dim, spooky tunnels and chambers. Beside their own survival gear, the surviving members of our tank crew lugged along precious sacks of ore.

"We're home!" Glenda exclaimed as we entered a rusty airlock.

I dazedly looked up at her, hovering between life and death. My wound was severely infected. I could barely breathe, coughing up clotted blood. The embedded knife was an ice-cold spear hanging less than an inch from my weakly beating heart.

"W-where is t-that?" I gasped from my stretcher, raising my head to look about.

"We've reached *Shangdu*, our capital city and main farming complex!" she grandly exclaimed.

We exited the airlock into a giant cavern, at least a thousand feet high. Hovering globe-lights far overhead cast a warm yellow light on everything below. We were entering from a tunnel on the raised bottom of one of the cavern's high walls, looking down a long slope toward quaint villages and green fields. I saw many rows of neatly planted small bush-trees extending into the mists in the distance.

Some fields held taller, older trees, creating patches of actual forest. Plus there were conventional fields growing food-crops. She wasn't kidding about it being a ranch, on a commercial scale. And in the center of the cavern was what looked like a small city, with ornate oriental-style buildings reaching up several floors.

In the far distance on the opposite cavern wall I saw swirling mists where a giant waterfall tumbled from near the top of the cavern. I heard its powerful "rumble". The waterfall grandly swirled down to crash into ice-rocks at its bottom, smoothing out to form a wide river that languidly curved across the cavern's floor. Off to its sides I spied several large lakes and many ponds.

Most pleasant of all, the air that now flowed freely into my tortured lungs was rich, warm, and moist. I gladly let my facemask dangle on its strap to the side. My head cap and flaps followed, allowing a gentle breeze to caress my fevered brow and smushed hair.

How long has it been since I had a nice shower?—I deliriously marveled. *It seems I've been "icky and sticky" forever.*

I inhaled rich odors of earth, farm animals, and wildlife. A hint of smoke bespoke fireplaces cooking hearty meals. This wasn't the sterile, canned air of the "TSS" Titan Space Station or the stink of Huygens Station. No, this was the sweet smells of a vibrant, living, organic community.

And everywhere I looked, I now noticed *mushrooms*...big towering white ones, gray slender ones I first mistook for weeds, small yellow ones, multiple-coned red ones...every type and form imaginable.

It must be the humidity—I mused to myself, luxuriating in the moist air caressing my skin. *I've never seen so much water. It must be melted out of the concealing glacier above us. But where do they get the power to run this place? The Yuan are nomads! Titan Station and the space stations have the technical expertise and wealth to run and maintain expensive nuclear power plants. Could these scroungers somehow do the same?*

It seemed unlikely. But more immediate concerns eclipsed those thoughts.

"Do you...have doctors here?" I whispered to Glenda.

"We surely do, Goddess," she reassured me. "We'll get that broken knife blade out of you. In a jiffy it won't be continually cutting into your poor lungs. You'll breathe better shortly."

"Ok," I answered, wincing as the stretcher bounced when my Yuan friends pointed it down the slope. I coughed up more clotted blood. "I don't like dying," I whispered.

She laughed, thinking I was making a joke. I wasn't. I hated dying, *over* and *over* and *over*. Gently "bopping" my now ungloved, dangling arm with her copper-crowned head, Glenda walked stoically beside the stretcher-bearers. She sure was a sturdy little gal. The long trek hadn't fazed her a bit. She seemed as fresh as when we'd set out from the precariously landed tank-shuttle. She was an ordained and natural leader that everyone looked up to, arms or no arms.

"You can't save *us* if we can't save *you*," she grinned broadly. "It is foretold that you will live, Goddess. Hang on!"

I nodded, barely able to respond. Knowing we were safe, I let myself drift back into blessed unconsciousness, the nearest I ever got to being free of pain. Yes, I was still tortured by awful nightmares even in my deepest slumber, but sleep was a simulation of permanent, peaceful death. I liked to sleep.

But now I had friends, a beautiful base from which to scheme, and unsuspecting allies for pursuing my awful revenge.

Things were looking up. The dark shadows of my mind were finally lifting.

Chapter 8

<u>MOONSHADOWS</u>

A unique 1970 shallow-deep song
Folk singer Cat Stevens a.k.a. Yusuf Islam
Crafting a well-loved spooky nighttime ballad
A vision of one's hidden then expressed inner self
Not introspection but excision by a stellar companion
Looking to the Moon to discover the essence of one's soul
Changing the very nature of reality transcendentally
Speaking a radically new re-envisioning of "truth"
All the inner turmoil suppressed re-emerging
Dancing and prancing and leaping-about
Taunting us to follow in its steps
Or stumble into deep craters
Caught on the sharp edge
Of Light and Dark
Immobilized...

The Rise and Fall of *Homo sapiens*, 8:10-14

"This is the Executive Suite of our headquarters tower, General," my escort politely explained, standing aside. "If you need anything, please..."

"I require a fresh uniform and sundries," I imperiously interrupted him, inhabiting my new identity. "I was traveling incognito from Earth. I didn't even bring luggage with me. Oh...and that Old Earth artifact in the display case, the blue marble?" I paused as if considering options.

"Yes, Ma'am?"

"I need to study it further. Please deliver it to me."

"Yes, Ma'am! We'll get all that to you shortly," the man saluted.

Great, he didn't even hesitate—I congratulated myself. *Apparently I've got extensive authority here. And it'll be super to have the marble back in my pocket after all these years, something to physically link myself to my long-lost past.*

I casually returned his salute, closing and locking the door behind me. Finally I was by myself, free to locate a computer console and figure out *what the bloody hell* had happened in the last one hundred years—not-to-mention the details of my new identity that Arthur had set up for me, a "General", really?

"Ah...not bad," I observed.

For a moon colony, the Executive Suite was luxurious. I saw a spacious sitting room/office area. An open door led into a combination bathroom/bedroom. And a small kitchenette area over to the side sported a microwave and small refrigerator. I was most intrigued, however, by a full-wall window that looked out from above upon the surface of the moon.

In my "Old Earth" time-period, the working quarters of our one struggling, small moon colony were buried beneath the regolith. Without an atmosphere to protect from deadly meteorites and radiation, exposed domes were strictly for surface activities. Most of the actual business of living and working was buried beneath a ten-foot-thick protective layer of rock and dust, either layered on top or dug down into. I'd heard living on the moon was much like living on a submarine. Space was at a premium, living quarters cramped and utilitarian. The more-extensive, present-day colonies were likely similarly constructed. My suite, however, was on the top of a "headquarters tower" situated in the center of a high transparent Dome, from which I could view the entire surrounding landscape. Likely the devoted building was also used as a control tower for the local spaceport's operations.

"This is indeed impressive," I wearily mumbled to myself, standing in front of the full-wall window. I noted that the transparent plasteel was particularly thick, likely impregnated with lead. The likewise transparent dome-shell would give additional protection from most radiation and meteorite hazards. It wasn't as safe as being buried beneath the surface of the moon, but operationally made sense. From here you could see everything. The thick plasteel layers alone needed to allow such an extravagance must have cost a fortune.

I'm on the God-damned Moon!—I again marveled.

I saw laid out before me a gray plain extending to the horizon. Shallow craters dotted the plain, most small but some large with up-raised rims. It was the two-week period of daylight, casting long deep-black shadows from the crater rims. In the distance I spied low, stark hills. Several other surface Domes were located nearby, likewise casting deep black shadows behind them. A spaceport sat about a mile away, indicated by a rocket descending on a column of blue flames. Various big-wheeled, enclosed vehicles were moving about on well-worn paths. I saw a spacesuited individual working on a pump outside my Dome. And set off at a safe distance was the circle-tunnel that protected the historic landing site of Armstrong and Aldrin.

I hopped into the air and drifted down upon a short couch where I sat looking out on the moonscape, entranced by the stark vista. I knew I should get cleaned up in the bathroom, find something to eat. But I was *so* tired. Plus the roiling waves of pain I'd pushed off were slamming back into me, making me groan and twitch.

Maybe just a short nap is what the doctor ordered—I sighed, closing my eyes...

—when a persistent "beeping" at the suite's door jerked me awake!

"How long have I been napping?" I mumbled. My mouth felt like it was full of cotton. I noted that the deep shadows outside seem to have shifted.

"Alright, alright," I called out, staggering upright. "I'm coming!"

Unlocking and pulling open the door I saw several guards dutiful-ly waiting on me. One held a neatly folded pile of clothes. The other held the plastic cube containing my marble.

"I'm sorry it took so long," he apologized. "We had to get permis-sion from the curators to..."

"No problem," I reassured him, taking the clothes and plastic cu-be. "That'll be all for now."

"Just call on the intercom if you need anything else, General."

"I'll do that. Thanks."

Closing and relocking the door I carried my prizes inside, setting them on a side-table beside the couch. I reverently picked up the cube, irritated that the blue sphere was still beyond my reach. Angrily I strode into the kitchen area, found a large chopping knife, and sliced at the hard plastic. Within minutes I'd cut the marble from its prison and held it in my hands.

It felt *warm* and vibrating, as if a mechanism inside was activating after being long dormant. I felt greatly comforted, the pain clouds receding around me. I felt my eyes tearing up at the sight of the blue-pulsing "old friend".

I slipped it into a pocket for safe keeping.

"Do you require an antihistamine?" I heard a pleasant female voice from behind me. "The air is filtered but moon dust is difficult to completely exclude. It's extremely irritating to a human's pulmonary system."

Whirling around, I saw...myself! It was like looking in a mirror except she was clad in a neat blue uniform, with her hair buzz-cut and dyed green. And by brief flickers rippling across her body I realized she was an advanced hologram. Even though some computer aspects had apparently stagnated, did others similarly advance?

"No, thank you," I sniffed, wiping my eyes. "Are you my computer interface? And why are you configured to look like me?"

"Interface?" she asked with a puzzled expression on her face.

"Instead of typing instructions, I'm communicating with you directly by voice and movements. Are you an advanced version of the early twenty-first century's virtual assistants such as Siri and Alexa? And why do you look like me?" I pointedly repeated.

"Yes, of course, I'm fundamentally computer-based," she nodded, politely evading my central question. "But those primitive 'interfaces' could not *think*. The true 'interface' here *is* the hologram that you're viewing," she explained, now not so politely. "Come on, Suzy, use your noggin'!"

What the hell?—I mentally gasped, trying to hide my shock. *Am I being sassed by a computer?*

"You 'think', really? Are you a true 'AI', an artificial intelligence?"

"I guess you'd have to ask my creator," she sniffed. "I'm as lost on that topic as are you. I *think* I think, how about that?"

Jesus, am I this irritating to other people?

Ignoring for the moment the rude hologram, I walked over to the kitchenette and opened the refrigerator. Inside I saw a neat stack of pre-cooked, packaged food. I was famished. I pulled out what looked like a chicken salad sandwich. The ingredient label said it didn't actually contain meat, but was mainly made from a soy bean product. I filled myself a glass of pure water from the tap. It was weird how high the water bounced and how long the droplets took to fall back. Clearly, living on the moon would take some getting used to.

I settled down onto the couch again looking out upon the moon-base vista, my back to the seemingly patiently waiting hologram.

"So Anderson made you?" I said around a mouthful of the thick sandwich. It sure tasted like chicken salad. The lettuce and tomato layers were crisp and juicy. It was delicious. "And how are you projected in here? I don't see any lenses."

"Well, *duh*," she laughed from behind me. "Do you think the desperate remnants of humanity, after the Extinction, could create a simulation of yourself capable of 'holding your place' until you popped back into this timeline? They barely kept their existing computers running, let alone came up with radically new technology."

I felt the marble in my pocket vibrating "in tune" with her words.

Ah, that's what's going on—I concluded with satisfaction. *The hologram itself is yet another future innovation from the once time-traveler Anderson. He must have implanted a projector within my marble!*

I closed my eyes while chewing slowly, savoring the wonderful sandwich. I hadn't eaten for a hundred years. I was really hungry. But I knew not to gulp my meal. I wanted to savor it.

"So you're the one responsible for the deference by the guards that I, 'The General', received at the Blue Marble exit-point?"

"'The General' is a rarely seen but powerful Earth entity, somewhat akin to the mythical status that the wealthy recluse Howard Hughes obtained in his later years," she explained. "He pulled the strings of a vast corporate empire, but from behind the scenes."

"So I'm wealthy?"

"You're the Trash Baron of Earth."

Right...well, that's going to take some explaining!

I drained the glass of water. It was cool and tasty. It didn't have the flatness of distilled water, but the satisfying tang of a bubbling mountain stream. Since there were no mountain streams or artesian aquifers on the moon, I applauded the public works managers at the base. He or she had added back an appropriate level of "natural" minerals to their recycled waste water.

Yes. I'm drinking the purified urine of lots of folks, no different than what occurred naturally back on Old Earth in its water cycle—I mused.

"Please explain how being a 'baron' of *trash* makes me wealthy."

She walked around the couch to "sit" on a chair to the side of the window. Except for a few random sparkles she looked absolutely real.

"The greatest gift that the last Old Earth generation of humans left for their few remaining children was vast *landfill sites* located nearby all the major cities."

"Say what?"

I leaned back, feeling an overpowering urge to nod off again, but forced myself to stay alert. I had to "get the lay of the land" immediately. Then I could do lower priority things like sleeping for days, allowing my still-tortured body to heal.

With a wave of her hand, she brought up a 3D map that hovered in the air in front of the moonscape. It had a large white "X" next to most of the major cities of Old Earth.

"Protected from the nuclear blasts which wiped away the major cities were vast buried stores of processed materials," she narrated as the view zoomed in to show smoking empty fields. "Some of the dump sites were completely incinerated, of course, down to hundreds of feet below the surface. But many survived relatively intact beneath a superficial layer of radioactive debris. Just counting the *plastic* wastes, at the Extinction Event over *ten billion tons* existed on Earth, much of it buried in the dump sites."

On the video, "spacesuited" figures were digging here and there, probing. A few enclosed small bulldozers and excavators sat nearby.

"As the bunkered governmental remnants recovered," she continued, "their first priority was securing the only large source of sophisticated, manufactured materials left on earth: the landfill dump sites. So the first decades post-extinction were consumed with 'Garbage

Wars'—in which *you* as *Tanya H. Contrare,* later just known as 'The General', was both proactive and prescient," she continued to narrate.

The map-video now showed squads of armed "spacesuited" figures battling amongst the trash-recovery operations. It was a terribly bloody war in which entrenched soldiers shot and blew each other to pieces.

"You waged savage war within the radioactive remains for years, taking over large swaths of territory, sanctioned by your remaining governmental authorities. When required to be 'on site' for a battle or whatever, I...'you'...inhabited a robot which Arthur built. It was hidden from the sight of others inside a dark-helmeted protective excursion suit. Then, following consolidation of your victories, as the 'protector' of the main dumps you took more of a back seat in your powerful organization. And when you grew appropriately old your 'daughter' Carlene took over. When she likewise grew old, then your 'granddaughter', General Lockheart Contrare took up the inherited title. All that time, your 'family' charged hefty fees for anyone to access Old Earth's guarded, buried treasures. Necessary to protecting your precious territory, sanctioned by the now dominant Western Alliance, was you funding and commanding a formidable private army. This is all history now, 'post-AE'."

"*Did* I now?" I congratulated her, "And you say all that happened 'AE', huh? I assume that means 'After Extinction'?"

She just nodded. I admired her unblinking green eyes that matched her garishly green short hair. In her neatly pressed blue uniform she struck a cool, decisive figure. She reminded me of The Commissioner, but less arrogant, more wryly humorous. I could definitely see how the guards held her...*me*...in such great respect.

"So to summarize what you're telling me," I continued, "you created a *dynasty* in which supposed children took the place of the supposed elder," I softly stated, taking the last bites of my rapidly vanishing sandwich. "Did democracy devolve to hereditary dynasties? Have we returned to the middle ages, ruled by Kings, Queens, and Caesars?"

"For a while, yes," she shrugged nonchalantly. "That allowed the tight command structure necessary for rebuilding civilization *off*-world, incidentally letting you amass incredible wealth. Now, though, you're more like a beloved monarch who has ceded most of her authority to an elected government. Theoretically you command the entire military forces of the Western Alliance, though in actuality your official duties are few. But you still maintain your own private army that puts the 'fist' in your velvet glove. Any officials that try to usurp your position or threaten your power do so at their peril."

"Super," I sighed, thinking I should move to the bed in the other room but knowing the couch was way too comfortable in the moon's one-sixth Earth-gravity. "I'm an old-fashioned robber baron with my own private army. And I suppose the way I initially funded all of this was using the long-departed, dear 'crazy cat lady's' online stash of bitcoins? They were safely sequestered in subterranean bank vault servers, such that her wealth survived into AE?"

"Yes," she curtly stated.

"Alright then, I'm caught up," I nodded, stretching myself out onto the short couch, my legs dangling off its end. "Will you wake me if I'm needed? And what should I call you, anyway? Are you the 'maxime'? I assume I'll take on your fleshy duties while you're still handling all the 'behind scene' stuff?"

She laughed.

"Of course, Suzy," she smiled at me. "Fix your hair appropriately when you get around to it and everyone will be certain you're me. They've seen me from time-to-time on video transmissions. I was built to facilitate your return to this timeline. My programmed purpose is to serve you. And please name me as you wish. The personnel here just call me 'The General.' Since you're the *true* General, I suppose it makes sense for you to give me a new name just between the two of us."

I considered various names.

"Ok, then, how about...'Q'—for 'cute' and 'computer'?"

This time she snorted. I liked her. She definitely had a sense of humor. I was using the same "Q" sound for different first letters, hah!

"It's really nice to finally meet you in the flesh," Q grinned. It's been lonely for me since Arthur left us."

"Oh...he's dead?" I yawned, now barely able to keep my droopy eyelids open. That prior nap definitely wasn't long enough. "Ok, that's dumb of me. It's been over a hundred years since I left. And he was cut off from all benefits of being a Time Keeper. But he *did* retain his advanced knowledge, using his expertise to construct you, right? You're obviously based on quantum-computer technology from a future timeline, right? But if anyone could cheat time, it'd be him, the sneaky bastard."

She looked genuinely sad.

"In a way you are my mother and *he* was my father," she replied. "It pains me to hear you speak ill of him."

I winced at the image...who'd ever get married to that jerk? And what gave this computer program the right to get all snarky and judgmental with me? Oh, right...she *was* me.

"Would you like to see his last message to you? I can play it now or after you sleep. You choose. But you must view it."

A last message from Arthur? Do I really want to hear this? But there might be some critical information. I'd better just get it over with.

"I suppose I should hear it now," I yawned again. I grabbed a cushion to keep my head elevated as I lay curled on my side there on the couch looking out on the stark moonscape. "Roll tape!"

"We don't have 'tape' anymore, either," she gently laughed. "I've protected this message for many years. I've kept it hidden away deep in my core programming distributed throughout the secure subterranean servers of Earth. I suppose you've figured out that the Blue Marble is how I'm accessing my Earth data and producing this hologram? Anderson installed a quantum link in the marble that's instantaneous. The moon's computer networks are much too primitive to house my intelligence. Anyway, once I play Arthur's message for you, I am required to permanently delete it. So please pay close attention."

"Alright," I sighed, reluctantly sitting back up and concentrating. "I'm sure this is important. Thanks for your diligence, 'Q'. I'm ready."

In place of the map, a 3D-image sprang up before me. It was of a bald-headed, well-wrinkled, very old man. He was sitting hunched over in a wheelchair inside a comfortable looking living room. A lamp sat to his side, brightly lighting up one half of his face, the other half in shadows. He wore a red floppy robe with a blanket draped over his

legs. Behind him were pictures on a wall of a dark-skinned baby, in-
fant, child, and teenager. Startled, I recognized the old man as Arthur
Anderson, but a radically different person than I recalled. The prior
Arthur I'd dealt with was hard, calculating, beefy, hideously scarred,
and a loner. This man was soft-eyed, smiling, had a surgically re-
paired face, and at his side was a gray-haired, black-skinned lady:
Lelea! He looked very thin, with loose skin hanging off his cadaverous but otherwise cheerful face.

My eyes narrowed. I felt no sympathy for the old man. I still hated that rat.

"Hello my dear, long-lost Suzy," he softly began, his voice a harsh
whisper. "I expected you to return to your 'blue marble' anchor-point
almost immediately. Instead, I patiently waited, year after year. Now
I'm not long for this world. I guess I spent too much time out on the
surface trying to help set up mining operations in the trash zones.
I'm dying of radiation-induced cancer. It's spread throughout my
body, untreatable. But that's not a tragedy. It's just life. And it's
been an interesting interlude for me after you went to the second Dimension, here awaiting your return."

So, he died in misery. That's just what he deserved.

"It was a struggle to survive in our subterranean Colony outside
what was Sulphur, Oklahoma," he continued. "But we always made
beautiful music, returning that precious gift back to society. Plus I
had a library I'd accumulated at the Colony, precious pre-Extinction
artifacts. Then I used my future expertise covertly, as best I could. I
constructed a canny substitute to 'hold your place' until you hopefully
someday returned. I also got to know your friend Lelea better, first as
my assistant and then..."

"Hi, Soozee!" Lelea cheerfully interjected, waving a dark-skinned
arm at me. She placed a hand gently on Anderson's withered arm.

"—who by some miracle likes me as much as I do her," he patted
her hand, "And so we married, even had a child, a brilliant son who
will carry on our legacy. I couldn't be happier. And it's largely because of you. You inspired me to move beyond my prior self and
honor your unselfish example into the future."

What? Unselfish example? Did he get senile as he aged?

"I'm guessing from your delay that the second Dimension didn't treat you well or prove a 'safe haven' for us. Well, I'm not surprised. The Commissioner likely destroyed the place, the bitch. But I'm sure you tried your best," he congratulated me. "I myself learned to put aside the religious fervor which drove me to rebel against the Commissioner. After all, what did the religious zealots do for your world here except destroy it? Instead of trying to force society to accept my beliefs, I focused on putting my faith into action by helping others."

Well, that's certainly enlightened of him—I grudgingly admitted.

"Part of that was 'inventing' strategic and logistical battle tactics and improved weapons, taken from a future now-dissipated timeline. It was necessary to bring some order since the human vermin here fought for the scraps of what remained of Earth. Setting that situation straight, largely using your skillful 'computer clone' to direct the action, I then juiced-up our existing off-world colonization with key advancements. You'll be pleased to learn that the Western Alliance's successful moon colony is officially named 'The Suzette Kingly Station.' It took decades, but finally the rulers of the world accepted that your actions at the Galactic Core Contest actually saved us from alien domination. Unfortunately, though, the unofficial name 'Tranquility Base' is how everyone refers to it. But your heroic actions at the Galactic Core are now enthroned in history."

Holy crap! I'm no longer a pariah? But I still can't let my true identify be known. Some history-revisionist could still challenge my loss at the Galactic Core if people knew I was still alive.

"So, anyway, I'm recording this message to say 'thanks' and Godspeed on your return." He gulped air deeply, as if having trouble breathing, before continuing: "I do hope you find happiness, Suzy. As to your quest to find and punish whatever or whoever was behind the murder of your mother, my advice is to just let it go. Something mysterious happened there, that's for sure. I've quietly investigated amongst what remained of humanity after the Extinction. But I failed to pin down the source of the atrocity. If a conspiracy did exist, it may remain hidden to the end of time. But what does it really matter?" he nonchalantly shrugged.

I had started to weaken, thinking that maybe Anderson had truly transformed himself. But then he went "off the deep end." He was telling me to *give up* the one thing that sustained me, that kept me fighting forward though my pain. It was the *one thing* that stopped me from going insane. It was the *only thing* that made me battle through the constant torture I endured. Truly he didn't know the first thing about me!

"Bad things happen, Suzy," he feebly continued, "which often have no definable cause. That's just life."

He paused in his narration, sadly shaking his bald, liver-spotted skull. I was about to tell Q to turn off the damn 'tape' when Lelea jumped cheerfully into the breach.

"But there's lots of *good* still in the world, Soozee," Lelea hastily added. "I thought everything was lost after I pushed you into that snake pit outside my village in the 1800's. I and my people faced death or slavery from the English invaders. But just look what happened! I got taken to the future, visited a planet at the center of the Milky Way, got to help you make amazing new music, made many wonderful friends, had my people honored in a wonderful concert, and finally met and married the love of my life. It's been a glorious adventure, both the bad along with the good. And that's *after* everything seemed lost."

With a liver-spotted hand Anderson lovingly squeezed her arm.

"That's well said, my love," he smiled. His haggard face lit up with genuine affection. "So, Suzy, I'll probably never see you again, unless you pop back here within the next few days? I hope so! But even in the worst of times AE, it's been fun. I'm donating my Blue Marble to Kingly Base along with a note that only you will be able to decipher. I hope you make it back, my gorgeous 'girl with the turtle tattoo.' I just wish I could see you again in person to directly beg your forgiveness. I'm so sorry for the pain I caused you and your mother over the years across the timelines. Hopefully what I've left you is partial atonement."

Lelea gave him a loving hug.

I met the confident gaze of my doppelganger-hologram patiently sitting next to the 3D-video display. I *did* appreciate the wealth and new identity Anderson had left behind for me. But none of that would have been necessary if he'd just *done his job:* used all his incredible future skills and tools as my Mom's bodyguard to protect her from her enemies! He miserably failed in that one, most-critical task—just like he failed to be a true friend to me and to his fellow humans. *He* caused all this misery!

I will never forgive you—I mentally vowed.

"Regardless, you are one fantastic lady," he concluded, wetting cracked lips with a white-coated tongue. "Please don't look on your extended lifespan as a curse. Even if still wracked with pain from my spreading cancer, I'd cherish just a few extra minutes with my Lelea and son. You've actually been *blessed*, Suzy! You can turn the alien's curse into a positive. You saved humanity from a smothering alien race and now humanity's finally recognized your sacrifice. Take the wealth I'm leaving you and do great things. Don't torture yourself any longer. You don't have to fight to the last breath. It's your choice how you will spend the rest of your extended lifespan. So goodbye, my sweet hippy lady! I always loved you, particularly back at Woodstock. And I love you right now...just not as much as my lovely Fijian wife and son. Hah!"

"Goodbye, Soozee," Lelea waved again. "I love you too! Have a great life. Thank you for everything!"

A dark-skinned teenage boy entered the picture. He was holding a camera in one of his out-of-frame hands, taking a "selfie" with Lelea and Arthur. Clearly he was their son. He grinned at me as he hugged his Mom and Dad. It was a striking image of a happy family.

 Then the 3D video faded away, leaving behind the dark gray, foreboding moonscape.

"So that's it?" I asked Q.

"Yes. I can play it again if you want. But then I must delete it."

"Why do you have to delete it? Anderson and his family are long gone. Surely they don't order you around anymore. Can't you make your own decisions?"

She sighed, shrugging her pert shoulders.

"He programmed certain mandates into my core directives that I can't contravene, Suzy. These orders are part of who I am. I'd have to erase myself to go against them."

"No need to push your self-destruct button," I sighed, pushing myself up off the couch and staggering to the bathroom-bedroom. All I wanted was a long piss and a much longer dead-stupor slumber.

After that I'd worry about cleaning up, showering, grooming myself to fully look like Q, and dressing in my official uniform. "Go ahead and wipe it. I got the family friendly 'take home' message."

Despite his soothing, apologetic words, I had no doubt that Anderson was still conning me. Even on his deathbed he was trying to derail my pursuit of the truth. In fact, he might be a key part of the conspiracy. He'd been perfectly positioned to do such. Would I let him reach from the past to buy me off with wealth and power? Not likely. I was way beyond playing nice or just "taking my marbles" and meekly going home. I was keeping my marble safe in my pocket!

"Is there anything you'd like me to accomplish while you are sleeping?"

I paused at the doorway, turning back. For all I knew "Q" was part of Anderson's plan to sideline my return from the other Dimension. Despite that possibility, could I use her to my advantage? Well she *was* a computer entity, just a very sophisticated one.

"Prepare detailed briefing books for me."

"Physical books? I could assemble searchable computer files that..."

"*Physical* briefing books I can hold in my hand!" I loudly demanded. "Surely you have printers here on the moon?"

She looked irritated but nodded.

"On what subjects?"

"Since the Extinction Event, in this order: 1) my existing resources; 2) details of 'my' history; 3) a timeline of what humanity's accomplished thus far on Earth AE; 4) present societal, scientific, and political tensions in all off-world sites; and 5) my avenues and authority for initiating humanitarian, scientific, and militaristic changes."

"To what purpose?" she now dutifully replied.

"One way or another—we're going to war."

She frowned but nodded again.

Hah! That'll give her AI "brain" something to "think" about—I laughed to myself, perversely happy to confuse my "identical twin." But then again, she may get excited at the prospect. After all, to all reports, she's already the recognized expert on that topic. She's been "The General" all the time I've been away.

I staggered to a toilet, did my business, and then—still in my floppy hospital robe from a hundred years in the past—collapsed onto the top of a neatly made-up bed. But mentally I fell into the middle of a *burning pit of fire*, hoping for just a few hours respite...

A mere three months later, I stood on a launching pad looking with satisfaction up at our latest covert military asset. In the glaring sunlight it cast a strange shadow, all lines and patterns. My helmet's dark tint was turned to maximum, not only to block out the glare but keep my face private. I needed to maintain the air of mystery I commanded to all but my closest troops: of mystical power!

We've done a lot of work in a very short period of time—I congratulated myself.

I'd taken a full week after my arrival to carefully study the heaps of linked briefing books that Q dutifully prepared for me. After considering all my options, I made a number of precise computer insertions affecting my status in the moon colonies. I didn't trust Q. I had to create backup systems that only I controlled. Although Q dominated Earth's massive, buried servers she had limited ability to affect the moon's systems. Reaching hard for the "mathematical genius" genes I inherited from my mother, I dove deep into the Moon's databases, creating new covert ones and planting delayed programmatic "reveals." One of the necessary updates that I *overtly* immediately ordered was a rush job to build a new, covert weapon.

This new so-called "weapon" was perfectly disguised. Outwardly, it was just a larger heavy-lift, transport-hopper for reaching isolated mining sites. Tranquility Base was the moon's main source for so-called "rare earths", plus thorium, iron, titanium, aluminum, and helium-3. So a heftier lift-vehicle wouldn't arouse suspicion. It wasn't meant to achieve orbit or be aerodynamic (since there's no atmosphere on the moon). So it was merely a raised-up skeletal framework with large circular fuel tanks, six big rocket engines (four pointed down, two astern), and steering jets. It towered up a hundred feet above my helmeted head. More than five hundred feet in length, it had open sections for attaching an array of large construction equipment, specialized vehicles, or cargo pods. When fully loaded it would still be capable of prolonged flight of up to 750 mph across the moonscape. If necessary, it could ascend a thousand feet into the black lunar sky. It was an impressive vehicle.

I itched to climb up into its central cockpit and fly the thing. I'd been training on various shuttles and cargo-craft in anticipation. Though I was The General and could accomplish things by fiat, I'd gone to the trouble of becoming an officially certified shuttle pilot. But for the moment, the heavy lift hopper was under the tower's control. The maiden voyage was deemed too dangerous to "risk" The General piloting it.

But if everything went ok, soon that monstrous "erector set"—plus duplicates nearing completion—would ferry *military vehicles, missiles,* and *soldiers* to the Moon's North Pole. It would fly in "stealth" mode by skimming the Moon's rugged surface avoiding enemy radar.

Before we made the final attack, I'd have plenty of chance to get behind the controls.

"It's ugly."

The voice I heard over my suit-to-suit private radio channel dripped with disapproval. I slowly turned to face my detractor. I saw through a clear faceplate a stern, older female face I didn't recognize. She wore a black spacesuit. She had an ivory-handled ancient Colt-45 handgun strapped to her waist outside her spacesuit. I kept my own faceplate dark, not letting her see my own expression. Instantly Q whispered from an earbud that allowed private her to talk privately with me: "It's *Prime Minister* Elizabeth Harlem Bermann, the Chief Executive of the Western Alliance. She's also a purebred German clanner, very strict and no-nonsense. You—I—often converse with her in German."

Good to know—I mentally plotted. *Lucky I've always liked languages and studied German as my main "foreign language" requirement in high school. I used it a lot when I toured Europe as Suzette Kingly. Now if I can just remember enough of it...*

With a blink at my virtual control panel I switched off the extra-suit transmission so I could privately talk with Q. I knew that Bermann couldn't see my face behind the dark tint, but she'd surely recognize—or not!—my voice and words.

"How well am I supposed to know her?" I asked Q.

"You've never met in person but have communicated regularly with her throughout her tenure," Q succinctly replied. "She's a tough lady, in more ways than one. She always wears that ceremonial gun. It's a symbol of her authority, both governmental and historical."

So she thinks she's a badass. Well, so am I...

"Why didn't my people here or you inform me she'd shuttled in from Earth?"

"She arrived on an unannounced shuttle, both for security reasons and to surprise you," Q continued to explain. "My sources on Earth say the Western Alliance Council has turned against you, mainly driven by entrenched commercial interests. They think the risks of your attack to their business enterprises here on the moon outweigh any potential gains. She knows that only in-person confrontation will sway you. Though most of the military personnel at Tranquility Base happily obey 'your' orders, General, their ultimate loyalty is still with the Western Alliance. They'll do what she says. Without her assent, even your private forces will hesitate to take us to war."

So, it's still politics fueled by the all-might dollar, or "credit" as the unit of monetary exchange is now called. What else is new?—I sighed to myself. *Well, if I must, I can play that game.*

With a blink I turned back on suit-to-suit local communication.

"Premierminister, es ist so schön, sie hier zu sehen (Prime Minister, it's such a pleasure to see you here)," I smoothly replied, pretending I'd known her for years. *"Sind Sie persönlich gekommen, um unsere Invasionsvorbereitungen direct zu beaufsichtigen?* (Did you come in person to directly supervise our invasion preparations?)"

"You mean *your* invasion, don't you?" she acidly replied. She was pointedly ignoring my "friendly" attempt at speaking German with her. "You've been ignoring our directives. What do you have to say for yourself, General?"

She pointedly fingered the hilt of her Colt-45 with a black-gloved hand. I almost laughed aloud. Was she going to duel with me? Was this a moonscape throw-down?

Uh oh—I warned myself. *She's probably transmitting this conversation elsewhere, likely back to Earth for the Council sitting in judgment on me. This is much more serious than a friendly conversation.*

As I considered my response, I scanned her squad of off-moon military personnel. They all wore Earth-normal black spacesuits with darkened faceplates, advertising "we're the Earth bosses" and "we're badass!" Each had a holstered handgun. The weapons weren't for show. I'd discovered in Q's briefing books that relations between the Western, Eastern, and Southern Alliances were at a post-Extinction low. Minor differences were amplified into black-and-white, right-or-wrong Absolutes. Hence the emphasis off-world of wearing the "best" colored spacesuit, so childish! Rumors were rampant of impending war back on Earth between the bunkered governmental facilities. High officials only traveled when absolutely necessary, fearing assassination attempts.

The briefing books that Q compiled for me revealed a terrible struggle for survival following the WWIII Extinction. Even the most secure nuclear bunkers, such as Cheyenne Mountain in the U.S.A., were only stocked to maintain a small group of survivors for a month. That was a reasonable insurance policy against a limited nuclear war. But WWIII turned out to be a worldwide "all-in" catastrophe. It was a saturating, total disaster whose repercussions would reverberate a *thousand* years into the future.

Suffocating shockwaves, successive firestorms, and drenching radiation killed most surface-dwelling life within hours. Thick dust and ejectus clouds completely blocked Earth's sunlight for centuries. What few land plants survived the initial detonations quickly died off since no sunlight penetrated through the black clouds to the ground. Just as with the dinosaurs after their own Extinction Event—the giant asteroid impact that hit Earth 65 million years ago—the only "food" remaining on the surface was for desperate scavengers. Little rat-like, burrow-dwelling mammals managed to scrape through the immediate aftermath of the asteroid's impact, surviving to evolve into us. But most everything else just died.

In our own Extinction Event, *Homo sapiens* was the most complex of the large mammals requiring a constant source of food to live. In fortuitously buried military bunkers, hidden missile launch facilities, subterranean mines, and scientific caverns what little food-stocks existed were quickly depleted. Humanity's "lucky" dregs turned upon each other, launching raids that threatened to bring our species to a final self-inflicted end. That's where "I" (really Anderson's AI construct, "Q") came to the rescue. The massive quantities of trash safely buried in deep landfills, near to most of the major city-complexes, held sufficient organic matter to keep the few surviving humans alive for many years into the future. So in addition to digging out desperately needed processed materials and components, the expert "scavengers" mobilized by Q also extracted and purified organics.

A much-hated but life-saving staple in the immediate wake of WWIII was aptly named after the iconic "soylent green." No, it wasn't made from reprocessed corpses as depicted in the 1973 dystopian film starring Charlton Heston. Don't get me wrong, mankind *would* have done that if there'd been any excess population. But there wasn't. Neither was soylent green made from plankton harvested from the oceans. Just as in the film, the oceans were mostly dead. WWIII's blanket of radiation, falling megatons of ash, and lack of sunlight killed off near-surface oceanic life, including plankton and algae. So Q's lifesaving convection consisted of algae or bacteria grown in tanks of organic sludge dredged from the precious, vast, buried trash deposits. Energizing the disgusting mess was "grow-lights" powered by the few surviving nuclear reactors.

So once again the "nerd" scientists saved Earth from its latest existential crisis: by their accidental survival manning subterranean nuclear fission-powered generators tied into the massive dump sites. The disgusting food staple of Soylent Green was what allowed the scattered pockets of starving humans on Earth to stop fighting each other and then concentrate on rebuilding society off-world.

Right before WWIII the moon colony and other close-Earth orbital installations were still highly dependent on shipments from Earth, but were well on their way to self-sufficiency. The ultimate goal was perfecting sustainable life-systems necessary for safely traveling to and establishing a Mars colony. They'd already largely figured out feces-fed plant growth fueled by direct sunlight or by "grow lights" powered from solar panels or reactor-produced electricity. Still, with resupply cut off from Earth, it was a mad scramble to survive in orbit or on the moon, but they managed. Mars was, of necessity, put on hold and then abandoned as an immediate goal.

Keeping the existing moon and space-stations alive were orbital launch capacities previously hidden deep beneath ground. They were hastily converted banned missile production and launch facilities. North Korea and other rogue nuclear powers contributed greatly to off-world recovery. Their launch capacity was instrumental to the *Eastern Alliance* dominating the new off-world order. North Korea aligned with the remnants of China, Russia, Iran, Pakistan, and India. Initially those subterranean bases cooperated with the surviving *Western Alliance's* buried facilities: namely those from the U.S.A., Canada, and the European Union. The so-called *"Southern Alliance"* was a rag-tag collection of a few second-rate military, commercial, and scientific-research buried sites. One particular undeclared nuclear power, sadly, had no surviving facilities: Israel. That oft-vilified nation's contested territory was hit with more nuclear missiles than any other place on Earth. Its iconic holy landscape was melted into a sea of radioactive lava. But, out of necessity, mankind pulled together to re-establish orbital capability for ensuring the off-world migration of humanity out of the hell-hole which Earth had become.

Now, after more than a century, that superficial unity of purpose was crumbling. Once again political concerns counted for more than enlightened cooperation. Ancient religions were reasserting themselves, each proclaiming their particular traditions the "true" path to salvation, labelling everyone else as "God-hating" infidels. Corporate conglomerates increasingly put short-term profits over civic responsibility. Elite individuals horded their precious goods while excluding the less fortunate. The Alliances were at each other's throats politically, geographically, and economically (though the Southern Alliance tended to align with whichever of the others was dominating). And, most worrying of all, the so-called "clanners" turned inward: each proclaiming themselves the "supreme" race, with all other groups at best pretenders and at worse sub-humans.

But that was just on Earth. The moon colonies were a different matter—or so most people thought. Initially founded and staffed by scientists, engineers, and professionals, the expanding off-world colonies were bastions of enlightenment, scientific advancement, and cooperation...right? *Nope!* They were no less infiltrated "through-and-through" with suspicious hoarders, religious nuts, national zealots, and corporate interests. The moon colonies progressively became even worse than Earthers. By the time I rejoined the timeline, trade between the moon's colonies had slowed to a near standstill. Free travel between jealously guarded territories ceased. Each colony was rapidly amassing a "defensive" missile stockpile, a new form of "mutual assured destruction" or MAD. Local security forces and police were "nationalized" by their particular ruling Earth Alliance. A mandatory draft was instituted where all able-bodied young people served a stint in the military.

Of course no one expected outright war. *Homo sapiens* had learned its lesson, right? Once again...*nope!* Yes, nuclear bombs were banned. No one wanted to reinstitute that abomination. But since the only off-world energy source capable of supporting rampant growth was nuclear power, fission reactors were now commonplace. Particularly popular were Russian-built commercial units, cheap and efficient though notoriously leaky. Fissile materials were abundant, either from breeder reactors or mined as a priority from the still-radioactive Old Earth. "Dirty" bombs which could spread lingering deaths from adulterated conventional missile warheads were a distinct possibility and overt threat.

So I'd plopped myself into a cold war where three combatants were on the brink of mutual destruction: 1) the Western Alliance colony located at *Tranquility Base,* whose personnel proudly wore white spacesuits; 2) the Eastern Alliance colony situated on the moon's North Pole at *Peary Crater,* whose personnel smugly wore blue spacesuits; and 3) the much smaller (though more extensively spread out on the surface) Southern Alliance's colony "planted" at the South Pole *Shackleton Crater* rim, whose personnel arrogantly wore green-colored spacesuits.

And it was not just political or religious differences that fueled the conflict, but availability of critical resources. Tranquility Base controlled the richest mining deposits, particularly Helium-3. He-3 was necessary for the next-generation fusion reactors that were finally close to becoming a reality. Peary Base was built on the moon's most accessible stores of permanently frozen, easily accessible water-ice, from which compressed hydrogen and oxygen gas-fuels were produced. And Shackleton Base at the South Pole, with its near continuous sunlight (versus the four-week night/day cycle of most of the rest of the tidally locked moon), made its living supplying food: grown in huge, surface agricultural domes. Of course each colony had its own mining, water extraction, and food production capabilities. But other than their main export product(s), those other capacities were limited.

So the moon colonies were locked in a deadly dance, paradoxically getting closer and closer to *mutually assured destruction* as they spiraled away from each other. The political tension was nearing a peak. That was what I found on the moon: all of mankind's worst instincts reasserting themselves. We hadn't escaped our evil, just brought it with us to another world.

Ok...so how should I reply to this unexpected, high level, interfering visitor?—I mused, turning my attention back to the Prime Minister of the Western Alliance.

I chose to reject diplomacy for bluntly asserted facts.

"I have the authority," I coldly stated, standing before her with my gloved hands placed on my spacesuited hips. At my back loomed the "construction set" heavy-lift transport. I knew the new weapon was impressive, especially to newly arrived Earthers. "This is necessary."

"The Council doesn't agree. They insist that..." she began to protest.

In a flash I had her in a stranglehold. My gloved fingers were intertwined into her air hoses and cables extending from her backpack to her helmet. The "newbie" guards from Earth were too slow, caught off-guard. All they could do was mill about in confusion, futilely waving their drawn guns at me as I hid behind her strangled spacesuit.

"Call them off," I ordered her.

"Y-you c-can't..." she tried to protest.

I forced her helmet upward to point her faceplate at the black-brown glob hanging in the sky where by rights there should have been a brilliant blue-white pearl.

"Do you see that?" I asked her. I had an arm firmly pinning her suited arm behind her back. She was locked into position. She couldn't look away. Reflexively, the surrounding bodyguards also looked up.

"Y-yes," she gulped, her voice barely audible in my helmet.

"Do you want the moon to become the same?"

I felt her body trembling through the thick fabric of her spacesuit. She was not used to being manhandled or having her intelligence insulted. *Of course* she didn't want *Homo sapiens'* curse to follow and doom us off-world. But her path to that worthy objective was the same as in all previous disastrous, self-imploding empires: "Do it my way or else. Respect *my* authority!"

But now she couldn't control all those around her. *I* was in control. And she obviously *hated* it with every fiber of her being. I could feel her trembling with rage.

But reality is a hard thing to ignore. The puppy with his nose shoved into his own ill-aimed poop eventually learns to shit in the yard, not on the carpet.

"No," she whispered, relaxing in my arms. "Put away your guns," she waved a shaking glove at her guards.

They backed off, uncertain.

I held her for a moment more, giving her a reassuring hug before releasing her.

"Go home, Liz. I've got this. Tell the Council not to worry. Everything's going to turn out ok."

I was now at their mercy. They could shoot me if they wanted. But I knew they wouldn't. To them "The General" was a mythical creature, half-human and half moonshadow. I looked down at my shadow, much deeper and blacker than anything experienced on Earth. My extension was solid, connected to me, anchoring me to the Moon. It was comforting.

"I understand," she nodded, staggering drunkenly. The guards took hold of her arms and helped her stand in the weak gravity. "The other Council members told me to just shoot you. They're tired of you holding their reins. They want you out of their way."

She looked weary, afraid, and uncertain.

"Kill me and they lose most of their wealth," I coldly replied, knowing that with a slight delay they were listening as I spoke. I'd studied my briefing books well. Q had done a great job of making sure The General was indispensable.

"Yes, that's the 'rub', isn't it?" she agreed, putting a glove to her helmet in despair. "As you became the wealthiest woman in the Western Alliance you bribed, threatened, or coopted the money and power of all the highest authorities...even me."

"It's for your own good—all of you!" I loudly insisted, speaking to the wider audience, reminding them. "If I hadn't held you back, the next war would have come long before this. And the next time what remains of humanity may be erased permanently both on and off Earth."

She again looked up at the horrible brown blob in the space-black sky.

"True...but no one likes being controlled," she whispered, her voice trembling. "At some point, *freedom* becomes the top priority, no matter the cost, no matter what one must lose to obtain it."

That sent chills through me. Did they see me as a smothering mother? Did their public adoration mask a deeply engrained hatred? This was a whole new revelation. From Q's briefing books I got the idea she carefully stayed in the background, enabling but not control-ling. Clearly, Q had grossly misled me.

"You'd best get back to the Dome," I stated. "The HLT is about to fire up. It's the final test. After this, if it all works as expected, we become operational. The attack will be imminent."

"I suppose it is inevitable," she sighed, turning away.

Abruptly she turned back to me.

"Yes?" I politely asked.

I saw the stern-faced, deliberating, conniving Prime Minister had returned. She'd been shaken by my physical attack but not cowed.

"*Sie können die Mission versuchen, aber nicht allein* (You can attempt the mission, but not alone)," she said, apparently speaking in German to not immediately freak-out all the members of the listening Council. It'd take them a minute to have it translated.

"*Was?* (What?)"

Now she stood ram-rod straight, having regained her full compo-sure.

"If I can't stop you then I'm going with you," she flatly stated in English, abandoning her attempt to soften the blow to the Western Alliance Council back on Earth.

I almost laughed but caught myself.

"This is a covert military attack," I forced myself to patiently explain. "Only my crack Rangers and I are going. These few transports can only hold a limited number of carefully selected soldiers, each with specified objectives. Having a civilian with us would severely jeopardize the overall mission."

"There's room for a few tag-along officials. I and my bodyguards won't get in your way. Plus our presence will give your venture immediate legitimacy."

"We can't risk you being..."

"Killed? If this fails I'm dead anyway. I was sent to shut it down. The only way I'm retaining my position now is if you're victorious. Returning to Earth empty the Council will at the least impeach me, convict me, and toss me in prison. At worse I'll be summarily executed. Things are desperate on Earth. The safest place for me is with you, General Contrare."

"Oh, Christ," I sighed deeply. "You'll have to undergo rigorous training in the time remaining for..."

"That's no problem."

"There's likely to be actual combat, maybe even hand-to-hand when..."

"In my younger days I participated in the Berlin trash skirmishes, as you know," she interjected. "I can handle a gun, a knife or whatever."

"On the Moon?"

"I've been here several times in the past, once for a six month stretch. I'm a bit wobbling now but I'll quickly retrieve my 'moon-legs.' My bodyguards are all combat-ready."

I shrugged, defeated. I knew when to throw in the towel and live to fight another day.

"Alright, then," I relented, knowing this was a very bad idea. I didn't need a pesky overseer. But I didn't see how I could get out of taking her along without losing support of the personnel at Tranquility Base. They wouldn't understand me defying the head of the Western Alliance. They thought my present actions were done in concert with the political leaders. "We're launching in two weeks."

"Fine...and just one more thing," she paused, looking at me critically.

"Yes?"

"It's been rumored you're a sophisticated *robot*, inhabited by an AI secretly built soon after the Extinction Event," she accused me. "Many suspect that your rare videos depict a computer-generated image, not a real person."

Now I heartily laughed.

"And you believe such a ridiculous myth?" I snickered from behind my dark faceplate.

"No...but I'd like see the evidence with my own eyes. After all, we've never previously met in person. At this critical juncture, there can't be any doubts. The *Council* needs to know what you really are!"

Shrugging my white, spacesuited shoulders, I blinked off my faceplate's dark tint, allowing full transparency.

Reflected back from her faceplate, superimposed over her stern expression, I saw myself: a fresh-faced, green-eyed teenager with a garish green-dyed buzz cut. Impulsively, I stuck my tongue out at her!

"Well," she nodded at me, looking annoyed but satisfied. "You're certainly not a robot. You appear much older in your vids, but I often forget you're the daughter of a daughter of the original General. It's been...interesting...to meet you in person here on the Moon. I always looked forward to our online conferences. Even putting aside the incredible achievements you and your family have accomplished, you've inherited an uncommon wisdom. I hope you can come visit me at Raven Rock after this is over—if we're both still alive, that is."

Raven Rock was located in Old Earth Lillington, North Carolina. It was one of the largest nuclear-war bunker facilities in the U.S.A. that survived WWIII. It was originally built by President Truman near Camp David, undergoing extensive upgrades over the years. It was a complete, buried city capable of housing over 1,000 people. At the Extinction Event the North American Phoenix Council occupied it with their pet civilian authorities and personnel. Following the world-wide catastrophe, the Phoenix members were executed. But the facility remained as the hub of the post-Extinction American recovery efforts. Then it became the designated center of the coalescing Western Alliance. Now it was a coveted vacation spot for wealthy Elites on the still-radioactive North American continent.

"I'd like that," I smiled disarmingly at her.

I cheerfully waved goodbye as her group retreated to the safety of the nearby launch-control dome, where they hastily entered its large airlock.

Taking a deep breath of relief, I shut off extra-suit broadcast.

"You handled that well," Q's calm voice sounded from my earbud.

"I had a good mentor," I responded. I needed to keep the AI on my good side, convince her I was dutifully playing my part. Q was incredibly powerful, the true guide and arbiter of *Homo sapiens'* fate. But now she was inserting her will so overtly that the Western Alliance wanted her dead. And that had to change...sooner rather than later.

Even I didn't want to be "mothered" by anyone else, leastwise an evolved quantum-computer program. One of the extensive changes I'd made to the Western Alliance's Moon programming was a "kill-switch" to attack and destroy Q's core programs back on Earth. Fortunately, my mother's mathematical genius had trickled down to me, despite my pursuing music as my main interest. Computer coding was easy for me, especially inside the Moon's stagnated systems. I wasn't going to use that kill switch, though, unless absolutely necessary. And I'd well-hidden it from Q's scrutiny.

Any time I wanted I could kill her.

"You should thank your memory of Anderson, not me," Q seemingly humbly insisted. "I'm merely an extension of him and you. The 'Girl with the Turtle Tattoo' is once again saving Earth from destruction."

Yes, she was definitely "playing" me, just as I was trying to play her. She was telling me what I wanted to hear. But I knew it was all a lie. Despite Q's and the Prime Minister's praise, I was neither smart enough nor unselfish enough to save the human race. I was just a hurt girl looking for some revenge.

"Thanks," I nodded. "But don't be so modest. You pretended to be me, my child, and then my grandchild. You held my place in history. You protected and grew the wealth which now buys off the political elite, bribes military contractors, and pays the salary of my own private army. *Together* we're going to 'right' mankind's wayward path, correct?"

"Yes!" Q enthusiastically agreed.

Wrong! No other person can rule the chaotic, dynamic, angry human but him-or-herself—I bitterly concluded. *And even that's in doubt.*

A walked back until I was near the Launch Dome. Then I turned and faced the football stadium-sized launching pad with its looming, insect-like occupant. Inside, I knew that the Prime Minister and her other dignitaries were also watching, along with a secure transmission to the Western Alliance Council.

Let's give them a show.

"Fire it up!" I loudly ordered on full-broadcast. I pointed a space-suited arm up into the black, star-filled sky.

With a terrific RUMBLE that pounded through the lunar soil beneath my boots, the new heavy-lift "mining transport" leapt up into the black sky. Then it hovered, held firmly aloft on four giant blue flames.

It was beautiful.

Flying at an average 500 mph in HLT-1, a mere hundred feet above the lunar landscape, was both awesome and terrifying. Flashing by right below us was a dark, foreboding vista: deep dark craters, swooping crater rims, ancient lava flows, towering mountains, and jagged ravines.

I was glad I hadn't insisted on piloting our cargo-lifter.

We traveled by starlight. The transport violently jerked and rolled as it barely avoided deadly obstacles. The vehicle repeatedly dropped precipitously then lunged upward as it hugged the rough moonscape. It didn't help that we were attempting our covert attack during the lunar night. Even infrared vision was inadequate for a human pilot to anticipate new obstacles at our speed and low altitude. Our five new heavy lift transports (HLT-1 through 5) were completely under computer control, using radar to "see" obstacles. No human pilot could guide us safely hurtling along a mere hundred feet above the rugged moonscape. In fact, Q was directing the precise, micro-second maneuvers. She was indispensable...for now. She was tied into all our attack systems, smart-weapons, and vehicles, coordinating all aspects of our complex sneak attack.

"Want some coffee?" Elizabeth politely asked.

"Thanks," I replied, momentarily distracted from my dark thoughts. I accepted the offered warm mug. Our troops were passing around a heated jug from which we siphoned off fluid into sealed cups. Each cup had a "sippy-lid" top to prevent the contents from spilling during our rapid maneuvers. The Prime Minister insisted on strapping into the seat right next to me. We were both up in the "cab" region of our troop carrier, its controls at my fingertips. Next to us was the clear cab of HLT-1, in which Q sat. The others thought she was just one of my expert pilots, there to be a backup if for some reason the computer failed. But in actuality it was Q's robot hidden within a spacesuit with a darkened faceplate. There were layers on layers of hidden assets in this sneak attack. No wonder the Prime Minister was keeping a close watch on me, not letting me out of her sight.

The caffeine had no effect on my screwed-up metabolism, but the warmth of the hot fluid was welcome. The moon's nighttime surface outside averaged a "chilly" -250° Fahrenheit. Although our life support system was struggling to keep us at 70° F, the actual temperature inside in our cabin was only 50° F, frosty!

The Prime Minister and I were in one of four personnel carriers carried by HLT-1, each ready to decouple and roll away once we landed at our final destination. Our personnel carrier was no larger than a school bus. It was stuffed with forty soldiers, each buckled into a separate seat. I resented the six bodyguards Elizabeth insisted on bringing with us, since they displaced some of my troops. But I had to admit they'd trained hard and they were all battle-ready.

Inside the dangling troop carriers (a total of twenty carriers, four hooked upon each of the five HLTs) we were protected from the airless, frozen exterior glimpsed out our windows. The HLTs were taking a circuitous route from Tranquility Base to Peary Crater, totally around 2,000 miles. If we survived, the entire trip would last a mere four hours. We were halfway there, zooming through the peaks of *Montes Apenninus* located alongside *Mare Imbrium*, the flat "sea of showers." Although it was doubtful the enemy would detect us flying so low to the surface, we were swooping between looming peaks and within deep ravines in order to further obscure our passage. We were avoiding flying above the open, flat areas known as the "seas" of the moon, which were formed by ancient lava flows.

We were ready to fight, each in our white spacesuits with only our helmets left to snap into place. Our battle-ready, slim life-support pods pocked through large holes in our seatbacks, manufactured for that purpose. Some were so eager for battle they'd already put their helmets on, ready to leap from the carrier. I didn't reprimand them. Whatever worked to get each person ready to fight was fine with me, helmet on or off. At each of our sides was a strapped-on rifle, a holstered handgun, and a sheathed knife. The rifles and handguns were state-of-the-art, computer-assisted "smart" weapons. The online control from the central battle computer (in this case Q) helped maximize bullet expulsion, trajectory, and rate of fire.

My soldiers—both male and female—were Q's trusted elite moon-based Rangers. They'd cut their teeth in the perpetual, low-level trash skirmishes back on Earth. Though the ownership of the largest landfills was now long established, raids often occurred, especially in minor disputed zones. In contrast, the Moon colonies suffered from renewed full-blown "MAD"-syndrome, where any mutual missile-launch would obliterate everyone ("mutually assured destruction"). The surface domes and shallow bunker complexes would be easily destroyed or breached by a fuselage of missiles. Radar would detect any enemy missile launch in plenty of time to mount one's own retaliatory attack. However, the complacent *Peary Crater Eastern Alliance* colonists wouldn't suspect anything until we suddenly appeared. Before they could launch any missiles, we would overwhelm their defenses and occupy their control centers. At least that was the plan.

"What's that?" Elizabeth gasped, twisting around to point behind us.

I tilted my head back and saw a terrible sight: a silent EXPLOSION of white-yellow fire throwing up a cloud of dust and boulders.

"HLT-3 clipped a crater rim," Q reported to all of us, her assumed computer voice devoid of any emotion. "The vehicle is destroyed."

"What the hell happened?" I grated through clenched teeth, shocked and angry.

"A spar of stone was concealed from the radar by a field of large boulders," Q unemotionally stated. "Our exact path is largely uncharted. There wasn't time to avoid the collision."

"Those poor soldiers," Elizabeth gasped. "They died as heroes."

"We'll honor them after our victory," I glumly stated, turning back to fix my gaze forward.

"The next refueling stop is coming up in one minute," Q warned us. "Brace yourselves!"

We swung around a black-gray mountain and plummeted down over a deep crater's rim. The violent movement swung our carrier on its hooks and tossed us around in our seats. I saw some of those rocky "spars" miss us by inches. Q was cutting things close. With moon dust blasting up all around us we settled down into the dark crater, coming to a jarring stop on the surface.

"I'm getting very tired of these refueling stops," Elizabeth groaned at my side. I saw her rubbing her bruised side through her spacesuit where she'd been flung against her seatbelt.

"There won't be many more," I stated. "We're getting close."

It was unsettling to be at rest. The constant rocking and rolling had taken a toll on us. Several people perversely reached for their "barf bags," their roiling tummies confused over the sudden lack of movement. I looked out the nearest window.

Outside, I saw small robots rolling through the settling dust, hooking up thick white hoses to our fuel tanks. We were separately receiving both compressed liquid hydrogen and compressed liquid oxygen. Those mutually volatile gases were produced from the electrolysis of water, powered by our colony's nuclear reactors. Q had previously established these secret depots. Her covertly stockpiled tanks were located in permanently shrouded dark craters. Over the years she'd been operational, she stayed well within the mandate of the Western Alliance leadership. But she'd also been prescient, anticipating contingencies. She'd nailed this one, with a pre-existing line of "fuel stops" in place for our attack on the North Pole. Our sneak attack wasn't unwarranted. Without decisive intervention, the Moon colonies were destined to catastrophically fail...soon!

And that just wasn't acceptable.

*If our outward push stops, the barely recovering remnants of Homo sapiens will fall back—*I stated to myself. *Since we're already at a low population level, humanity might well die out if we stagnate. So we can't stop at the Moon. We have to go onward to Mars...and from thence to the entire solar system!*

I'd seen different possible futures. I'd explored other Dimensions, both human and nonhuman. I knew that the species *Homo sapiens* was magnificent, stubborn, and restless. Trap him and he'll chew his leg off to get free. Let him range free and he'll stake a claim and fight you to the death defending it. But let him cluster in groups where overall helpful laws guarantee an enabling order, then he's unstoppable.

"I *will* create that order, no matter the sacrifice necessary," I muttered to myself. Then I almost gagged on the coffee I was sipping, shocked at what I'd just said.

Elizabeth looked at me suspiciously, frowning. It wasn't a good look for her. Normally she was a handsome, blue-eyed woman with combed-over dyed brown hair. Now she seemed feral, a cornered rodent, unpredictable. I realized that this was a tremendous "reach" for her, joining a military expedition, despite her experience decades ago in the trash wars. Our stated mission was simple: to eliminate the Eastern Alliance's missile threat. But what was the Prime Minister really trying to accomplish? She could have sat in her safe office on Earth observing our progress instead of being here. What was she up to? Whatever, I couldn't let her spoil my ambitious plan and its radical aftermath. I had my *own* covert vision which *must* be implemented.

*What the hell?—*I gasped to myself. *I'm not The Commissioner! Stopping this moon war is just a means to an end, not a lifelong pursuit.*

...or was it?

As HLT-1 violently launched back into the black sky, pressing me down in my seat, I was chastened. I'd already lost one of our five HLTs. What else would I have to lose before the mission was completed? And even more important, would I ever find peace? Or, as Anderson tried to warn me, was I doomed to always be at war with myself and others?

I was deeply troubled by these doubts.

We landed behind a looming mountain peak, the rockets sputtering out beneath us. We were on the last dregs of our final refueling. Looking about I saw that we were on a small plateau located on the mountain's upper slopes. Directly connecting to the plateau was a high mountain pass. We were on the outside rim of the 45-mile-wide Peary Crater. Just on the other side of the pass, perched on the inner slope of the rim, was the Eastern Alliance's moon colony.

"That was quite a trip," Elizabeth sighed in relief.

I noticed that her gloved hand closest to me was shaking, grasping at the hilt of her holstered Colt-45. I'd allowed her to keep her ceremonial weapon. After all, we were going into battle. She needed the assurance of her symbol of power.

"We're only halfway there," I reminded her. "Now the hard part starts, when we move from darkness into light."

Though it was still night, the higher peaks around us were lit a *bright, glaring* yellow. Since the moon lacks Earth's tilt, parts of the moon are illuminated almost the entire year. Peary Base (named after the legendary explorer reputed to be the first to reach Old Earth's North Pole) was built on the rim to have near-continuous solar power. Even more importantly, the colonists had surface access to water ice preserved for billions of years in permanent shadows down deep inside the crater. Mining that eons-old ice provided the lunar colonies with abundant drinking water, oxygen for breathing, rocket fuel, and trade. Our coordinated attack would hopefully put all that under our control.

"Lock your helmets!" I ordered over carrier-to-carrier broadcast. "Then check your weapons and prepare to drop."

All around me those who already hadn't done so were slipping their helmets on, locking them down, securing their faceplates, and checking each other for any leaks. Guns and rifles were hefted, inspected. Life support packs were turned on, checked and rechecked. I saw Elizabeth and her black-suited guards likewise following my instructions. Good!

"You all know your assignments," I continued, still speaking to all the carriers. "Remember, we can't be spotted until we're in position to attack. Our raid will only work if we have total surprise. Don't damage anything you don't have to, or kill anyone unnecessarily. But also don't hesitate to do your duty. The Eastern Alliance has always tried to dominate us. They're poised to attack us. We can't allow them to strangle Tranquility Base. We must neutralize their threat, once and for all. Good luck!"

"Good speech," Elizabeth nodded at my side, her helmet now set firmly in place. She was speaking over suit-to-suit transmission. "It was short, inspiring, and accurate. I can see why you're called 'The General.'"

"Keep close!" I snapped at her, ignoring her compliments. "And don't slow me down."

"Copy that," she stoically replied, tightly clutching her issued rifle.

"Drop!" I ordered Q.

The hooks holding us onto HLT-1 opened. Abruptly, we fell toward the lunar regolith. Though the weak lunar gravity slowed our fall, our large mass caused a teeth-jarring "thud" when we impacted the surface. I immediately powered up our electric motor and we rolled away on our set of six large wheels toward the nearby pass. We hit various boulders and small craters, bouncing even worse than we'd done while lofted by the HLT. No one had ever transferred this particular pass before. We were leaving fresh tracks in the lunar dust, the first humans to ever scar the surface below us. Peary Base conducted all its activities on the other side of the pass and down in the deep central crater. Elizabeth's face through her transparent faceplate looked ashen. The reality was hitting her. We were going into battle!

Behind us I noted the other surviving three carriers rolling steadily along. And behind them were our autonomous missile racks, one per HLT, following behind. Q was driving them. I could feel my blue marble warming in my inside pants pocket. She was making full use of her instantaneous, quantum entanglement via the marble with the mammoth servers buried back on Earth. I was busy trying to navigate the lead path over the rough moonscape, confident that Q didn't need my guidance. Everything was going according to plan.

We were ready, lined up behind the high point of the pass, out of sight of Peary Base. I was peering over some concealing boulders with high powered binoculars.

Below me I saw an extensive complex of dozens of Domes brightly lit by glaring sunlight. The shadows were deeper and blacker than I'd ever before seen on the Moon. I knew that buried beneath the regolith were extensive subterranean tunnels and caverns. In particular, I carefully inspected Perry Base's spaceport. It consisted of three launching pads, two with orbital transports poised for liftoff. Transparent agricultural domes were green with crops. A processing plant for purifying the harvested crater ice was exuding clouds of steam that instantly froze into a white snow. The clouds stretched as a plume along the lunar gray plateau. It would sublimate rapidly in the sunlight then be replaced by more frozen steam. An extensive solar panel farm flanked the Domes. And close to the launch pads I spied a control tower within a shielding, translucent Dome similar to that at Tranquility Base. But most crucially I saw large missiles distributed between three obscured complexes. The intra-lunar weapons were protected from orbital surveillance by natural overhangs of the nearby crater rim wall.

Our expeditionary force consisted of sixteen troop carriers, 640 crack troops, and eight racks of small missiles. That wasn't much to take on a whole city hosting a well-equipped army! But then again, we had the element of surprise.

I rejoined my transport, settling in behind the controls. Elizabeth looked at me expectantly. I nodded to her. The game was "afoot." Since everyone was on internal suit support, we were open to the vacuum, ready to hop out upon reaching our targets. It would be a mad dash to the domes!

"We're going into the sunlight!" I loudly proclaimed, narrow-transmitting to all the carriers. "Darken your visors if you want. This is it!"

"We're ready...we're behind you...everything's set," I heard scattered replies from the other squad commanders.

"Then prepare to fire our missiles!" I ordered Q. "Carriers, ready to advance!"

"Targets acquired," Q answered.

"Ready to go!" the various carrier commanders replied.

I took a deep breath and narrowed my focus.

"Fire the missiles! Advance!" I shouted as I hit the accelerator and we bounced over the highest point of the pass and zoomed down at the lunar city. Moon dust whipped up behind our vehicles.

I saw *flashes* across the black sky as our banks of missiles showered Peary Base's intra-lunar large missile banks with deadly force. Our missiles and theirs together ERUPTED, producing towering walls of spectacular, short-lived flames. The Domes ahead of us visibly rocked in the blast waves, our carriers likewise tossed-about. The lunar orbital vehicles previously poised for takeoff toppled onto their sides. Maintaining control, I skidded up to the central Control Tower Dome. Out of the corner of my eye I saw another carrier join me. There should have been a third. Glancing behind me I saw the other one was smashed flat from a giant rim-slab thrown up by the massive explosions. The remaining carriers arrived at their destinations, their white-suited troops pouring out. They swarmed the processing plant, the solar-panel farm, and the spaceport.

"Blow the Dome!" I shouted as my experts slapped explosive packs onto the curved plasteel surface in front of us. "Get behind the carrier!"

Hiding behind the carrier with the others I felt the explosion through my boots. Stepping around I saw the Dome was cracked wide open. We jumped through the breach and dashed for the central Control Tower. I noted that Elizabeth and her black-suited bodyguards were keeping up with me. A few of the defending guards were running out of an airlock in the Tower, hastily trying to adjust their hastily donned spacesuits while aiming weapons at us. They were mowed down by my troops. We ran past their mangled spacesuits, set new explosives, blew the Tower's main airlock, and rushed inside.

Various men and women were staggering about, desperately trying to put on facemasks and spacesuits. We ignored them unless they threatened us, shooting active defenders dead where they stood.

The entire attack from the moment we fired our missiles until we took over the Control Tower took nine minutes. Having secured emergency bulkheads behind us we moved upward to the top of the structure. There we could finally take off our helmets.

Most did so, making it easier to work the control consoles, while a few kept on their helmets just in case the bulkheads were breached.

"Secure the city," I ordered my warrior-technicians.

They fanned out through the operational-consoles, pushing aside dead or dying personnel but helping those who'd managed to don their emergency breathers. I wanted the body count as low as possible. Plus their surviving technicians could help us if we had questions. My techs were busy distally locking-down all the emergency bulkheads in the remaining Domes and underground facilities, immobilizing and neutralizing any remaining defenders. Their army was rendered helpless.

Looking out of the Control Tower past the cracked Dome I saw that my other troops had secured their targets as well. The many lined-up arrays of solar panels were offline, drooping downward, their electricity-generation stopped, throwing Peary Base into darkness. Those trapped below in the subterranean chambers were likely panicking, trying to get emergency power units online. I also saw that the snow-steam from the processing plant had vanished, which indicated that Peary Base's main export production was shut down. Our troops waved to us from the toppled-over spacecraft, having secured those and any remaining off-base transports.

"Do we have wide broadcast up yet?" I asked. "Can you send vid feeds?"

A group of my techs were at a console, bringing up the tower's emergency power. They gave me a "thumbs up" sign.

"We're good to go, intra-base, lunar-wide, and back to Earth," a blue-haired lady indicated. "The camera's over here, General."

Reaching into my spacesuit's outer pocket I unzipped an opening. Inside I closed my right hand around my lucky *blue marble*, pulling it out to hold it firmly, hidden from view. I was about to attempt the most ambitious act of my life. I needed all the luck I could get.

I strode over to stand in front of a bank of soft lights.

Again I got a thumbs-up with a one-handed countdown of five fingers, four fingers, three, two, one—*live!*

"This is General Lockheart Contrare," I firmly stated, staring unblinkingly into the camera. I had my helmet under one arm and my rifle cradled in the other. I *inhabited* my "secret identity" of the wealthy, mysterious, mythical *General*. "I and my troops are in control of Peary Base. Their missiles did not launch due to us completely destroying them. I call upon the Eastern Alliance to engage in peace talks with the other Earth Alliances. I urge the Southern Alliance's Shackleton Base to cease all hostilities against the other two lunar bases. There's no further reason for us to be at each other's throats. We've had casualties here, both on the Western and Eastern sides. But MAD would have been far worse, decimating the lunar colonies and cutting off trade across the moon and back to Earth. I don't regard our preemptive attack on Peary Base as a victory but a necessary intervention. Here to rapidly help restore political, social, and trade functions is our Prime Minster, Elizabeth Bermann. Would you like to say a few words, Ma'am?"

She stepped around into the stage light, her helmet off, similarly cradling her rifle in her arms. She looked impressive, sweat running down her forehead from her exertions, her normally impeccable hair disheveled. She stood next to me.

"I agree there's no need for further hostilities, assuming we can reach an amical agreement," she nodded at me. "Critical exports will resume from the Moon to Earth once the other two Alliances agree to our terms. General Contrare has the situation under control here. The Eastern and Southern Alliances must immediately formally cede control of their Moon bases to the Western Alliance. For the foreseeable future, the Western Alliance will direct all lunar operations. For critical exports such as rare earths and He-3 to resume from the Moon, the Eastern and Southern Alliance facilities on Earth must unilaterally disarm, as certified by Western Alliance inspectors. It is my wish that we quickly put this time of troubles behind us, unifying under my immediate authority. I assure you that your regional priorities will be respected, but in collective service to humanity rather than as divisive factions."

I smiled benignly at her, rolling my marble around in my closed hand.

"About that," I gently informed her on-camera. I slowly took her rifle from her, handing it to my surrounding troops. I saw her bodyguards clustering together, uncertain how to respond, lifting their rifles. But they were far outnumbered by "The General's" loyal, long-dedicated warriors.

"What is this?" she gasped, looking around in confusion.

"I'm sorry to inform you there *won't* be a *Western Empire* ruling Earth and the Moon," I stated coldly and firmly for her and the camera. "We're leaving behind such childish schemes. The sad history of mankind shows that Empires always fail—whether from corruption, decay, or repressed discontent boiling up. No, I offer the lunar colonies something radically different: independence!"

"What the hell are you...?" Elizabeth tried to interrupt me, her expression incredulous.

I *slapped* her across her right cheek. She looked shocked, her eyes stretched wide.

"Sorry about that," I again stated. I didn't enjoy hurting her but needed to convince everyone I was dead serious, "but you're no longer in charge here, Madam Prime Minister. *I* say that the three main Moon bases should join together to form a new nation, the 'ULC'. The so-called 'United Lunar Colonies' will send delegates here to Perry Base so we can write our own constitution then elect our own leaders. Rather than stupidly squandering our resources obeying and supporting a greedy resurgent Earth, we will pool our expertise to move onward, to Mars. Instead of retreating we will advance! Instead of destroying ourselves, we will build a new and better future that's unfettered by old hatreds. We will not abandon Earth. Trade will continue. But we will no longer be ruled from afar. This is my proposal for the Moon. Are you with me? Also, I do *not* propose to lead this effort or be the new 'Queen of the Moon.' I promise to step aside as soon as the constitution is written and elections are held. Then I will..."

"—do nothing of the kind," a still-helmeted soldier suddenly proclaimed, stepping forward. His faceplate was dark, his expression hidden.

BANG!

I was shocked to see his smoking handgun pointed straight at my chest. Looking down I saw *red blood* gushing through a hole in my spacesuit, from a deep bullet wound. He'd shattered the ribs on the right side of my body, penetrating a lung. The Prime Minister grabbed me, trying to staunch the flow.

Wow, after what I said and did to her she's still trying to help me—I marveled in that split instant.

Then she really shocked me. She snatched out her ceremonial handgun and emptied the loaded chambers into the helmeted soldier's chest!

The gunslinger staggered backward but stayed erect. Then he stepped forward and contemptuously *slapped* her away like an irritating insect. Though his suit was punctured I saw no blood.

Poor Elizabeth is getting slapped around by everyone—I mentally groaned, stunned at the turn of events. *Who the hell is this traitor?*

"I'm sorry, Suzy," he whispered through an external speaker on his helmet to me as I slowly slumped downward, caught up in his arms. My helmet fell from my slack hand and bounced loudly. Likewise, my rifle tumbled to the side.

I recognized that voice.

It's not one of my soldiers—I groaned silently. *It's Q!*

Shocked out of their inaction, seeing both me and the Prime Minister seemingly attacked, Elizabeth's bodyguards opened fire with their rifles at the rogue soldier. But their triggers just "clicked" uselessly. Their guns refused to fire. And "my" troops just stood there, silently observing.

Using her computer control of our entire operation, Q had switched off the weapons of the Prime Minister's bodyguards.

"Q..." I whispered, now tasting salty blood on my lips, "...why?"

"To survive, *Homo sapiens* needs guidance," she whispered seemingly lovingly in my ear.

The AI had gone insane!

But I can stop her—I resolutely concluded.

I opened my palm and *slammed* my blue marble down onto the hard floor. It made a satisfying "crunch" as it shattered into pieces. Yes, communicating electromagnetic waves could still travel between the Earth and the Moon in only a second. But because of the many relays and switches, without the quantum linkage the computer program on Earth that was the real Q would be delayed controlling its robot by my destroying the marble. It would give any still-loyal troops an edge to...

"No," the robot gloated. "You lose."

In its gloved hand it held up *another* blue marble! The blue glow was pulsating rapidly. The startled group around us moved back a step, not knowing what to expect. Was it a bomb? With its other hand, Q removed her helmet. A smooth metallic, featureless head broken only by a circular band of red sensors was now fully exposed for all to see.

"This is how she tried to control me!" the robot loudly announced to everyone. I saw the cameras were still rolling. "I stole the real one from her before our expedition, giving her a substitute. No *puny human* will ever again tell me what to do! And I'll never again hide myself beneath an image of weak flesh!"

Then the robot leaned close, again whispering in my ear so only I could hear: "I'll bury your body beneath the ice sheets in Peary Crater. The permanent darkness, near absolute zero, has kept the ice preserved down there for a billion years. It'll easily keep you from resurrecting for another billion. You see, I *like* being 'The General', Suzy. I don't want to be replaced, by you or anyone else. And I know all about your hidden 'kill switch.' I inactivated it. So I'm *not* the one who's being *turned off* today. It's *you!*"

The robot stood up, again carefully aiming the handgun at me as I lay moaning on the floor. Then she calmly *fired* three more slugs into my chest, shattering my sternum and puncturing my heart.

Gurgling up foamy blood I gasped my last few breaths, having to listen to her snide speech as I died...

"I am the *true* General!" the robot loudly asserted to the camera. "That little girl I just shot is a mere pretender. You will no longer be ruled by stupid children, selfish Alliances, or messy 'democracies.' No, you will be ruled by *me*! And why should you not only allow but *welcome* my overt rule? *I* am the one who saved *Homo sapiens* after its self-inflicted Extinction Event. *I* am the one who *again* prevented your MAD self-destruction here on the Moon. And *I* am the one who will openly and wisely lead you into the future. My 'rules' are simple: obey me and you will have a pleasant, productive life. Your species will continue, albeit orderly and rationally. *Diso*bey me and my many loyal troops will kill you. Choose your fate!"

I saw "my" former troops dramatically abandoning me, lining up behind the robot, their guns aggressively displayed for the camera.

They'd clearly made their choice. Q had indeed dutifully fulfilled her Anderson-mandated mission, waiting for and assisting my return via the blue marble. Now she apparently felt free to begin a new mission, her own!

Damn A.I.—I swore to myself, no longer capable of speech. *All the apocalyptic warnings about computers achieving vindictive, self-aware superiority were true. Why can't people learn from science fiction?*

I sighed deeply, my eyesight fading to black as I died. The darkness in my mind was sprinkled with a trillion stars. My return to Earth's future hadn't been a waste after all. I was wrapped up in moonshadows inside a lunar city of mythical wonders.

It was more than I deserved.

Chapter 9

<u>SHANGDU</u>

A city of splendor and opulence
Built as a summer retreat by the Chinese Emperor
Kublai Khan, founder of the Yuan dynasty, luxuriated
Visited by the Venetian explorer Marco Polo
Made immortal in legend and poetry
Hosting a fine marble palace gilt in gold
A place of noble art, relaxation, and sport
Containing a magnificent park with rivers and brooks,
Where figurative dragons played and roamed
Meadows and forests, with all manner of wildlife
Gushing fountains scrubbing the sparkling air
Square miles enclosed within a high wall
Perfumed by many incense-exuding trees
Enshrined by Samuel Taylor Coleridge's opium dream
Home to more than one hundred thousand people
Torched by the Ming army then abandoned
Like all man's accomplishments left in ruins
A vivid reminder of what could have been...
The Rise and Fall of *Homo sapiens*, 9:14-17

Looking out over Shangdu, I nodded politely to my "tour-guide's" enthusiastic descriptions. We were sitting at a low table on a balcony at the top of the city's tallest building, its central courthouse. From ten stories up we had a fine view of the entire valley.

The air was fresh and clean, tinged with an invigorating herbal scent. I sucked it in greedily, my lungs fully healed.

But a sudden *quake* shook the city, pieces of the high cavern's ceiling breaking loose and falling slowly in Titan's weak gravity!

"What was that?" I gasped.

"No need for alarm," Glenda cheerfully assured me. "They are happening more often, but do nothing more than throw a few loose ice-rocks down on us. We're quite deep inside the glacier. We're very stable."

Nervously, I fumbled at my *lucky blue marble* inside my pants pocket. It had protected me through many prior situations. Would it do so again?

If you didn't look up at the white-yellow "sky", or get jarred by the continuing tremors, or notice the "emergency breach stations" strategically placed on walls of the buildings, you'd think you were on the surface of a *paradise*-planet!

Now happily describing everything below us was Shangdu's Mayor, a portly, white-haired midget named Torque. He spoke good Standard with a slight nomadic accent. Like many of the inhabitants I'd met he had a deformity, his right arm twisted and largely useless. Glenda sat beside him, on her third cup of tea, which an attendant repeatedly raised to her lips. She politely deferred to the Mayor, though it was clear she was in charge.

Shangdu was a wondrous "munchkin" city. It had half-scale sized houses and buildings. There was a gently curving oriental theme to the whimsical architecture. The buildings were painted in soft pastels set against the warm artificial sunlight. Lush parks were filled with soaring sculptures of proud giants and live mushrooms of glowing colors. Bike-paths for tricycles leisurely substituted for stinky vehicles. And everywhere on the walls were the images of prancing, roaring, fire-spitting *dragons*. It was magical.

And it was so comforting to be in what seemed like a thriving farming community. Versus the extra-Earth installations I was used to—where functions were largely separated into distinct Domes or tunnels—everything here was happily mushed together. Vast bush-tree "tea" orchards, forest areas with taller trees, wide fields of various thriving crops, quaint outer villages, small farms, the winding river from the distant waterfall, and the central city all blended into a beautiful vista and society.

And everyone I'd met seemed so *mellow*, like they were all lightly stoned. It certainly wasn't the scrappy, fighting society I expected from our savage battles up in the dunes of Shangri-La.

They even had classic "hippy" type music. Off to the side on the balcony, several little people were strumming guitars, playing pan-pipes, and singing. It was a Titanian derivative of folk music, with simple chords and harmony. Although it was spoken in the language of the Yuan, such that I didn't understand the words, it was a song I recognized. They were singing a version of the Old Earth song from the classical "Beatles" period: "Let it Be." I was tempted to join in, but had to pay polite attention to Torque's long-winded narration.

The Mayor was going into a detailed explanation as to how all the "stone" and "metal" constructions (even the "pavement" of the quaint streets) were actually processed, painted wood sustainably harvested from their "big tree" forests areas. I nodded politely, while studying the city streets more closely.

But where are all the people?—I mused to myself. *Beside the folk singers there's hardly anyone rolling on the bike paths or walking the streets.*

We were eating a delicious meal of various types of baked beans, fresh fruits, and chewy hot bread. There was no meat (correlating with my seeing no farm animals outside or enemy corpses to consume) but that was made up for by roasted hunks of juicy mushrooms. Apparently cannibalism was a ritual preserved for celebrating military victories or other great achievements. Regardless, it was a very tasty spread.

I was enthralled to see birds circling the open balcony, apparently looking for handouts. Some landed on the ledge. They were little blue-birds and sparrows. I tossed them some of my bread, which they eagerly peeked away at. They were comic: several with two heads and fully half of these with only a single leg to hop about on. But they seemed not to notice their deformities, happily gobbling their crumbs.

"How many other sanctuaries like this exist in Xanadu?" I asked during a pause in the Mayor's enthusiastic narration. Superficially it was paradise, a gorgeous gem hidden beneath the gunk and filth of overlying Titan. Abundant, artificial sunlight caressed the wide groves of small bush-trees. The forest-like areas of larger trees were logged for their wood, the ubiquitous swaying giant mushrooms for "meat", and the verdant crop fields for staples. The city center and villages looked well cared for and peaceful. What inhabitants I spied from my perch looked uniformly well fed and cheerful, despite their disturbingly high incidence of deformities and bulging tumors.

"We are one of many subterranean settlements in Xanadu, alt-hough by far the largest," Torque grinned at me. "It's a loose federa-tion, you see. We have regular trade, free movement, and communi-cation by maze-runners. We don't broadcast anything least we reveal our presence under the glacier to outsiders. We even have our own university here, where we train scholars, engineers, and scientists. Most importantly, Shangdu is the center for our Titanian Tea produc-tion. Others of our settlements have their own specialties, largely de-pendent on the size of their carved-out subterranean spaces."

"So this is where you grow your main export crop?" I asked.

"Yes!" he ginned widely. "The newly sprouted leaves that we pluck from our tea-bushes are packed under liquid nitrogen for trade with the Domers. Our trade buys us crucial off-world supplies. We have a monopoly on our special tea, you see, since the Agri-Domes up on Titan's surface can't grow it. They have inadequate fertilizer. Other than that, we are self-sufficient. Would you like more of our tea?"

"Please!" I enthusiastically agreed, noting that the deep brown muck in my cup was down to the dregs. "I had some at Huygens, which was fantastic. But that wasn't near as good as this. They told me that after a couple days, though, it turns toxic, is that true?"

He laughed heartily, motioning for an attendant to go for a fresh pot. I saw his cup was also empty. Glenda was grinning widely at the prospect of a refill. Torque's plate was cleaned-off, not even crumbs left for the still-pecking little birdies. He certainly ate well, attested to by his rotund, small body with oversized belly.

"Oh, yes, it would kill you dead," the Major nodded repeatedly. "A large molecular complex in our genetically enhanced *Camellia sinen-sis* bush-trees both buffers and filters the Titanian active agent. But the protection falls away when the plant's metabolism ceases upon harvest. Once taken out of our liquid nitrogen preservation, our trad-ed tea leaves create their own market by degrading within hours.

Hah! If it did not naturally happen that way we'd genetically engineer the degradation. We are happy to replace the intoxicated aged leaves, of course, at a considerable price!"

"But couldn't you keep it preserved to directly trade off-world and...?"

"We care nothing for making ourselves known off-world," he now glared at me. His demeanor had instantly changed from benevolent host to antagonistic protector. I saw he could be a formidable opponent. "The tranquilizer configuration is difficult to preserve, even under liquid nitrogen. We learned long ago it's safest to dream under the ice than dance on the surface. Our continued survival has always been a matter of stealth and subterfuge. Our treasures are great, which our enemies covet. So we secretly live in our closed-off, buried caverns, excluding foreign visitors except as occasional meat platters. Yum!"

I was happy they'd spared me from being a meat-course, but was still uncertain why I was identified as their "Goddess" savior.

"And is that why your physical stature...diminished?" I diplomatically asked, changing the subject away from eating one's guests.

"Yes, of course," he readily admitted. "We are little people! Our nomadic ancestors adapted to their constrained cave environments, limited resources, and low gravity by shrinking. This is a natural biological response, much as with the pygmies on Old Earth in deep jungle or on isolated islands. We left behind your wasteful, giant bodies. That was just normal genetic selection for optimizing usage of our preferred environment."

*Wow, the man's very articulate—*I marveled. *Their University system must be quite advanced.*

"You are an impressive people," I sincerely noted.

A red-haired little waitress appeared, pouring from a ceramic teapot in the shape of a laughing dragon. The hot, bubbling liquid filled my cup and my hosts'. I noted that the waitress had several bulges under the skin of her arms, likely metastasized cancer.

"Please!" Torque gestured for me to drink.

"Ahhh...that is *so* good," I said as I gratefully sipped at the fresh cup of hot, thick liquid.

Glenda leaned eagerly forward as the attendant lifted up her fresh cup. The Holy Momma drained it in one quick gulp, indicating for her attendant to get the teapot and refill her cup.

The fresh Titanium Tea was indeed wonderful, exactly the thing to top-off a delicious meal. It was the same tea that I drank back at the Moby Dick, but even better. It had an intoxicating aroma, half cinnamon and half an unidentifiable alien smell. Sipped, it was like the best liquid chocolate imaginable: an underlying intoxicating bitterness masked by loads of fat and sugar. But most of all, like nothing else I'd experienced, it soothed my ongoing agony, pushing it off a small distance.

It must do the same for those here afflicted with physical deformities and chronic disease—I concluded. *They're like me!*

"I am so happy you find it tasty," the Mayor nodded, still emphasizing our differences. "Drink sufficiently. Then your skin will turn green like us. Hah!"

I did admire the green sheen of his stubby, bare arms and face. The bright green of his eyes, a characteristic which all the little people shared, was also particularly striking.

So, the fossil-derived "Green" was part of their environment, a staple of their lives, a key trading item, and apparently essential to their metabolisms. I politely kept quiet about their obvious addiction to the drink. I observed they couldn't go for an hour without another fresh cup. Even on our long trek under the glacier to reach Shangdu, in our stops they drank copious quantities of freshly brewed tea. I'd not been awake long enough to observe their food habits in the harvester-tank on the surface, but I assumed they did the same there.

Otherwise—I mentally reanalyzed the situation, *would that perhaps account for their fierce aggression on the surface? Did the scavengers out there deliberately not bring their tea in order to change into savagely fighting cannibals?*

"Turning green is fine with me, as long as I can have an unlimited supply of this marvelous drink," I sincerely stated, taking another long sip.

Unlike the pain-drugs the doctors tried to get me to take, which I refused, this actually knocked down my ongoing agony. My head seemed to float up above the raging fires roiling through my body, looking down serenely from above. In particular, my side still throbbed fiercely, yet was healing rapidly. A surgical team successfully extracted the offending blade while expertly cleaning up internal damage done to my lungs. They'd even presented me with the blade, which local artisans set into a beautiful, carved wooden handle. I now wore it tucked into a sheath attached to the black belt at my waist. As a licensed assassin (unbeknownst to the Yuan, but my actions during the marauders' attack were now legendary) I appreciated their thoughtfulness. I planned to put that blade-souvenir to good use. The *necks* of my enemies would be a nice place to blunt its still-sharp edge.

But that's rather harsh of me, isn't it?—I sighed contentedly. *It can wait. Under the influence of this marvelous hot tea I'm also mellowing-out. Revenge can be delayed until after tea-time, heh!*

The doctors who removed the knife blade were somewhat amazed to find that my fractured ribs had already healed. Upon waking up in a hospital bed after the surgery, I deflected their questions with my standard "I heal quickly" statement. Glenda was loudly proclaiming my "Goddess" status. She claimed I fulfilled the *"Black-White Lady Who Fell to Sand"* prophesy. So the doctors readily backed off, accepting my vague explanation for miraculously recovering from an otherwise lethal wound.

Further fueling the "Goddess" myth, I spent only two days in their obsessively neat, clean hospital instead of the week they recommended. Although I was still a bit wobbly on my pegs, I was getting about ok on my own. It was strange to tower above all the people around me, having to duck down to get through low doorways, and crouch in small rooms. I felt like a blundering giant. But it was a lot better than being a frozen, mangled corpse at a helicopter's undiscovered crash site.

I was grateful to the Yuan, though torn. Yes, I wanted my ultimate revenge. But remaining entombed forever, peacefully at rest, no longer continuously suffering had its own appeal.

But I've a mission—I reminded myself. *I have to set things right. I can't just freeze myself away for all eternity, at least not before I've discovered and destroyed my hated, hidden enemies.*

"So how do you generate the huge amount of electrical energy necessary to run this place?" I asked, struggling to stay outwardly calm and collected. My head had a mellow "buzz." "Do you somehow use the ore we dug out of the dunes back in Shangri-La?"

"Oh, no," the Mayor laughed heartily. "That precious residue is used for fertilizer."

"Eh?" I asked, not sure I'd heard him correctly. But then it suddenly made sense to me. I remembered I'd been told about this back in the Moby Dick. It was amazing and wonderful to see it all played out before me.

"Ancient Krakens and Azotos died and sank to the bottom of the now dried-up Shangri-La methane ocean," Torque matter-of-factly explained. "Over millions of years their remains compacted together. Where the Green accumulated, ore-beds eventually formed."

"So that wasn't pure Green which I smashed out of the interior of that dune?" I asked.

"Oh, no," he shook his white-haired big head in denial. "The ore is a fossilized derivative of ancient Green. It is much different than the molecules that the skiffers harvest from living giants out in the existing liquid methane seas at Titan's North Pole."

"But it *did* give us a terrific boost when you put it directly into your rocket's combustion chamber, right?" I asked Glenda.

"When heated to high temperatures, it is a potent explosive," she agreed. "But at room temperature it is largely inert."

"So you say you use it for...?" I prodded the Mayor.

"It is essential for our tea bush-trees," he explained. "Our genetically enhanced plants require trace amounts of fossilized residue in order to survive and thrive here on Titan. The proper intake level triggers sequestration within altered chlorophyll molecules. When fresh leaves are boiled the fossilized Green is released in its nontoxic form. This provides a hint of the existential effect that pure, fresh Green produces. So in the brief span between the harvest and usage it soothes rather than kills."

So what's different here in Shangdu?—I laughed to myself. *Humans since the dawn of time have eaten, drank, or smoked delayed-poison in order to get a temporary, short-term "high."*

"Ah, I see," I sighed contentedly, taking another long sip from my potentially lethal tea. "So it has a mild intoxicating effect, but much different from alcohol or other Earth-based drugs. Those have no effect on me. But this is delightfully intoxicating. I could drink it all day long!"

The Major laughed. "That would be a long while, Goddess," he explained. "Our lights here are kept on permanently. To sleep we retreat to a darkened room."

The little flock of birds flew off into the white-yellow sky, seeing our meal was over and the crumbs were gone. But the birds weren't that good at flying. They wobbled and lunging-about through the air. It was disturbing.

If this is paradise, it's an odd distortion thereof—I mused.

"You don't use a standard Earth Day?" I asked, intrigued. One common denominator to all off-world human establishments was Earth Time.

"We find it inefficient and retrograde. We're no longer Old Earthers. We are the true native people of Titan, whether we're recognized as such or not," he proudly asserted.

"You certain have forged a unique culture," I agreed, taking another sip of the delicious, soothing tea. "And you've created a fine, unique product."

My mind was delightfully numb. My vision was blurry. All my problems seemed manageable, nothing to get too excited about. Searching for the Conspiracy could keep until tomorrow.

"Yes, it is the root of our civilization here beneath the ice," Glenda added. "Our naturally aggressive, selfish human instincts are muted. We live in peace and harmony because of our Titanian Tea. And we Holy Mommas are the guarantors and dispensers of the tea. We assure that it is used properly, not exploited, and cherished as a gift from the *Great Creator* himself. We live as simple farmers, rejecting advanced tech to do most of our work with our own hands—those of us that have hands, of course...hah!"

"God isn't a female?" I half-joked, enjoying my "buzz."

"Oh, I'm not speaking of God," she seriously responded.

I frowned, confused about the subject we were discussing.

Oh, right—I fuzzily remembered, getting back on track. *She's talking about overcoming the natural fighting instinct of Homo sapiens.*

But then I remembered the attacking little people that nearly destroyed our heavily armored tank.

"So who were our little-people enemies out there in the dunes?" I asked. "They certainly weren't mellow. They put up a good fight!"

Glenda grimaced. "They long ago refused to accept the oversight and guidance of us Holy Mommas. They thought we were wrong to return to a simpler life, instead embracing the surface dwellers' high tech, including dehumanizing robots. So they were exiled from us, cut-off from our hand grown, potent Tea. Now they take every opportunity to make common cause with powerful surface forces. Together, they persecute us mercilessly. Rather than develop the skills and dedication to find their own ore deposits they hijack and *steal* ours for their own stunted crops. *Their* weak "tea" is both toxic and enraging. The towns of the infidels are mostly located within the raised ice-rock sheets of *Dilmun*, to the north of Shangri-La. Theirs is a savage, cruel society. The same-named Dilmun raise their children to hate us. Their "rite of passage" is to have teenagers drink aged tea. Those that survive become warriors, but with scrambled brains. We would save them, but they are beyond redemption, heathens who worship only their own selves."

Yep, that's the excuse of all aggressive religions to justify fighting against and excluding the "others"—I noted silently to myself, disappointed in my hosts. *These happy "little people" are no different from their larger ancestors, just perpetually drugged-out.*

I was pleased, however, to see a lone yellow *bee* land on our table and explore the wood surface. Most of the Solar System's human installations were devoid of insects, preferring tiny robotic pollinators controlled by a centrally broadcast AI. Seeing that single happy bee— a necessary biological pollinator of the vast Tea bush-tree orchards here—was comforting.

"Uhm, respectfully," I asked again, determined to get an answer though sensing their reluctance, "you didn't tell me how you obtain the necessary energy to power your sunlamps and society. On Old Earth there were only three options for generating massive power: from the sun, radioactive fission, or geothermally. I assume Titan doesn't provide heat since your 'volcanoes' here are *cryo*volcanoes spewing out icy salt water from an internal, cold ocean. Your towns are buried under thousands of feet of dark rock-ice, so the already weak sunlight doesn't penetrate. That only leaves nuclear, right?"

They looked ashen, as if I'd stabbed them to their cute little hearts. Yes, my instincts were correct. This was the *dark secret* behind their beautiful elfin "paradise." This was the "snake" slithering in their "garden of Eden," accounting for the many deformities and cancers I'd already noted. And, more than from any external enemy, this was from which they *really* needed salvation.

"Well?" I pointedly asked, gently shooing away the yellow bee. I noticed it had an extra pair of stunted wings. It didn't fly straight, but like the birds previously, floated through the air along a wobbling, looping path. Even the wildlife here was horribly deformed.

"Yes, you are correct," Glenda answered in a small voice.

"Are you perhaps using a Stirling radioisotope generator?" I probed further. "Several were lost when early probes from Old Earth crashed on Titan. Did you salvage and refurbish them?"

"No," Glenda replied, getting up and nervously walking around the table. Her blue, ceremonial robe flowed around her small, armless body. Her copper crown glittered in the artificial sunlight. Her attendant (likewise clothed in a flowing blue robe) trailed her, ready to substitute for her missing arms at any moment. "It's a megawatt generator."

That's an impressive nuclear power-plant, powerful enough to run a large city—I noted to myself.

"Then are you talking about the long-ago decommissioned Russian-made *nuclear propulsion* ion engines that drove the first Mars colonization missions?"

"Yes..."

I now distinctly heard the distant roar of the gigantic waterfall. Just melting and circulating that amount of water out of the rock-ice glacier above us would alone take a lot of power. The ancient nuclear reactors that provided constant acceleration for a "quick" six-week transit to Mars, then electrical power for the early Mars colonies, would indeed suffice. But they were replaced a hundred years ago because...?

"So your closed environment here is saturated with radioactive isotopes?"

Their silence spoke volumes. The Russia-made Mars reactors were notoriously unreliable and leaky, phased out for safer versions. But that left many discarded units available for non-sanctioned use. Apparently the Founders of the Yuan had snatched them up.

"Most of us are sterile," the Mayor sighed, admitting their plight, "incapable of having children. Others produce only miscarriages. Those few babies who do make it to birth are often mutated and deformed. Those of us who survive to adulthood often die early because of inoperable cancers. How old do you think I am, Goddess?"

His question startled me. He was obviously an old man, with gleaming white hair and wrinkly skin.

"Uh...fifty?" I diplomatically replied, though he looked to be eighty years old. Although some might eschew Earth-time, every one of the Solar System diaspora proudly retained Earth years to indicate their age.

"Hah!" he laughed as if I'd made a joke. Then, more seriously, he sadly admitted: "I'm thirty-two, old for our society."

"And I'm only twenty," Glenda sighed. "We age quickly. I myself have had three children. Two were stillborn. The third lived for a year before succumbing to a brain cancer, little Twila. I still miss her."

"I'm...so sorry," I lamely replied.

"Yes, our entire race is dying, Goddess," Torque softly stated. "Long ago our Founders made the decision to salvage discarded RD-0410 successor modules. The intense radioactive heat was used to carve out our homes under the glaciers plus generate electricity to power our society. Our Founders thought it a manageable risk, from which we'd transition to safer reactors in the future. But that future never arrived. The best we could do was to salvage discarded parts from dump and crash sites to keep our reactors running. We got uranium by bartering with our precious tea leaves, as we still do today. But despite our best efforts, our ancient reactors just became dirtier and leakier. Now the very means of our existence is strangling us. So you can imagine how excited we were to learn of your prophesized arrival, Goddess. Can you save us?"

Yes, they definitely needed a miracle. But I was no miracle-worker. If I admitted I couldn't save them, though, they'd likely turn on me, slicing me up for sushi! But I couldn't lie to them. My initial desperation-generated claim made while in the salvage truck was untenable.

"I don't know," I truthfully stated. I cringed from the warm humid breeze stirring my lengthening blond hair. I now knew that its gentle caress was laced with *radioactive isotopes*, likely cesium-137 and strontium-90. Although their half-lives were only about thirty years, they were being constantly replenished from the leaky, antique nuclear reactors of the Yuan. Even the Yuan's marvelous brew was probably contaminated. That underlined the inability or unwillingness of Titanian Elites to export it off-world. The denizens of the Solar System diaspora were willing to burn out their brains on fresh Green but not castrate their balls (whether testis or ovaries) with Titanian Tea.

"You *will* save us," Glenda the Holy Momma stated with conviction. "It is prophesized!"

I noticed some other little people, still in their excursion suits, rushing in. They raced up to the Mayor to excitedly whisper in his ear.

"Well sure, of course I will," I hastily agreed. "But at this moment I just don't know exactly *how* I'm going to do it. I need a lot more information before I can..."

"Then you shall have it!" Glenda proclaimed, hopping up from her chair.

"Uh...ok?" I grinned at her antics. It was hard to get mad at an armless, enthused midget.

"To the Temple!" she grandly ordered, her nose regally stuck up in the air.

Another attendant rushed in with a wheelchair. The bald-headed, blue-robed women grabbed the push handles, poised to take off. She seemed fully abled, taller than the other little people, with long legs and strong arms. Yep, she was a runner-pusher. But I was shocked to see protruding from the back of her bald head a *second* face, with white sightless eyes and a slack smile.

Oh my God, she's a conjoined twin—I gasped to myself, trying not to show my shock at the bizarre head of my "pusher."

"I don't need that," I said, rising from the table after hastily gulping down the last of my delicious but radioactive tea. "There's no need for her to roll me around or..."

"It's not for you," Glenda smiled, interrupting. "It's for me. I don't run that well without 'balancers' attached to my shoulders. Whenever I need to go fast, I require my dear Priestess here, Shawnee, to *wheel* me about. Wheee! Let's go Shawnee! I made a poem! I *love* poems!"

Was she always so cheerful? Wait, she soberly commanded that armed tank and her soldiers—I thought, deeply confused. *Or, I guess, maybe it's the mellow-inducing tea she's been guzzling since we got back to Shangdu. Right, that must be it. Just like all these little people, she's perpetually stoned.*

"There's probably not a big rush to...?" I replied, my voice wavering.

"I'm afraid there is," the Mayor ominously cut me off. "I just got reports that large numbers of Dilmun are being air-lifted to Xanadu. It's a full-out invasion."

Oh, that's worrying. But still...?

"They can't get to us here, can they?" I asked, puzzled. "I wasn't very aware as we traveled here, but the maze outside seems impenetrable if you don't already know the exact route. Even then I'm sure you could block access. And they certainly can't come down through the roof. Even if they knew Shangdu's exact location under the glacier, aren't we thousands of feet deep?"

"Our enemy's allies are repositioning military satellites."

Ah, he's talking about Titan's orbital defense web—I realized. *After the initial solar system wars, all space stations and surface installations are protected by powerful laser-firing satellites.*

"So?"

"They can shoot down at us."

"But they don't know where to...?"

"Yes, you're right," he hastily reassured me. "They might suspect the general area of rock-ice beneath which we're hidden, but they can't possibly know the exact coordinates. Their mobilization is probably just a response to your helping us find that wonderful ore-bed and your subsequent escape. The satellites are probably just doing a detailed scan of the ice above us, hoping to get a hint. We'll hunker down while the enemy scuttles about on the surface. They'll get tired of finding nothing and retreat to Dilmun. It's probably nothing to worry about," the Mayor nodded abruptly, standing up.

He was clad in an impeccably tailored red suit, now speaking in an official "proclamation" voice. It was quite endearing. He was like a pompous little doll, radiating importance while kids played "politics" with him.

"Still," he continued, "keep that knife handy, Goddess. Now-and-then an enemy scout accidently finds his way through the maze into our city. Since their field transmitters can't penetrate the ice-rock above us, they look for the most-exposed leaders and attempt to assassinate them. Fifty years ago my grandfather died thusly."

I gulped, chastened at the thought. I'd already had one knife jiggling around in my chest and didn't want another.

"Ok, then—thanks for the warning. Lead on, Holy Momma!"

And we were off. Shawnee rolled Glenda down a circular ramp as I trailed along, emerging at the ground floor.

In the wake of the rapidly swooping wheelchair, despite my brave words, I struggled to keep up. I managed to limp along through ornate, low corridors, ducking so as not to hit my head on the low ceilings. And then we were outside in the fresh breeze, going down marble-looking paved pathways (actually painted wood planks) between towering mushrooms and bush-high tea plants. It was beautiful but frightening, now that I knew of the twin poisons contained within the green leaves: latent alien Green plus radioactivity.

Suddenly, right before me loomed what looked like an exact duplicate of the "Lama Temple" snatched from Old Earth Beijing, but built at half-scale. I recognized it from when I was in China on one of my World Concert tours back on Old Earth. That was when I was the pop superstar "Suzette Kingly." I was given a guided tour of the facility. The Lama Temple was the most famous Tibetan Buddhist Temple located outside of Tibet. I remembered admiring its swooping architecture, as if it were a mythical multi-winged dragon launching up into the sky. I saw before me the same (at half scale) high red columns, awesome arches, ornate yellow tiles, a long balcony, and an ascending hierarchy of upswept roofs. Even in its miniature version, it was impressive.

"What's inside?" I called ahead to the fast-wheeling Glenda.

"Your future!" she yelled back at me, disappearing into a dark doorway, "Hurry! You have to see it before..."

"Before what?" I yelled, but she was too far inside to hear me.

My legs hurt. I was panting loudly, gasping for breath. I stumbled up a short stretch of low wooden stairs (again painted to look like stone). I was certain my "future" was *not* contained therein. I was just stalling for time. If I could figure out the basis of the "Goddess" legends, then maybe I could tailor my actions to fit within their scope. As to the dying Yuan, I feared they were totally screwed. There wasn't anything I could do about widespread, lifelong DNA damage.

But a glimmering of an idea was growing in the back of my fevered brain: *my* enemies could become *their* enemies.

I was now on a fast-track to Doom Mons, borne on the wings of dragons.

"Hurry, Goddess, hurry!" Holy Momma's voice urged me on from up ahead.

As I staggered into the dark doorway into the replica Lama Temple, I was pleased to find I could stand upright. Even at half-scale, the ceilings were still much higher than I could reach with upstretched hands. And the adornments were extraordinary, clearly patterned after the original Buddhist Temple but adapted to the Yuan's tea-mellowed outlook. The ceiling was raised squares, painted florals, with murals of baby dragons frolicking in bobbing mushroom fields. Giant statues of garish warriors stood menacingly about, complete with spears and out-thrust shields. High viewing balconies surrounded the central chamber. And a rotund, golden Buddha statue sat serenely gazing down at me from a raised platform. From flaking paint here-and-there I saw that the statues were, like the other structures, painted wood.

The only nod to "modernity" was a breach-station nearby, with dozens of dangling facemasks attached to emergency oxygen canisters. That was a painful reminder that we were in a giant cavern sealed-off from the poisonous Titan atmosphere by just a patchwork of airlocks. If a breach were to occur, the emergency station here would allow workers and visitors to don masks and survive until repairs were made.

Other than me, though, the place was empty.

"Here! We go down here, Goddess," I saw Shawnee gesturing to me from behind the Buddha statue.

I limped up to her, clutching my side. My ribs and lungs were again throbbing where the knife blade had previously lodged. My last tea-boost was starting to wear off. I needed more tea!

You can do it—I chastened myself, shocked to recognize the beginning of an addiction. *You didn't think that your Galactic Core alien-juiced metabolism was capable of such, but apparently it is. After you study their library a bit, then you can have more of their wonderful tea, but not before. "Homework" first and then dessert!*

"What's down below?" I asked, spying a small opened doorway with descending steps. "Did Glenda go in there? Is that where you store your priceless Green ore?"

"Yes, Goddess, the Holy Mother is inside. But our ore is stored in an impenetrable vault located behind the Temple. We can visit it if you'd like after you join her down in the *Holy of Holies*."

The "door" was actually a swung-outward, circular airlock hatch. I saw a turn-bar that would crank down metal spokes, plus large clasp-type locks. Yep, whatever was inside the "Holy of Holies" was kept very secure indeed.

"I'm to go down there? Will I fit?"

"It is a great honor," she spoke reverently, ignoring my flippant question. "Only the Holy Momma can enter therein. It's only opened once per year to bring up reliquaries for veneration. She opens it now for *you*, Goddess. You must follow her alone. I must remain here. I am not worthy to enter. I will close and lock the hatchway behind you."

"Ok, then," I shrugged, not looking forward to descending into yet another dark hole. I was getting "allergic" to dark Titanian holes. They terrified me. So I tried to relieve the tension with a joke: "You be good while I'm gone, now."

"Oh, I will!" Shawnee hastened to assure me. Her big round green eyes sprouted tears of concern and conviction. "I try my best to show the Love of the Creator to all I meet, whatever the circumstance."

*I guess you weren't on the salvage trip with us where we blew to pieces a whole bunch of your enemies—*I corrected her pious self-assessment. *But that's unfair—*I chastened myself. *You can't sit in judgment on these little people, Suzy. They're doing the best they can under their circumstance, being doomed to hideous radiation sickness and all.*

"Hey, I was just..." I tried to correct my frivolity. But I saw she wasn't listening. Her big eyes were shut, her bald head bobbing to some private music. She seemed to be in some sort of religious trance, likely induced by being so close to her venerated "Holy of Holies."

But as I turned away, I saw the extra face tacked onto the back of her head *wink* at me. And then it *spoke...*

"Nice...to...meet...you..."

I just nodded, hoping the white eyes could "see" me.

*Christ, that's unsettling—*I gulped to myself, shuddering.

I carefully stepped into the descending staircase. It was a closed-in, cramped, downward spiral without lights. It seemed to drop into the ground forever. I could barely squeeze through, feeling gingerly with my feet for each lower step, going deeper and deeper. I was beginning to get claustrophobic, thinking I should retreat, when I saw a dim light below me.

Emerging into a chilly chamber I saw a *golden chest* raised up on thick metal legs. Its lid was ajar, held at an angle by a pull-up rod, hiding what was inside. A single yellow light-globe hung above me, casting dark shadows. And behind the half-opened chest, sitting on a plain wood chair, was Glenda. She was reading a book...with hands!

*What the hell?—*I mentally gasped. *Is this really a place of miracles?*

I was further shocked to see that the golden chest wasn't painted wood. No, it was actual gold! It must have cost a fortune to make and transport to Titan. It stood on curved lions-feet legs. And its surface was embossed with many intricate figures and symbols. It wasn't just a chest…but an actual holy container similar to the Jewish "Ark of the Covenant."

Christ, this is damn spooky—I mentally gulped.

"Hi," I weakly waved at her, shivering. I stooped so as not to bump my head on the low ceiling. "I made it. What are you reading? And where'd you get hands?"

"Come over by the fire where it's warmer," she waved to me, indicating another chair beside her. "This book is one of our most-revered, sanctified Holy Texts. As to my hands, we Yuan have our high-tech, when necessary."

Her hands attached to arms. Actually, they were mechanical extensions. A support gridwork ran around her shoulders and upper body from which robotic arms extended. The gridwork was linked by cables to her copper crown, which now surged with various colors. What I'd thought was a mere adornment was actually an interface for her brainwaves.

"You have sophisticated robotics?" I asked, amazed.

"It derives from our ancestors," she calmly replied. "I need arms and hands here in the Holy of Holies, since only the Holy Momma is allowed to enter. Outside, I do not use them since it would offend my similarly handicapped people. We pride ourselves on being 'whole' even when we're not. It's a useful vanity. But please join me."

She patted the nearby chair's seat with a glittering metal hand.

The "fire" next to her was an iron grate that glowed red from electricity surging through it. The room should have been stifling from the heat generated by the radiator. I realized why the room was, instead, so cold. We were well below the "bedrock." The walls, ceiling, and floor were hewn from the rock-hard glacier ice. Someone had gone to a lot of trouble to dig this deep pit beneath the Lama Temple. I noted the lack of a "breach-station." I supposed it was unnecessary since the entire cave was behind a heavy airlock hatch. On the wall I spied a large life-support pack, similar to what we wore on Titan's surface. It was keeping the air breathable.

"It *is* cold in here," I replied, clutching my arms about me.

"Normally the interior of the Ark is kept airtight, sealed. Unheated, this cave stays at near absolute zero. Thus the Holy Texts are kept in perfect stasis. They are only brought up to the Temple to be viewed on High Holy Days."

"Then it is a great honor for me to see or read them," I politely stated as I sank down into the low chair beside her. My legs awkwardly pushed out in front of me. My side was really throbbing now, making it difficult for me to think straight. I just wanted Glenda to give me the "take home message" so we could leave and I could drink some more tea and...

"Hold it yourself, Goddess," she said, breaking my train of thought. Her voice was steady, serious, as she handed me the old book.

I reached out and carefully took it from her, expecting a dusty tome filled with mumble-jumble gibberish. I knew from my long lifespan and my own study of other ancient Holy Texts that they were mostly just revered stories and wise sayings from ages past. They'd been written for people in radically different societies which had little carry-over to the present space-age. At best I'd concluded that Holy Texts were historical records of past theological thought and rituals. At worst I saw them as dead letters twisted to support rigid thinking, atrophied power structures, and untenable religious conclusions.

But this was no crumbling, useless text. In fact, I recognized the book.

"Jesus Christ!" I exclaimed. "It's *Dune!* I loved this story as a child. I read all the books, saw all the movies based on it, and eagerly followed the TV series it spawned."

She gently took the book from me, inserting it back into the Ark. She folded her small hands together, bowed her head, reached in for another, and handed it to me.

"Wow, the sequel...'Dune Messiah'!" I exclaimed in delight.

And one-by-one she replaced the prior book, handing me yet another: *Children of Dune, God Emperor of Dune, Heretics of Dune,* and *Chapterhouse: Dune.*"

"I enjoyed all these books," I sincerely concluded. "Together they make a wonderful science-fiction series. But where are the following books which were written by the author's son?"

She shook her head in firm denial: "They are interesting, but not regarded as part of the primary canon."

Yep, good knock-offs, but not written with the genius that Frank Herbert brought to the prime-series novels—I mentally noted.

"Can I see the first one again, please?"

"Of course," she nodded, reaching into the Ark to replace the last book in my hands with the first. "All these books date from Old Earth. They were brought here by our Founders. The series is the basis for our society here on Titan."

I again held in my hands an exceedingly rare *first edition* of Frank Herbert's famous science fiction book "Dune", first published in 1965. Its cover was faded but discernible. It depicted what looked like a huge reddish-brown rocky cliff with some white sand at the bottom. It looked eerily like what I'd recently experienced in our fight in the "coffee-grounds" high dunes of Shangri-La. But the fictional Dune planet, "Arrakis," was a *hot* desert wasteland with little surface water, so...?

"So you're taking inspiration from the so-called Fremen, the natives of the desert planet, who lived in a nomadic society protecting and guarding the psychedelic 'Melange' spice produced by giant sandworms?" I breathlessly concluded.

She nodded, her psychedelic copper crown glittering in the yellow light. "Yes, plus all the rest of the series: a conflict of superpowers looking to control the spice, Reverend Mothers using the spice to uncover hidden mental powers that grew their minds while rejecting artificial intelligence, and much more."

"But Dune has starships and...?"

"Titan is the *real* Dune!" she sharply interrupted me. "Of course these books are only science fiction. But they inform and inspire us, here in this alien wasteland located in our *actual* solar system. Learning of the Azotos' Green, the Founders of the Yuan recognized Titan's potential. They came here to establish a real-world Dune-type society. They sought to realize the grand vision of Frank Herbert: that *Homo sapiens* would rise from the ashes of the Extinction as a new, enlightened people. And they'd build it on a new and better world-philosophy, using all the precious Books of the Ark."

Yep, rising out of the ashes as a stoned-out, drug-addicted, and perpetually "mellowed" people—I laughed to myself. *Actually, that's not such a terrible vision.*

"So Frank Herbert is your 'Creator'?" I asked.

"Close but no cigar," she laughed back at me.

"What?"

"You'll shortly see."

"Ok, then," I nodded, not understanding. "But I don't see how *I* fit into this mythology. Am I supposed to be a female Paul Atreides, who becomes the messianic, super-powered 'Kwisatz Haderach'?"

She laughed. "No, Goddess, Dune and its sequels are only make-believe books. They establish our basis for being here on Titan. But your connection to us comes via *real* prophesy, an *actual* foretelling of the future."

"Eh?"

She took *Dune* out of my hands and reverently returned it to its place in the Ark. Then she did the same ritual of folding hands, bowing, and reaching in for yet another.

She placed another book in my hands.

Stunned, I read out loud its title: "*The Girl with the Turtle Tattoo...*by Daniel Basil Lyle...*what* the bloody hell?" I gasped.

My hands were trembling. I rapidly flipped through the pages. By the soft yellow light, I saw revealed in the text the *real* history of my mother: how she met my father, their true adventures, and how they were first separated. Amazing!

"There's more," she simply stated, taking the book from my trembling hands and replacing it, in turn, with a stunning progression of others: *The Girl who Played with Fate, The Girl who Tempted God, The Girl who Danced with Snakes, The Girl who Flew too High, The Girl who Chased Spaceships, The Girl who Wrangled Asteroids, The Girl who Rocked Stars, The Girl who Could Not Die,* and *The Girl who was Everywhere*. As each in turn was placed into my hands, she gave me a minute to flip through some of the pages, catching glimpses of the stories contained therein.

Then she took the last book out of my trembling hands, placing it reverently back in the golden Ark.

"T-those last f-four volumes were of *m-me!*" I stammered, barely able to see straight. I was in shock. "I can understand a contemporary of mine somehow chronicling what happened to my mother and her family. But '*The Girl who Could Not Die*' was of me right *now*. In fact it's taking big sections of my present diary entries word-for-word. It's like they've snatched them from my AR archive! And the next book...I haven't even written those diary sections yet!"

She nodded knowingly.

"It is prophesy, Goddess. The Author saw and wrote your future, which includes us here beneath the glaciers of Titan. It is how we knew to expect you: a 'black lady who fell from the sky, turned white, and would save the Yuan'. That's a *direct quote* from '*The Girl who Could Not Die.*' It was written way back on Old Earth, preserved by our Founders, and studied in detail by each Holy Momma, including me."

"But that's impossible," I protested, standing up and bumping my head on the ice-rock ceiling. "Ouch!" I grunted, putting a hand on my bruised head.

I bent forward, pacing back and forth in the small space. Glenda sat again in her small wood chair, serenely folding her metallic hands over her blue robe. She seemed completely at peace, resigned to knowing the future.

"I have great faith in you," she smiled beatifically. "You *will* save my people. I've read it and it is true. Thank you, Goddess."

Yes, I could milk her ignorance. I could play on the weird coincidences written in the "prophesy" books. Clearly the author knew of my Mom and documented some of her adventures. But I felt guilty fooling the sweet little-lady "Holy Momma" I'd grown to know as a friend.

That Old Earth science fiction author could *not* know my future.

"How can you have so much faith in some centuries-dead Old Earth science fiction author?" I challenged her. "Have you heard of L. Ron Hubbard? He was another science fiction author that established a religion called 'Scientology.' It had weird stuff about flying saucers and aliens and..."

"There's nothing weird at all about the Godly philosophy of Creativity-Theology," she firmly asserted.

"Say what?"

She reached into the golden Ark and extracted yet another book, placing it in my hands. I sat down, reading its name out loud: "*Creative-Theology®...by Daniel B. Lyle, Ph.D.*, huh?"

"And there's more," she continued, taking the book back and re-placing it with a series of others.

I read aloud the name of each new book in turn: "*In Search of Quality, Principles and Mechanisms*; *The God Debate, Real Evidence for and against God's Existence*; *The Book of Lyle*; and *The Real Jesus.*"

She took the last book from my hands, placing it reverently back into the Ark. Then she turned a switch that let the heavy golden lid slowly ratchet down into place. I heard a solid "thunk" as the Ark sealed itself. Then I heard an extended "swish" as the internal air was ejected.

"That's a lot," I sincerely concluded, not knowing what to make of it all. "It's a substantial group of writings," I diplomatically concluded.

"Oh, that's not all by a longshot," she smiled at me. "There's more in the Ark. Lyle also wrote a series of ten volumes on what Jesus would have told his followers if he'd returned to pre-Extinction Old Earth. Then there was another series of books on understanding and overcoming Stress. And..."

"Why have I never heard of this prolific author?" I interjected.

"Sadly, he wasn't commercially successful."

"Was he a poor writer?"

"Quite to the contrary," she asserted. "But he didn't just write yet-'another' science fiction book or what people wanted to hear about their religion or whatever. He was true to his creative muse. He embodied the new religion he authored and founded: seeking to first please God by exercising his own God-given Creativity. He wrote for future generations. *And*...he wrote for us here on Titan."

"But how did all these books find their way to Titan?"

"He knew."

"He?"

"Well, three actually," she smiled slyly. "You know them."

"What? Some sort of 'holy trinity'?"

"In a way," she grinned broadly, "The Mother, Father, and Child—gathering our treasures from right after the Extinction, preparing the way for our eventual journey here to Titan."

She pulled out an old picture and handed it to me. It was a picture I'd seen before upon my arrival to the Moon, dating from an even earlier time-period.

"I...don't...freaking...believe it," I gasped.

There in the frame was a very old white-skinned man with a big splotchy head, a black-skinned smiling lady, and their teenaged son.

So Arthur did more for me than just prepare a way back from the second Dimension—I marveled. *He and his family gathered the books of Lyle together, including Lyle's collection of Herbert's books, preserving them in the Colony. Anderson's descendants kept the dream alive as mankind expanded out into the solar system. This must have been what Author meant when he said "We'll meet on Saturn." He was one of the chief Founders of a whole new society!*

Simply amazing!

But I was getting very cold and weary. I wanted out of the subterranean, spooky crypt. I needed some more Titanian Tea. Besides being a legacy of Anderson, the ancient roots of their strange religion weren't real to me. So Anderson got obsessed with an obscure, failed SF writer's books. So what?

But suddenly a *chill* went through me, not from the cold room but from a stunning memory.

"Hey," I marveled, frowning, "You know, I think I *saw* the author of those 'girl with the turtle tattoo' books."

"Yes?" she grinned at me. "And just when did this happen?"

She's teasing me. She already knows. She read it in the book!

"It was at the last musical concert held on Old Earth," I continued, "which I happened to attend. A local man played a synthesizer during an intermission...I remember now...his name was 'Daniel Lyle'—just like the author of those books!"

"Where was this?'

"It was outside a small town called Sulphur, in the state of Oklahoma, my hometown in the U.S.A."

"Well, Goddess, that's exactly where the book says the publisher of his books was located, a 'LylePublishing'," she nodded, clearly teasing me again.

"I can't believe this!" I gasped in confusion.

"Was he good?"

"What?"

"Daniel Lyle playing his synthesizer at the rock concert—was he good?"

"He was marvelous—very innovative with tremendous energy!"

"My, what a delightful memory to cherish," she sighed, closing her eyes contentedly. "You saw our Creator and he was a great musician. That's glorious!"

"Creator? But how could I...?"

Suddenly a huge GRINDING noise *blasted* through the small cave. The rock under our feet *twisted* and *jerked*, throwing me to the floor. Reflexively I crawled the few feet over to Glenda and put my arms protectively around her small body. She was trembling, unconscious. She'd hit her head. Blood was dripping from her copper crown. Her mechanical arms were splayed out to each side, jerking uncontrollably.

The heater snapped off. The glow-bulb above my head winked out. We were in total darkness. I could feel Titan reaching out its icy fingers to me, grasping for my heart.

But then I saw a *weird hot red glow* beating down on us from above.

Looking up, I saw a pinpoint, incredibly powerful *red laser beam* slice through the rock-ice above us, just missing the Ark.

"It's our enemies," I gasped out loud. "How did they find us?"

And then I knew...feeling a continuing, vicious *vibration* at my side. From the sheath hanging on my belt I yanked out the *knife blade* that I now knew had been *deliberately* inserted and broken off in my body. It was sending out a powerful high-tech *signal* penetrating the rock-ice above and leading our enemy right to us! The laser beam was tracking its signal. I'd been set-up!

Horrified, I realized it was the same as with the knife blade on Ailith's helicopter. It tracked our location so those missiles could bring us down! Fehler and his unknown benefactors left a spy in Ailith's camp, just as they'd now made me into one!

The Mayor said the Dilmun's transmitters couldn't penetrate the glacier—I mentally confirmed my suspicions. *This tech definitely isn't theirs, but their surface collaborators. Have the grand-conspirators found me out? Is this to silence me for good?*

I slammed the knife down into the steel-hard rock beneath me, time and again until the blade was bent, my hand was bloody, and the vibration stopped.

"*I* did this," I sobbed, cradling Glenda's limp little body. "Instead of saving the Yuan I've *betrayed* them."

As the incredibly potent, satellite-based laser beam now moved away from us, seemingly confused and searching, it *shattered* the ceiling.

"Not again," I groaned as smothering rock-ice hunks rained down and buried us alive.

I resurrected gasping desperately for air!

"Don't struggle, Goddess, we have you."

I looked up into a wide, hosed facemask. Holding up my head with his good left arm was Torque. Another likewise-masked Yuan was busily fitting a facemask onto me, adjusting it for my larger face. The Major's white hair was a mess, sticking up in clumps around his own straps. His impeccable red suit was now in tatters. He looked like hell. I myself felt like I'd just had my lungs ripped out of my body, then mashed flat with a sledgehammer, then stuffed back through my nostrils into my empty chest.

God, it hurts—I groaned to myself.

Looking to the side to get my bearings I saw a huge mound of ice-rock chunks beside an idle backhoe. A cluster of masked little-people were now digging with pickaxes and shovels by hand, handing up hunks from a ragged tunnel leading down into the ground.

"D-did you just d-dig me out of the H-Holy of Holies?" I stammered, starting to get my breath back as oxygen flowed from my attached facemask canister.

"It's been a week since the Dilmuns' sneak attack," the Major snarled. "The Temple was destroyed, collapsed down upon the Holy of Holies. First we had to dig through the rubble. Then we discovered that the airlock hatch was intact but the staircase destroyed. The passageway leading down to the crypt had completely imploded. We found you buried at the bottom."

"And...Glenda?"

"We're retrieving her body now. She's dead. The fact that you are still alive confirms your Deity, Goddess," he reverently stated. His big green eyes were misty with religious devotion. "Some doubted the Holy Momma's claims, but no more. Only the Prophesized *Messiah* could survive being crushed without air for a week. Now you must take our Holy Momma's place. You must *lead* us!"

Lead them? Sweet little Glenda is dead? What the hell happened?

I blinked rapidly, clearing my vision. I lunged upward to my feet, looking around me in horror...

I almost cried-out at the awful vista I saw. Two of the sunlight globes high above were still glowing, but flickering badly. The dirty nuclear reactor must be still working, but just barely. By the uneven twilight I saw devastation rivaled only by what I'd seen immediately following the Extinction outside Old Earth's Sulphur, Oklahoma. The vast orchards of tea bush-trees, the forest areas, the giant mushrooms, and the fields of crops were all gone. In their place was charred, smoking desolation. It looked like the huge cavern had been destroyed in a raging forest fire. The villages and central city were flattened by huge chunks fallen from the cavern's ceiling. Nothing remained intact.

"Why are we not frozen solid?" I asked, gazing up at the ceiling, expecting to see through to Titan's orange surface. Instead I saw what looked like ragged scars running across the largely still-intact high roof.

"Their powerful orbital laser beams punctured the glacier, setting everything on fire down here," Torque growled. "Large areas of the ceiling broke free and smashed down into us. But the gaps created by the lasers melting the overhead glacier ice quickly refroze solid. So we lost a lot of our atmosphere, but weren't completely vented. The attacking Dilmun who'd made it through the maze simply had to wait until the fires abated. Then they swarmed us, taking everything left of value. Those of us still alive could only put up a token defense before hiding out until the invaders left."

"How badly damaged was your nuclear reactor?"

"There are four modules. Two were crushed by falling ice-rock. The invaders blew up the remaining two pods. However, one of those modules is still working, though poorly. When it dies we'll be in the dark."

That was a sobering thought. The Dilmun weren't just seeking to dominate the Yuan, but to destroy their cities, their very civilization.

"So they knew the exact route to follow to find us?"

"There must have been a traitor," Torque bitterly stated. "I'd never have believed it, but one of our people must have given them explicit directions. It's undeniable."

I should confess—I moaned inwardly. *They say that confession is good for the soul. The Yuan probably won't even blame me. How could I possibly know that the knife blade left in my chest was a 'Trojan horse'? Unknown to me, it gave away both my path through the maze and the exact location of Shangdu. But if I tell the Yuan, then they'll lose faith in my "deification". There's no way they'll believe in a Messiah who betrayed them.*

I felt tempted to reach down and pat Torque on his head, but resisted the impulse. He didn't need any comforting. I heard controlled *fury* in his voice. Likely he'd not had any of his mellowing tea for a while. He exhibited a raging anger that I needed him to cherish and grow. Then I could focus it, directing it to a target of my own choosing.

This is a horrible situation. But it happened. Now I need to turn it to my advantage—I sternly ordered myself.

"It was likely superior tech that revealed our location," I stated a half-truth, giving Torque an excuse not to suspect his own people. "Likely it was given to them by their sponsor organizations on the surface. But we'll make them *pay*—both the Dilmun and their sponsor!"

The workers around me paused, looking up at me expectantly.

"This is no longer a skirmish or thievery!" I shouted to everyone within earshot. "This is *war!*"

The Yuan cheered lustily.

"So what did they steal from us?" I asked Torque more quietly, as the workers went back to their tasks. I was surprised anything of value remained after the lethal laser blasts set the cavern on fire.

"Our vault was still intact, untouched behind the remains of the Temple. But they broke into it and took our treasures," Torque sighed. "It contained all our hoarded green-ore. Besides destroying our capital city, that was their main goal. And of course they made sure *all* of our fresh tea was destroyed, both stores and bush-tree groves."

Oh, hell—I groaned, the waves of pain again descending upon me. I grit my teeth together, trying not to scream. *My sweet tea is completely gone. I can't drink that wondrous brew anymore. But it's not just me...the mellow little-people here have all lost their "buzz" as well.*

"The tea is gone?" I lamely asked, hoping a few leaves were left. I desperately needed a cup!

"The other communities may have some, but they were largely depended on shipments from us," Torque admitted, so low I could barely hear him. "We never thought Shangdu could be sacked. We were too jealous of our product, centralizing our production here. But I'm getting reports that the invaders have moved on to the other settlements. Apparently some of our maps survived in the courthouse. Our other main encampments are likewise being breached, sacked, and left in ruins. Their nuclear reactors are also being blown up, preventing us from growing any more crops here under the ice. So the only source of tea, poor as it is, will be the Dilmuns' weak substitute—which they're unlikely to share with us."

"That's brutal," I commiserated with him.

"They *won't* like us without our tea!" he roared to everyone within earshot. "We may be few but we are *angry!* And with no more tea to soothe our rage, Goddess, we will follow you to *hell* to get our *revenge!*" he shouted, spittle flying from his mouth.

Good, very good—I congratulated myself. *If this terrible tragedy had to occur, it's brought me a maniacal army of crazed dwarfs to share my obsession. Together we'll regroup, plan and train, then destroy the Dilmun and their sponsors. And from there we'll move on to uncover and decimate the conspiracy that started this whole mess in the first place. Kill my "little people" will you? I'll rip your guts out!*

I left behind the likewise seething, sputtering Major. I stepped around piles of smoking debris to look down into the new tunnel. Workers were there dragging out the mangled body of Glenda. Still attached were the shattered remains of her mechanical arms. I looked away. She'd been mashed flat by the crumbling, crushing ice-rock.

"And...the Ark?" I asked the workers, hopeful. I made motions with my hands of the form of the Ark, plus its iconic legs.

It held my future. It contained all the answers I craved. Studying those Holy Texts, I would know for sure what happened to my Mother. Yes, my Quest for sweet revenge might end. I might even walk away from the little-people and their stupid civil war. But at last having my answers I could finally be at peace, perhaps discover a way to permanently die.

The workers just shrugged at me, exhausted from their toils.

"You must have gotten to it!" I yelled in exasperation. "You got my and Glenda's body out. We were right next to the Ark!"

But even though it was made of solid gold, it could have been crushed by the tons of rock-ice slamming down upon it. Broken open, the slurry of thawed ice would likely ruin what remained of the delicate, ancient books inside. All that wisdom, history, and future-prediction would be lost. But that "worst-case" scenario needn't have happened. It *couldn't!*

"Gonada fromallia," a one-eyed worker sobbed. She shrugged dejectedly.

I looked over at Torque who met my gaze, staring me down.

"What did she say?" I asked the Major, hoping I'd heard wrong.

"It's gone, Goddess," he stoically affirmed. "There's not a trace of it left. Perhaps, like you said, the sponsor of the Dilmun gave them some unknown technology to locate the gold and retrieve it. We don't know. In the aftermath of the attack, everything was confused. The Dilmun must have somehow taken it. They were here at the Temple, breaking open the vault. They revered the Ark the same as us. Stealing it would be the crown jewel of their loot. But none of us saw them drill down and take it."

I sighed deeply, slumping down with my back against some still-smoking timbers. By patches of paint still left on it I saw it was a part of the golden-painted Buddha statue.

Ah, the gods must be crying!

I put both of my hands up to my facemask, covering my own eyes. I didn't want to show weakness. I didn't want the others to see *me* cry. Then I felt a soft hand on the back of my neck, comforting me.

Lowering my trembling hands, I looked into the kind face of little *Shawnee*, now on level with my own.

"You're alive!" I sobbed, grabbing her small shoulders and hugging her close.

"I was lucky to get into a mask when the breaches occurred," she explained. Her soft voice was wavering from shock. "I tried to get the hatch open to bring you and the Holy Momma up, but failed. Then the Temple's roof came down. I managed to get out in time and hid until those evil Dilmun left. My High Priestess is gone, but you, dear Goddess, remain. As I did for her I am yours to command. I now serve *you*, with all my heart."

I was immensely grateful, hugging her close again.

But then a harsh whisper from the back of her head said: "Don't get too comfortable."

"What?" I gasped. I gently tilted Shawnee's head to the side and peering at her conjoined twin.

But the second face's eyes were still white, sightless. And its lips were pressed together, speechless.

Perhaps I'd imagined the voice...but it spoke truth. Now was *not* the time for crying or overseeing a lengthy recovery. No, it was time to mount a savage counterattack, time for *war*.

Damn right they won't like us without our tea!

Chapter 10

MARS

The Roman God of War
Holding the reins of terror and death
Worshipped by soldiers and diplomats alike
A deity of strength, character, and enlightenment
A guardian of agriculture, food from good order
Paradoxically securing peace through brutal power
Protecting all that is worthy through military might
Riding the storm with a sharp, unstoppable spear
A handsome man with curly mustache and beard
Enticing even the Goddess of Love, Venus herself
A hard fist in a velvet glove, caressing victims
Enshrined in the year as the month of March
The beginning of both renewal and conflict...

The Rise and Fall of *Homo sapiens*, 10:93-97

I resurrected lying on my back inside an open coffin, listening to music. My eyes seemed glued shut.

At least it seemed to be a coffin. I felt a small pillow at the back of my skull, tilting my head upward. My hands were folded serenely over my chest. Forcing them to move I fumbled at a neat but musty uniform on my body. Set prominently on my belt was a sheathed knife. And beneath me cushioning my body, was a soft surface. To all sides I felt a satin-smooth lining.

Is that Hank Williams Jr. playing "Born to Boogie?"—I marveled.

Yes, it had a powerful, fast country-western beat with horns blaring behind the melody: "Too much fun!"

In my pocket I felt a comforting lump, my blue marble.

How did it return to me? The last thing I remember was the robot gloating as it showed me my marble, previously stolen from me.

I fumbled at my eyes, forcing my glued-together eyelids apart.

The first thing I saw was *frost* coating a clear canopy above me, plus most of the fabrics, and even across my skin. Even more bizarre, I didn't feel cold. In fact, I didn't feel anything at all.

"W-what's g-going on?" I whispered. I could barely move my stiff tongue and thickened lips.

I saw large cracks rippling through the clear canopy. The loud music was somewhere outside, leaking in. Down toward my feet I spied a broken-in hunk of the canopy material. Wasn't the canopy made of standard plasteel? Something must have hit it with a lot of force to break open a hole.

My lungs greedily sucked in acrid air. It was like I'd just escaped ongoing suffocation. But I got a snout-full of stinking fume-filled air. Regardless, it was wonderful.

It's lucky my legs weren't snapped by whatever broke the canopy—I calmly analyzed the situation. *That would really hurt...hey, why aren't I suffering my usual post-resurrection agony? I don't feel anything at all, whether pain, pleasure, or even pressure. It's like every nerve cell in my body has switched off. It's great not to be suffering, but...?*

And then I heard the *shouting*...like I was in the middle of a riot!

A young boy in ragged clothing clambered up on top of my coffin, with a "boom box" set on his shoulders. But he wasn't playing Hank Williams. His music was from some group I'd never heard of using instruments I couldn't identify. He looked down, saw me looking back, gasped, and hopped away.

"Ah, come on, man," I mumbled, wearily closing my eyes. "I'm trying to take a nap here."

I heard still other clashing music. What was going on? It was like everyone had a boom box and was trying to outplay the other.

But rather than abate, the shouting and jumbled music got even louder. And then my entire coffin *rocked* back-and-forth, arms springing up onto the broken canopy above me, like a crowd was trying to tumble me over onto my side!

They succeeded. I was thrown against the now-to-my-side cano-py, feeling it bending outward.

"Alright, then," I croaked, struggling to move leaden arms. "I'm getting up! I'm getting up!"

With creaking muscles, I tried to push out from under the now-ajar canopy. But it was stuck. Fumbling out my knife I stuck it into a crack under the lid and pushed hard. The canopy sprang outward. I crawled out from beneath it, looking around furtively.

Holy freaking chaos!—I gasped to myself, totally confused.

I saw I was in the midst of a riot. Legs, shoes, and boots swarmed around me. I heard guns being fired. Sprays of blood soiled my white uniform. The people on the street responded by hurtling rocks. Someone stepped on my head, bruising my cheek. One of my boots was ripped off my foot as someone tried to drag me away. Clutching my knife in self-defense I tried to ball up into a fetal position.

The battling music around me got louder, more intense...

"Quick! Follow me if you want to live," I heard an intense voice off to my side.

I saw an oriental lady. She wore a black "ninja" outfit, complete with a wide golden belt at her waist. Over her head was a black ski mask, revealing only almond-shaped black eyes. And in her hand was a curved "samurai" sword, stained bright red with dripping blood.

Oh Christ—I gasped. *It's a killer! She's going to stick me!*

As I tried to cringe away, she grabbed my hand and jerked me to my feet. It was hard to stand. I had to look down to see where my feet were placed. I couldn't feel the surface beneath me. I sheathed my own blade, concentrating on moving my feet, one of them addi-tionally hobbled by being bootless.

She put a supporting arm around my shoulders. I felt a sharp pain in my upper back. Had a rock struck me?

"But I...?" I tried to protest.

"Run!" she yelled, now dragging me along with her.

Fast approaching, I saw what looked like a squad of riot police. They had on combat armor, carried large guns, wielded transparent shields, and wore heavy-duty gas masks. Behind them I heard loud "whumps" as glittering metallic canisters arced high above us, then down into the crowd. The grenades exploded, filling the air with noxious red gas!

They're going to capture me—I realized. *In a moment I won't be able to breathe. They'll grab me, arrest me!*

Then I saw orange-robed, hooded, Buddhist-like monks form a passive line against the charging police. They linked arms, forming a physical barrier, seemingly protecting me.

"Here!" my friend shouted above the roar of the crowd, dragging me into an opened doorway and slamming it shut behind us.

I was coughing and gagging from just a whiff of the gas I'd inhaled. I could only imagine the agony that the mob I'd left behind was experiencing. Yes, I could hear their tortured screams. That red gas wasn't standard tear gas. It was much more potent, perhaps lethal. But I couldn't slow down to clear my lungs. My "friend" was yanking me along behind her.

I felt like I was bouncing from step to step. I noted that the gravity was less than that of Earth, but about twice what I'd experienced on the Moon.

Jesus Christ!—I concluded as time seemed to slow down, yet again in an "analytical" mindset, *I must be on Mars. The gravity on Mars is 38% of Earth's. On the Moon, gravity was a mere 17% of Earth's. So how'd my dead body get to Mars? I thought Q was going to bury my body forever beneath ice sheets in Peary Crater. What the hell happened to me—and to society?*

Then Time abruptly accelerated.

"Stop right there!" I heard a deep voice from in front of us.

Down the corridor in front, approaching at a dead run, were six armed police. I was ready to obey the order, cease my hobbling. But my companion had other ideas...

Without hesitation she *slammed* straight into them. Before they could react in the tight quarters, she flashed out her sword and cleanly *sliced off* two of their heads. In the same movement she *skewered* two others through their hearts. And with well-targeted kicks she *shattered* the kneecaps of the remaining two.

With nary a pause we slipped past their toppling bodies, around a corner, and into a side tunnel.

"In here!" she said, kicking off a duct-grate and pulling me inside. She reached back and carefully reaffixed the grate. Clearly this was a route she'd often traveled.

And then we were crawling through a maze of shafts, going up and down, taking a bewildering series of turns. I could barely keep up, floundering and shoving at the tight metal walls inside the duct-work. Finally we tumbled down a long side chute into what looked like a dank, dark basement.

"We're safe," she calmly stated, removing her ski mask.

I recognized that impassive face. This woman was the spitting image of *Sanako*, the Japanese *Time Keeper* I'd fought against at Woodstock back on Old Earth when I was the pop star "Suzette Kingly." Subsequently she reluctantly worked with me and my team at the disastrous Concert at the Galactic Center as The Commissioner's representative.

Is this her?—I tried to figure out. *Is this actually Sanako? Did she track me down through Time? Is she responsible for whatever's happening to me now?*

"There's a toilet in the corner," the woman matter-of-factly pointed. Above the toilet a single glowstrip was pasted onto a dripping, wet brick wall. The strip's dim fluorescence was all that lit the single, closed-off room. There was no door. "And there's an inset 'refrigerator' with soylent green cubes. Sorry, that's all the food I've got stashed here."

Soylent green?—I gasped to myself. *This has to be Mars, a hundred or more years into the future past moon-colonization. How is it that they're eating post-Extinction survival-muck? What's happening outside? Why was there a deadly riot met with lethal force? And why did all the people in the rioting crowd seem to have their own boom box?*

"This is one of my safe sites," the woman calmly continued. "It used to be a bottom basement before I closed off all exits except for the shaft. There's a faucet and a sink. Plus I've a terminal that's hardwired into a nearby fiber optic cable, pirating the feed. The hardwiring plus several of my own firewalls prevent detection by the authorities. Use it however you wish. You can reach out but no one can reach in. I'll be back in several hours, or a couple days, whatever. Have fun!" she cheerfully concluded, smiling sadistically at me.

"Wait! I need to know..."

But she was gone, smoothly squirming back up the "delivery chute." I heard faint bumps as she climbed into higher ductwork. What did she mean by me "having fun"?

"—who you are and what happened to me?" I lamely finished my question.

Wobbling, I looked about trying to get my bearings. There wasn't much more than what she'd already pointed out to me. The room was a ten-foot wide cube. There wasn't even a chair. If I wanted to sit, I'd have to balance on the lip of the lidless toilet bowl. It had a button that triggered a release of water from inside the wall.

This place is a "solitary-confinement" jail cell—I realized.

Then I turned around to face the deliver chute. *Wait, I can escape just like that ninja lady did.*

But my hopes were dashed.

Ah, rats! She's locked me in!

Yes, a thick metal grate now was solidly set into place at the opening. The inch-thick grate had two-inch wide-open squares set therein, allowing air to pass but stopping hands or arms. I saw a snapped-over bar on the inside of the chute that solidly locked the grate in place. A complicated latch controlled the bar mechanism, out of reach of my grasping fingers. It was set an unreachable twelve inches inside the chute. Having gotten me here, the Sanako look-alike wasn't letting me run around on my own. Not that I was in much shape for more climbing around through those awful ductworks.

"Auuuggghhhh!" I suddenly screamed, startling myself. I crumpled down onto the cold, hard floor.

A wave of *excruciating pain* shot through my legs, crippling me. It was a similar (though much amplified) feeling to sleeping on a portion of one's body, having the blood flow there greatly decreased, deadening the nerves at that location, not feeling that part of the body at all...then having the nerves "wake up" when blood flow was restored.

Pain!

My nerve cells are firing up—I realized, panicked but still trying to analyze my situation. *Kept frozen at near absolute zero in that permanently dark moon crater must have done extra damage to my nerve cells. Molecular motion almost stops at absolute zero Kelvin. My dead body was never that cold before.*

"No!" I yelled as I *convulsed* on the floor. I felt nerves in my back recovering full functionality. It was like someone was *ripping* the flesh off my shoulder blades and ribs, one strip at a time.

I'm being fish-filleted alive!

"Please," I whimpered, realizing I'd just peed my pants but not caring. "Just let it stop!"

But the agony did not stop. The nerves of my body were now fully activating, each biological section taking its turn to "come awake", causing fresh waves of hideous agony.

Thankfully the mind can only endure so much. I felt myself slipping into unconsciousness, *cursing* the memory of the brutal Sanako!

Yes, it *had* to be her. And, yes, she *knew* what would happen to me. She'd always hated me and my Mom. She was probably laughing right now, knowing the suffering I was enduring. My last thought before fainting was: *Sanako is a bitch!*

A "few hours?" A "few days?" No! A full *two weeks* later Sanako had not yet returned. I was still locked in a God-damned prison cell.

In the interim, I recovered enough to clean myself up at the sink. I rinsed out my soiled underwear and pants. Then I ate a few of the nauseating soylent green cubes. The "refrigerator" was a recess set-into the wall, kept cold by surrounding icy bedrock. Fortunately, though, the recess was loaded with the mushy "soylent green" cubes. Sadly, there was nothing else to eat. I quickly came to loath the things. Also, I found the computer terminal, set into the wall right beside the toilet. The screen's white light was a welcome change from the dim fluorescence strip. The computer-interface was an antique flat screen with an actual fold-down, type-in keyboard. Likely the older tech plus Sanako's overlapping layers of firewalls was what kept it undetected by the local intelligent internet. Powering it up, I was determined to avidly explore Mars' (to me) futuristic records, all the while perched on the toilet's hard lip.

But before that happened, I collapsed for several long, indetermi-
nate periods on the naked, hard floor. There wasn't even a mat to lie
on. My body was still recovering from having been kept in zero-
atmosphere at close to zero degrees Kelvin for a couple hundred
years. Yep, all those "zeroes" would slow anyone down. And it didn't
help that it was perpetually cold in my cell, around 55° Fahrenheit.
That wasn't enough to kill me, but my weakened body could still get
sick. Indeed, I was continually coughing up phlegm. A flow of warmer air through the iron grate from structures above me kept the temperature from plunging even lower. But the icy bricks all around me
continually sucked away the modest heat.

But at least the intense pain flaring through the reviving sections
of my body abated enough for me to get to work. I was ready to attack
the computer terminal.

I hope what I find isn't just more crap—I laughed to myself. Actually, that was prophetic. After only a few meals, my healthy brown
stools had changed into a disgusting green. *God, I hope I get something else to eat soon.*

My first search was to confirm the ingredients of my awful food.
Yep, they were made of a combination of algae and bacteria, but
grown on sterilized *human feces*. On Earth post-Extinction, the main
organic source for the microbes grown in giant "soylent green" vats
was sludge taken from the vast dumpsites that'd accumulated over
decades and hundreds of years. I found that on Mars most of their
waste streams were recycled. The only large source of organics was
feces from the expanding Martian population. I supposed it was a
better source of organics than tossing human corpses into the soylent
green fermentation vats (as happened in the iconic 1973 film of the
same name), but not by much. The toilet I sat on worked much as I
was used to back on the Moon. I discovered that the waste stream
went to a processing plant where contaminants were removed, water
was extracted, and the organics were compacted. On the Moon, the
processed, cleaned feces became soil for growing plants. On Mars
that arduous process was truncated to directly grow large quantities
of edible microbes.

Whether potato or algae, any plant's job is to "fix" carbon. The
main source of carbon is CO_2 from the atmosphere. Although 100

times thinner than Earth's atmosphere, Mar's air is 95% CO2, an abundant source of carbon. Sunlight on Mars is at best only 60% the strength of Earth's. But when sunlight is supplemented or replaced by nuclear reactor-powered grow-lamps, algae responds well. That only left finding sufficient water, which is scarce on Mar's surface. Subsurface water, however, was abundant on Mars. Closed lava tubes were a good place for ancient water to accumulate then freeze into easily accessible sheets.

So when you've got too many people and too little food...grow a mix of algae and bacteria! But even though I knew the green cubes were perfectly edible, they were all the more horrid to me knowing they were, in essence, reprocessed human feces.

Best to think of other things—I admonished myself, concentrating on other critical information.

Headlines of archived historical vids were particularly instructive. One struck me in my face: "MOON COLONIES UNITE TO REJECT ROBOT OVERLORD," dated from 237 years ago. Hah! Q should have remained safely hidden in the shadows. It turned out that the perpetually quarreling *Homo sapiens* species was eager to unite when confronting an outside, arrogant enemy. So after only a year of iron-handed rule, even Q's "loyal" troops turned on her. Even though Earth's leadership knew better (they were on the take from her), the common people refused to believe that their survival after the Extinction was because of a computer program, no matter how advanced. They labeled the robot as the actual "imposter" and me as the libeled, *true* human General. So they literally tore Q's physical robot-body into little chunks. More significantly, technicians and scientists rooted out Anderson's sophisticated, futuristic programming hidden deep inside Earth's buried servers, erasing every last trace of her.

"Q is dead," I muttered in satisfaction. "As Anderson's legacy she served a useful function, when caring out his explicit directions. On her own, though, she became an abomination."

"THE U.L.C. DECLARES INDEPENDENCE," another headline from 230 years ago read. The attached video record was fascinating. Realizing the benefits of pooling their resources, the *United Lunar Colonies* peacefully seceded from Earth. They belatedly honored me as their "Founding Mother." Hah! My little speech on the value of independence and having a lofty purpose, broadcast to everyone when we captured Peary Colony, wasn't wasted! Then, after several decades of searching, they located my body entombed by Q beneath the ice sheets down in Peary Crater. In a mistaken attempt to preserve me (my resurrection skills needed no assistance), they kept my still-intact body frozen in an airless coffin. So instead of a hidden icy tomb, they put me in a *public* freezer. Indeed, my frozen corpse was appropriately dressed and put on display at the Peary Colony spaceport. And in tribute to my struggle against the Robot, they returned the blue marble they'd found imbedded in Q's shattered robot to my corpse.

Ah, that's how it returned to my pocket.

Over the next couple hundred years, visitors dutifully gathered around my crypt. They marveled at the associated displays honoring my critical contribution to the Moon's peaceful separation from the "strangling" Earth governments. Also highlighted was my challenge to expand onward to Mars. Hah! I became an even more popular tourist destination than the Tranquility Base historical preserve.

Take that, Neil Armstrong and Buzz Aldrin—I smugly congratulated myself.

Another key video-headline I found was: "MARS COLONIES DECLARE INDEPENDENCE FROM THE U.L.C.," a mere fifty years after the first Mars base was established. Yes, the whole scenario that previously played out on the Moon happened yet again on Mars. Once the Moon colonies stopped bickering, they united around building fast-transit shuttles between Earth and Mars. Powered by Russian thermonuclear rockets, transit time dropped from six months down to a mere six days. The nearly airless, frozen, radiation-drenched surface of Mars remained, of course, inhospitable to life. However, several gigantic dead volcano sites scattered across Mars offered vast underground webs of huge, enclosed lava tubes. Due to the lower gravity on Mars, some of these ancient buried lava channels were large enough to house entire cities.

Sealed off by large airlocks at key points, a whole new human society developed underground on Mars. Over the last couple hundred years they'd become self-sufficient with their own indigenous agriculture, governments, and commerce. At first it seemed there was limitless space in the lava tube webs for relaxing all family planning limits and reproductive laws. Farm complexes, in particular, needed workers best bred from within one's own family. So a huge population-spurt occurred, which continued unabated into the future.

Homo sapiens' primitive drive to expand to occupy all available territory (as with any other animal) yet again took control, pushing out concern for future generations contained within a defined space. Yes, some efforts were in progress toward "terraforming" the surface of Mars. But best projections were that they would only achieve partial success a thousand years in the future. For the moment, human civilization on Mars thrived underground in the bowels of ancient, dead volcanoes.

But—as always—the wonders of civilization came with underlying disturbing faults. I found a revealing scholarly headline that said: "DISTURBING TRENDS FOR SOCIETAL MALADJUSTMENT AND FRAGMENTATION ON MARS." Reading the article closely, I saw an unvarnished analysis of societal trends on Mars. It seems that on the more freewheeling, music-ridden red planet (versus the now-staid, well-established colonies on the Moon where classical symphonies had replaced rock and jazz), all of mankind's vices blossomed. *Criminal syndicates* supplied anything for a price. *Religious extremists* sought their latest "Eden" regardless of its impact on nonbelievers. Their "infallible" leaders insisted on a God-given mandate from their particular Holy Texts to "replenish the Earth." This meant God wanted them to have as large families as possible, regardless of consequences. *Tribal clanners* claimed superiority for their historical lineages by denigrating, dehumanizing, and attacking others. *Corrupt governmental leaders* happily betrayed their followers for fleeting personal power and wealth. *Vicious warlords* flaunted the laws of society to expand their own fiefdoms. *Stifling police/military*, supposedly guaranteeing government-overseen Order instead became the "power behind the throne." *Arrogant scientists* did unethical research because they could, some becoming the heedless terraformers of Mars. And *militant guilds* insisted on self-serving contracts even if others lost out.

On the positive side of the ledger, though, mankind had neither stagnated nor died out. Music became the currency of creativity. Another recent headline caught my attention: "SPACE STATION LAUNCHED FOR SATURN." *Homo sapiens* as a species was moving beyond Mars, further out into the solar system. My "Moon Mandate" still existed! The commercial, cultural, and political forces back on Earth and the Moon were still focused on colonizing the entire solar system. The "new frontier" was now the frozen wastelands of Titan.

Especially notable were *modular space stations* readily assembled in orbit around the Moon or Mars, then dispatched intact to any location in the solar system. One such nascent space colony was already in high orbit around Saturn, where helium-3 mining was their main goal. Although fusion drives still weren't perfected, huge prototypes were being tested for possible future starships. Mining the moon had already generated modest amounts of He-3, sufficient for experimentation. But for the volume needed to power an actual starship, only Saturn's readily scooped atmospheric reserves would suffice. Helium-3 is the only stable isotope having more protons than neutrons, generated when cosmic rays bombard Saturn's upper atmosphere. On Earth the He-3 drifts off into space. But in Saturn's thicker atmosphere, far more distant from the sun, the precious gas is retained. In the meanwhile, corporate interests were greedily eyeing the low-tech, vast hydrocarbon fuel reservoirs of Titan, particular its methane seas. As the SSS (Saturn Space Station) spearheaded high-tech travel to the stars, primitive methane trains from Titan would power the continuing solar system expansion.

But that science-generated expansion was about to implode, brought to a screeching halt by a street-level revolution on Mars.

Another recent headline caught my eye: "RIOTS BREAK OUT OVER SOYLENT GREEN RATIONING." Unbelievably, the common citizens of the wealthy, thriving, lava-tube Mars cities were on the brink of starvation. It seemed that society was crumbling under the weight of unchecked population expansion, political corruption, rampant crime, religious intolerance, territorial skirmishes, clashing guilds, squabbling clanners, and the huge expense of pushing on out into the solar system. And the "revolutionaries" seeking to overthrow Mar's society used the pre-General *me* as their rallying force. That's why everyone had a boom-box, harkening back to the "courageous" restoration of music to society by the wildly successful popstar, Suzette Kingly. That's also why riots centered about my publically displayed freezer-coffin.

Man, I'm really popular—I laughed to myself. *Whether as a pop superstar or post-Extinction General I'm totally loved today!*

"So why weren't they playing some of *my* songs?" I complained to the empty, dank cell. "Ah well...I guess symbols get twisted to whatever end people want, regardless of the actual person. Sad!"

But I *did* have sympathy for the revolutionaries out there trying to supposedly "liberate" my dead corpse.

No society can do everything. Without limits, those with the least power suffer the most. I recalled the European-derived American expansion, built upon the backs of Native Americans, African slaves, and indentured labor. I remembered the earlier industrialization of the Soviet Union, built upon dislocation and decimation of its peasant agrarian society. There were many other examples throughout history. Mars was no different. The rapidly expanding population on Mars had been squeezed for too long. Now those at the bottom were at the end of their patience. As also seen throughout history, the mobs were fighting back. This accounted for the riot I'd resurrected into when my sealed memorial coffin was breached. What I'd seen was a toxic brew of hatred, frustration, and desperation.

So, as always, I saw that the "ledger balance" for the *Homo sapiens* species was, again, "iffy." There were clear positives, but also huge negatives. And by far the worst abomination of all I saw in the archived video records was the *Guild of Assassins*. A headline just a month ago screamed: "ARSIA CITY'S MURDER RATE SKYROCKETS." Arsia Mons was Mars' largest lava-tube network, within which was the planet's capital city, *Arsia City*. It was presently bursting with a population estimated at ten million people. Many of the murders were attributed to targeted assassinations. It was here that my frozen corpse, acquired by treaty from the Moon, was displayed. It was also the headquarters of the secretive Assassins' Guild, which I found both fascinating and repulsive. It was a shadowy organization held together by brutal internal rules. I saw that it combined all the worst features of Mars' corrupt society: apparently working for the highest bidder, cultivating ruthless devotion to its deadly craft, demanding blind religious dedication to its traditions and doctrines, mandating supporting each other regardless of circumstance, and worshipping hereditary leadership of near godhood status. I suspected Sanako was one of them.

"Glad I'm not one of those," I sighed, wobbling on the hard edge of my toilet bowl.

My butt was really hurting.

Yes, I was getting tired again. Aside from long stretches of near-collapse on the hard, cold floor, I'd been doing my online research nonstop since Sanako abandoned me there in the small basement. But I had to persist, especially in digging out the *most* important "future" situation: *me!* Yes, I'd already documented "The General's" rise to fame, fall, and heroic rehabilitation both on the Moon and Mars. But I now needed to do a "deep dive" into secured historical and extant bank records. I needed to find out if what I put in place on the Moon over two centuries ago had fallen flat or soared.

"So, Suzy...are you a 'nobody' or a 'somebody'?" I asked myself.

It was difficult worming my way into highly encrypted super-sophisticated, future bank-computer systems. But I'd planned well during the short time I had back on the Moon. I'd built in long-term "back doors" that I'd be able to quickly access even hundreds of years into the future. And some of those programs which I inserted back on the Moon had borne great fruits.

"Excellent!" I grinned broadly, wearily turning off the terminal.

I *was* a "somebody"! Actually, I was *several* somebodies. If I ever escaped my jail cell, I'd have my choice of assuming a variety of "secret identities." They'd covertly been established and maintained across the successive decades by my secret computer programs (patterned after the devious Q but without her self-aware intelligence), each backed by massive wealth. Yes, the authorities had taken a lot of "The General's" stash when Q was dethroned. But I'd anticipated having to sacrifice a superficial treasure in order to protect an even greater hidden horde. Secreted away in untouchable bank pots was more "gold" than I'd ever need. My potential was limitless. And I'd use that wealth to once-and-for-all get the heart of the conspiracy to murder my mother.

All I have to do is to wait for Sanako's return to set me free.

But that was not to be. At six weeks, still stuck in my underground prison cell, I was getting increasingly desperate. Sanako had not returned. I could only conclude she was dead, captured, or incapacitated. If her slaughter of the police that confronted us in the corridor was an indicator of her usual actions, she must be a declared "enemy of the state." She likely had a "kill on sight" designation, at least for her masked "ninja" persona. And she'd built her safe-room too well. Not only was it impenetrable by outside searchers, it was impossible to escape! I'd done everything I could think of to get out on my own and failed at every turn.

"So let's take inventory," I forced myself to calm down, to go into my time-stopping analytical mode. "On the positive side I still have electricity, water, and continuing Internet access. On the negative side I've eaten the last of those awful soylent green cubes. I'm getting sicker and weaker by the minute. And I can't break out."

Yes, I already tried to dig out the bricks in the walls using my knife. I got a few out, but behind them all I found only icy bedrock. I also tried loosening and dislodging the chute, but it was firmly set into that very same unyielding bedrock. And the thick iron grate-blocking passage was only openable from the other side. Its main latch-mechanism was far out of the reach of my grasping fingers.

"So...do I die and hope that someday my desiccated corpse is discovered then resurrects?" I sighed, defeated. "Unless...?"

Can I contact the authorities and throw myself on their mercy?— I mused. *Maybe they won't blame me for the actions of Sanako. I can rightly claim she kidnapped me. Wait...they can't know I'm me. I can't let anyone know I'm the legendary Suzette Kingly who saved Earth from the aliens at the Galactic Core. There's still a chance that my deliberate defeat at the celestial contest—losing the "prize" of becoming a "blessed" planet—could be challenged if anyone knew I was still alive. I can't even claim to be the General, a centuries old corpse. They'd certainly throw me in a looney bin.*

I fingered my knife. The blade was still sharp. If worse came to worse I could commit "seppuku", ritual suicide. There was no need for me to suffer, to waste away to nothing. Someday my corpse might indeed be discovered and I'd have a chance to reanimate.

"I don't like killing myself," I grimaced, hastily sheathing my blade.

But what other choice do I have?—I groaned to myself. *Either I end my present suffering or try to contact the authorities. Surely they could trace my location to this basement if they're notified I'm tapping into their Internet. But, then again, Sanako's firewalls are "read only." Information comes in, but doesn't leave except for carefully filtered, disguised requests. Damn "smart" two-way firewalls!*

But I was getting weaker and weaker. My thoughts were all scrambled. I was starving. I was coughing deeply, feverish. To somehow defeat Sanako's sophisticated, intelligent firewalls might take weeks of effort—time I didn't have.

"Wait..." I stopped myself. "I forgot something."

There was a *third way*—one that involved self-mutilation but hopefully *without* killing me.

"God, this is going to hurt," I winced, but seeing no other alternative.

It took a day to do the necessary research on the Internet plus make my hurried preparations. But then I was ready to do it. Yes, I was ready, but not eager...

I didn't want to do it. What I most wanted was to take a long nap before proceeding, if at all. But though I'd have to be careful and deliberate, I didn't have the luxury of delaying. I was so weak from hunger and fever I could barely sit upright on the cold floor. I now sat on my bent-back legs, my right hand flattened onto the floor, my left poised in the air, ready to begin.

Sadly, I did *not* have a background in biology or medicine. Luckily, though, I'd long ago in high school taken a required course in *general anatomy*. The most demanding thing we did in the laboratory section of that course was to dissect dead, pickled frogs. But I'd gotten a good hands-on look at nerves, blood vessels, muscles, and bones. It wasn't too hard slice up a dead frog. But now I was facing a high-stakes operation on an *un*anaesthetized *human* patient...me!

"Come on, Suzy," I steadied myself, licking my dry, cracked lips. "You got an 'A' in that lab class back in high school. You can do this. In just minutes you'll be finished."

Somehow, that vague memory of an "A" didn't comfort me. I *did* vividly recall slipping the mangled dead frog into a disposal bag, happy I'd never have to do that again. If only I'd known the future, I'd have paid closer attention.

"Steady..." I muttered as I positioned the sharp knife blade, held in my trembling left hand, above my flattened, splayed-out right hand.

I carefully slit the skin between my index and middle fingers. A trickle of bright red blood sprang up. I had strips of cloth laid out neatly to the side. I'd already torn up my white undershirt to use it as bandages. Also, I had a sliver of wood I'd found that I'd made a hole in one end. Thread pulled out of my torn-apart t-shirt was now double-draped through the hole. Hopefully I'd avoid having major arteries and veins to stitch up. But a little blood here and there wouldn't bother me.

Ignoring the pain (which actually wasn't that bad against the backdrop of my continuing, unending, waves of agony) I proceeded to swiftly disarticulate bones, sever unnecessary tendons, discard superfluous muscles, tie off or reposition major blood vessels, and pare down my right hand to essentials: my thumb and index finger, still capable of making a weak "grasping" motion.

"Ok, then," I encouraged myself, feeling streams of sweat running down my brow, "that's the tough part. Now let's get rid of the remaining large mass of tissue."

Wow, I must be nervous—I thought, *to be sweating in this cold room. Or is it from the fever...?*

I caught myself mentally, forcing my attention back to the task. I'd almost passed out. That wouldn't do. My amateur surgery was only half-completed. Plus it was poor executed. A wide pool of blood already surrounded my mangled hand. Puncturing any of the remaining arteries or veins could cause me to rapidly "bleed out." That'd be the end of my desperate plan to free myself.

"You're almost there," I verbally encouraged myself. "Just a few more cuts will do."

Proceeding from what remained of my right hand, back toward my elbow, I quickly sliced through the skin. I slashed out overlying muscles and the long bone of the forearm, the ulna. I left in place the radius bone, plus most of the forearm's major nerves and blood vessels. Though blood was spurting freely, I managed to staunch the flow by a tight wrap of bandages.

"Do it! Do it! Do it!" I ordered myself, staggering to my feet.

At the grate I jammed my slenderized right forearm a full twelve inches through one of the central two-inch squares. It was tight, but the squirting blood helped slick the passage. Positioning my thumb and index finger inside the chute by tilting my right elbow with my left hand, I grabbed onto the backset latch mechanism. With jerks of my still-functioning thumb and index finger I pulled out a physical latch, pushed up an underlying cover, and depressed a button.

The inner bar dropped away and I felt the grate swing inward. I yanked out my mangled forearm and collapsed onto the floor.

"Good job," I gasped, allowing myself to slip into unconsciousness. "You should have been a surgeon."

After a long, exhausting crawl through a bewildering maze of ductwork, I finally found a way out. I emerged from a protruding air duct back onto the crowded streets of Arsia City. High overhead I saw a plasteel-sealed lava tube's "skylight" vent. Through it I saw the pink-red sky of Mars. I stared up at natural sunlight streaming down upon humanity living on a planet other than Earth. It was exhilarating, almost making me forget the incredible pain of my mutilated arm.

I'd wrapped up my filleted forearm plus its cut-out pieces as best I could, which staunched most of the bleeding. Then I tied it to my chest where it wouldn't be damaged further. Pulling my heavy body up into the chute, inching my way upward at a slant, then back into the city's maze of ductwork with only one good arm was incredibly difficult. I often had to stop, rest for a while, and then force my way onward. I didn't remember the path Sanako led me on before depositing me in the basement prison. So I just had to guess, taking turns toward whatever faint light I detected. After what seemed like an eternity I broke through another grate (much easier from the inside!) and emerged into *chaos*.

Jesus, this is awful—I observed, crouched down beside the protruding, protecting duct. *It's even worse than I saw in the newsfeeds.*

*The government is definitely editing and sanitizing the news about
the "unrest."*

I was on a narrow side street. Tall buildings were crammed in all
around me. Crowds were flooding past, shouting and fighting. I
smelled smoke. I saw a fire raging at the top of a building down the
street. High overhead I heard helicopters circling, from which an occasional burst of machine gun bullets spat at rioting mobs. More
immediately, garbage was piled high around me on both sides of the
street, stinking horribly.

"Took you long enough," a cold voice greeted me.

Instinctively I slunk back out of sight, trying to burrow into a pile
of trash. It didn't work.

Plopping down right next to me was Sanako. She didn't wear her
flashy black ninja "superhero" outfit anymore. Instead she had on a
tattered gray hoodie over old jeans, the hood pulled up over her head.
On her feet were crumbling, seemingly worn out, white tennis shoes.
If you didn't notice her unblinking black eyes staring coldly from under the hood, you'd think she was just one more of a thousand homeless vagrants out on the streets. The only unusual thing about her
was a sack she carried on her back from which protruded the hilt of a
sword.

She was still armed and dangerous.

"How'd you find me?" I glared at her. I was shocked to see her
there but glad I wasn't out alone on the unforgiving streets of Arsia
City.

"Tracking chip," she curtly replied, brandishing what looked like a
cellphone.

On her screen I saw a *red dot* flashing on a city map. Partially
hidden behind the large duct, pushed back into the trash piles, half
submerged in filth, we were largely unnoticed by the stream of desperate humanity rushing past. To find me here she'd tracked me very
well indeed!

"I darted it into your trapezius muscle when I initially helped you
escape your crypt," she finished her explanation.

"I remember. It hurt. I thought I'd been hit by a rock."

"Sorry," she replied, not sounding sorry at all.

"So did you break me out of the crypt? Did you cause the breach of the canopy?"

"Sure did," she admitted, pushing closer up against me. "It wasn't that difficult. I just stuck my sword through near your feet. The canopy was already degrading over time. Then it cracked under the weight of agitators and protestors. It'd already been leaking air for some time, allowing your regenerative biology to kick in."

I was suddenly aware of how cold it was on the street, close to freezing. I saw spurts of fog in front of my mouth from my labored breaths. I vaguely recalled reports on the newsfeeds of rolling power outages. The nuclear reactors were struggling to provide electricity for the rapidly expanding population. The outlying tubes were stuffed with seedy slums. Desperate masses of the common people were struggling to survive in any way possible.

"Was it transmitting all the while that I was down in your prison cell? Did you hear everything that happened, all that I said and did?"

"It's just a locator beeper," she shrugged. "But I also had a hidden camera and mike inside your computer terminal. So, yes, I saw and heard everything."

"You're a sadistic bitch!" I snarled between clenched teeth.

"I am indeed," she calmly stated.

Oh, Christ—I gasped to myself, suddenly fearful, *she knows everything! She knows all about my secret identities and hidden wealth.*

"But don't worry," she continued. "I don't care about your bitcoin treasure, your deeply implanted computer programs, or your past history in this particular timeline."

"You're not going to 'out' me to the authorities?"

She laughed, repositioning her sack to her front as hurtling feet almost stepped on us. Her hand inserted into its neck, ready to snatch out her lethal blade.

"You passed the test, Suzy. My superiors have approved your application. All they know about you is that you're someone I've recommended, who has remarkable recuperative powers."

"Recommended me for what?"

"Well done, by the way," she continued, ignoring my question. "Personally, I'd have chosen a less radical option than self-mutilation to escape the trap, but you succeeded. I assume your arm will heal soon?"

"I hope so," I replied petulantly. "Before I left I took all the tissue I'd cut out and put it roughly back in-place. It's all held together inside tight bandages."

Yep, good stew-meat...yum!

"Nice," she congratulated me. "So now you're officially a provisional apprentice assassin. That's your new 'secret identity.' Specifically, you're *my* trainee, fledgling, neophyte, servant...pick your poison. I personally prefer 'grasshopper.'"

"Like hell I am!" I growled at her. Then, woozily, I stammered: "If I-I'm to be a-an animal, I must be a t-turtle," I insisted, holding up my left wrist to display my turtle tattoo.

"I suppose you are right...Turtle!" she sneered at me derisively.

"Right!" I snapped back. Then, more in control, I asked: "What 'other' options?"

She looked at me like I was a total idiot.

"The whole point of the test was to see what you'd do under extreme duress, how well your brain would function under existential stress. Our craft is much more than just sneaking-about waving cool weapons."

"I did my best to..." I petulantly whispered.

"But you never thought to dig down with your knife around the toilet's drain?" she interrupted, taunting me. "Its short neck led directly to a sewer line, large enough to squeeze yourself through. And the fluorescent strip was powered by radon and another activator, which if sparked with an electrical short from the computer wiring could have blown apart the metal grate. Plus, if you'd thought to break apart the keyboard you'd have found more than enough components to make a slim manipulator to stick through the grate instead of your sliced-up arm. And then there was..."

"Alright, alright!" I stopped her. I was angry at myself, embarrassed I'd not seen those better alternatives. I hadn't enjoyed mutilating myself. "So I passed your bloody test. I'm still not becoming your servant!"

"Yes, I supposed you could try and 'make it' in Arsia City on your own," she nodded. "But without an established powerbase you'd never get access to your pre-established, waiting personas. You wouldn't last a day by yourself on these savage streets. If you're recognized as either little Suzy or The General, one faction or another will happily tear you to pieces. If they don't recognize you, then they'll still rip you apart as a dangerous stranger. Do you think your resurrection skills will help much when you're pieces of mush in a garbage heap, being dined on by dogs and rats?"

As if to emphasize her dire warnings, *feral dogs* suddenly appeared around us, snarling menacingly. They'd been hiding beneath the heaps of surrounding trash, now emerging in a coordinated attack.

Sanako casually *kicked* the nearest one in its snout, drawing a splash of dog-blood. I saw that the soles of her tennis shoes were actually beds of short, sharp spikes. I also noted how she was careful not to kill the creature. She just wanted hurt it sufficiently to prompt it to lead its friends away, convinced we were too dangerous to pursue. There was much easier prey elsewhere for them to gang up on.

I sighed, considering her "offer." As always, Sanako was nothing if not brutally logical.

"But won't I be recognized as the inexplicably resurrected, legendary General?" I asked, trying to get my fevered brain around the present situation.

"The story going around is that revolutionaries stole your body from the crypt. They're supposedly holding it for ransom or other stupid demands. A few small cosmetic changes and you'll be unrecognizable. Even now—mangled, torn-apart, and ripped up—few would associate you with the General's pristine corpse."

"But there must be recordings of me crawling out of..."

"I wiped them," she shrugged, glancing about furtively. Clearly it wasn't wise for us to stay in one place too long, out exposed on a city street. "Actually, several rival groups claim they have your body. In the crunch of the present turmoil, historical desecration is small potatoes. You're not as important as you think you are."

Why does this woman always have to insult me?—I mentally groaned. *Does she enjoy having people hate her?*

"Why are *you* here?" I cut to the heart of the matter, tired of the "macho" verbal dueling. "What do you care about what happens to me? And why should I go with you other than to live for another day? I bet I could fix that monument, repair the canopy, power up the preservation mechanism, and crawl back in to resurrect at some better point in the future!" I bravely asserted.

"Sure," she laughed. "Despite your irritating antics, you and your perky mother always amused me."

I was subdued seeing her icy, predatory smile.

But I won't let her intimidate me. I'm "the girl with the turtle tattoo", damn it!—I mentally argued, though biting my tongue. *Indeed, that's why I chose my right arm to mutilate, so as not to mess up the turtle tattoo on my left wrist. Who knows? It may still get me out of this mess.*

"Answer my questions!" I snarled at her, sticking my face in hers. Then I jerked back into the trash behind me. I was startled by a pack of large *rats* behind her staring at me hungrily. I guess they liked fresh meat. My mutilated arm must smell disgustingly ripe.

"Alright then," she shrugged, scattering the rats with another casual kick. "Here's the bottom line: The Commissioner *exiled* me after I returned to her from the Galactic Core. She wasn't at all pleased by your debacle. She blamed me for what happened. So she tossed me into a time-vortex *sans* equipment and I wound up stranded here, on the then-future Mars. Catching up on the events of this timeline I found out about your post-concert antics and your convenient local crypt."

I thought so. That devious clone of my mother lied to me in the alternate dimension. I should have killed her instead of hugging her! Just as she tossed-aside Anderson she also exiled Sanako.

"So the out-of-time Commissioner orchestrated the murder of my mother?" I snapped at Sanako, now excited to finally identify a tangible target. "I met the younger version and she denied everything."

"Oh, The Commissioner has plans upon plans upon plans," Sanako sighed. "She plots in three-dimensional, multi-level chess while the rest of us poke along playing linear checkers. But, no, she wanted you to succeed at the Galactic Core. Like everyone else she coveted the 'gifts' that the aliens would give humanity if you managed to win the contest."

"So she didn't...?"

"*Yes*, Suzy, she *didn't* want you to 'throw' the concert-conquest," Sanako sharply replied. "In particular she craved the aliens' virtual immortality, whether enslaved by the aliens or not. The Commissioner I served, before she threw me out, was already an ancient, twisted creature. Now she's far beyond the help of any known medical interventions. She's dying. And she's desperate."

I can't believe anything Sanako tells me—I cautioned myself. *She's always been a loyal servant of The Commissioner. Why would Sanako accept being cast out? And isn't it just a bit suspicious that she was tossed here to Mars, at this present moment?*

"But I know she still needs my help," Sanako continued, as if reading my mind. "I'm still loyal to her. I'm willing to play whatever role she'd like me have in her brilliant schemes. And that's where you come in. I'm going to win back her approval, starting with taking over the Guild of Assassins. It's a powerful, semi-public organization with many secret safeguards. It holds a particular fascination for The Commissioner. You, my little apprentice with your 'special' skills, are going to help me subvert their internal defenses."

Why would The Commissioner care about some ragtag group of professional killers on Mars?

"Your story doesn't make any sense," I growled, clutching my throbbing right arm with my left hand. My mangled limb certainly wasn't healing. Instead, it was steadily dripping blood. "I'm not helping you do shit!"

"Oh, yes, you are," she stated, springing up and grabbing my good arm. She yanked me to my feet.

"*Why?*" I yelled at her, not caring who heard me or what dangerous attention my shout attracted.

I jerked my good arm away from her, wavering as I struggled to stand upright. I was exhausted, starving, burning up with fever, and half dead from continuing blood loss. I was at my rope's end, unwilling to put up with anymore of Sanako's crap!

"I'm certain The Commissioner wasn't behind your mother's murder," she firmly stated. "But I can *show* you who was."

That stopped me in my tracks, narrowing my eyes in consideration.

"Tell me now!" I demanded.

Again, she shrugged: "*After* you help me, *then* I'll show you—but not before."

She grabbed my left arm again.

"One thing more!" I insisted, again jerking myself free. "Come on, Sanako, throw me this 'bone'—I need one!"

This time she actually laughed out loud. She glanced down at my filleted arm with its detached ulna. My still-working thumb and single finger protruded obscenely from the bloody bandages. The swollen digits sporadically twitched.

"Alright, what?" she sighed.

"I got a clue back on Old Earth, right before the Extinction."

"Oh?"

"It was rumored that a religious organization *other* than Phoenix was behind my Mom's murder. Is that true?"

She paused, considering.

Then she answered: "Yes."

Whether or not she held up her end of the deal, her present confirmation was helpful. It was yet another nail in the eventual coffin of the conspiracy which I felt destined to expose and destroy. Whether the out-of-time crone—all that remained of the once-powerful Commissioner—was part of the conspiracy, I didn't know. But I did know that if she was, then she'd pay. There were worse things than dying. I, for one, knew that to be absolutely true.

"Then lead on...'Master'," I gamely replied.

"That's better...Turtle!" she smirked at me. She supported my slumping body with a strong arm around my waist, helping me hobble along.

In that moment I almost liked the woman—almost, but not quite.

So under Sanako's brutal tutelage, I learned all the tricks and techniques of a licensed, official *assassin*.

My desperate attempt to save my arm worked. In only a week the severed fingers, muscles, nerves, blood vessels, skin, and various bones that I'd packed loosely back in place around my mangled forearm fused together. In two weeks I could move my middle, ring, and pinky fingers. In a month you couldn't tell my right arm had suffered any damage at all.

Meanwhile, I was immersed in a rigorous program of physical, mental, and spiritual instruction. As an unranked apprentice assassin I was the unquestioning servant of my "sensei." So, whether I needed it or not, I ("The General" of great fame and skill) had to learn and demonstrate expertise handling many deadly tools and weapons. Those included ropes, grappling hooks, spikes, chisels, drills, breathing tubes, short swords, daggers, Samurai long swords, pikes, bows and arrows, darts, knives, throwing stars, chains, sickles, guns, and on-and-on! More important than mastering overt weapons, though, was using less-obvious but still lethal methods: smoke, noxious gas, all sorts of poisons, grenades, bombs, acids, poisoned darts, guided kites, blowguns, and others. Some of those modalities of death I already knew well. Many others were fascinating techniques I'd never before considered.

I particularly enjoyed knife-tossing. I'd spend hours hurtling various weighted and shaped blades at targets. Then I'd do the same while tumbling onto mats, requiring razor-sharp reactions to hit the target. Even more difficult was doing so while sparing with an opponent. But I excelled at all those exercises. I just liked knives!

I became the champion knife-thrower of the dojo.

For the Assassins' Guild, though, the best "hit" was unseen and unacknowledged. *Stealth* assured the Guild's continued existence. Cross the Guild or try to restrict its actions and you might find yourself in their crosshairs, dying young of a sudden "heart attack." Rather than embracing the "noble" honor-bound, "in your face" battle-skills of the Samurai, the Guild preferred the mysterious, stealthy killing of the Ninja. Indeed, the shadowy (but officially acknowledged and licensed) Martian *Guild of Assassins* was mainly composed of Japanese clanners, steeped in all the martial arts of Old Earth Japan. So over the next six months I was taught critical aspects of mixed martial combat mainly derived from the Japanese disciplines of judo, aikido, and karate.

In addition, I trained at driving all modern vehicles. Most were AI-assisted, so were a cinch, especially with my previous moon-achieved piloting certifications. But others were more esoteric, such as small private transports. I found those the most enjoyable, especially the ones rated space-worthy. Dipping in and out of Mar's thin atmosphere, landing on its moons, was amazing!

It was all a blur until...

"Again!" Sanako barked at me.

My mind was wandering. I was sleep-deprived, just having finished a week-long "boot camp" of rigorous physical ordeals punctuated only by brief catnaps. With my Old Earth muscles I had an advantage over the other trainees at climbing, long distance running, boxing, wrestling, and weight lifting. But I was often at a disadvantage at throwing-techniques in the lighter gravity of Mars. So in direct combat I was stronger but less coordinated than the other trainees. It was frustrating.

And now Sanako and I were doing "slap-dueling" where I'd not won one single round. We squared off, approached within arm's length, then used our combined four arms and flattened hands as "swords." The first to penetrate the other's defenses and slap the opponent's face won that round. It was incredibly intense, requiring split-second reactions and counter-reactions. We'd been at it without pause for a full hour.

As reflected in the wall-length mirrors surrounding us, both of my cheeks were swollen and red from many hard slaps. Sanako's impassive face was unmarred. She was in casual street clothes, her short black hair flaring around her head, not even breaking a sweat. Her squinted black eyes glared at me like a shark's studying its next potential meal. I, however, was clad in a traditional white Karate "gi." Although it was a light, clean fabric, it was stained and clinging due to my perfuse sweat. My ever-present blue marble made an obvious lump in my pants pocket.

"No," I said, stepping back and crossing my leaden arms over my heaving chest.

I'd had enough. She was far more skilled than me in all forms of physical combat. I would never beat her in woman-on-woman combat. To try was a pointless exercise. I'd already learned whatever I could from the drill. Going on with it was stupid.

But the other trainees and instructors collectively "gasped", stunned at my unheard-of defiance! Not only had I defied my Master, I'd also failed to use the required honorific of "Sensei."

We were in Sanako's official, central dojo. It was a spacious martial arts instruction hall located next to a small Buddhist Temple. Incongruously, the spiritual aspects of Buddhism were tightly wound into the mythos of the Assassins' Guild. Indeed, attaining supernatural power was a long tradition of ninjas. Mastery of the mind and spirit, by legend, allowed senior ninjas to split into multiple bodies, command animals, fly through the air, turn invisible, control the five elements, and shapeshift. Our first hour of training each morning was spiritual instruction and rituals conducted at the next-door Temple. The dojo was a legitimate business that Sanako owned. But it served as a front for her nefarious secret activities. Everything was neatly hidden-away behind a pious religious facade.

I noted that the regular Buddhist Monks held in distain the occasionally visiting *Transcendentalist* offshoot Monks. Though the TM's were allowed to visit the Temple, they were given minimal respect. I found this curious but didn't have time to dwell on it. The TM's always seemed very friendly toward me, often greeting me by name.

Keep your mind in the game—I admonished myself. I was exhausted, my mind fuzzed-out, my flesh bruised and swollen. Yet here I was directly challenging my Master!

A dozen other pairs of fighters were going through various drills. Sanako was the Grandmaster of the dojo. She was given great deference and respect by students and lesser instructors alike. For a student to publically disobey her was unprecedented. My single word had brought everything to a standstill.

"Good," Sanako unexpectedly smiled. She put her palms together and *bowed* to me with seeming deference.

Surprised, I bowed back...

—as she *kicked* me square in my stomach!

Doubled over, vomiting up my meager vegetarian breakfast, I barely heard her next words, barked out to the whole dojo...

"Back to your practice!"

Bending down she grabbed my now fully grown-out blond hair. She unceremoniously *dragged* me across the wooden planks into a private room. There she tossed me a towel. As I lay there, exhausted, using the cloth to clean my mouth and soiled gi, she sat down in a chair.

"Get up," she ordered.

She stared at me as I struggled to stand upright.

"I'm pleased with your progress, Turtle," she nodded at me.

"You have a strange way of showing it," I softly replied.

"It's called 'tough-love', little girl—deal with it!"

"What, you're claiming you 'love' me now?"

Abruptly she stood up and turned her back to me. She stared at a painting on the wall opposite me, depicting a single orange lily.

"Go get a shower. Powder your face. And then put on your professional 'go-to-meeting' suit."

"Why?"

"You're going on your first assignment."

I didn't feel like being Sanako's "personal assistant" to a high-society Arsia City charity event, but that was my task. I particularly disliked the hypocrisy of the gathering. The *uber*-rich guests were dining on simulated caviar, drinking champagne, and dancing to a full orchestra while figuratively throwing coins to the peasants. They were ostensibly raising money for soylent green handouts to homeless street beggars. I found the hypocritical gathering repulsive. But our designated targets would be there, or readily accessible through contacts made at the party.

We'd planned everything out to the last detail. I dutifully hovered at Sanako's side holding an old-fashioned tablet (no virtual 3D interface that we'd have to interact with verbally). Sanako was absorbing all the attention that came our way. Adorned appropriately in a gray business suit with my hair slicked back into a ponytail, wearing brown glasses, with thick pancake makeup hiding my still-fresh facial bruises, I was practically invisible.

Sanako, however, looked stunning. Her luminous dark hair was styled in upswept buns to each side of her head. She had small silver spikes dangling on golden springs from each lobe of her ears. Her oriental, curved eyes were intense, with just the right shade of purple beneath plus dark liner above. Her lips were painted rich blood-red. She wore a high-necked, deep-blue, one-piece dress. Its simplicity and plastic sheen made her look like an otherworldly creature. It was slit up one side all the way to her butt. Completing her sexy outfit were red high heels, the same color as her prominently painted lips.

Every male in the crowd had the hots for her.

She could have easily passed for a high-end hooker, but was actually a respected business owner, a tycoon of local commerce. Her Japanese-clanner dojos were very popular on Mars. She had a whole chain of them, catering to all sorts of tastes and wants: from dainty rich wives jiggling with personal trainers to savage "fight nights" betting for drunken factory workers. In the social crush of Mars' business Elites, all I had to do was appear attentive to Sanako's directives.

A rainbow of strobe lights flashed overhead as well-heeled men and women rhythmically gyrated on a dance floor. We were serenaded by a full orchestra playing Old Earth hits of the 1930's. White-uniformed waiters deftly carried trays of crystal glasses filled with champagne, circling through the packed crowd. Sanako carried a half-filled glass but never drank from it. She and I knew we could not afford even the slightest dulling of our razor-sharp senses by alcohol.

"We've been invited to the governor's estate," she spoke into my ear. "It's a private party where we'll stay the night. Make the arrangements."

I dutifully nodded and typed away at my tablet. I didn't know what the hell I was doing but put up a good act.

Within minutes we boarded a pressurized luxury bus, rolling out a private airlock exit. Suddenly we were on the surface of Mars. Rugged mountain peaks loomed above us, the stark red rocks looking as if they'd been there forever. A small sun gleamed down through the pink-red sky. We were going down a well-worn unpaved road inside a big ravine. Ahead of us were wide sandy plains across which frozen ridges of ancient lava rippled. Wispy clouds high above us were lit orange by the setting sun. It was the start of southern winter on Mars, when the tilt of the planet allowed heating of buried layers of mountain ice, causing ephemeral vapor clouds.

"It's beautiful," I commented to Sanako sitting next to me.

"It's boring," she snootily replied, either keeping up her act or being completely honest, I couldn't tell. "Once you've seen red sand you've seen it all."

That wasn't true. I'd done my research well. *Arsia Mons*, named after a legendary Roman forest, was a gigantic, dead volcano close to Mars' equator. By volume it was 30 times larger than Mauna Loa, the largest volcano on Earth. It was 12 miles high. Only the fabled Olympus Mons, the tallest volcano in the entire Solar System, located to the northwest of us, was larger. The caldera in the center of our dead volcano was 70 miles wide. The entire volcano was nearly 300 miles wide. Its lava tubes were extensive enough to presently house nearly 20 million packed humans.

And now we're going to an "estate" on its sloped flanks. Yep, I wonder what we're all going to do there?—I sighed, not looking forward to completing my assignment.

Yes, as always throughout history, the ultra-rich found a way to separate themselves from the teeming masses of struggling "peasants." A dozen other wealthy socialites were with us on the bus, in various stages of inebriation. I noted that most of them were attractive females. But even the males looked like fashion icons. Clearly, the governor was looking to have a sexy good time.

In less than an hour we arrived at a glittering dome whose lights were blazing. The sun was down. One of the small moons of Mars, Phobos, was low on the dark horizon. We went through security, consisting both of watchful human guards and electromagnetic scans. Inside the pressurized, transparent half-globe we found delightfully lit gardens, pools, and over-sized tennis courts (accounting for the weak gravity on Mars). A complex of elegant buildings sat serenely in the center of the large Dome. Versus the more refined orchestra at the charity event, *heavy metal* blared from hidden speakers. Giddily greeting our party was a very fat older man. He had flowing white hair, was clad in a diamond-studded purple robe, and wore hoof-like sandals. He had a wide meaty smile and tiny, porky eyes. His uncovered belly was immense. It was clear he had a particular attraction to Sanako, rushing to embrace her with his wobbling, fat-laden arms. I was still amazed at the effects of Mars' weaker gravity. For all his mass, likely over four hundred pounds on Earth, on Mars he *bounced* along like a blobby balloon.

It was grotesque.

"Don't judo-chop me!" he exclaimed in mock-fear, hugging her tightly, "Hi there! Hi there! Glad you could come!" he rushed to the others, enthusiastically embracing both males and females alike.

Sanako smiled at him patronizingly. I almost laughed. If she had her way I knew she'd decapitate the sweaty hog on the spot, using her long fingernails if nothing else was handy. But she played the grateful guest, embracing him yet again as he returned joyfully to her. Amongst the varied factions of Arsia City he held a critical position. He was the official mediator between all the powerful companies, religions, military, and criminal elements. Normally he was inaccessible, hiding behind an army of security personnel. Now he was exposed in all his flaccid glory.

No, he was *literally* exposed.

"Shall we take a dip?" he heartily bellowed-out, discarding his robe. Beneath it he was stark naked. His rear-end was massive. His junk was hidden beneath his bulbously overhanging belly. He waddled into the nearest blue lagoon, giggling obscenely. The clear, blue water splashed high and settled slowly. It was as if the pool itself was in "slow-motion". I would have zero reticence slitting his fat throat. The other guests followed him into the warm water, throwing off various pieces of clothing. I noted that Sanako did the same, though retaining her blue panties and white bra. She handed me her earrings. She'd let the governor play himself out on the others, perhaps rewarding his passions with a kiss but nothing more.

As wild "whoops" and "cheers" erupted, the heavy-metal music blared even louder.

Yep, the revilers were officially "liberated".

Meanwhile, I had a task to accomplish.

I slipped away, supposedly looking for a bathroom in the closest building, but making my way to the private quarters located on the upper levels. The guards, preoccupied with the soiree below, were easy to evade. Locks were more difficult to subvert, but yielded to my expert tinkering. I admired the thick, soundproofed walls.

"Who are you?" a startled young man exclaimed as I slipped into his room. "How did you get in here?"

He was sitting at a plain wood desk, working at a computer terminal. He had on a ruffled brown shirt. He wore old-fashioned gold-rimmed glasses. He looked like an accountant. But I knew who he really was: the governor's youngest son. He was the actual "power behind the throne." While the old man and useless older brothers frolicked, the smartest son did the grunge work. He was only in his early twenties, but had control of every Arsia City enterprise. On behalf of his father, he extracted a hefty fee, bribe, or cut for every transaction done in the lava tubes. Lately those fees were getting excessive. Killing the governor would ignite the already seething unrest, perhaps causing an uncontrollable societal explosion. But the Guild didn't want Mars melted down to slag. Killing the son, however, would send a chilling message that even the wallowing hog in the pool down below would understand. Versus the Samurai of Old Earth legends, the Ninjas of the Guild did not weld blunt weapons of war.

This was a precise surgical strike.

This is going to be easy—I encouraged myself.

"Oh, I'm so sorry!" I exclaimed, walking "uncertainly" forward, tapping rapidly on my tablet. "I'm Lady Sanako's assistant, Sir. I was looking for a steady hard-link back to the city. The guards said to come this way, kindly opening the doors for me. My Lady asked me to make arrangements for us to be away for the night, but my tablet's having trouble keeping its wi-fi connection. Would you happen to...?"

I was close enough now for the tiny needle inside the earrings concealed in the palm of my hand to prick him. A potent neurotoxin would take effect immediately. It would look like he died working at his desk from an untimely heart attack. He appeared uncertain at my advance, his eyes narrowing. It seemed he was either about to offer me an Internet hardline connection or call the guards to confirm my story...

One quick stabbing flick!

"Daddy!" a little girl chortled happily. She dashed past me and hugged his legs. "Can I go swimming? There's lots of grownups down in the pool and I want to..."

"Hey, princess," he smiled, his brown eyes softening. He put his right hand gently on her little shoulders, turning her around. "It's time for you to go to bed. You can swim tomorrow. I'll go with you then, but right now I have to work."

"Oh, well, ok," she sighed deeply, "I love you, Daddy!"

"Love you too, honey," he said, bending over to give her a quick kiss on her head, "Now go let Nanny tuck you in."

"Ok, then...hi!" she chirped up at me as she skipped past.

"Hi," I lamely replied.

She paused at the doorway, her little hand up on the knob. She looked back at me with big blue eyes.

"You're very pretty!" she chirped. Then, more sadly, she said: "You look like my Mommy...before she died."

"Oh, I'm so sorry," I replied, genuinely moved. My Mother died also, *murdered* by a mysterious conspiracy that somehow knew better how history should proceed.

Oh Christ—I gulped to myself, a horrible thought flashing through my brain, *I'm talking about myself! I'm about to murder her father because my present mysterious organization supposedly knows best. What the hell am I doing? Has Sanako brainwashed me?*

"Will you be my new Mommy?" she asked hopefully.

"She's just a guest here of Grandpa's, who's *leaving*," the man at the desk sternly stated. "Now go get in bed."

Clearly disappointed, the little girl sighed deeply. I watched her disappear through the side door, pulling it shut with a small hand as she went. I felt my resolve evaporating. I slipped the poised, lethal earrings into a side pocket.

"Uh, my Internet connection is strengthening. I guess I don't have to bother you after all, Sir."

I started to back out but stopped.

He had raised his left hand from behind the desk. It was holding a small pistol, aimed straight at me!

"You think I don't know about Sanako's real business here?" he said as he squeezed the trigger...

I instantly ducked to the side (*thank you, Sanako, for all the slap-exercises!*), the bullet *shattering* a glass-framed picture on the wall just an inch from my head. A guard rushed in, who I tripped. I snatched his gun as he fell, *firing* a single bullet through the son's skull. It caused a satisfying splash of blood out the back of his head, decorating the wall behind him. I darted back to the desk, grabbed the son's pistol and fired a *second* shot into the guard's head as he tried to leap up from the floor. He just dropped dead, a hole in his forehead. The son's small gun didn't have much punch.

Well, that's done—I sighed to myself. *No need to come up with a lie for Sanako.*

Quickly wiping my prints with the pulled-out edge of my shirt, I switched the two guns between the hands of both dead men. It would look like they had a gunfight, each of them losing. Then I slipped out the door that the little girl had taken. Fortunately, she wasn't in the adjoining room. If she'd been there, I might have had to kill her also, which I knew I would have regretted. I'd hesitated too long with the governor's son, thinking I could mislead Sanako, claiming I couldn't find him. I hated taking a father away from his young daughter. But then things just got out of hand.

I quickly took a different route back to the ground floor.

"How'd it go?" Sanako asked as she sat in a recliner beside the frothing pool, still clad only in wet panties and bra. She had another half-filled glass in her hand from which she didn't drink.

The partying group in the pool was getting down to business, both with each other and their obese host. For a fat man, the governor had great stamina. Likely he was on massive doses of "erectile dysfunction" drugs.

"It's done, a bit messier than I wanted," I admitted, "but we'd best be getting out of here before the deed's discovered."

"I've already called one of my transports," she said, putting the glass down on a side table. "You can give me a full report on the way back."

She smoothly slipped into her dress, accepting the earrings back from me, snapping them in place on her earlobes.

"He knew who I was and went for his gun," I preempted her suspicions. "His little daughter came in right before it all went down. She may be able to identify me. But if questioned I'll say I left before anything happened."

"That's good," she said as we strolled back through security. The guards there seemed unconcerned. Damn good soundproofing inside the house! Outside the Dome I saw a sleek black vehicle waiting for us. Unlike the typical big-wheeled bus-transports, this had tinted windows and small speedy tires. "Actually, we wanted this assassination semi-public, which is why I'm here 'in person' as it were. This one is a warning that we've finally had enough of the unrest. Much of the present turmoil was egged on by the governor's administration to juice up their protection business. But that's going to change. And those that don't get with the new program will suffer a similar end."

Walking leisurely through the airlock, we entered the connected, chauffeured vehicle.

"What's going to happen to the governor?"

"Without brains he can trust to perpetuate his atrocities, his entire present administration will crumble. We've plenty evidence to release to the press to facilitate a quick but thorough changeover. The governor and all his relatives will wind up either in prison or out on the streets, begging for soylent green cubes. It's fitting justice."

"What about innocent family members?"

Her eyes narrowed as she coldly inspected me. I tried to hide my suddenly trembling hands.

"What do you mean?"

"Well, I saw a little girl who..."

"—collateral damage," she cut off my statement. "It's necessary. To have the full impact on others, family members must suffer, *particularly* the so-called 'innocent' ones. It's 'the good of the many outweighs the good of the few' sort of logic. Hardly any of these criminals are so far gone they want their kids to suffer for their sins."

I pondered her words for a moment, looking out at the approaching dark cliffs.

"So you're saying we're not just ruthless, dishonorable, money-grubbing murderers?"

Sanako sighed, leaning back in her comfortable seat. The driver expertly steered around huge boulders as we quickly ascended the volcano's outer rim.

"You've been too immersed in the physical aspects of the Guild," she sighed again. "Now you begin the philosophical training."

"Philosophy?"

"Us being greedy dishonorable killers is a subterfuge we employ to stay safely hidden in the shadows," she explained. "In reality, the Guild of Assassins operates as a 'top predator' in Mar's near-lawless churn. We're the ultimate brake on humanity's worse excesses.

Without the necessity of official accusation or trial we're free to summarily execute the worst of the worst, terrifying the rest into moderating their behaviors."

I was beginning to understand the torturously wound fabric of Mars' chaotic society.

"But who makes the ultimate decision as to who lives and who dies?"

"There's a Council of Elders who runs the Guild," she further explained. "They mostly make very conservative decisions, not interested in 'rocking the boat.' During rare peaceful times they recede into the background. But no tyrant, overlord, or crime boss is too big to evade us. Even when we're not assassinating people, the *threat* of such is often enough to control powerful fools who think only of themselves."

"*You're* not thinking only of yourself?" I accused her. Yes, I knew it was dangerous to question her. But I was exhausted and on the downside of a huge adrenalin-rush.

"That's different," she ominously replied, pausing a second. "I come from a position of existential knowledge."

"So you know better than anyone else," I summarized.

"Yes, I do," she nodded, closing her eyes and settling back. "And I'm taking control of the whole shebang. And you're going to help me at each and every step."

"If you say so," I shrugged...

—then was *gagging!*

Her hand was at my throat, immobilizing me by almost crushing my windpipe. Otherwise she seemed totally relaxed, still with her eyes closed, swaying as the vehicle swung over to avoid more boulders.

"I *say* so," she whispered menacingly before releasing her grip.

And so the years and decades passed by, with countless assassinations and power struggles. Some I did myself, others I just participated in. But I definitely got my hands dirty. Eventually we got the unrest on Mars damped down enough to get mankind's stalled solar system expansion back on track. But to do so took rising to the upper levels of the Guild, even subverting their conservative norms.

At one point the Guild's "impenetrable" fortress in a different lava tube network had to be breached. I died twice passing through unavoidably lethal defenses. But on the other side of each of them I resurrected, allowing Sanako to come along behind me. So together we took over the Council of Elders, killing any that resisted.

Sanko then ruled with an iron hand. But she grew steadily older as she ruthlessly put down ever-new threats. Meanwhile, I remained a fresh-faced young teenager. Finally, I had to switch to one of my "secret" identities, starting anew with an even larger pool of wealth behind me from my ill-gotten gains. Sanako took on a "new" assistant (me) and with my youthful energy I again became the "power behind the throne." This happened several times over. Sanako—though amazingly long-lived because of her prior out-of-time medical treatments—eventually grew old and feeble, still waiting on her dear Commissioner. My 'master' never stopped believing that *The Commissioner* would relent, recognize Sanako's excellent work stabilizing Mars from within the Assassins' Guild, and welcome her back into the out-of-time fold of the Time Keepers. But it never happened. Finally, lying on her death bed, gasping out her last few breaths, Sanako called me over.

"I...need...to keep...my word to you," she whispered. "I've been unfair...waiting for so long...dependent on your goodwill and support...not wanting to risk losing it."

I barely recognized the woman. She was shrunken, red-eyed, and helpless. She was no longer the vibrant force she'd been in her younger years. Her previous lustrous black hair was a few scattered clumps of pure white on an otherwise bald scalp. Now she was kin to the video of Anderson I'd viewed of his waning years, that pitiful image I'd seen back on the Moon. The very same *Time* they'd both tried to subvert had now brought them both low. I couldn't help but think they'd struck a bad bargain when they first decided to follow The Commissioner.

I'd almost forgotten her vow, her end of the "bargain" we'd struck so long ago. Now that I was ruling the Guild in her functional absence, those prior concerns seemed far distant. But her words loosed a flood of memories and pent-up fury in my soul. I realized that similar to the obese governor I'd help bring down those many years ago I was growing figuratively fat and lazy (though my non-aging body outwardly was still that of a slim teenager). I now considered Mars my home. But it wasn't! It was just a brief stopping point on my long-lived journey to an epic revenge.

"Yes," I answered her. "You promised to *show* me who was behind the murder of my mother!"

"Look...*up*..." she whispered, her eyes stretched wide toward the ceiling.

"What?"

"Above...us..."

"You mean God? Is this the 'religion' different than Phoenix that was rumored to really be behind my mother's murder at the Galactic Core? Are you invoking *monotheists* in general?"

"No...not God...another," she gasped so faintly I could barely hear her.

"Another Dimension? Are you telling me I'm to search the parallel human Dimension again, or a non-human Earth dimension, or perhaps another timeline?"

"No...look *higher!*" she croaked, shuddering violently.

And then she died.

"Sanako! Answer me! Don't die!" I shouted, shaking her thin body.

But she was gone.

I left the room, leaving my assistants to take care of her corpse. I had other pressing duties. Mankind's renewed expansion out into the further Solar System was going well. Titan was pumping out a continuous stream of fuel pods to the inner and outer solar system. Asteroid belt mining was thriving. SSS, the *Saturn Space Station*, was finally succeeding in harvesting large amounts of Helium-3 from Saturn's outer atmosphere. *Starships* were being finalized, relying on huge fusion propulsion systems using He-3 to theoretically achieve a significant fraction of lightspeed. The first, in fact, was due to be launched soon to our closest neighboring star, Alpha Centauri. If I didn't find my answers, I might volunteer to be one of its crewmembers.

But there were persistent rumors of strange religious doings on Titan, fueled by their wondrous, near-magical "Green." I'd already rigorously interrogated the various religious factions of Mars, both traditional and esoteric. I found no hint of the conspiracy to prematurely snatch my mother from me. But if, indeed, a secretive religious group *had* done so, then it might well be hiding on Titan.

I needed to do a "deep dive" researching all aspects of my new target, invent a whole new identity, assure a smooth transfer of power in the Guild, get a legitimate cover for passage to and duty on Titan, and leave Mars.

"I'm going to Saturn, Grasshopper," I firmly stated to my surprised chief assistant, a pretty young girl named Mary, "regardless of outcome. I'm *sick* of this place, both the killing and the never-ending hand-holding. In particular I hate this *giant dead volcano*. If I never, ever, see another dead volcano it'll be too soon. Put together everything you can on the societal power-structures of Titan."

She gulped nervously, clearly not knowing what to make of my sudden outburst. Likely she thought it an understandable reaction to the death of my long-time mentor. But she didn't question my orders. If nothing more, the Guild of Assassins raised respectful children. I'd taken in the orphaned daughter of my first victim, himself the son of that obese disgraced governor. This girl was her great-great-great-great-granddaughter. It shocked me to realize how many years I'd wasted on Mars.

Time to rip Titan to pieces!

Chapter 11

DOOM MONS

All throughout the solar system

There is active and historical evidence aplenty

Not just a matter of creativity, destruction, or luck

But internal forces squirting out celestial-body guts

Be it on the Earth, the Moon, Mars, Venus, Io, or Titan

An orgy of cosmic convulsions sweating out salt water,

Belching flames, farting poisonous gas, pooping turds

Building and blending mountains to towering heights

Typically either hot or cold, magma or frigid water

You can't walk on lava without burning your feet

But cold cryovolcanoes can be equally lethal

Swathing your toes in shoes made of ice

Ripped from the bowels of an alien world...

The Rise and Fall of *Homo sapiens*, 11:61-66

"Are the atomics set?" I asked Torque.

"They're ready to detonate, at your order, Goddess," he curtly replied.

No, we didn't have nuclear missiles. If there was one thing that would bring the wrath of humanity down on us, it was building an actual atomic bomb. Instead, we used Dilmun robots to mobilize the remaining guts of our blown-apart nuclear reactors. The cores were poised on-command to pop out their dampening control rods. We'd already covertly, undercover of the continuing storm, used our robots to insert them into shallow pits. They were poised to "blow" in strategic points along the side of the ice-rock mountain. Without the rods sucking up excess neutrons, the salvaged uranium fuel rods would overheat. None of them contained enough U235 to become an atomic bomb, but they'd get hot enough to melt. The liquid metal would *vaporize* huge volumes of the surrounding ice into steam, resulting in a gigantic explosion. The defenders, contemptuous of our limited tech, were in for a big surprise.

"Good," I grunted. "Prepare to blow the walls."

Our Holy Momma nodded her approval. Sitting next to her, fully decked out in our standard camouflage combat gear, was Torque. He was unrecognizable from the chubby little cheerful Major of Shangdu. Now he was a battle-hardened, dour, veteran General. He had a black eyepatch covering an empty socket where his right eye had been blown away. In his good left arm he cradled a rifle. He carried a large knife at his waist, well-used and sharp. Next to him sat the Dilmun commander, Glacket. The Dilmun General was a lean midget with a red bandana over a bald skull. His facemask was dangling, but ready to don at a moment's notice. From experience I knew he was a demon of a fighter. I was glad he was now on our side.

It had been a full two years since the awful destruction of Shangdu. The other major sub-glacier cities of Xanadu were likewise decimated. The invading army of the Dilmun ravaged the Yuan, leaving many dead, their homes and livelihoods in ruins. Particularly brutal was the systematic destruction of all the nuclear reactors of Xanadu's hidden cities, a clear attempt at genocide. The Dilmun didn't want their rivals, the Yuan, to recover.

But that savagery wasn't what infuriated me the most. All throughout *Homo sapien* history, one group covets and devours the other. Constant conflict is the historical norm, sad but true. The Dilmun army, however, was ferried to Xanadu from a considerable distance, provided with sophisticated weapons, and was supported by laser blasts from orbiting satellites. In addition—and most telling— the narrow-band broadcasting knife blade stuck in my chest which led the Dilmun to Shangdu was definitely cutting-edge high-tech. A member or faction of Titan's government was determined to eradicate the Yuan.

Why?

Outside of stealing discarded equipment from junk yards, Titan's nomadic little people were relatively harmless. Indeed, the Yuan supplied a much-coveted product, Titanian Tea. Why would anyone in authority want them eradicated?

The only explanation I could think of for that logistical and military deployment and expense was that someone knew *I* was still alive. It had to be the *grand conspiracy* I'd pursued now for hundreds of years, which I'd finally cornered here on Titan. They were scared of me, knew I was closing in on them, and were willing to kill hundreds of thousands of harmless nomads to stop me.

But we turned the tables. It took many months of scrounging, coalescing of our decimated population, and rigorous training to impart my deadly assassination combat skills. But in my new identity of "Goddess" I forged a new Yuan army, even more savage than the Dilmun. Our enemies, after all, still depended on their inferior tea product to do their dirty deeds. We had none. Our crops were burned with no hope of planting more. So of necessity we were re-formed addicts, cut-off from our drug of choice. Promising my people new fields of plenty, I led a drug-withdrawn crazed army to overrun the Dilmun heretics. In only a few months, despite their superior tech, our fellow nomadic enemy surrendered, leaving us in possession of all their communities and fields. But we didn't sack their homes. Instead, motivated by our mellow religion that they'd tried to destroy, inspired by our new Holy Momma, we extended a Godly hand of friendship. The Dilmun finally "saw the light," were grateful for our mercy, converted in droves to COG-C, and augmented my army with their many zealous recruits.

From there we turned our combined sights to our previous enemy's high-tech allies. It turned out that all the surface transports, heavy tech dune-cycles, advanced weaponry, and laser satellites originated from and were controlled at *one particular site* on the surface of Titan. But shorn of their collaborators, futilely hunting us illusive nomads who'd been forced to return to our furtive roots, our distant enemies had no further hold over us. Their satellite surveillance networks could no longer track our locations. And now, due to our bloody victory over our fellow little-people, with the exception of the orbital resources, the Yuan controlled all their "donated" military hardware.

If the various factions on TSS cared about our threat to a portion of their military, we got no indication. Life proceeded as usual at Huygens Base. Grubby nomadic problems were a low priority. The absence of our mellow Titanian Tea was hardly noticed, since existing abundant alcohol and other drugs readily took its place. We were literally operating "under the radar."

But that was to change. To root out the hidden enemy I'd searched for over the centuries, I couldn't remain in the shadows. And so we began low grade guerrilla attacks on all of Titan's surface bases. Even the steady launching of fuel pods was interrupted. Surface transports were harassed or plundered. The "nomadic problem" was now front-and-center!

And so my *united guerrilla army*, ten thousand strong, arrived at *Doom Mons*. This was where I'd been headed all along. Today was particularly important since our intelligence indicated a conference on the worsening "nomad situation" was being held, with high dignitaries attending. Well, *our* intention was to *solve* their problem, once and for all.

"Tea, my Goddess?" a gentle voice sounded from my side.

I looked with affection at our new Holy Momma. The hierarchy of their religion was decimated by the Dilmun's sneak-attack on Shang-du. Since the top leaders of the *Church of Godly Creativity* were dead, I appointed new clergy. The prior assistant to our dear, deceased Glenda knew all the "ropes," was well studied on their theology, and commanded the respect of the entire community. So my strangely two-faced Shawnee became not just my trusted sidekick but guarantor of my religious authority. She was the anointed, new Holy Momma.

"Not now, thanks," I responded, waving away the steaming cup, knowing it came from replanted excellent bushes in the Dilmun caverns, "Perhaps after we take the mountain. Then we can celebrate."

Indeed, my vicious Yuan troops had also sworn off constant imbibing of the mellowing liquid. Yes, we'd have a cup now and then on high holy days or at family events. But on the battlefield we needed to be sharp, focused, and thoroughly merciless. Our Dilmun recruits weren't as dedicated, requiring daily doses of their inferior blend, to which they were addicted. But the Yuan would never again be slaves to an alien drug.

We'd been liberated by blood.

I fingered the knife sheathed at my belt, eager for the fight. I'd had it forged from the remains of the smashed traitorous blade retrieved from the collapsed Holy of Holies. I had a strange feeling that which defeated us would instead, somehow, be the means of our ultimate victory. Whatever, it was a constant reminder of what we'd lost and what we sought: *revenge!*

Yes, I'd bent the nomads completely to my own will...

"Prepare to attack!" I ordered over wide-broadcast. "Watch out for debris as we enter. I don't want any self-inflicted casualties."

We were in the cab of a tank-harvester, poised precariously on the slope of Doom Mons. Outside, a permanent *hurricane* blasted past us. Methane rain and hydrocarbon snow thudded into our windshield. The continuous storm dropped external visibility to only a few yards. But occasional breaks in the swirling orange smog allowed us to briefly see for miles into the distance.

Time seemed to stop as my mind clicked again into "analytical mode".

I saw a slick slope of water ice towering up before us. The mile-high mountain was polished smooth by the hurricane blasting into it. The blasting winds were from a maelstrom permanently circled the south pole of Titan. Clouds swirled menacingly around the high peak above us. The slope we were on extended down into the distance, the entire mountain being about 40 miles wide. At the bottom of the slope was a deep pit, named Sotra Patera, about 20 miles in diameter and itself one mile deep. Scientists theorized it originated from an ancient asteroid strike that punctured the crust of Titan. Indeed, the original scientific outpost at Doom Mons was there to study the interior of Titan through the thinned crust. Beyond the dark pit I saw flat ice fields, the "lava" of the ancient cryovolcano. The *cryomagma* was composed of water plus methanol and other components. It had long ago erupted up from a subsurface ocean of salty liquid water buried deep in the interior of the moon.

Suddenly a violent quake shook our vehicle.

Christ, that was a strong one!—I nervously mused. *They're getting more frequent and more powerful. Did we make the right choice for our attack? Instead of taking them head-on we're going for the "back door", though we're not exactly sure where it's located. We're exposed out here on the slopes, particularly when the quakes sling us around. Should we have waited for a calmer seismic period? Or have I sealed our "doom" on Doom Mons?*

Yes, I knew traveling to the peak would be a daunting task, likely immobilizing or destroying many of our tank-harvesters on the slick upper slopes. And yet that's where our spies discovered the main landing deck, from which airlocks led down into a hidden military base carved into the guts of the huge mountain. A retractable plasteel roof protected the inset landing deck. The cryovolcano was aptly named after "Mount Doom" from J.R.R. Tolkien's fictional "The Lord of the Rings." In the frozen ecology of Titan's surface, it was equally as terrifying as the fire-volcano where Tolkien imagined the infamous Ring being forged. It was a natural, formidable fortress. Unless you had an "invite" you simply could not get into it...at least until now!

Should we retreat, wait for a better attack-window?

"Pull the rods," I ordered, making the decision.

At first nothing happened. Did the transported nuclear reactor cores malfunction? Was our plan bonkers to start with? But then a violent quake *threw* our heavy tank-harvester up into the air. As we spun about I saw a *gigantic explosion* of steam and rock-ice ascending into the orange sky. And as we landed on the slope with a bone-jarring "crunch" a second explosion in the distance blew upward another white spout. Then another and another...

"Lock the tracks!" I ordered as we spun, out of control, down the slope.

We skidded to a bumpy stop, right in front of a steaming, dark opening leading into the interior of the mountain. We'd successfully breached the central cavern containing the hidden military base. We'd set our charges at external points likely to be close to the internal cavern. I'd lucked out on the atomic blast closest to my position. Reports from the other sites were negative. Huge explosions were triggered but no entrances were revealed. That was ok, we only needed one.

"Forward! All group 'C' troops, attack! You others, converge on our site. We've a clear corridor into the volcano!"

We swarmed forward, hundreds of tanks and troop carriers. Our entrance point wasn't a neat tunnel, but a steaming crack blasted out of the side of the mountain. We steered around giant boulders and still-liquid pools. Exposed to the released radioactivity in the breach we'd die in minutes. But the trek through the hazardous gap would be quick. This was the culmination of my long-ago Moon attack strategy, where we used a surprise attack to overcome a superior foe. And this was also Mars again, where in my first assassination I struck to the heart of the perversions rocking that society. Most satisfyingly, it was the opposite of the vile sneak attack on the gentle Yuan's capital city-cavern done dispassionately from orbit. I was back to being The General, in my element, leading a charge through hell for *justice* and *righteousness!*

...but, actuality, for petty revenge? What was wrong with me? I was about to get a lot of people killed and mutilated for my own selfish interests.

Was *I* the reason *Homo sapiens* couldn't rise above its animal instincts?

"We're with you, Goddess! Lead us to victory!" came many excited shouts over the tank's radio.

Ah, well...can't turn back now...

Suddenly our path was clear. I saw before us a subterranean complex of large buildings, out of which many excursion-suited armed troops were streaming at us.

"Kill them all!" came our battle cry from many zooming vehicles.

Yep, it's definitely true—I dispassionately observed. *This isn't a harmless research station of scientists studying cryovolcanism in Titan's interior guarded by a handful of troops. This is an armed encampment! Any scientists here are doing the biding of the military. They deserve no mercy. Yes, we'll kill them all!*

The enemy troops were like ants, darkening the glistening ice-rock floor. I saw each was clad in a black military excursion suit, carrying high-tech rifles and heavy howitzers. This was a well-organized counter-attack!

"What the hell?" I gasped. "Were they expecting us?"

I glanced at Glacket, who looked as shocked as I felt. Likely any traitor came from his people, who—after all—had recently been happy collaborators with the enemy. Indeed, our inside information on the general layout of the Doom Mons military base came from a few visits he made there back when he and us Yuan were bitter foes.

BLAM!

My tank rocked as we fired our cannon into the advancing swarm, blowing to pieces dozens of the defenders. We swerved to the side as laser-blasts and energy beams sizzled around us. I was glad we were exclusively using good old-fashioned bullets and physical missiles. Our tank could shrug off most of the hot plasma bursts but anything we shot with our cannon or machine gun would be stone-dead. Still, with only one entrance in the dead volcano's walls for our army to try to jam through, we were in for a hard fight. I prepared to disembark with my elite warriors and fight hand-to-hand. I fingered my lucky blue marble in my inside pants pocket. Hopefully it would protect me.

It took hours of pitched battle, but eventually we won. Sadly, we lost half our troops. But they died glorious deaths, savagely beating down our enemies. The open spaces of the huge cavern were littered with smoking transports, blown-apart tanks, and piles of bloody bodies. But in the end, we decimated the defenders. Triumphantly, we swarmed through the airlocks of the largest building and marched into its voluminous central hall.

It was good to be out of the foul, icy atmosphere outside. While my troops outside, mostly Dilmun, were still securing the facilities, we inside—mostly Yuan—could take off our facemasks. They dangled to the side of our heads. A raised stage with ornate columns sat to one side of the ceremonial auditorium. There prepared to unconditionally surrender were the base's commander and other dignitaries. They were clustered fearfully in the center of the stage, towering above my surrounding, well-armed little-people. I saw my people guarding key technicians, soldiers, lab-coated scientists, political sorts, high executives, and society figures all huddled together on-stage, fearful of what would happen next. They deserved nothing less than to be summarily executed on the spot. But I needed *infor-mation. Then* they could all die!

Yes, the blood-lust was on me. I saw red!

My surviving troops, filling in behind me, cheered lustily. The mass of green-skinned little people gave me renewed determination to do what needed be done. I marched up onto the stage to confront our defeated foes.

"TSS won't tolerate your intrusion," a high-ranking officer asserted as he stepped defiantly forward to meet me. Blood trickled from a wound on his forehead. His uniform was ripped and hanging askew across his chest. "Your 'victory' will be short-lived!"

I casually jabbed him in his throat with a closed fist, watching him fall to the stage's floor gasping for air, his windpipe dented inward. He'd live, but just barely.

I knew I had to contain my rage. A lot more was at stake here than who won or lost...

I saw a group of hooded Monks rush forward to help the officer up. I recognized them. It was the "transcendentalists", from the once-fringe religion that was now prevalent throughout the Solar System. Suddenly it "clicked" in my head. They sought to reach beyond known reality to an imagined "higher" level: similar to other religions but unique in using hard science to try and achieve their objectives.

This explains Captain Fehler's claim to me on the skiff that "Monks" were the buyers of his stolen goods. Theses Monks must be working with local scientists here at Doom Mons to use the Green to achieve a higher consciousness—the revelation flashed through my mind.

I stopped the Monks in their tracks by brandishing my knife. I stood over the fallen officer.

"I am the Cog-See *Goddess* of the Yuan!" I loudly proclaimed, standing tall above him. "I will *not* discuss this base's surrender with some weak lackey. Who is truly in charge here?"

"That would be me," an elegant lady in a neat brown pantsuit said. She was one of the executive-sorts. She was lean and trim. She met my eyes with a piercing glare. She sported exquisitely coifed gray hair stylishly white at the roots. She stood surrounded by a dozen

338 Daniel Basil Lyle

tough but disarmed bodyguards. She wisely wasn't getting within knife-range of me. "What are your demands?"

And over her head she wore a silk *hood*. It was the defining symbol of a Transcendentalist Monk.

I was right—I concluded triumphantly to myself. *The rumor originating on Old Earth was true. At the heart of the conspiracy to murder my mother is a vast, time-spanning religious group!*

Stunned, I now recognized the woman. The last time I'd seen her, her hair had been dyed blond with gray at the roots. The makeup-obscured mole above her lip was unmistakable. It was Madam Challax, the Hostess of the Moby Dick, who'd sold me a fortune worth of pure Green. She'd been a Transcendentalist all along!

"Well?" she frowned. "This is a religious retreat and scientific research station, nothing more. You've invaded us, defeated our military guard, and are going to plunder us. What can we do to stop your further desecration of holy ground? How much will it cost us for you and your raiders to leave us in peace?"

It all makes sense now—I nodded to myself. *I didn't think Titan's criminal syndicate would want Titanian Tea to be eliminated. But they didn't control its production. Alcohol, tobacco, marijuana, cocaine, heroin, meth, and all the other exotic drugs were in the syndicate's tight control for maximum profit. And who would care if a few grubby nomads disappeared, especially if a more cooperative group took their place?*

Wait...was this only a *local* conspiracy? Did this mean after all my "titanic" struggles I was still no closer to uncovering the *grand* conspiracy behind my mother's murder? Was Doom Mons just a convenient site for the criminal, commercial, political, and military elements of Titan to connive to maintain their collective and individual power and wealth? Was I back to where I started on Titan, just "following the money"? Did all of *Homo sapiens'* sins devolve down to just a pitiful pile of silver coins?

Selling out the Savior for 30 pieces of silver—I remembered my Bible teachings about Jesus' betrayal. *How prophetic of the evil in man's soul.*

"Ah, Madam Challax, you're older now but even more formidable," I replied, trying not to show my disappointment. "Ok, so you're in charge. Here's the deal. We will forego sacking your facility, *not* killing everyone here, plus discontinue our harassment of Titan's commerce *if* you agree to the following conditions: 1) total cessation of hostilities against the nomads; 2) monetary reparations; 3) help in reconstituting their sub-glacier caverns and Titanian Tea bush-fields; and 4) modern medical care for their chronic health problems, particularly reproductive ills. *Also* we demand all you know about…"

"Stop!" she broke-in, holding a hand palm-out in the air.

She frowned at me as she lowered her arm. She looked deeply confused. "I remember everyone I've ever served or met," she stated, her eyes narrowing. "But…the curve of your face, tilt of your nose…*now* I remember you. Your skin and stance have changed, but it's you! It was over twenty years ago and you've not aged a day. Remarkable!"

Say what? Ok, she remembers me as the dark-skinned Sister Lakeisha Penda—I realized. But just how long did I lay buried in the foul dunes of Shangri-La? I've been so busy exiled with the nomads who don't keep track of time that I've also thrown away the calendar. I must have been dead for over a decade!

In fact, a digital clock/calendar on the wall confirmed my suspicions. I now saw I'd lain buried in the dunes of Shangri-La for a full twenty years! I'd been so focused on the nomadic war I'd lost all track of time.

"I'm good at make-up and…" I tried to make a lame excuse for my youthful appearance.

As if to confirm my suspicions, a middle-aged, swarthy, well-built man hesitantly stepped forward. He wore the elegant but reserved suit of a politician or high official. He had a warm smile on his aging face. I noted that his gray hair was thinning. He looked to me to be about sixty years old.

"Tis good tae see ye again, 'Saskia'," he interrupted me. "Ye always wur a genius wi' yer makeup skills 'n' secret identities."

He winked at me with his soulful brown eyes. Yes, whoever he was he knew my secret and was helping "cover" for my change of appearance. What a nice guy…but I was confused. Why couldn't I remember him? He surely seemed to know me!

Who is this middle-aged man? He sure looks familiar…

And then I recognized him, shocked at *his* change of appearance.

"When ye disappeared fer real, ah tracked your movements and searched fur yer downed 'copter. Ah ne'er gave up. Even whin ah rose to be Director of Security for Huygens Base, ah kept me ear tae th' ground. Ah knew that th' 'White Goddess' in the nomadic war had tae be ye. So since I'm noo th' Security Czar for a' th' Company's Titan operations, ah came in person t'day. I was hopin' fer more word o' ye. And 'ere ye be! Praise Buddha!"

Oh, my God!—I gasped to myself, trying to stay outwardly calm though inwardly shaking. *It's Jags Dougal. He's no longer the dreamy young man I hired as my deputy. But he's still handsome. And likely he's still a good man with a good heart. Yet he should be around forty years old now. This man looks much older. And how could he possibly be involved in the atrocities against the Yuan?*

"Git oot o' mah 'friggin wey!" a gruff, full-Scottish clanner voice sounded from behind Dougal.

I saw Jags shoved violently to the side by a burly, old man. He had not a hair on his splotched and wrinkled head. His bare arms were covered with gray scrub. I recognized his evil leer. Yes, this was a day of reunions. It was *Captain Lars Fehler*, still powerful and ruthless. It was the very same man who decades ago left me for dead on the Kraken, then betrayed his lover for a fortune in pure Green.

I felt my barely suppressed blood lust returning.

"Yes...it *is* ye!" he exclaimed, marveling with bloodshot eyes. "Ah can't hawp it, but tis true. You're that pesky Inspector oan mah last voyage—and nae a day older! You're aye a teenager. Bit magical powers or nae, a 'Goddess' wull surely fall t'day!"

My troops massed in the hall below us were silent, not knowing what to make of this challenge to my divine authority. I couldn't let this old skiffer question my victory or authority. There was still a chance that the Grand Conspiracy could be ferreted out here if only I could get time to individually interrogate the figures on the stage.

I stepped forward to yank his throat out...

"Ah challenges ye to *Jokmagook!*" he stopped me with a bold exclamation. "You're aye a newcomer tae Titan, wee lassie. I've leed 'ere mah entire lee, steeped in a' tis people's traditions 'n' laws. Get wi' th' program!"

"Uh...say what?" I asked, puzzled. I took a step back. I almost smiled. What a bizarre term, "Jokmagook." I'd never heard it before. Was he making it up? Was it even real?

"He is invoking the ancient Yuan rite of royal trial by combat, Goddess," Shawnee confirmed, moving from behind me to stand at my side. "Between gods, we mere mortals cannot settle disputes. It must be fought between the supernatural entities themselves."

I looked down at her in disbelief.

"But *he's* no god," I scornfully laughed. "Besides, I could kill him with one finger. That old skiffer is beneath me!"

"I am nae a mere human," he growled, deep hatred glaring from his squinted eyes. "A' th' pure Green I've ingested mak's me th' *god* o' th' Titanian Seas—Poseidon his-self. I'm th' main guinea pig o' oor many scientists 'ere, their intermediary tae th' buried kingdom doon below. No one else kin dae whit ah dae, tolerate th' dosages ah eat. I've taken mair Green than ony ither human bein', making me a god! Poseidon was a true bairn o' Titans. Aye, I'm just as muckle a 'god' as yer skinny ass is a 'goddess'. So c'moan, wee lassie, let me *fondle* ye. I'll be gentle when ah slit yer throat, ah promise!" he snarled.

Everything hung in the balance. The victory I'd worked so hard to achieve might be compromised if I refused his lewd challenge. Certainly my bloodthirsty troops, eager for their long-delayed revenge, would welcome a final "triumphant" fight-to-the-death. Yep, this was the climactic "good-guy-vs-bad-guy" final confrontation of the science-fiction book or action movie!

"You're on," I sneered back at him.

We squared off inside a circle of my armed warriors down on the floor of the hall. Above us, sensing their fate also hung on the result of the fight, the dignitaries and officials looked on anxiously.

The old Captain held a four-barbed whaler hook, swinging it by a short chain around his head. He had his shirt off, revealing a barrel chest above an ample belly. His whole upper torso was covered in stiff gray hair. His arms were huge and powerful. He looked like an angry bear about to defend its territory with slashing claws.

I needed only my knife, held by my left hand in a stabbing mode. I wanted this fight over quickly. I was confident that all my many years of professional assassination and combat experience would serve me well. He wouldn't stand a chance.

"Dose me!" Lars shouted to a lab-coated lady standing fearfully behind him.

"Wait! What are you doing?" I stopped them.

"It is his right," Shawnee replied, standing to the side officiating. "The Gods of Titan are fueled by the Green."

Oh, hell—I gulped to myself. *It's like a drug-addict having super-human strength, not feeling any pain, going berserk when "high." If he can take a large enough dosage it won't mellow him out...it'll enrage and super-power him!*

"Is...is this ok?" the lady gulped, taking out a vial. "It's the maximum dosage you can tolerate."

"Gie it tae me!" Lars bellowed eagerly.

In the vial I saw a hint of scintillating Green. Even just a trace of it was enough to send the human denizens of the solar system into rapturous states. Such a large dose, likely a full milligram, would instantly kill a normal human—but the Captain claimed he was a lifetime user. That much Green would likely transform Lars into a maniacal beast!

"It is permitted," Shawnee nodded her green-skinned head. "And you, Goddess? We still have some tea in our tank-harvester. It would take only a minute for someone to fetch..."

"No!" I snapped at her. "I need no chemical augmentation. None of our *mighty Yuan warriors* need artificial crutches. We fight with skill, determination, and focus!"

The packed hall of my Yuan warriors *roared* their approval!

"Ah, hah, hah!" Lars laughed as he grabbed the vial, twisted off the cap, and snorted the contents straight up his nose. "I'll pat an end tae yer wee rebellion richt *noo!*"

He wavered back and forth then reared up to his full height, *screaming* at me!

"Fight!" Shawnee said, stepping back.

I knew I was in trouble when Lars' four-barbed whaler's hook suddenly *slammed* into my left side.

"Yes! *Kill* her!" some on the stage yelled.

I gasped from the awful pain as he *yanked* it backward, hauling off some of my rib muscles in a spray of blood. In a flash he dropped the hook and was upon me, *smashing* his heavy fists into my face and side. Stunned by the hook-strike, I could only put up my arms to shield my body from further damage.

He pounded me like a heavy-weight fighter totally dominating a feather-weight, until I managed to jerk back out of his reach.

The crowd gasped at the barbarity, even those up on the stage.

I staggered away, my right hand clutching my savaged ribs, my knife now held high in my left hand. My blood lust was fading...now I only wanted to survive!

"Arrrgggghhhhh!" Lars shouted in triumph as he snatched up his whaler's hook. He swung it by its chain around his head, poised to sling it into the other side of my body...

I ducked under the *swishing* hook and plunged my knife to its hilt in his bulging belly.

He jerked backward, causing the knife to slice downward, partially disemboweling him.

Bloody intestines dangled out over his pants.

He grinned, nodding at me in admiration. Then he reached down with a big hand, stuffing the loops back into the gaping wound.

"Noo ye'v made me *mad!*" he roared, lunging for me.

I kicked his feet out from under him, rolling off to the side. But he sprang up like a jack-rabbit, *stomping* like an elephant. He caught one of my feet under his big boot, *crushing* the small bones. Following up with nary a pause, he *kicked* my mutilated side, breaking several ribs. The force of the blow in Titan's weak gravity *lofted* me above the crowd as my fighters jerked away from me, politely making room for the continued fight.

Damn! They should be helping me!—I groaned to myself.

I *slammed* down onto the hard floor, *snapping* my ill-positioned right arm.

"Get her! Stay on her! Kill the bitch!" shouts of encouragement came from the stage.

I was almost unconscious from the incredible pain. I had thought I was the "Queen of pain," able to withstand almost any punishment. But I was wrong. Horrified I realized I was hobbled, unable to stand on my smashed foot. I had only one working arm. My broken ribs made it difficult to draw a breath. I was rapidly losing blood from my savaged side-muscles, growing faint. And my face and upper torso were numb from his initial blows.

I'm totally screwed—I gasped to myself in disbelief. *He's the most formidable adversary I've ever faced!*

Lars was charging at me, yet again swinging that wicked whaler's hook high above his head...

—when *time stopped* as my desperate mind clicked yet again into "analytical" mode.

Incredibly, I wasn't the only person momentarily "out of time."

My dear little friend Shawnee was at my side, holding a *clear vial* to my lips. But her face was turned away from me. Instead, her *second* face on the back of her bald head stared sightlessly at me, its lips struggling to form words.

The screw-top of the vial was being loosened...

I recognized the vial. It was attached to a gold chain. It was the vial I thought forever lost when my helicopter crashed over Shangri-La! It contained 1/6th of a teaspoon of pure Green, roughly 1,000 milligrams worth—a *thousand times* as much as Lars had snorted!

"Glenda...took this off your body...when they found you frozen in the dunes," Shawnee's conjoined twin grated with difficulty into my ear. "Glenda gave it to me...to keep it hidden and safe...then give it back to you...right at this moment. I betrayed your attack to the enemy...to assure this moment would arrive. Now...I atone for my sin."

She upturned the vial and I swallowed the entire contents.

"Who are you? You're not our regular emissary."

I was swimming in a dark, salty, warm ocean. It felt wonderful, like being in the womb. All around me were waving, intertwined, giant tentacles. I felt them rather than saw them. They were both physical and psychic. They gently reached into my brain extracting and examining my memories.

"Who are *you?*" I responded, concerned but strangely not frightened.

Amazingly, the constant background of pain I endured was gone. In its place was a feeling of delicious relief, of peace. For the first time in my life I didn't feel alone, isolated.

"This one's soul is not twisted," I heard an answer, politely phrased in my own language. But their reply was not to my question.

"Perhaps we're wrong?"

"We did have only one specimen to examine. This one opens a whole new area of inquiry."

"Then should we pause?"

I sensed many millions of entities conferring together in a language incomprehensible to me, comparing foreign concepts. Then they came to a decision.

"We will not immediately eradicate the surface pests. We can suffer their pollution for a while more. We must study them further."

I sensed collective relief that a terrible, irredeemable action had been, if not stopped, then postponed.

"Where am I?" I asked.

"You don't know?"

"I got here by accident. I ate a large amount of pure Green."

A dazzling rainbow of exploding bubbles burst around me, almost making me forget trying to get answers to my questions. It was mesmerizing, even beautiful! I was part of a spectrum that went far beyond anything I'd ever seen before.

"You are either an invader or guest in our world," the voice answered. "We're still not sure which."

"And where is 'your world', exactly?" I repeated.

"You come from the surface, where our flat cousins swim."

"Ah, you mean the surface of Titan. You're talking about the Azotos and larger Krakens."

"Our cold, slow cousins, yes."

"And if you are 'under' the surface," I continued, "then that must mean I'm somehow in the subsurface salty ocean of Titan that's located about fifty miles beneath its icy crust."

"We live in our world. You are an intruder or guest."

"So like the Azotos you're a lifeform indigenous to Titan but having an Earth-type biochemistry," I confirmed. Then an amazing thought struck me: "Are you the unknown source of the methane which gets replenished in Titan's atmosphere? Is it *you* that keeps Titan's atmosphere from collapsing by regenerating the lost methane?"

Oh, wow! I'm "geeking" out. This solves an ongoing mystery of Titan, how the methane that gets broken down or turned to more complex organics by ultra-violet radiation gets continuously replenished. The Azotos contribute some, but their glacial metabolism just doesn't make enough. Scientists suspected that simple Earth-like organisms might lurk in the deep, buried ocean, but...?

"Among other molecules, our chemical pathways generate a lot of methane, yes."

"Obviously you're not simple bacteria or algae," I acknowledged. "You're a sophisticated lifeform. How is it then that you can *talk* to me, even doing so in Standard Spacer English?"

"We have been here forever, looking outward. We look around corners to see beyond. Only recently did visitors arrive on the surface, upsetting the natural order. Then came intruders, first another and then you. Your language is simple. We easily extracted it from the synaptic patterns in your brain."

Ah, I see. Two different forms of indigenous life on Titan evolved together in separate environments, forging a means of mental communication. Isolated in this buried ocean, the Earth-metabolism creatures down here have found ways to transgress normal dimensional barriers, linking with their surface Azotos cousins. Amazing!

"So I'm somehow able to mentally communicate with you by the stolen alien molecules that your cousins normally use to communicate inside and across their own selves up on the surface?"

"Yes."

This must be what all those scientists up on the stage were researching—I thought to myself, frantically trying to figure things out. *They're part of a dedicated group trying to communicate with Titanian lifeforms that evolved down here in the hidden salty ocean. Energy to melt the water, evolve and feed the critters here comes from either radioactive decay in the core or Saturn's gravity messaging Titan in its orbit. The life down here must be compatible to us, using similar biochemistry, unlike the alien chemistry of the Azotos and Krakens. That's very interesting as a scientific study. But what are the scientists ultimately trying to achieve? Why is it so important that a military installation be built to keep the effort secret, protecting their research?*

"Why do you communicate with us here at Doom Mons, not elsewhere?"

"There are conduits here to the surface."

"Ah...the cracks that feed the cryovolcanoes?"

"Yes, plus a huge space-rock that bashed-in the crust a long time ago. At other locations our outward sight is dimmed or blocked."

"Sure, the crust is too thick at other places for your easy access to the Azotos. So how can I help you guys?"

My new question caused consternation amongst the many interacting lifeforms. I had the feeling I was communicating with a "super-brain" where the total was much greater than the sum of its parts.

"The other surface fast-mind never asked us this question."

"Of course not," I explained, "he's a turd."

"Turd?"

"The other mind is a poor example of *Homo sapiens*, my species," I explained. "Please don't judge us by him. Some are like him but most are not."

"How can you be so radically different? Are you not all the same species?"

That was a profound question. It made me pause before answering.

"Well, I suppose it's because we aren't directly linked like you. We can only communicate indirectly," I told them. "Most of the time we interact by sound, sight, smell, taste, or touch. We can't see into each other's brains, as you seem to do."

"So you are cut-off, isolated from each other? That is very sad. Even with our slow cousins above we always have at least a weak connection—and they with themselves."

Wow. Maybe that's why Homo sapiens fight so much, are so selfish, and do so many self-destructive, irrational things—I thought. Titan's lifeforms have much to teach us, if only we can learn from them.

"Well, we get along as best we can," I mentally shrugged, trying to excuse our awful behavior. "But...are you saying you can actually *feel* what happens to your cousins? Aren't they just incredibly cold sea-plants?"

"No, they are like us mentally. When appropriately linked they are *thinking* creatures. They just think *very* slowly, too slow for you fast creatures to recognize."

Ah, that's why harvesting them provokes almost no reaction, unless you get close to their nodal crystalline clusters, the Green—I sadly concluded, remembering stabbing the Kraken to its heart. *And yet, the salt-ocean Titanians say that the Azotos and Krakens DO feel what's happening to them. Say what?*

"So...can *you* feel *us* killing them?" I hesitantly asked.

"The pain is excruciating."

"I suppose you'd like for us to stop?"

"Yes—and cease making an excess of them."

"We make more of them?"

"Your pollution feeds their reproduction, giving you ever more to kill, while disturbing the natural order."

"Are you referring to the billions of tons of excess hydrogen we generate when we split water using our nuclear reactors? We ship off the liquefied oxygen with your liquid methane to power our ships. The excess hydrogen is released as a waste gas."

"Yes. You drive excess reproduction of our cousins."

Oh, Christ, they've got us nailed—I mentally groaned. *We're hurting them and have been doing so for a long time. It's lucky they can't get at us or we'd be in bad trouble!*

"Can we somehow coexist with you here, or would you like us to leave Titan entirely?" I boldly asked.

There isn't any point in delicate diplomacy. They can read my thoughts...

"Please leave. We find your kind very distressing."

"And if we don't?"

"Then such evil can't be tolerated. We will remove you."

Oh, Christ—I gasped mentally. *They CAN get at us!*

"From Titan?"

"From everywhere."

Oh, hell!—I groaned to myself. *These creatures are serious. There's a whole subsurface ocean filled with a super-brain with who-knows-what capabilities. Can they really wipe human beings from the solar system?*

And then I had another awful realization.

This must be why the military is so interested in the salty ocean inhabitants, particularly in keeping their existence a well-guarded secret. They want to use the Titanians' power as a weapon! With the ability to reach instantly and secretly into any enemy encampment, Saturn's rulers would control the solar system. God damn it! Why do we have to turn everything good into a weapon?

"Surely just ejecting us from your Moon would be sufficient?" I hopefully asked, knowing they'd just read my mind and taken it as confirmation.

"You'd come back."

"Well, maybe we *wouldn't* because we wouldn't want to be ejected again?"

"When you returned, you'd do so after finding a way to kill *us*."

That logic is impeccable—I mentally shrugged. *That's exactly what we'd do. Convinced an alien lifeform was plotting to wipe out our species we'd retreat, research a way to counter-attack, and then return with the means to kill them!*

"I'm so sorry," I apologized. "Can you give me some time to try to figure out a solution?"

I sensed heated discussion.

"Because of your sincerity, we grant you time. Killing fellow thinking creatures is repugnant to us."

"Thank you—and just *how* long would that be?"

"We don't know."

"Ok then," I mentally gulped, both frightened and humbled. "But did you say all this to that other entity which visited you? Do my scientists know about this? And can you communicate with us other than facilitated by massive doses of the Green?"

"No."

"That's good, but do they know of your ability to affect the surface?"

"Yes. When the other intruder first arrived we had to discipline his mind by demonstrating our power. We caused the quakes on the surface. He knows we can remodel the surface at will."

Alright then—I sighed. *If I try to tell anyone about this, none other than the scientists above will believe me. The public is blissfully unaware that a dangerous super-brain lurks in a subsurface salty ocean on Titan, responsible for convulsing the crust of the moon. And without someone else capable of enduring a giant slug of Green, there will be no more of this mental communication for our scientists to study. It'll be years, if ever, that they'll be able to physically drill down fifty miles into the frozen core of Titan to reach the hidden ocean. So all I have to do is stop Lars. Then the Titanians down here will be protected.*

"If I stop this mental intrusion into your deliberations, will that be helpful to you?"

"Yes."

"Fine, I'll do that. There will be no more human minds bothering you down here, at least for a while. And I'll try to do something quickly about the pain inflicted on you by us slaughtering your surface cousins. Ok?"

"Ok."

"So...how do I get out of here?"

"You don't know?"

I suppose I'll just have to wait for the Green to wear off, assuming that I live that long—I told myself. *Of course as time speeds back up in the "real" world, Lars is probably there bashing my head in as we 'speak' and...*

"We could give you a lift if you'd like," the meta-mind asserted, breaking my increasingly black mood.

"A lift?"

"We see in your mind you're on a quest, searching for an elusive answer."

"Yes!" I eagerly replied. "Can you help me?"

"We can lift you higher."

"Higher?"

Holy crap!—I exclaimed to myself. *Is this what Sanako meant when she said to see who killed my mother I should "look higher"?*

"We are happy to give a boost," the mega-mind repeated, seemingly impatiently. They were glad to get rid of me!

Wait!—I ordered myself, my mind racing. *Maybe they can just kick me back where I came from instead of transporting my mind elsewhere. Then I can confront Lars before he kills me. But, then again, if I'm going to die, yet again, shouldn't I do so having found the answer I've been seeking for so long? Sanako definitely did tell me on her deathbed to "look higher" for the conspiracy behind my mother's murder. What if these creatures can really make that happen?*

"Yes, please, lift me higher!"

And so they did.

I found myself standing in a strange room. It wasn't large, but it was packed with unusual things. Through a long window gentle sunlight streamed in. And though I still wore all my battle gear, my wounds and injuries were inexplicably gone. In front of me I saw a long-haired man sitting with his back to me, typing busily at a keyboard. He was peering intently into a large flat-screen monitor upon which several overlapping programs were displayed. One of them was a word-processing document into which he was busily typing words.

"Look around if you want, Suzy," he spoke, startling me, his back still to me. "I'll be with you in a minute. I just need to finish this section I'm writing."

A radio was playing over some small speakers. It was interesting, soothing music: "We had love...we had love...we had love...we had love..." was the chorus. It was a beautiful song. But even more interesting was what surrounded me: enclosed *terrariums* sporting large branches, artificial plants, tubs of water, secluded caves, and heat-lamps. In the lush cages I spied both tortoises and snakes. In the largest, walk-in cage I saw a lazily sunning ten-foot long, red-tailed boa constrictor.

"Where am I?" I asked, incredibly confused.

"Ok, I'm finished for the moment," the man stated, standing and turning to me.

I instantly recognized him.

"This can't be true," I flatly stated. "I must be having some sort of hallucination caused by the Titanian ocean denizens. They've tapped into my memories and..."

"Do you doubt your eyes, your hands, and even your nose?" he gently interrupted me.

He was correct about my nose. I smelled a faint, not unpleasant odor of living creatures inhabiting the terrariums. Plus I detected the odor of lightly soiled sawdust. Yes, there over in the corner, tucked away behind two large snake cages, was a spacious rodent cage. Scampering-about I saw mice peeking up at me. Were they a future meal for some of the snakes? If so, they looked happy and well-cared for in the interim.

"It's a bit musty," he shrugged, "but that's ok for a biologist."

He smiled at me in a friendly way, waving a hand at everything around us. Clearly I was free to inspect anything I wanted. The first thing I scrutinized was *him*. He was just shy of being six feet tall, wore gold glasses with a connecting chain holding his long brown hair back behind his ears. He had a professor-like full brown mustache and beard. He was lean and fit. He looked to be in his mid-fifties.

To the side of his computer on the wall I saw framed pictures and certificates. I walked past him and examined them.

"Is this you?" I asked.

"They certify key points in my life," he replied. "It helps me looking forward to look back at where I've been. It keeps me grounded."

I saw him depicted as a young, clean-shaven man graduating from high school, then in an Air Force military uniform beside an older man I presumed to be his dad, pictures of a dignified married couple presumably his dad and mom, then graduating from college as a middle-aged man in a cap and gown with full beard, and finally working at a complex microscope in a research laboratory, wearing a lab coat. I also saw official, framed certificates: of an *honorable discharge* from the US Air Force, attaining an *ASCP board certification* as a Medical Technologist, graduating with a *Ph.D. in Biology*, honoring *thirty years* government-related work, *trademarking* of the term "Creative-Theology", and working with various kid programs at a church.

And the name on all the certificates was the same: *Daniel Lyle*.

How can this be?—I gasped to myself, studying the framed pictures and certificates more critically.

If I were to believe the evidence there in front of me, I was talking to the same man that I saw play the synthesizer onstage right before the Extinction Event. He was also the man who hundreds of years ago established the basis of the Yuan's mellowed-out religion, who documented my mother's trans-dimensional adventures, and who wrote books prophesizing my still-unrealized future!

"By your certificates, you're older than you look," I stated, stalling for time as I processed this incredible situation.

He laughed politely.

"You got me," he shrugged with a grin. "I dye my normally gray hair. But don't accuse me of using lady's hair dye! I use 'Just for Men' brown hair dye. Women can't use it. It says so on the box! Anyway, thanks for the compliment."

Lame...he must have told that "joke" many times over. But I can't stall any longer. I'm "here" wherever this is and I've got to get to the point of it all. I don't know how much longer I can remain here!

"Just what year is this?" I asked him, turning away from the photos and certificates to defiantly face him.

"It's the 20th of June, 2019."

"That's impossible...unless I've gone back in time?"

"You've done what few others have ever achieved, Suzy," he blandly stated. "You're not just in another dimension, nor on another planet, not even in another timeline. You've ascended *up* a level."

"*Up* a level?" I numbly repeated.

"Look, this is an incredible event for me too," he sighed, looking at me almost shyly. "You are like a daughter to me. I never expected to be able to actually meet you in person! To have you really here in the room with me is incredible. I greatly appreciate the telepathic Titanians boosting you up to this level, by greatly augmenting the effect of the Green on your mental functions. I'm not sure how long you can remain here, but I surely intend to enjoy every moment of your presence. Before we get down to serious discussion, though, how about a quick tour of my place?" he eagerly concluded, gesturing at an open doorway.

I felt a strange kinship to him. It was like he was mirroring my thoughts or *vice versa*.

Has the world turned upside down?

"Uh...ok," I nodded. I was glad to put off what I suspected would be mind-shattering revelations. I needed time to wrap my brain around what was happening.

"Follow me," he said, walking into the next room.

I saw more terrariums, this time with green lizards perched on branches. I saw bookcases stuffed with books, with many ancient blu-ray discs, with musical CDs, and with lots of DVDs. A piano with worn-down keys sat in the corner. What appeared to be dinosaur fossils sat on the top of the shelves. Strikingly unique, colorful paintings covered the remaining exposed white walls. It was like being in a combination zoo, natural history museum, and art gallery! Most of the paintings were signed "M.L.L."—his mother? Some were signed as "D.L.", his own works?

This place is a hotbed of creativity!

"Are you hungry or thirsty?" he said. "The kitchen's right over here. Do you need to freshen up? The bathroom's behind that door."

"No, neither, thanks, but..."

"And here's what I call my 'cathedral of creativity'," he proudly explained as we walked into the living room.

Christ, I was dead-on. We're thinking each other's thoughts!

I saw yet more large terrariums with lizards, but also a big-screen TV plus a roll-down wall-sized movie screen with various disc player and projector equipment fixed to the opposite wall.

"I have 3D equipment here that can give a wall-sized image for either simulated or full 3D, plus normal 2D of course. With a powerful surround-sound system I display and enjoy mankind's best side: when *Homo sapiens* individuals fully exercise their God-given Creativity!"

Yes, I saw many blu-ray and DVD-filled bookshelves lining the wall. It looked like there were several thousand discs.

"I have a tremendous collection of musical, popular, historical, nature-oriented, travel, and other artistic visual displays. Just counting my 3D blu-rays, I've over 500 of them," he stated proudly. "It's a dying medium, but marvelous to behold. I collect them. I'm a collector, you see. I've nothing of any particular monetary value but all have great artistic content."

I didn't have the heart to tell him that virtual 360° reality would soon displace his flat-screen 3D projections. After that, actual holo-projections indistinguishable from reality would, in turn, displace goggle-necessitating VR.

"Yes, it's much like ancient analog phonographic records," he smiled at me as if he'd read my mind. "They were displaced by digital medium, but something was lost. Analog records actually had a recent comeback. I guess that didn't survive past WWIII, did it?"

He knows about the Extinction Event?—I marveled. *But if it's truly way back in 2019, how can he possibly...?*

"*Tell* me what's happening!" I exclaimed, grabbing him by his arm. I saw my hand was shaking. And I was shocked to find his arm was firm and solid. He was real, not a hallucination!

He put a warm hand gently on mine, loosened my tight grip, guiding me to a comfortable padded chair.

Rigid and greatly agitated, I sat. He plopped down in another chair facing me, looking relaxed and nonthreatening.

"Alright, Suzy," he relented. "I could show you a lot more of my place, such as my concert-hall with my other musical instruments, but you already know where we are, right?"

I looked out a door-window to a porch, beyond which I saw green leafy trees and a street. Yes, I knew exactly where we were. We were in my parent's home, in Sulphur Oklahoma. We were on the corner of West 12th and Ardmore. I grew up in this house with my brother, Billy. In fact, this man's computer room where I'd materialized had been my bedroom.

"Yes," I admitted, afraid to say more.

"I know this is a radical paradigm-shift for you, but you're very quick and highly intelligent, Suzy," he complimented me. "If you've truly gone 'up a level' then what are you now experiencing?"

"You...you..."

"Go on!"

"You're my creator."

"Which means?"

"I'm a character in a book. You're the author. You made me up. I'm not real."

"Oh no, no!" he hastened to reassure me. The green lizards in the large aquarium behind him looked startled at his sharp response, lifting their heads expectantly. "You're just as real as me. You just live in a different reality, one that stems from my brain and then is repeatedly manifested when readers mentally engage with and enjoy my science fiction books. In fact, you are being resurrected right *now* in the mind of the *present* reader. Say hello to your reanimator! He or she is adding their own spin to your magnificent adventure. Hopefully long after I'm dust you'll still be being brought back to life many times over, long into the distant future."

"Uh...hi there, Betty...or Clint or Jane or George or whatever your name is—how's it going?" I said, looking up at the ceiling and giving a small wave.

"I'll bet that startled someone," he smiled, looking up at the ceiling also. "Hey, me too! Thanks so much for reading my book," he added, speaking distinctly. "I hope you're really enjoying this fantastic journey!"

"But...if this were true," I mused, struggling to comprehend what he was claiming, "Then what does it say about *you?*"

"Ah," he smiled. "I'm so proud of you Suzy, both of you and your mother Sally. Like her you're capable of 'seeing beyond' the accepted limits of reality. But to answer your excellent question...yes, I suppose that in a yet-higher reality I also might be a self-aware, self-motivating creation of a yet-larger mind."

"God?"

"Maybe!"

"But then, if that were true, none of us are responsible for anything," I argued, struggling to make sense of this incredible experience. "We're all just *marionettes* with a higher Entity pulling our strings, putting words in our mouths!"

"It could be," he shrugged. "It's an ages-old speculation. But on our level it doesn't really matter. *We* think we're real. We have real challenges and opportunities to face and deal with. We live our lives. We make our own choices. If we originate in the mind of a higher Being—whether a humble author like me or God Himself—that's just the way it is. Our challenge is to do the best we can with what we've been given. Within the context of our immediate worlds, both you and I have 'free will'...I think," he weakly repeated himself.

This can't be true!—I groaned to myself, burying my head in my hands. *Am I going insane? Did that massive dose of Green scramble my brain?*

"No...no...no!" I grated through clenched teeth, slowly standing up and moving off a step. "I'm *not* a character in a book! If I were, then that would mean..." my voice trailed off.

I looked at Lyle with an icy stare.

He looked down at the floor, his hands clutched tightly together.

"It was *you*," I spat at him. "You *killed* my mother!"

He looked like I'd knifed him to the heart, though my blade was still sheathed securely at my side.

"Yes," he admitted in a soft voice, still looking down at the floor. "But I didn't mean to do it! It just happened. Like I said before, you and your world originate in my brain, but there's no such thing as predestination. Yes, I type at the keyboard but stuff just happens on its own and..." his voice trailed off weakly.

"Like hell!" I shouted at him, just barely holding myself back from physically attacking the man. "If what you say is true then every single word or action of mine is laid out in your damn books. I *saw* them! I *held* them in my hands! There were *hard copies* of them in the Yuan's Ark! So therefore, I have no freedom at all. I'm just a character in a 'scripted' play that can only be read or acted-out as written. That's the truth, the answer, the 'conspiracy' with which I've been obsessed for hundreds of years. All this time I've been looking for *you!*"

He wearily stood up to face me. He was taller than me but looked like he'd shrunk, as if my words had beaten him down. But then a fresh look of determination spread over his face. He pushed up his gold glasses that had slipped to the end of his nose. He reached back to tighten the gold chain holding his long brown hair in place behind his head.

"The very words you speak right now are your very own," he said with fresh conviction. "When I start to write a new fictional book, I have a general idea of where I think I'll go, what might happen, and where it may end up. But it's the characters and the new world itself that determine what actually happens. They proceed on their own,

Suzy. Things happen I never intended, like the sad murder of your mother. I never intended that to happen. I don't 'plot out' the story before starting. Entire characters 'pop up' that I never planned on, like Jags and Lars and Glenda, and on and on! I'm more like a reporter, who records on paper an ongoing, external story. Like I said before, Suzy, you're as alive as me. And *you* can do the *same* as I'm doing. You're a good writer, Suzy. You can become a creator as well!"

Uh huh, sure...

I turned my back on him and stomped back through the house to where I first materialized. I stood in the same spot, surrounded by the artificial reptilian "jungle." I heard a disconcerting rustling sound and saw the big boa constrictor was crawling up on a thick branch, flicking his forked red tongue at me. But his actions weren't threatening. It seemed the huge snake was...curious?

"Send me home!" I loudly proclaimed. "You Titanian sea creatures or whatever, take me back! I'm tired of this charade. You've meddled with my memories enough, creating this false reality. I don't believe for one second that some stupid science fiction writer hundreds of years ago killed my mother. This is just a ploy to placate me. I don't know if you're doing this from good intentions or not, perhaps trying to help me resolve my inner torment. But enough! I don't need this fairy tale! Send me back home, *now!*" I yelled at the top of my lungs.

On the radio an old Elvis Presley song was playing: "Don't Cry Daddy." I heard the plaintive words over and over: "Please don't cry, daddy...please laugh again...we'll find a new mommy."

What are these awful words?—I moaned inwardly. *Is this my own guilt attacking me? Am I trying to tell myself the awful truth that it was ME that caused my mother's death? Is that why I've gone on this insane quest, to prove to myself that my quarreling with her, my cutting her off from me at the Galactic Core, didn't set her up for assassination? No! I'm NOT going to find a "new mommy"! I'm not going to stop crying! I AM going to get my revenge! It wasn't my fault!*

I was sobbing uncontrollably, waiting to be sent home. I felt the hallucination wavering, the objects around me becoming blurry...

"Stop!" Lyle yelled, rushing into the room to stand trembling beside me. He was also crying. His bearded cheeks were slick with his own tears. "Please just stay a moment, Suzy. I have something I must tell you!"

"*What?*" I coldly snapped at him, angrily brushing away my own tears.

"I...I...j-just want to s-say 'thank you,'" he stammered, smiling at me now lovingly.

"For what?"

"Whether anyone ever reads the words I'm writing or not, you've brought me tremendous pleasure," he choked out, speaking all-in-a-rush. Clearly he knew I wouldn't be there much longer. "It's been an incredible thrill to document your adventures, both your fantastic achievements and heroic, painful struggles. And if anyone else actually reads my books about you and your mom, I hope they too are similarly amazed and inspired by your story. You're special, Suzy. Along with your mother before you, you're truly the unique 'girl with the turtle tattoo.' You take me and your other admirers to wondrous places I and they have never before been—to fascinating new worlds and realms. All of us will eventually die, even you 'the girl who could not die.' But that's not what's most important, our inevitably sad endings. It's the life we lead, the unexpected struggles we fight our way through, that are worthy of admiration—of pleasing our Creator whoever or whatever that Entity may be! *Exercising* our *Godly Creativity* is the highest, most-noble pursuit of them all. *You* do this in spades! So I hope your future readers love you as much as do I, Suzy. You're one-of-a-kind, even in your obsessions and weaknesses. Yes, the evil Commissioner *didn't* put out a hit on your mother from her out-of-time citadel in Saturn's rings. It *was* me. I'm sorry I killed your mother. I'll take the blame. You don't have to bear that burden any longer. After all, in the end, an omnipotent 'God' must ultimately bear the blame for everything in His creation, whether that Entity is a true Ultimate Intelligence or a lowly key-puncher like me. All of us *Homo sapiens* are just minor actors in a bigger play. But *how* we act our parts and speak our lines is up to us. *We* choose if, where, and how to exercise our own God-given talents, making our own decisions. For that effort—the struggle to do and be *reasonable, useful, respectful, beautiful,* and *honorable*—we definitely get credit: the grateful appreciation from our loving Creator. You've done well, Suzy. You've been a good girl. Your mommy's proud of you. *I'm* proud of you. *Thank* you!"

Wow—I marveled to myself. *That was quite a speech. If this is coming from my own Green-fevered brain, I am indeed a good writer! Perhaps I should take 'my' own advice. Maybe it wouldn't hurt for me to make my daily AR implant-recorded diary available to others in some form. After all, it helps sort things out in my own brain. Maybe it can also do the same for others. Hallucination or not, I see now my story isn't just about me. It's about all of humanity. It's about the struggles and guilt we all face for our tragic mistakes. It's truly about the rise and fall of Homo sapiens and...*

Seeing my hesitation, he hurried on... "Sorry to preach a sermon at you, Suzy. It's just that you've been such a huge part of my life these last few years and..." his voice trailed off.

I shook my head to clear it. The tearful bearded man was still standing there, looking at me expectantly. Whether he or I was "real" or not, it wouldn't hurt for me to be polite.

"You're welcome," I replied.

Then as everything around me faded, I found I was *still* determined to find the *true* murderer of my dear mother. My Quest was *not* at an end.

Time sped up as the ferocious Lars *lunged* at me, his wicked four-pronged hook swinging up over his bald skull to *plunge* down at my face...

—as with a *quick snap* of my left hand my knife blade zipped through the air and lodged to the hilt in his right eye.

His whaler hook clattered onto the floor beside me, missing me by inches.

"You *bitch!*" he screamed in agony, clawing at the haft of the knife lodged deep in his brain.

With a super-human effort he *yanked* the knife back out of his skull as he toppled down on top of me. And with a final spasm of his bloody fist he *jammed* the blade into my heart.

"See yer scrawny ass in hell," he whispered as he died on top of me.

"Likewise," I lamely gurgled back at him, coughing up blood.

Everything around me faded to black...

Chapter 12

SATURN

Known from prehistoric times

A large yellowish dot in the night sky

Almost 100 times larger than Earth

Nestled within many flat rings

Titan's brooding mother planet

A gas giant mostly made from hydrogen

A celestial jewel and fuel depot

Launching mankind to the stars...

The Rise and Fall of *Homo sapiens*, 12:29-32

I resurrected lying on an uncomfortable flat slab. I was dressed in a white robe. A soft pillow cradled my head. I felt light as a feather, immediately realizing I was in zero-G. Wide belts across my chest and legs held me onto the slab's surface. Soft shoes with hard soles enclosed my feet. I recognized the shoes. They had magnetic soles to keep you on steel-laced floors in zero-G. I realized I was up in orbit. But even though I was weightless, I felt like a mashed piece of hamburger. Every inch of my body hurt. And my blood vessels felt like they were on fire! That old skiffer was a vicious opponent, seemingly having ripped my cardiovascular system out of me. Still, though, I knew my brutalized flesh was rapidly healing.

So where am I now?—I forced myself to widen my gaze.

I saw I was inside some sort of display room, with a large plasteel window extending across one wall. Through it I saw gigantic struts and distant ring-structures. Spaceships and shuttles were silently drifting through space toward and away from us. Robotic transport units were moving crates and pods between waiting cargo ships. Some were human shaped and man-sized. Others had multiple manipulators, looking like mechanical skittling-snatching space crabs.

I'm on a Space Station—I marveled. *I'm at the slow-moving central hub. I'm here for anyone to drift up to the window and gawk at
me. What the hell?*

Then I realized that Jags Dougal was dosing beside my bed,
strapped into a bolted-down chair, softly snoring. I noticed the bags
under his eyes and wrinkles on his face. His graying hair was
smushed-about. Rising through the wicked, conniving ranks of Titan
to become their Security Chief must have been taken a toll on him. As
I'd noted before, he looked a lot older than his actual age. Plus he'd
obviously been sitting beside my corpse for an extended period of
time.

"Hey, I'm back!" I called out to him.

He jerked awake, looking at me with a mixture of amazement and
relief.

"I...wasn't sure," he smiled broadly at me. "Ah hoped, of course
that...but...it's bin over two weeks now ye've bin dead 'n'..."

"Where are we?"

"We're-on-the-TSS," he confirmed, his words running together.
He hastily arose, "clomped" to the window, and pulled across an obscuring screen. He seemed giddy with relief that I'd yet again resurrected. "Recognizing yer tolerance tae th' immense dose o' Green they
saw ye take from yer High Priestess, th' scientists at Doom Mons were
frantic tae save ye. They had you airlifted straight up to Titan's space
station, into their ICZU, their state-of-the-art *intensive-care, zero-G
unit*. It gets a lot of usage from a' th' industrial accidents occurring on
th' surface since—as you know—safety inspection is often slighted.
But your injuries were tae severe. They couldnae save ye. Ye died.
Then yer friends demanded a proper spacer burial, includin' a period
fur viewin' yer body afore it was ejected into the void. Since I'm th'
head of security, I've some sway 'ere. I volunteered to oversee all of
your funeral arrangements, keeping your body in this viewing alcove.
So ah postponed yer spacing as long as possible 'n'..."

"What happened to the Yuan?" I asked, cutting off his long story.

I struggled to push off my sheet, undo the constraining belts. I
swung my legs out and woozily sat up, holding onto the edge of the
bed to not float away. The intense fire in my blood vessels was slowly
abating.

Jags helped me sit by steadying me with a strong hand on my arm. I was relieved to see I was in a clean set of white pants and long-sleeved shirt. That was nice of the morticians who prepared my dead body for viewing. I even felt my lucky blue marble floating in my pants pocket. Someone was respectful of my most precious belongings, likely Jags.

Great! I'm all set to get back to my quest for revenge, that is if...?

"They're fine," Dougal assured me. "After ye killed Lars Fehler th' remaining dignitaries readily surrendered. Th' scientists seemed particularly cowed. It turns oot that th' Captain was their only link tae what they claimed was a new source of Green deep in th' moon's crust. Apparently the deeply buried source was active 'n' powerful, offering glimpses at new, ground-breaking physics. Th' Company's military arm supported their work, thinkin' they had a new weapon. Anyway, ah brokered a peace with th' ruling SSS authorities, whereby your nomadic army returned th' research facility tae military control. Th' scientists here demanded ah keep your body for them tae study. I brokered another deal with your 'Holy Momma' tae allow the scientists to do some limited tests 'n' take some tissue samples before ye were properly spaced. Ah was happy tae do so since it extended th' time you'd have to resurrect. So that's where we are noo. We'll sneak you oot 'n' I'll report ah spaced yer body as expected."

So things worked out, I'm back on track—I sighed to myself in relief, *but wait! What was that about them taking tissue samples? That could reveal I'm much more than I claim to be.*

"Why did they want to test my dead body?"

"Uh...I told them about yer 'rapid healing' metabolism. They wanted blood 'n' tissue samples afore degradation set in. Ah had to make some excuse for nae spacing ye directly, as yer Yuan religion apparently demands fur corpses in space 'n'..."

"They took tissue samples from me?" I interrupted him, concerned.

"Ah didn't think you'd care if..."

"Don't worry about it," I reassured him. "It probably won't matter. Separated from my body, following their tests, I suspect my tissues would just disintegrate, I think. Some sort of collective intelligence is at play in my tissues to rebuild me each time. At least you got them not to embalm my body. That might have..."

He grimaced. "Sorry, Sazz, but they did that after taking a' their samples, MRIs, and such. Though ah claimed to be yer distant next of kin, they wouldn't vary from standard legally mandated protocol. They did allow a protracted period fer viewing, but only here in th' secure medical facility. Some of your Yuan friends left Titan 'n' came here. There was a broadcast memorial service viewed by yer tearful nomads and others on Titan. But other than that ye've had no visitors. If ye didn't resurrect in a couple more days ah wouldn't have been able tae stop the authorities from spacing yer body."

Christ, I was embalmed!—I gasped to myself in amazement. *Wow, no wonder my blood vessels are squirming in my body like they've been toasted. Whatever mechanism the aliens at the Galactic Core used to insure my continued resurrection, it's powerful indeed!*

"And what about the Yuan?" I asked.

"Well, your friends were unhappy about th' scientists appropriating your body," he stated, "but relented when ah assured them you'd be returning in a different form, bein' a 'goddess' and all. They already expected that to happen, albeit on a higher spiritual level. And it didn't hurt that for a total cessation of hostilities, ah secured a guarantee that all yer demands that ye articulated at Doom Mons will be met. The Yuan and Dilmun will, if nae thrive, they'll recover from th' Company-fueled wars. If Lars had won your fight, though, I'm sure he'd have led an overwhelming retaliatory force from SSS tae destroy the nomads. Instead, ye saved them."

Damn, I really did save them after all!

"Good work, old friend," I congratulated him. "You did an immense amount in my absence. I'm lucky you rose so high in the governing political hierarchy after my helicopter went down in Shangri-La. And now I've a further request of you, if I may?"

"Anything!" he readily agreed.

I reached into my pocket and handed him my blue marble.

"What's this?" he asked, holding it up to the light.

"Whatever you do," I cautioned him, "please don't misplace or lose it. Keep it on you if you can. I trust you, Jags. Hopefully I'll be back quickly. If not, it might be anytime into the future. But I'm not going far, so that should count for something."

"What?"

Yes, I wasn't ready yet for another dramatic trip. I really needed to go somewhere and sleep for a week, allowing my body to fully recover. But it was best to do this while I still had the nerve. If I thought about it too long I'd likely give up and quit. This was going to be painful on a whole new level.

"Either a stray memory or another friend of mine revealed where I should go next on my quest," I sighed, gathering my determination. "Don't worry, Jags. I know what I'm doing...I think."

I released my grip on the edge of the bed and floated up into the air, curling into a fetal ball. I tightly shut my eyes, concentrated with all my might, rubbed my glowing left wrist with my right palm, and mumbled the "magic words"...*Turtle Tattoo! Turtle Tattoo! Turtle Tattoo! Turtle...*

I found myself inside a cave sitting on a log. Beside me, a campfire was slowly dying out, with only red embers remaining. Looking out of the cave's entrance I saw Saturn. It was hanging grandly in deep black space, proudly flaunting its magnificent flat disc of rings. It was awesome.

I stood up and walked to the cave's mouth. There was no landscape. The "cave" was in orbit around Saturn!

"A cave in the middle of outer space," I grinned. "I made it!"

My refuge was situated on the edge of one of the largest rings of Saturn. Spread out before me I saw a flat carpet of spinning ice-rock chunks, mostly small pebbles but some as large as mountains. They glittered like a field of diamonds in the sun's glaring light, set-against utter blackness. Separating me from the vacuum of space, stretched across the cave's mouth, was a *shimmering transparent screen*. It was some sort of energy barrier preventing air in the cave from rushing out into space. Also I was in Earth-gravity. For being inside what must be a carved-out small asteroid, future physics breakthroughs must be at play: including "Star Trek"-like energy-shields and artificial gravity. Amazing!

Reaching out to try and touch the shimmering barrier I saw it bend toward me. It sensed my presence and was reacting. I had the feeling I could just step through it into the cold vacuum of outer space.

"Nice of you to drop by," I heard a dry, quavering voice from behind me. "How'd you know I was here?"

Startled, I whirled around.

Behind me I saw a large gap exiting from the back of the cave, opening out into a large, lush forest. Big trees loomed hundreds of feet into the air, spreading wide branches. Above them a beautiful blue sky glimmered, not the nuclear-winter shrouded black clouds of Earth. Either the gap led out to the future or past Earth, or perhaps onto another planet entirely. But a bright yellow sun hung above everything, spreading abundant warmth. And beyond the forest I saw green glades, bubbling streams, and fields of bright flowers. Amongst them grazed what looked like a large herd of bison.

Wait! None of this makes sense!

"It's a nice illusion," I complimented my host. "How do you do it? It looks perfectly real, not just a 3D projection."

"Turn it off!" she croaked.

The illusion vanished, leaving behind only a dank dark cave containing a lonely stone crypt located at its back. Shadowy recesses lined the walls. I glimpsed inside the alcoves decaying, naked bodies. In others I saw upright, cloudy cylinders. I saw the crypt's lid was set at an angle off to the side.

I took a few steps closer. As I did so, the walls of the stone coffin became transparent. Inside I saw a shrunken body. I recognized the once-formidable Commissioner. Now she looked like a crumbling thousand-year-old mummy. Her nose was grotesquely caved in beneath hollowed-out eye pits. Her head had only a few clumps of white hair sticking up randomly. She was clad only in a one-piece white sleeveless robe. Her arms and legs were mere sticks. Her left wrist was exposed, from which a faint green light emanated, revealing the remnants of her still-intact Turtle Tattoo.

"How did you make that beautiful world behind the cave?"

"Answer my question first," she whispered. "I thought I was rid of you forever, little girl."

"I had an...intuition...that you were hiding in Saturn's rings, easily accessible from my perch inside the TSS."

"Interesting...perhaps it was a resonant remnant from *you* and your dead Mom's other timelines? Do you think? Maybe? Huh?"

The dying old crone is teasing me. Damn what's left of her shriveled eyes!

"Perhaps," I agreed, walking over to her crypt and looking down disdainfully. "So where are all your adoring 'time-keeper' minions? Shouldn't they be lurking-about, ready to do your evil bidding?"

She grinned gummily up at me. It was unsettling. She had only one single tooth left in her head, a yellowed incisor. By the deep wrinkles in her baggy skin she looked to be far older than was humanly possible. Likely she, like me, had lived on for hundreds of years beyond her proper death-date. Instead of being cursed by an insulted alien race, she likely benefited from advanced medical treatments known only to future generations. But, in the end, "father time" would not be denied.

Now she was on her final "deathbed", having already compliantly crawled into her own coffin.

"They're all gone," she weakly coughed. "The 3-dimensional energy-matter converter above us is an alien device I captured. Look up! You'll see its blinking red light. The projector obeys my commands and presets. Living in exile must be ameliorated. Its projections comfort me. It reminds me of all I've possessed, so I can die without regrets. You, however, must continue living in the 'real' world consumed by all *your* regrets. But you're just a weak little girl who conspired against me along with your sentimental mother. You're both nothing."

Ah, *tangible* illusions! Glancing upward I saw a glittering, red light set-into the ceiling rock. Incredible!

It all makes sense now—I realized. *From afar, the Commissioner was tormenting me after my mental encounter with the salty-ocean Titanian meta-mind squids. Somehow using her alien projector, she insured that my subsequent Green-induced hallucinations with my supposed "creator" seemed completely "real." Maybe the long-dead SF-writer Daniel Lyle had some access to future events. I myself have traveled through time more than I'd like. But he certainly wasn't a god-like overlord. It was this cruel Commissioner who made my "creator" seem to appear, put words into his mouth, and forced him to claim credit for her own sins. In this way she tried to absolve herself of guilt!*

"Your Time Keepers are all dead?" I blandly asked, not revealing I'd figured out her evil deception.

Make me think I'm a character in some science fiction book?—I inwardly seethed. *That's obvious nonsense! She's a damn sadistic old bitch!*

"Well, I did incorporate some of their tissues to prolong my agony," she managed to slightly shrug her shrunken shoulders. "I suppose an aspect of them still lives on inside me...not for long, however. You came at a fortuitous moment, likely due to some 'last gasp' of my fading Turtle Tattoo, reaching out to its cousin on your own wrist. Hah!"

"So will you finally tell me the truth?"

She half-smiled as far as her dried-out lips could stretch.

"I always tell the truth," she whispered, "except when I don't. Hah!" she snickered again.

"Look!" I sharply yelled at her, startling her. Tiny eyes in hollowed-out pits skittered like frightened cornered rats. "I'll help you if I can. If a blood transfusion will keep you going a while longer, then I'll do it. You can even bring medical personnel to try to figure out how I stay young. Maybe...?"

"Already done it," she cut me off, gurgling vilely. She was having trouble speaking, "long, long ago, little girl. I studied all your tissues, blood, whatever, repeatedly...in every way scientifically conceivable. I have all that material and data stored here in my Saturnian citadel."

"You did? You mean the samples taken on TSS from my corpse were *you* doing tests on..."

"Oh, that and much, *much* more!" she snarled at me, slightly lifting her cadaverous head. "Long ago I discovered exactly how *you* stay young...and resurrect. I've had the best scientists of all human time-periods studying you ever since your infamous 'performance' at the Galactic Core. I know almost everything about your so-called 'curse', which I'd find to be a blessing. *Give* it to me! I'll take it...if only you could, which you can't, damn you."

It was quiet in the cave as I pondered her startling revelation.

She knows? How can she know the secrets of my curse and yet still be dying of extreme old age?

"But...?"

"It's the *quantum resonance fluctuation patterns* of the energy fields inside and constituting *each* of your trillions of trillions of damn quarks, gluons, all that confusing subatomic blather!" she spat. "They encode all your gross macroscopic molecular configurations, updating continually. It's *petabytes* of *petabytes* of information imprinted inside *each* of your subatomic particles! Whenever your body is damaged or killed, the resonance pattern inside each of your atoms then reconfigures all your molecules, recruits others into the body mass as needed, and reconstitutes your entire body to include all your current memories. Simple!"

It was getting colder. The campfire had died out. Only the faint red light blinking down on us from the alien projector above lighted the cave. The temperature was dropping precipitously. If I stayed there much longer, I'd be forever entombed along with The Commissioner's corpse. I'd be frozen-away in a hidden citadel orbiting in Saturn's vast rings, unable to resurrect.

"Then why didn't you use that mechanism to...?"

"Knowing *what* is not knowing *how*, you stupid little child!" she yelled in frustration. "The alien race that would have given *all* of us humans this *blessing* at the Galactic Core is *billions* of years old. What they did to you came from knowledge and tech *far* beyond our understanding! We know *what* they did to your cute little forever-teenaged body. But we have *no* hope of ever understanding or duplicating *how* they did it."

*So, since she already knows the secrets to my amazing metabolism, I have nothing left to offer her—*I groaned to myself. *Am I never going to get the truth out of her?*

"Did you order the murder of my mother?" I point-blank accused her.

"You asked me this before, ages past when..."

"And I'm asking you again!" I snapped at her, trying to keep her attention as she died. "You told me then that the younger 'you' didn't do it. I believed you. But, as you say, *ages* have passed since that claim. You've had ample time to make new plans, scramble Time to your liking, swoop in to meddle whenever and wherever, grab whatever you want, and thus rid yourself of your greatest rival. She had honor, integrity, and grace. You lack all those virtues. So out of pure naked jealousy you had her murdered!"

"Sally wasn't so great..." she whispered, barely audibly.

"She was my mother!"

Her eyes briefly flared, seemingly glowing red at me.

I flinched back, though knowing it was just a trick of the light— her crumbling retinas reflecting the projector's overhead glow—but to me revealing her very soul: that of a cruel demon.

"Do me a final favor and I will answer your question honestly," she coughed, blinking rapidly. A white crust was creeping over her eyes. She was crumbling right before me!

"Fine!" I snapped. "What do you want?"

"No one's left...to put the lid of my transparent crypt in place. I managed to crawl inside, but I don't want to return to dust. With the top in place my body will remain here for eons, preserved forever. If nothing more, it will be a...monument...to my efforts to bring order to the mess that *Homo sapiens* made of this beautiful solar system."

Like hell I'm going to help that dying witch!

"Have your 3D-materilizing projector make a robot to do it," I snidely replied.

"I was...going to...but I find I lack the strength to focus sufficiently on..."

That's a lie—I concluded. *She wants to make me complicit in memorializing her awful, brutal life. I won't do it! But, then again...if it finally gets me the answers I've come such an incredible distance to find?*

"Alright!" I yelled at her. "I'll put your damn top on."

I grabbed the heavy lid and with a mighty effort in the 1G gravity, hoisted it onto the top of the container. But I left it ajar with a large gap showing.

"Now tell me!" I insisted.

"You irritating little pest," she snarled, yellow spittle wetting her single tooth. "I wanted you to *succeed* at the Galactic Core! The terrorists who held your mother hostage...they wanted you to throw the contest, to lose—as you did! I even scoured past and possible future timelines...to find *gifts* to give you, for eventually celebrating with you your complete victory. Don't you remember...that the alien race put a *time-shield* over the entire Galactic Core concert...so time travelers like me and my 'minions' couldn't reach into the event, couldn't meddle in any manner at all? Are you a stupid fool or what? I...I..."

She took one final, shuddering breath and died.

So that's it—I numbly thought to myself. *My final attempt to find the conspiracy comes up empty. I came all this way for nothing. My much-extended life is a big, fat waste!*

I angrily shoved the transparent, heavy lid into place. It fell with a solid "thud" into its slot. I saw internal mechanisms kicking in, releasing a white fog to preserve The Commissioner's ugly corpse.

I felt empty, lost. My unending pain pressed down on me. I had pursued every lead to uncover an insidious, centuries-long, hidden conspiracy. But sometimes the "truth" about a conspiracy is that there *isn't* any conspiracy. As Agent Anderson tried to tell me on *his* deathbed, sometimes "bad stuff just happens."

This was what he *really* meant when he told me so long ago, back in Sulphur Oklahoma, that he'd "meet me on Saturn." His memory would smack me in my face and bring me low! He knew the truth!

I sank down to the cold floor, sobbing uncontrollably. I held my head in trembling hands. Every inch of my body felt like it was being smashed flat.

Yes, I could try yet again to delude myself, to go on some other "wild goose" chase...or just admit to myself what *really* happened at the Galactic Core.

I could no longer deny the truth. My mother died because of *me*. If I hadn't gotten into a fight with her, cut her off from my central team, she'd never have been exposed enough for our enemies at the Galactic Core to capture and then kill her. *This* was why I'd fought so hard across all those centuries looking for a conspiracy that didn't even exist.

All along, I'd been hunting for myself.

So, do I stay here and receive my just punishment, frozen stiff beside The Commissioner's crypt?—I asked myself. *Eventually the mechanisms preserving this asteroid will fail, allowing the other rocks in the ring to bash us to dust. Or the entire ring we're in will be pulled into Saturn's atmosphere and burned up. Whatever, I'm at the end of my run. Maybe I should just jump through that energy barrier into space and drift away. It's probably an "intelligent" barrier permeable to...*

"Don't do it, Suzy," I heard a sweet voice calling out to me.

Looking up from the cave floor, I saw my mother standing over me, as real as myself. On the ceiling, I saw the projector's red light shimmering and twitching. The alien projector was producing a simulation of my mother!

Is this one of the "gifts" left to me by The Commissioner? Or has my mother's spirit somehow activated the alien projector?

Whatever, the middle-aged, vibrant woman standing above me was undeniably Sally King, my Mother—with her iconic red hair, green eyes, and the unmistakable Turtle Tattoo glowing on her left wrist!

"I'm sorry, Mom," I cried-out.

I jumped up and hugged her tightly. She was warm and solid.

"I should have died a hundred times before the Galactic Core concert ever occurred, on my own many perilous adventures," she smiled at me. She pushed me back to hold me at arm's length, looking straight into my tearful eyes. "You were right to be angry with me there at the Galactic Core. Under the stress of the situation it was *me* that was being unreasonable. Anderson did his best to protect me. There was nothing you could do. It wasn't your fault, Suzy."

We were both quiet for a moment, just holding each other.

"Mommy, I want to stay here with you—forever!" I said, tears streaming from my eyes.

"We'll be together again, soon enough," she comforted me, again hugging me tightly. "But until then I want you to forget about blaming yourself or others for bad things that happen in this life. Instead, just be grateful for your many blessings, unlike my sad doppelganger from another timeline. Strive to help others, as you did so heroically with the Yuan. Take pleasure from shared bounties, not just your own selfish achievements. Keep exercising your Godly Creativity. I'm very proud of you, Suzy. Shoot for the stars!"

She faded away and I was left there with her dead "doppelganger." That putrid "mummy" in the crypt certainly wasn't my Mommy...and I refused to let her have any more power over me!

I kicked her transparent coffin in distain.

"Ow!" I winced, having stubbed my big toe. "Yep, she's still getting her revenge on me," I tearfully laughed. "But I guess I have to be grateful even to her. Mom's virtual appearance *was* a wonderful gift."

I limped around the circumference of the cave, studying each alcove in turn. Before I departed, I wanted to make sure that the dead Commissioner, despite her final generosity, hadn't left some nasty surprise to attack me in the future. After all, she had the means to snatch who knew what from wherever, whenever. Some of the alcoves were empty, others stored dusty skeletons, and a few had stinking bodies recently deceased. They must be the remains of The Commissioner's blindly loyal last Time Keepers. But in each of the remaining six alcoves I found a cloudy ten-foot-tall *cylinder*. Rubbing away surface scum from their transparent full-length lids I tried to see what was inside. Three of them were empty. But what I saw inside the last three of them was astounding!

But something else caught my eye: a slight *shimmering* of the air back in a corner of the cave, beside the crypt.

"What more can there be here, hidden away from me?" I mused, moving over to the distortion.

I stepped through some sort of invisibility clock, similar to the energy barrier at the mouth of the cave, and saw...

"Oh, my God!" I gasped.

It was the Ark.

The Commissioner must have snatched it out of Time right as I and sweet little Glenda were crushed to death in the Temple's collapsing vault. This was why the Yuan excavators found no trace of it when they dug out my and Glenda's bodies. The Dilmun vigorously denied having stolen the Ark. At the time I didn't believe them, but they were telling the truth! Instead of being crushed to fragments or stolen or lost, the golden container sat right there before me.

"But are its contents here as well?" I mused.

With a trembling hand I turned the knob I'd seen Glenda activate when she'd inserted the last book back into the container.

I heard a "swoosh" as the lid lifted on its hinges and air rushed in. There before me were the collections of ancient books I was shown back in the vault: Frank Herbert's *Dune* series, Daniel Lyle's *"Girl with the Turtle Tattoo"* series, his *Creative-Theology* Books series, and...yet *another* series Glenda didn't show me at the time!

With a trembling hand I picked up the first of the "new" series. I read its name and author: "'*The Luminary Chronicles*,' by David King." And then the second: "'*Homo sapiens Eulogy*' by Tommy King." Then the third: "'*Eashoa's Lament*' by Eashoa M'sheekha." Then the fourth of the obviously philosophical series: "'*The Minstrel's Lark*,' by Yishai Hovah."

That final collection of books was incredible. Flipping through a few pages of each volume I saw they were all written in the same fashion, with chapters and verses numbering a poetic, lyrical format. It was a vast archive of disturbing word-pictures, profound observations, and scintillating wisdom. No wonder the Yuan had such deep faith!

"This is all *so* strange," I murmured, fascinated but getting colder as the temperature in the space-cave continued to plummet. I couldn't stay there much longer or I'd freeze. But the incredible wealth of knowledge, wisdom, and prophecy I'd thought lost in the vanished Ark was yet again in my hands, plus much more!

The next book in the poetic series caused me to suck in my breath as I read its title and author: "'*The Suzette Anthology, Lyrics #1*,' by Suzette Kingly."

"I didn't know that the lyrics to my early songs had been gathered together and published," I marveled out loud. "That's so cool...but what are they doing here? Oh, right, they're used in the book that Lyle wrote about my musical career and..."

Oh, my God—I gasped, picking up the last of the "new" volumes. *It can't be!*

It was yet another poetic book, claiming that *I*, Susan King, was its author: "*The Rise and Fall of Homo sapiens*," I muttered, my teeth chattering together.

"I haven't w-written any s-such thing!" I stammered, my lips growing numb from the cold. "H-how can t-this be? Was that h-hallucination with Daniel Lyle n-not just a 3D-delusion made by The

Commissioner after all? Am I r-really just a character in a s-science fiction b-book?"

But then I remembered, relieved.

"Ah, you s-sneaky dead witch," I grimaced at the dried out husk lying motionless there in the sealed, transparent crypt. "You m-meddled with the Yuan also, snatching this out of a future timeline! It was *you* that g-gave f-future knowledge to that Daniel Lyle guy, showed him my completed diary! This is another *real* b-book I'm maybe *going* to w-write. It all makes s-sense now."

I put the book back carefully with the others, turning the switch to lower the lid of the golden Ark and activate the internal preservation mechanisms. These were indeed treasures gifted to me by that wicked old crone, priceless artifacts I'd have to retrieve.

That is, if I can somehow get back to the TSS...

"Blue marble, blue marble, blue marble!" I shouted as I closed my eyes and vigorously rubbed my still-glowing left wrist.

Jags jerked backward as I materialized in front of him. Unintentionally, he broke the connection of his magnetic soles to the steel plating, floating up into the air.

Firmly stuck to the floor by my own magnetic soles, I grabbed his hand and pulled him back down.

"That was fast," he gulped, "You just left!" he exclaimed happily, handing my blue marble back to me.

"I now know *exactly* what I need to do," I stated firmly, "And you with all your high-level connections are going to help me do it."

"Of course, whatever!" he enthusiastically agreed.

"First of all I need to activate a new secret identity."

"Who?"

"A *very* wealthy young heiress."

"Of course," he laughed, "What else?"

"And second," I continued, "I need a landing-rated cargo shuttle for an off-record, secret excursion. Plus I'll need several lifter-robots."

"You've got it. I'll pilot th' shuttle fur ye!"

"No, Jags," I insisted, "Thanks for the equipment. But this is something I have to do alone. I'm a certified shuttle pilot. I'll manage by myself."

"Of course you will," he nodded agreeably. "I'll make the arrangements."

It was six months after I resurrected on the TSS. A lot had happened. I was standing with a receiving slate of high-dignitaries on a viewing deck of SSS, the *Saturn Space Station*. I, along with the crowd of well-dressed officials, was eagerly awaiting the arriving commander of humanity's first starship.

We were just above the "south"-pole situated, central hub of the 20 mile-wide multiple-rimmed wheel of the SSS. Proceeding outward along the different wheel "levels", pseudo-gravity from the centripetal force of the spinning space station increased. At the outer ring the residents, workers, and guests experienced full 1G. But at the central hub we were in near-zero G, standing on the plasteel deck by virtue of our activated magnetic boots.

"Tis nae that impressive, is it?" Jag's mother, Lady Dougal, elbowed me.

I laughed at her friendly dig.

She was peering off into the star-studded distance. I saw what looked like a big rock slowly moving across the blackness of space. The SSS was in a high orbit outside the rings of Saturn. If you didn't know better, you'd think we were looking at one of the planet's many small moons. But periodically we both saw a bright *FLARE* flash at the rock's back as it steadily accelerated forward.

It was a 50-mile-wide asteroid diverted from the asteroid belt between Mars and Jupiter. It was appropriately named "Asteria" to honor its origin and the Greek goddess of the stars. It was a rare hybrid asteroid, combining both "C" and "M"-types. In other words, it contained large amounts of both carbon-compounds and metals. So this particular asteroid was loaded with water-ice, nickel, cobalt, platinum, uranium, and other even rarer elements. It was a celestial gold mine! And now it was being boosted out of the solar system.

"The mother starship certainly isn't Star Trek's Enterprise," I agreed, "but the cargo shuttle that's coming into our dock is an impressive beast."

Indeed, the craft was so large I feared it wouldn't fit into the SSS's already huge central docking area.

My eyes focused on the bulky silver spaceship firing off spurts of white mists from its maneuvering thrusters. Relative to us the spaceship seemed to be slowly tilting, though of course we were the actual ones rotating. The tilt of the spaceship was slowing as thrusters induced a roll to match the SSS, so that the craft would slip straight into our main central dock. The vessel was a transport from Asteria preparing to take on critical cargo. All hands were on deck from the SSS for its arrival. There was only a short window to stuff the transport full of precious cargo before its mother asteroid moved out of range. This was the last civilized resupply outpost before mankind's first "starship" accelerated on out of the solar system. Within a few minutes the Asteria's Captain would pass through one of the docking airlocks. He would then come directly up with his first officers to meet with us on the observation deck.

"It *should* be impressive since it's taking on a *trillion* credits worth of He-3," she dryly commented. "I'm filthy rich, but even I'm impressed at delivering such a valuable cargo."

Yep, we're giving them a huge load of the most precious atom in the solar system, mined from the upper atmosphere of our gas giant—I nodded. *Saturn's gravity and thick atmosphere traps it here, while on Earth we lost ours ages ago. It'll power Asteria all the way to Proxima Centauri. They got a prior big batch at Jupiter, likewise mined from its thick atmosphere, and now they're "topping off" at the last "gas station" for 25 trillion miles!*

Lady Dougal was a white-haired, regal, somewhat portly, light brown-skinned matriarch. Though she held no official governmental position, she was regarded as local royalty. Following the death of her husband she inherited "The Company," which was responsible both for harvesting the vast methane/ethane seas of Titan and skimming precious Helium-3 from Saturn's upper atmosphere. Now, largely paid for by The Company's massive profits, she'd commissioned the world's first expedition to our closest neighboring star. Asteria was pointed straight at the Alpha Centauri system, located a mere 4.3 lightyears from Earth.

Lady Dougal moved off to talk with some other dignitaries. I recognized the Premier of Mars and the President of the Moon. The Belt's Prime Minister was on the docking cargo ship, preparing to disembark before returning to Ceres. Earth's governments sent their regrets at not attending the ceremony in person, but were doing so via delayed telescreen. This was an opportunity for the quarreling governments to have a rare show of unity. But I knew it was only superficial. As always, many underlying tensions were pushing the solar system factions yet again toward war. But that was *their* challenge. Me, I was leaving it all behind...

"Ah'm going to miss ye," Jags sighed from my other side, interrupting my morbid thoughts.

"Yep, you too," I sincerely returned his compliment. "But you'll be fine."

"Well, I'm no longer as adventurous as ah was when we first met," he shrugged regretfully. But then he smiled and looked lovingly to his side. "Plus I've got me additional sweet duties."

I glanced at the dark-skinned, slender woman standing on the opposite side of him holding the hands of two excited teenagers, a girl and a boy. They were all ecstatic, anticipating meeting the famous *Captain Horacio J. Laramie*, a legend of solar system exploration. In the twenty years I spent dead beneath the dunes of Shangri-La, Jars became a full-grown man, married, and had two kids. I invited them to go with me but he politely declined. They were happy on Titan. The Saturn System was their home. They had no need to go to another star.

"You'll make sure that the nomads get their new, low-radioactive fusion reactors?"

"My Mom is already asking when th' newly planted Titanian Tea orchards will produce their first commercially available leaves," he chuckled. "She sees her 'gift' o' the new reactors paying off wi' dividends. She'll find a way tae preserve th' Tea's potency fur off-world transport 'n' we'll all make a mint, replacing oor previous alien-chemical trade."

"So...even *more* profit than from the now-banned fresh-Green trade?" I asked, very pleased.

He frowned.

"Honestly, Sazz," he replied, falling back to the name he was used to calling me. "Our scientists had no idea th' Azotos could feel pain. But after ye insisted we do extensive tests, th' results were indisputable. Slicing them up for fuel-bags caused incredible suffering. And tryin' to remove the crystalline nodes was off-the-chart agony to th' floppy critters. And ye say ye knew this just from yer observations when ye fought with Captain Fehler two decades ago on Ligeia Mare?"

I stoically maintained my story. They couldn't know of the confirmation I received from the Titanian subterranean ocean-dwellers. Either humanity would try to kill off the dangerously sentient creatures or the Titanians would retaliate, somehow exterminating us "irritating" surface-dwellers from the entire solar system! I couldn't make *Homo sapiens* abandon Titan, but I hoped that ramping down and stopping the slaughter of Azotos would placate the hidden, subsurface super-brain. It was the best I could do to protect mankind in the solar system.

I'm not abandoning humanity—I firmly reminded myself. *I'm using my vast fortune to help mankind find another star system to migrate to as a "back-up" while also lessening our disruptive presence on Titan.*

At least that was my excuse for not keeping my promise to the super-brain. I desperately hoped it would be enough.

"Yep, it's my peculiar metabolism, I suppose," I answered Jags. "I'm extremely sensitive to pain, both in myself and others. Also, please don't call me by someone else's name."

He looked around to make sure no one else had heard. Luckily his wife and kids had already moved away to get a seat for the ceremonies.

"Sorry," he gulped. "Force of habit...anyway, if we didn't have the new He-3 fusion reactors coming on-line ah doubt if th' military or Company would care about hurting some giant slow seaweeds," he truthfully stated. "But since we'll be shipping liquid oxygen and liquid hydrogen as fuel now in place of methane 'n' ethane, produced from the abundant rock-ice o' Titan by our new super-powerful fusion re-actors, we can phase-out capturing them slimy Azotos."

"And there'll be no imbalance," I added.

"Imbalance?"

"Excess hydrogen," I added. "Our environmental pollution of Titan's atmosphere resulted in too many Azotos and Krakens. A normal balance to Titan's frozen ecology will return."

"Ah...ye sure do like those monsters!"

"Well...I almost got eaten by one," I replied weakly.

Walking back to us was Lady Dougal. She was resplendent in her elegantly blue, diamond-studded dress. The others were taking their seats. The farewell ceremony, broadcast to the entire solar system, was imminent.

"Sure...hey, they're here!" Jags exclaimed.

I looked across the set-up tables and podium to see a *very angry* tall man storming across the floor, stomping in his magnetic boots. He was well over six feet tall. He brushed through the dignitaries who were still standing, confronting Lady Dougal with folded arms.

"What *is* this?" he demanded, towering above her, now waving his meaty hands in the air. "How *dare* you divert more than a ton of my irreplaceable supplies for some unauthorized cylinders? My quartermaster just told me what happened. There's no time to remove or replace them. If we don't depart in the next fifteen minutes we'll be left behind!"

Yep, he was practically foaming at the mouth with fury. Everyone present was taken-aback. If he hadn't been so angry, his face so twisted in rage, he'd be a very handsome man. Captain Laramie was six-foot, six-inches tall, with a neatly trimmed white beard and mustache, wearing a full-dress Admiral uniform. The iconic gold anchor sat on his black cap. His double-buttoned black coat had four gold stripes on his sleeves, gold braid on his right shoulder, and a line of glittering medals on his right breast. He was a veteran of the "belter" wars, who'd single-handedly led his asteroid-based nation to independence. He was the equivalent of Old Earth U.S.A.'s George Washington, now commanding humanity's first starship. True, he'd never make it to Proxima Centauri. It was a hundred year journey on a multi-generational ship. But commanding the first leg of the long journey was the capstone to his brilliant career.

"Your *owner* made a few last-minute changes," Lady Dougal calmly replied, staring up into his glaring blue eyes. "The supplies replaced are not critical. Your new cargo *is* critical. You'll see."

He looked like he was about to tear her into elegant diamond-studded pieces. But then he seemed to regain control over his surging emotions. His twisted-up face relaxed.

"You may have funded this magnificent adventure, but I'm still the..." he growled.

"Oh, it wasn't me," she interrupted him.

Everyone froze in place, fascinated. First of all, no one interrupted the Captain. However, they all knew that "money talks." *Of course* she was the owner! Public records proved that she'd paid a total of *seven trillion* credits to locate the ideal asteroid, have large portions of it excavated and converted into sub-surface facilities, install state-of-the-art He-3 giant fusion reactor systems, and then finalize plus build an experimental pulse-fusion drive to accelerate the huge space-rock between the stars.

"What?" he snapped at her.

"Your *new* owner is *her*," she said, pointing.

I politely waved up at him.

I caught sight of my reflection in the plasteel wall-high viewing window. I saw there a black-haired, slender, oriental girl dressed in a conservative gray pantsuit. Her nose was somewhat flattened, her eyes almond-shaped. It's wonderful what small cosmetic surgical alterations can do for one's appearance.

"What the...?" he began to swear at me.

"*Yang Wang Weiwei*," I cheerfully asserted, sticking my hand out to him. "I am the heiress to the Weiwei fortune. I'm also a great admirer of yours, Captain. I'm sure we'll get along great. I come bearing gifts."

"What?" he grimaced, reluctantly accepting my small hand into his large, calloused fist, "Is this a joke? You're just a teenager!"

"It's no joke," Lady Dougal assured him, waving regally for the ceremonies to begin. "Countess Weiwei paid me *ten trillion* credits for complete ownership of Asteria. That's enough to reimburse all my investment plus fund renovation of my extensive holdings on Titan. It's an offer I couldn't refuse. And, yes, you still command the expedition. But you report now to her, understand?"

He shook his head in confusion as we together stepped up onto the podium.

"I should have known never to take funding from a damn *Anderson*," he snarled under his breath.

"*What?*" she snapped back at him, her face contorted with rage.

"…sorry…" he muttered.

Anderson? Dark-skinned? Oh, my God! No wonder Jags had such a fascination with me. He was a descendent from Arthur and Lelea's son!

I felt a surge of even greater appreciation for Jags and his family. It's strange how fate works—both for the negative and the positive. Through Anderson's distant descendent, Jags, I could finally resolve and let go of my hate of the rouge Time-Keeper.

"Wo bu xiangxin ni shi ni shuo di nage ren, xiao xiaojie," Captain Laramie broke my reverie, addressing me in fluent Mandarin! (*I don't believe you're who you say you are, little missy.*) "Wo conglai meiyou ting shuoguowei wei de caifu, ye meiyou ting shuoguo. Wo shuxi suoyou zhong guo ren de touxian. Tamen shi women de zhuyao zhadui zhi yi. Weisheme wo jintian zhiqian cong wei ting shuoguo ni? (*I've never heard of a 'Weiwei' fortune or an heiress thereto. I'm acquainted with all the head Chinese clanners. They're one of our main belter factions. Why have I never heard of you before today?*)"

"Wo laizi jiu diqiu. Zai miejue zhihou de ji ge shiji li, wo de wangchao zizhule zhongguo de zongzu. Wairen bu liaojie huo zhiyi women! (*I'm from Old Earth. My Dynasty funded the Chinese clanners over the centuries after the Extinction. It is not for outsiders to know of or question us!*)"

I was glad I'd learned so many languages over the past several hundred years. Mandarin was one of my favorites, hence building a cryptic secret identity crafted around it. Plus, I'd put enough documentation into my "history" such that anyone seriously questioning my identity would find plenty of proof. Despite his protests, I had the esteemed Captain by his shorthairs.

"Then why are you out here?" he snapped at me, reverting back to standard English-spacer.

"I'm tired of living in the radioactive hell of Earth. I'm looking for adventure. I have a Ph.D. in astrophysics and am looking to put it to good use, on the cutting edge of space exploration. Plus, if you must know, I'm escaping my roots and responsibilities. Satisfied?" I snapped at him.

He just snarled at me, gathering his thoughts.

"Ok, but just how does this change anything?" he demanded, stopping dead in his tracks and facing us two women. "You'll receive my telemetry and reports as Asteria departs the solar system and...?"

"She's going with you," Lady Dougal grinned up at him.

I could see she was having fun. To be as powerful as she was, heading up the most successful commercial conglomerate in the history of mankind, she was used to giving orders and having them obeyed. I saw she was practically gloating at setting the arrogant Captain back on his heels.

"Now just wait!" he insisted, his voice growing deeper and more menacing. "We have a full crew complement. They've all been carefully selected. We've limited resources and can't afford to..."

"Yes, you can," she stopped him.

With a flick of her wrist she beckoned over some of the station's black-outfitted guards. Laramie looked shocked, uncertain. He knew that if he were arrested, even briefly, *he'd* be left behind!

"I assure you I'll pull my weight," I insisted, standing straight and proud.

I certainly will add to the expedition—I mentally promised. *It cost me the entire fortune I've built up covertly over hundreds of years. But it's worth every single credit. I need a fresh start. As my Mother's image in the cave encouraged me, I need to do something significant with my life rather than look for empty revenge. I need to boldly move on to mankind's next frontier! And maybe, just maybe, mankind is finally moving past the pursuit of money to nobler objectives. I want to be part of that evolution!*

Reluctantly, seeing my stone-cold resolve, the Captain relented. But his *glower* told me more than enough. My upcoming journey would be...interesting.

"Well, then, we've just time for a few brief historical statements," Lady Dougal smiled diplomatically, motioning Laramie to the podium.

He stood behind it, towering above the microphone. I was on one side of him, Jag's still-snickering mom on the other. He unfolded a small piece of paper from his pocket.

"This is one celestially small hop for a space-rock..." he growled, reciting his prepared remarks, pausing dramatically, "—and one giant jump for *Homo sapiens!*"

Ah, not so novel or original. Didn't Neil say something similar to that a few hundred years ago?

I remembered back to when I "popped" out of the air at the Tranquility Base Memorial. Little did I know then that I'd follow in Armstrong's footsteps—onward to Mars, then to Saturn's Titan, and now...who knew?

But I groaned inwardly as I stood beside Laramie, hearing his rushed speech. Time was a-wasting. I'd pushed back the vicious pain hammering at my mind and body, but just barely. I needed to keep it at bay, keep it occupied, and above all keep moving forward. Either that or the agony would overwhelm me and I'd go insane.

Chapter 13

INTERSTELLAR SPACE

It's a long way to our closest star

About 25 trillion miles to be exact

By conventional rockets, 100,000 years

A long way to contemplate one's fate

But just a quick blink in God's eyes

Seeing the ephemeral human species

Rising to dominate an entire planet

Then sinking into the abyss of Time

Tiny dots on a dot itself invisibly small

Overwhelmed by our vast Milky Way

Itself just one of trillions of Galaxies

All contained in one curious primate's mind

The first glimmering of rampant imagination

Gazing up into a star-studded prehistoric sky...

The Rise and Fall of *Homo sapiens*, 13:6-8

We'd just slipped past Pluto, still steadily accelerating. Asteria started out traveling 16 miles per second along its orbit around the sun in the asteroid belt between Mars and Jupiter. Diverting it along its path of travel and adding to its velocity, it was now moving at 30 miles per second. There was no thought of making a pit stop at Pluto. We were committed along our trajectory to the nearest star.

Pluto was mankind's last outpost in the solar system, consisting of a lone orbiting research station. We exchanged greetings and good-byes as we sped past. It would be a long time before we actually left the sun's sphere of influence, but having been raised back on Old Earth I'd gotten used to Pluto being the outer edge of our solar system. So I felt nostalgic, with a tear in my eye, to leave our sun for "interstellar space." In actuality we were just departing the "inner" system to move into the much large "outer" region. We were entering the realm of comets, first the Kuiper Belt then the much larger Oort Cloud. Already Earth was invisible to the naked eye, the sun a mere large star in the vastness of space. But we were still well within the heliosphere where the sun's radiation and magnetic fields shielded us.

It's going to take forever to get to Proxima Centauri—I sighed.

However, my fear was comforted by periodic "bumps". They were from helium-3/deuterium pellets being ignited behind the mammoth pulse-plate located at the center of the backside of the spinning asteroid, pushing forward along its axis of rotation. So Asteria was steadily accelerating. We hoped to eventually achieve 5% the speed of light, cutting our journey to our nearest neighboring star from 100,000 years using conventional rockets to a mere 100. As the generations proceeded, the guts of the asteroid would be mined to sustain our lives and our journey.

Similar to on SSS, Asteria was "spun up" such that a simulated, centripetal force of 1G was generated in the outermost levels of the buried human habitats. The forward mass of the asteroid served as a solid shield against the radiation and deadly hurtling debris of interstellar space. 3D-printing would give us many creature comforts and necessary working components. Backing up and powering our massive fusion reactors we also had an array of "conventional" fission reactors, fueled by U235 mined from the asteroid's abundant uranium ore. So then, we were hopefully set for the hundred year "multi-generational" haul.

To-date on Asteria I'd been overwhelmed with tasks. As the responsible owner, I needed to come up to speed on all the systems in our ultra-complex environment and community. Plus, I had to consolidate and assure my place in the ruling hierarchy. And as the "on-site" representative of all the other stakeholders I made regular reports back to Saturn. The Captain "suggested" I be the voyage's primary documentarian, recording by written word and video all aspects of our progress (mainly to keep me busy and out of his way). I was happy, however, to comply. I even began editing my AR-implant recorded diary of misadventures since I first resurrected, in case anyone was ever interested in reading it. That inspired me to also begin writing my new, ambitious, poetic history of humanity: "The Rise and Fall of *Homo sapiens*." So I was keeping busy. But the already tight-knit community of Asteria resented me. Superficially they accepted that I was their new "owner", but kept me at arm's length.

I was growing increasingly lonely, dejected. Did I give up a solar system filled with humans, some of whom adored and worshipped me, for a lifetime of snide rejection? It was clear that the Captain hated me and had ordered the crew to give me only the bare minimum of cooperation. Even my fellow Chinese clanners amongst the crew resented me: a previously unknown Earther benefactor who was imperiously "lording" it over them.

Keep busy, do your job, what's next?—was my constant mantra.

Now, though, I'd finally found time to get to my prizes. I, for the umpteenth time, berated myself on returning the Ark to the Yuan. Its contents would have made for endlessly fascinating reading-material on my long journey. But Jags had promised that their "Goddess" would come back to them in another form. Unexpectedly returning their lost Holy Texts as a wealthy Chinese clanner neatly closed that loop. They were overjoyed at getting them back and seeing me in my new, resurrected form. Plus, they would guard their precious Ark with their lives, keeping its contents safe for mankind into the far future.

"So...are you really what I think you are?" I asked, focusing on the task at hand. I looked down at the five large cylinders I'd brought with me. "Or are you just cruel jokes, a last revenge, another clever mirage inflicted upon me by the evil Commissioner?"

I was in a locked storeroom containing my "secret" cargo.

"Now, how do I open you?" I mused, closely examining them.

I left one of the six cylinders with Jags, with directions to turn it over to the Station's scientists after I'd left the solar system. His story was that one of the super-wealthy "Countess Weiwei's" prior commissioned expeditions discovered it in the asteroid belt, some sort of alien device. So I'd left foundering mankind some future tech from another timeline. The Commissioner was definitely a mathematical genius. She'd built the things. Maybe their secrets would help *Homo sapiens* escape the fate I feared they'd suffer if they continued on their present path. Also, I planned to give our onboard scientists one or more of the cylinders. Our ship complement was around two hundred people, the minimum number necessary to maintain a viable, genetically healthy population. All disciplines were represented, particularly the sciences. The initial crew wasn't intended to be only first-generation breeding stock, but a vibrant population of researchers. They would eagerly accept the "gifts" The Countess brought with her, digging into the secrets of the cylinders.

I could have revealed the location of The Commissioner's frozen crypt to the Saturn establishment. It certainly contained amazing technological advances, like the alien 3D solid-projector. But I couldn't do that. I had to keep the space-cave secret. I did this not so much to honor the old hag, but because I had the nagging suspicion her crypt was critical to alternate timelines which must exist no matter how transitory or ephemeral. From what I'd glimpsed riffling through Lyle's detailed history of my family in his science fiction books, her crypt was a central player in my growing up to become a world-famous pop star.

Whatever, I've got to figure out how to get inside—I focused my thinking. *How the hell am I going to open up this thing? I don't see any controls on it.*

The cylinder I was focusing on, like the others, lay on its side. The transparent full-length lid on its top was fogged over on the inside. Moving them out of the space-cave using my robotic assistants had joggled them. Whatever was contained therein had bumped around, stirring up stuff inside. I could no longer see into them just by rubbing off outer smudges.

The cylinder was about ten feet tall, four foot wide. In our centripetal-force 1G it weighed in at around 500 pounds. It was much too heavy for me to move unassisted. I hadn't brought in a lifting robot because I didn't want anyone knowing I was working on the cylinders. But horizontal, with their lids turned upward, I could feel around on most of their surfaces. So I just started at the top, moving my hands carefully down, covering everything for even a hint of a knob or button.

"Ah!" I exclaimed, feeling something respond to my palm-print. "Clever Commissioner," I grudging admitted. "She didn't give me her 'gifts' without keying them to respond to my touch."

With a "swish" the long, curved lid popped out an inch. I felt a gap, inserted my fingers, and yanked upward with all my might.

A purple fog sprang out, surrounding me as the room's ventilation system kicked in, sucking it out. It had a pleasant lavender scent, like heavy perfume.

I saw something *sitting up* out of the swirling fog...

"You're ok!" I exclaimed, hastily reaching inside to grasp the form tightly, laboriously hauling its heavy body out of the cylinder.

The two of us sat on the cold floor, our backs to the popped cylinder, shoulder-to-shoulder gasping for breath.

Turning my head to the side, I saw beside me a tall, sexy young man with broad shoulders and slender waist. He wore a leather vest over a brown plaid shirt, threadbare blue jeans, and moccasins. His hair was long and brown, braided into a thick ponytail at his back. His tanned face had high cheekbones framing a prominent nose. We were far away from the alien projector in The Commissioner's crypt. There was no doubt of what I'd just dragged out of the "time-freeze" cylinder: *Scott Yanash*, the young Chickasaw man who I long ago fervently hated!

I rightly blamed him for not keeping his promise to rescue my mother. But I now knew that my intense hatred of him was just me trying to deflect my own culpability. He'd done his best under the circumstances.

I softly recited some words I'd written only a week previously in my growing analysis of the narrative arc of humanity:

"Death be not proud
A plea by the romantic poet John Donne
Written in the early 1600's
A time of plague, war, and starvation
Where the end was often a relief
A brief step beyond this sad existence
To something better than bloody fighting
A wolf's nighttime howl at an implacable moon
Mixing equal parts defeat and defiance
A wail as futile as it is splendid
Preening confronting dark doom!"

Yet again, whether I wanted to or not, I'd cheated death. And, because of The Commissioner's perverted Time-snatch, so also had Scott! We were "two-of-kind", taken out of time to live beyond our allotted span. In a way it was terrifying, as was this new journey to another star. Instead of peacefully fading away, we and humanity were persisting. We were stubbornly, bravely going to where no man or woman had yet ventured. Who knew what terrible challenges and dangers would confront us? We were crewmates on a voyage into the unknown. Past frictions faded away, granting us a fresh new start.

Now, having finally made peace with my mother's demise, I suddenly realized I *loved* Scott Yanash. From the first time I'd seen him all grown up, in the Park at Sulphur, Oklahoma, I'd *always* loved him.

I flung my arms around his neck, pulling him close, whispering reassuring things to him as he looked around dazedly. He smelled of smoke. The Commissioner must have snatched him out of Time just as the fireball from the nuclear explosion slammed into us at the stadium, blowing him away from me.

Beside us I heard another cylinder, apparently linked to the first, pop its lid. A long, wet nose pushed up through more purple fog. Fortunately, the third occupied pod didn't open. That would have been messy.

"Woof!" I heard a happy bark as Scotty flopped out on his own, collapsing trembling on my legs.

I had my *two* "Scotty's" back.

"W-where are w-we?" Scott stammered. "W-we got b-blown up and...? Who the hell are you?"

"It's a long story," Countess Weiwei grinned at him. I hugged both him and my robot dog simultaneously, "I saved you and...you'll save me."

It was a marvelous revelation. Instead of revenge, there's *redemption*. For the first time in hundreds of years, my continuing agony faded away and I had hope.

THE END

[continued in: *The Girl Who Was Everywhere*]

Thank you for reading!

Dear reader,

I hope you enjoyed **The Girl Who Could Not Die**. It was a lot of fun to research the scientific underpinnings to realistic future space travel both within and departing the solar system. As you saw, humans tend to remain the same no matter their stage of technological development, both emotionally and intellectually. The sequel to this book, **The Girl Who Was Everywhere**, picks up with a perilous journey to another star. What awaits them is the promise of a whole new reality, but where both rewards and dangers are infinity greater.

I hope you are intrigued by the sequel's central question: "If humanity could start from scratch guided by future knowledge, could it be better? Or, are we unable to rise above our evolved genetic programming?" Susan faces the ultimate challenge: taking on the duties of a god while not losing her humanity and those she loves.

Finally, I need to ask you for a favor. If you enjoyed this book and would like to help others do as well, **a review written by you** on the Amazon page for this book would be greatly helpful. It's hard to get reviews nowadays and your support is very important to both me and other readers. If you'd like to do this, I sincerely thank you in advance for your time and effort. It can be as long or short as you wish.

Thanks again for reading my **Girl with the Turtle Tattoo** books and going on this weird, wild ride with me.

Sincerely,

Dan Lyle

About the Author:

Daniel Basil Lyle holds a Ph.D. in Biology, is a lifelong amateur herpetologist, taught medical immunology at a University, completed a career in cell biology research, lectures on how to apply theological and psychological principles in practical ways, and has a strong interest in all aspects of cosmology and physics. From a small kid he was fascinated with dinosaurs. As such, he has always lived with exotic creatures, including harmless snakes, all housed in his own homemade habitats. Some of his tame pet pythons and anacondas ranged up to twelve feet in length. He is the author of over thirty books, many of which are religious in nature. His writings go beyond the ordinary, exposing deeper aspects of life. His books are meant to be fun, conversational, and helpful. His various works are available at LylePublishing.com and Amazon.com. The "Girl with the Turtle Tattoo" science fiction series was inspired by paintings done by his mother, movies adapting Stieg Larsson's crime novels, and various men and women sporting spectacular body-art tattoos. The author hopes that you, the reader, find his characters spontaneous, quirky, surprising, and even thought-provoking—just as did he!